RISE FROM THE ASHES

ISBN: 979-8-9875300-0-9 *(paperback)*

Edited by Steven Moore
Cover illustration by Fiverr user Bobooks
Interior illustrations by Sonali Aheer

RISE FROM THE ASHES

Maria Ruiz

Chapter 1

The sounds of thundering gunshots and shattering glass tore through the silence that surged across the streets of our worn-down town in early August. Another monotonous day for many was interrupted by yet another wolf chase; a Deviant Hunter chasing after a fleeing rebel. I chased after that deviant like my life depended on it. I ran senselessly through multiple narrow streets, but the young rebel in the red tunic ran faster than I could; a result of the everlasting hunger for life we humans carried on ourselves.

Every breath of faintly radioactive air I inhaled invigorated my love for the thrill of capturing those who lived only to taint this nation and what it stood for, which they ultimately ended up dying for too. I'm an Executioner and Hunter in this town, which meant that I did the dirty work. I captured and executed rebels on stage for the masses, as each and every eye feasted on the sight of their blood painting this gray town red.

As we negotiated a sudden sharp turn, the woman lost her balance for a second, and the tanned skin on her slim arms met with the jagged walls of a concrete building. She slowed down for a second, and that one second was all I needed. The growing frustration from my inability to catch up to her made me oblivious to my surroundings. I felt my leg get caught on an inconveniently placed pile of wooden planks, but the fall didn't even faze me. The adrenaline that accompanied a rebel chase was like a drug- addictive and numbing.

Dammit! I cursed, not realizing we were in a construction zone. Before the rebel could get away, I reached for my rifle as quick as I could and aimed it right at her head. She turned briefly, and in her coffee brown eyes I saw the same doe-eyed look every victim had when their eyes settled on the barrel of my gun. Her reaction was perfectly aligned with my finger as I pulled the trigger. She swiftly darted to the side, dodging the first bullet by a hair, and it made my pride shoot through the roof.

"Try escaping this one!" I shouted as I aimed the gun perfectly at her unwounded arm, and once again pulled the trigger.

I heard her cry out as it pierced through her lower bicep. I tried to get up and seize the opportunity to capture her, but nonetheless failed. She ran into the deep, dark forest most wouldn't dare go into, and my prey had gotten away.

I forcefully punched the ground in defeat. Splinters and shards of glass were scattered all over the ground from the construction, so punching it wasn't the smartest idea. I stood up slowly, trying not to force my aching leg. A minor injury managed to break through my crimson knee pad, and it hurt to even take a step. The adrenaline high had worn off, and pain was once again a concern. I picked up my rifle, defeated, and took in my surroundings.

Dozens of faces belonging to concerned civilians examined the disappointing scene, and I could feel their eyes crawling all over me. It burned me inside to know I'd let this many people down. Their disappointed, scared, and worried looks were clear and lit by the many torches and streetlamps around us. I breathed out a long sigh of disappointment and dusted myself off before I began limping my way home. I hadn't made it too far when a gray man, seemingly in his forties and covered in dust, approached me.

"Are you okay young lady? That was quite a blow you took to your knee," he asked me in a raspy, tired voice. I sensed sincerity in his eyes.

"I'm fine," I vaguely responded, forcing a smile to make it seem more convincing. The tension in the crowd began to dissipate and I carried on.

It was careless of me to forget that there were currently a multitude of repairs ongoing throughout all the nation's districts. The rebels have been acting rather reckless these days and have adapted a new custom of blowing up buildings whenever they're in town. They claim this is their way of silently declaring war, but I doubt it. They are, and always will be, nothing but *cowards*.

Instead of heading straight home, I decided to drop by the market area to get a quick bite before it got too dark out. My house was located in the remote outskirts of the town, and it was a far hike to walk on an empty stomach. I hoped the news hadn't reached this part of town yet, though it was unlikely, since news traveled quickly in this small town; it was truly maddening sometimes. As I walked, I tried to push aside the aching pain in my knee, but that was easy since ignoring pain was luckily one of my specialties.

I walked into a small, wood-built diner in the middle of town, as I figured it would be pretty empty at this time. I scanned the building and saw only a few young teens at a corner table and an old man at the bar- covered head to toe to protect himself from the frigid temperatures. I tried to hide my limp as much as possible as I walked over to the bar. I sat down on an empty stool a seat away from the old man. I'd noticed a thick tension as soon as I walked in, but that tended to happen in the presence of an Executioner.

"The days only seem to get colder," the old man mentioned as he stared at his drink on the bar, "I remember the last time summer was actually somewhat warm- probably thirty years ago," he added, still submissively avoiding eye contact. It caught me off guard that he'd spoken to me considering most people tended to hold their breath around Executioners- particularly elders, I've noticed.

"And now?" I asked, but only for the sake of being polite.

"Summer is a curse," he answered wistfully before chugging the rest of his drink and walking out without any further elaboration.

His words lingered in my head as I tried to piece together what he meant by that. It was frustrating to not comprehend something so simply phrased, but I brushed it away and instead pondered on what to order. My brainstorming was suspended after I felt a cold hand roughly grip my shoulder. I turned my head a few degrees, and in the corner of my peripherals I spotted the last person I wanted to see right now- a person I've always dreaded seeing. I hesitated on turning around completely, but I did nonetheless.

"I didn't think you could be more of a failure, little girl, but you prove me wrong every time," came the most aggravating voice which belonged to the most aggravating scumbag- Bryce Miller.

We were both nominated for the position I now have as a Hunter, but my skill ultimately surpassed his. He's detested me for as long as I can remember, but winning the position only deepened that resentment. I remained quiet and looked down at the ground, because deep down, I knew he had the right to say that after I'd foolishly let a rebel escape. *I guess the news did spread quickly.*

I attempted to cut off this confrontation by heading toward the exit, but I was immediately stopped by Bryce's strong arm blocking the door.

"I'm not done talking," he said. His pale, freckled face displayed a grin at his own remarks. "You know, if you're gonna be a Hunter, you actually have to catch the deviants, hun."

My eyes immediately gravitated toward the crow sitting on the window frame, and my body suddenly felt much colder . . . *He's listening.* I heard the teens at the table chuckle at his snarky comment and my cold face now burned with irritation. I had heard enough of their obnoxious laughter, and certainly enough of Bryce's voice, so I pushed Bryce away from the door with so much force I knocked him off his feet. He fell onto one of the wooden tables, which caught his fall, and all laughter ceased as I walked away from that humiliating scene and began to head home. *I suppose there's nothing wrong with eating at home.*

It took some time due to my leg injury, but I managed. All I needed to do was cross over a small hill, and my house was situated right on the other side. As I struggled up the hill, I noticed it was nearly nighttime. I only knew this because the haloed, black sun was beginning to dip below the horizon, and the faint glow on the horizon was fading. I looked over the hill and dozens of little lights turned off as everyone prepared to shut down for the night.

The eclipsed sun that set and rose each day on this desolate, gray land always begged for all eyes to see it- at least mine never failed to. I've always felt especially drawn to that blinding light behind the eclipse. That dark veil hid a million untold secrets, unanswered questions, history, and all the light along with it. It was such a ravishing mystery, but perhaps it remained better untold.

I sat down and watched the dark sky transform into a blend of dark blues in a matter of minutes. It's a hobby of mine to sky watch, my way of making myself feel human, even after every inhumane thing I do. In today's case, it was a good way to stray my mind away from the day's disappointments- including the stressful conversation at the market.

I observed the multiple crows that scattered the land as they flew around and pecked at whatever they found intriguing. They were like the all-seeing eyes; they saw every sin you committed and spared no one from their retribution. They watched our every move; from each breath we took, to each mistake we made- like the eyes of *God*.

Faintly in the background I could hear the strings of The Bardman playing- that's the name I gave him at least. He wore a long black tunic and cape, along with a mask that covered his entire face except his eyes, which were covered anyways by shades- hiding all traces of his identity. All I knew about him was his music which I always heard playing in the distance. The sounds that danced inside his old, wooden guitar released out onto the earth and created the most beautiful of music. His strings made this run-down town feel like home. Nobody really knew who he was, nor did they seem to care- people here only ever worried about themselves.

I lay on top of the deteriorating grass, and it crunched beneath me. Grass was always brittle and never truly green. They say it's from the residue that remained in the air from the nuclear attack almost a century ago- but I doubted it; radiation didn't impede plant growth. My best guess was the lack of light- artificial light could only do so much- and the dropping temperatures, which seemed to be dropping even lower these days. I couldn't tell for sure though- the world has always been quite frigid.

I closed my eyes for a second, then I heard footsteps crinkle the grass, along with a string instrument. This time it wasn't the Bardman's guitar- it was a *violin*.

"Why are you out here sleeping when your house is right over there?" came a small voice.

I opened one eye and saw the green-eyed Hunter and her smiling, freckled cheeks; they always reminded me of how the stars freckled the night sky. Her chestnut hair framed her small face, which was upside down right now. Aurora Francis: The Emerald Hunter and Executioner who was also my squadmate. She was the second youngest Hunter and the only other girl besides me in the main league. I sat up to face her properly.

Her uniform was identical to mine- a black leather jumpsuit, lightweight bulletproof vest, a few ammunition belts, weapon belts, plus knee, shoulder, and elbow protection pads. She also had the same honorary gold pin with an engraved picture of a crow, which signified our municipal role as Deviant Hunters and Executioners. The only difference was that her pads and straps were green, while mine were crimson. The most distinguishing of Aurora's factors was probably that she used a bow and arrow; something none of us in the league are good at utilizing besides her- it earned her the nickname in town and amongst the league of, "*The Archer.*"

"Did you manage to catch the deviant?" she asked innocently. It seemed like a genuine question, but I couldn't help but feel taunted. It was provoking, but she is and always has been quite naïve. I couldn't possibly be mad at her.

"No . . . she managed to escape," I answered. Her question threw me back to reality and reminded me of how frustrated I still was about being unable to catch her.

"It's okay, we'll get her sooner or later. One of them had to slip away eventually." She tried to console me, referring to my perfect catch rate until now. "Are you ready for the mass execution on Sunday? Turns out they caught all four leaders from Rebellium in the invasion yesterday," she informed me, which caught me by surprise.

"Rebellium? As in the notorious rebel group?" I asked, still shocked.

"What other Rebellium is there?"

I found it surprising that they would hold the execution so soon after catching them. They had just caught them yesterday, today was Friday, and mass executions were held on Sundays. Only two days from today, we were going to kill them, strip them of their freedom, humanity, and life. *But that's what criminals like them deserved.*

"I'm ready as I'll ever be," I answered monotonically. I began to feel unexplainably unmotivated to do my job, but I assumed it was a result of the failure of today.

We continued our small talk for a while longer; she was always easy to talk to. Aurora and our other two squadmates were the closest thing I had to friends in my life, but we were technically co-workers, so that could easily be the reason for our bond. A sudden silence overcame the conversation, and then out of the blue, something fell right out of the sky and landed in between me and Aurora. We both gasped and instinctively drew back. It took me a moment to peer through the darkness due to the limited light around us. Torches and lamps became scarcer the further you were from the town center, and since we were in the outskirts, it was rather dim.

On the ground, a small crow lay in front of my very eyes, motionless and *lifeless*. We glanced at each other to make sure we were both seeing the same thing, and we were. The guardians and observers of this land- our Savior's vision- had just fallen dead in front of us. The eyes of God had just been forcefully shut.

"Let's pretend like that didn't just happen," suggested Aurora as we both stood up. She rubbed her arms to keep warm from the frigid temperatures, which each day seemed to get colder. I remembered the words of the old man; *summer is a curse.*

"I think I'm gonna head home, it's getting quite cold. Tomorrow we're sleeping in the base, so we'll have all weekend to chat," she said with a smile, which had to be one of the most comforting smiles on this planet. She picked up her violin and started to walk in the direction of her home. "And don't worry about the crow, I'm sure it was an accident. It probably flew into a torch or something," she reassured before finally waving goodbye and walking down the hill.

I looked back down at the black bird on the floor and adjusted my focus enough to notice something peculiar on the bird's body. I knelt down to examine the corpse, and I swore I saw what looked like a burn mark on its small body. It was getting really dark now, with nothing but the dim silver gleam of the moon and a few lamps and torches lighting the terrain. I scanned closer and my eyes were right; the tips of its feathers were burnt, and some were completely incinerated. I could see the bird's pink flesh had also fallen victim to the flames. *Who would do such a thing?* I asked myself, *and did they not know the consequences?*

I stood up steadily, trying not to force my knee too much. I had absolutely no clue what to do with the dead crow in front of me. *What do I even do in a situation like this?* I wondered. I wasn't sure who, but I knew I had to catch the person who'd burned it. Before I could even ponder another solution, I heard the sound of the grass rustling right behind me. *It has to be the deviant who burned the crow,* was my immediate thought. I hovered my hand over my pistol without completely drawing as I gradually turned my head around. Once I had, my eyes could not discern what they were seeing.

It was an ominous sight; someone in a burnt white robe idly standing there. They wore a white mask covering the top half of their face, but it was no regular mask; it was a mask with a long beak. It looked an awful lot like a bird, but it wasn't a crow, it was another

8

type of unfamiliar bird. The eeriest part about the whole costume was that they wore the mouth mask deviants wore while being killed. I stood there flooded with confusion and unease, and the deviant took that as a chance to run into the town, and they ran fast.

I snapped out of my trance immediately. "You won't gonna get away from me!" I shouted, trying to intimidate them, but they were far ahead. My words probably didn't even reach their ears.

I pulled out my pistol and chased after them. The pain in my knee immediately cried out, demanding me to feel it. My body wanted me to stop running, but I couldn't; I couldn't let another rebel escape again on the same day. I kept aimlessly running for minutes until I accepted that I had lost the rebel. I cursed myself for letting two deviants escape on the same day, and I fell to the ground, so frustrated I wanted to scream all the air out of my lungs. I punched the ground, as I had earlier, with my already sore hand.

After cooling off to some degree, I noticed something glowing on the ground; a small light I thought could've been a match or something. The light suddenly morphed into something that resembled a butterfly- a glowing, flaming butterfly. Its fragile light lit up the open air, disrupting the darkness around it with every flap of its small, delicate wings. Its bright contrast to the darkness reminded me so much of the little stars that lit up the night sky- the same stars I admired so much. It flew towards the forest, and my curiosity brought me back to my feet. I followed without a second thought.

I followed it blindly, and the more I thought about it, the more I realized how bad of an idea this could be; I could easily be falling into a trap. I abruptly stopped and began to process everything. There was an unusual sensation in my chest and a lot of emotions fighting in my head- frustration, pain, annoyance -but the dominating feeling was *curiosity*. As much as I wanted to chase it through the forest, I knew I needed to go home. I forced myself to pretend it was a hallucination, *but was it?*

I turned around and let out what seemed like my hundredth sigh of disappointment today, when suddenly my chest started getting extremely hot. For only a fleeting moment my heart felt like it was on fire, but it was enough to bring my knees to the ground. I clutched my chest in pain, until I realized there was no pain. Confusion came over me, overpowering any curiosity. I know I didn't imagine *that*.

The abnormal sensation from before was becoming concerning; *did I need to see a physician?* I panicked internally. This weekend was going to be the most important in my career, and I could not miss it for anything; the world would have to *catch on fire* for me to miss it. My internal conflict was interrupted by the freakish butterfly circling me. I was indecisive on what to do next; *was I supposed to follow it?* I thought as I glanced into the forest- the dying yet always growing forest. I liked to think I lived life on the edge, but for once, something actually felt truly dangerous.

I might not know much about nature, but I know enough to know butterflies don't glow, nor do any insects exist that appear to be made of fire. I was conflicted, but there was only one right option in my mind. I stood up from the gravelly ground, faced my fear, and followed it into the deep, dark woods.

I walked with heavy steps and a heart rate probably too fast to be healthy. I walked along the lonely, unwritten trail in the woods that would eventually lead me to the answers to all my questions. I looked around and swallowed nervously when I noticed there was not one single crow in the perimeter. I had heard rumors on the street that the forests were completely unsurveilled, and that's why no one but rebels went in, but surely The Crow must've set up some eyes around here. *Why wouldn't he?*

The more I thought about it the more I regretted following the damned thing, but I still felt inclined to follow. I just hoped whatever was waiting for me on the other side was worth the risk. I was quivering in fear, not to mention the addition of the bitter cold temperatures. After a while, I felt like I almost didn't need the butterfly's guidance anymore. For some inexplicable reason, it didn't feel like my first time walking this exact trail.

The walk dragged out forever, but I eventually reached a peculiar area void of trees. There was a burnt patch in the heart of the forest- no trees, no grass- just scorched dirt. My eyes scoured the perimeter, and through the profound darkness, I managed to distinguish the rebel from before looming in the very middle of the treeless zone. The glowing butterfly flew back to the deviant and circled around them the way it had with me. I've never felt so intimidated in my almost eighteen years of living. I wanted to run away at that moment, but I breathed in and resisted; *it was a deviant, and I had to kill them before they killed me*, I convinced myself.

"Thought you could hide here? District Four Hunter and Executioner- surrender your little game or I'll shoot right here, right now," I threatened as I pulled my gun on them.

I tried my best to conceal all traces of fear, and I think I hid it proficiently. The rebel ignored me and dropped something from their robe- another dead crow, also burned to death. I had to wonder how bad the bird must've suffered before it died. I swallowed hard and my eyes shifted from the crow on the ground back to the rebel. I failed to find their eyes, but I could feel them staring not *at* me, but *inside* me.

"You're the one playing," they murmured in a gritty, feminine voice that shook me to the core.

"Give it up. Distractions are futile," I threatened again, but it was such an empty threat.

I attempted to put together their words and I found myself slumped. *The one playing what exactly? Did they know me?* Either they were out of their mind, or I was losing mine.

"The truth will catch up to you, and when it does, you will pay the price of knowing too," they replied. Their gritty, sinister voice sounded sick and fragile.

"What?" I asked, genuinely confused. I was still aiming my pistol, but they didn't seem threatened or intimidated in the slightest.

"The Prophet will reignite burned-out flames," they said before a brief pause. "The Phoenix will *rise from the ashes*," they finished, right before my hand acted on its own and pulled the trigger. The bullet shot straight through their chest, and I was surprised to see the bullet pierce exactly where I'd aimed considering how much my arms were shaking.

I didn't want to hear any more of it; the situation was making me anxious all of a sudden- something I hadn't felt in years. It was like my ears wouldn't allow me to listen anymore and my brain had begun to reject every word. My heart raced and my head spun. They lowered their head, staring down at the wound, and then looked back at me. Their arm rose to touch the wound, but when the sleeve slid down-

A hand never came out of the sleeve.

Chapter 2

I came here looking for answers, and I was going to leave more confused than ever. No blood dripped out of the wound, nor did a single stain tarnish the white robe. *How were they not injured?* I wondered, and of all the feelings I could've felt, I felt furious. I was enraged because I let a deviant evoke such emotions out of me; because I let a deviant affect me so much. My fury overthrew my fear, and I darted towards them and pulled the white robe off. I wanted to see the damage I'd inflicted without a barrier of cloth in between; I wanted to watch them as they bled out.

I didn't know what I was expecting to find behind the robe, *a person, maybe? But there was no one there.* After I yanked the robe off, there was nothing- not a human, not an animal, *just nothing.* The mask and the mouth cover dropped to the ground, and random embers shot from out of nowhere, delicately floating in the air as they dimmed one by one. I drew back, shielding my face from the embers, and I looked around me. There were no more surprises; no more people, no more embers, no more weird butterflies- there was absolutely nothing. Nothing but me, the darkness, the silence, and her words echoing in my head.

Did I hit my head earlier? I genuinely wondered as anxiety and madness weighed my feet down. I didn't know any better than to run, so I forced my muscles to move, and I ran. I ran from the forest, from the deviant, her embers, the butterflies, her lies- and I didn't look back. I pushed my legs to move faster than they could and forced my lungs to use every last bit of air. I hit a number of branches as I ran, but I felt none of them crashing against my skin.

I didn't stop running until I got to the wooden fence situated outside my house. I jumped over it, not even bothering with the gate, and tumbled upon landing. My chest was tight and begging for air, and my knee would've given out if I had run even a second longer. I gasped vigorously for air, and I could see my breath in the frosty air each time I exhaled. I turned my head and looked behind me and saw nothing but darkness and perpetual silence; no weird apparitions or burning butterflies.

Maybe I was hallucinating from hunger? Stress maybe? I tried to conceive an explanation. I've gone so much longer without food, and I've been under way more stress, yet nothing like this ever happened. I went back and forth in my head until it started hurting. I decided to go with the whole scenario being a mere hallucination, and that the threat only ever existed in my head; fear only existed in our weak minds.

Instead of going straight inside, I sat down on the paper-like grass to reflect on everything. I felt as if I hadn't gotten enough of nature's simple beauty for today. Even if it was barely visible at night, I still knew it was there with every breath of cold air. Reflection for me was a risky game, because it made me think, and thinking inevitably made me *remember.*

I stared up at the night sky and its flashing lights for what must've been the fifth time today. The wind blew and sang the whistling song I loved so much. I closed my eyes and hoped it would blow me away with it. Even as the sharp wind gusted against my eyes and made them water, they remained glued to the sky. My mind trailed off and began to ponder all the things this world didn't have the answers to.

I asked myself the usual questions, like, *what did the rest of the stars look like up close? Were they all like our sun?* I knew they were trivial questions, especially because I would probably never know the answers, but there's always one question that no matter how hard I try to push away, the curiosity always comes back up; *has our sun always looked this way- dark and eclipsed?*

I walked up to the front door of our house, and I struggled to unlock it with my shaky hands. We had a decent house, decent for the outskirts of this beat-up district. It had a large main room and four small rooms surrounding it; the main room was a kitchen, dining room, and living area all in one, and the smaller rooms were a bathroom, and three bedrooms- one each for me, my mother, and my grandmother. The second I entered I was immediately greeted by the mouthwatering smell of my mother and grandmother's cooking coming from the kitchen in the corner.

"Welcome home." My mother took a brief glance at me as she greeted me, then quickly shifted her attention back to the boiling pot on the stove.

"Thanks," I replied, making my way towards the dining table and sitting in my designated chair.

My mother was undoubtedly beautiful, and although my grandmother claims I resemble her a lot, I disagree and believe I must've inherited a lot more of my father's genes. I didn't have her infamous, emerald eyes, nor had I even a fraction of her beauty. She did share a few things though- like her petite stature and wavy, coffee-brown locks.

My mother was incredibly young for being the mother of an almost eighteen-year-old, but that's because she had me at the age of sixteen. Although I didn't exactly know all the details of how I was brought into this world, I knew it wasn't exactly a joyous, heartwarming story. I've never met my father, and my mother claims she doesn't remember him enough to spot him in a crowd. I don't know his name, his face, who he is, or where he lives. He probably doesn't even know I exist, making him just another mystery in my life.

One thing me and my mother do share in common, is that neither of us really knew our fathers. I don't know who my grandfather is either, but I don't ask, nor do I insist on knowing. It's pointless to know since he just abandoned us as well.

My grandmother turned her attention from whatever was in the oven and came over to the table to give me a hug. She wrapped her arms around me and pulled me into a tight, comforting embrace that never failed to warm me, however, this time I felt perhaps *too* warm. Another inexplicable shot of heat burned through my chest like the last one in the forest had. I groaned quietly and jolted away from the hug to grip my chest, but the pain was gone before I could even fully process it.

"What's wrong, honey? Did you get heartburn or something?" my grandmother asked ironically. In my peripheral vision I also saw that I had captured my mother's attention.

"I guess you could call it that," I answered.

"What the hell happened to you? You look like you were thrown off a hill and ravaged by branches!" exclaimed my mom as she scanned me from top to bottom.

I hadn't seen myself yet, but I knew if I saw what I looked like, I would probably agree. *How do I explain that I fell in glass and splinters after letting a rebel escape, and then ran for my life in the woods after having a creepy imaginary encounter with a rebel?*

"It was a rough day," was all I could really say. I didn't feel like having that conversation with them.

My mother sighed and turned back to the kitchen to grab a few cups and silverware. She set them on the table as my grandmother served us the food. They had made some sort of stew followed up with some sweet bread that was fresh out of the oven. As soon as I saw the food, I was glad I came home to eat instead of eating in town. My mother rummaged through the cabinet our small television sat on while my grandmother and I had already begun to eat. She didn't take too long to find what she was looking for, and she came back to the table with a first aid kit in her hands.

"After you eat, I'll wrap you up," my mother said.

"Don't need it," I rejected coldly as I spooned the stew into my mouth.

"Why are you pushing us away more than usual?" she asked with an attitude.

"Why are you pushing *me* more than usual?" I refuted and looked her in the eyes.

"Don't be rude, *Phoenix*," Mother scolded sternly, and I almost spat out my dinner.

"Don't you dare call me that-" I began to speak, but something caught my eye which made me choke on my words.

My gaze landed on the window, more specifically the crow watching from the window's ledge. My heart felt like it stopped beating for a good second. I've never feared a crow surveilling me, but after everything that took place today, I didn't know if I could still confidently say that. To make matters worse, I'm almost certain the crow heard my mother just now. I swallowed hard and looked down at my stew, swirling it nervously with my spoon and praying that nobody would ask what had happened today for the rest of the evening.

The air around me was getting thinner, and even in these cold, August temperatures, I was sweating bullets. I imagined that it was solely from the sudden panic, until once again, I felt my chest rapidly heating up- only this time, it dragged out longer than usual. I grunted and shriveled into myself, firmly gripping my chest. I managed to lift my head up, knowing the crow was still at my window, watching me as I reduced to ashes. I saw its small, dark eyes scan the room and watch me like a circus attraction. I scrutinized each of the black feathers that gripped the bird's small body, and I studied each of those pristine feathers *as they went up in flames.*

Everything played out in slow motion, and the air around me refused to enter my lungs. I heard voices shouting close by me, but I understood none of the words being said. I watched the sublime creature fall from the window after being incinerated alive, then I too felt myself falling. My grandmother turning to look out the window was the last thing I saw before tumbling down with the world around me.

I couldn't move, but I could listen. I heard my mother rummaging through the first-aid kit to bandage my knee. I couldn't move, but I could feel. I felt a soft blanket and mattress underneath me, so I knew I was in bed.

"I saw it with my own eyes, Cordelia! This is not a mere coincidence!" I was finally able to hear and decipher words again when I heard my grandmother shouting at my mother.

"Quiet down or you'll wake her. And no- I won't let you tell her," my mother stated to shut her down sternly. I feigned my unconscious state a little longer to figure out what they were arguing about.

"Ignorance *isn't* bliss Cordelia . . . I won't keep this façade up any longer and I know deep down you don't want to either," my grandmother replied, "or can it be that they've finally gotten to your head as well?" I began to feel as if the longer I listened, the more confused I was getting.

I felt my mother tighten the bandages on my bare knee. I tried so hard not to move or twitch.

"She's *my* daughter and I want her to live a normal life. I don't want her to end up like us, trading our lives for a hopeless cause," my mother continued.

"It's not hopeless, Cordelia, and she deserves to know as well. I know you remember that day-" my grandma began before being interrupted.

"And if she is to find out about it, what do you think she'll do? You do realize who she is, right?"

I decided to cut her off right there by dramatically jolting awake. Whatever nonsense they were arguing about, it somehow came back to me, and I didn't want them to argue because of me. I opened my eyes and I saw my grandma immediately shift her gaze down to the floor. I looked over to my mother at the end of my bed, her angry, intense look diminished, and her emerald-green eyes widened while she nervously fixed her long brown hair.

"I'm glad you're okay," she said, her voice shaking a bit, "you scared us there."

"What happened back there?" I knew perfectly well what had happened, but I wanted to hear what they would come up with.

"A crow coincidentally bur-" my grandma started before my mother cut her off.

"You were eating your dinner when suddenly you got flustered and your chest started hurting. You must've passed out from the pain and overstimulation," she rushed the explanation, leaving no room for elaboration.

She continued to fix my bandages without looking at either of us. My grandmother submissively listened and remained silent. She slowly walked towards a small chair in the corner of my room, distancing herself a bit. There was an awkward silence for a while until my mother broke it by initiating small talk.

"How was your day?" she asked, and I decided I was going to respond to her question more explicitly.

"Well, I chased a deviant today. She was a young woman, probably mid-twenties, and I chased her down quite a few blocks. I almost caught her, but she managed to escape- not unwounded though, as I shot her in the arm," I began, and my mother simply nodded. "Deviants are so desperate to cling onto their insignificant lives," I added in a menacing tone, looking straight at her.

"They sure are," she replied and swallowed hard, still avoiding eye contact. She shot a glance at my grandma, who returned it.

19

"You'd never be like them, would you, Phoenix?" my grandmother asked out of the blue. Suddenly the tension grew so strong it could be cut with a knife.

"First of all, don't call me that name-"

"But it's your name, is it not?" She cut me off almost mockingly, and I glared at her. I felt insulted that she would even ask such a ridiculous question and then follow it up with *that goddamn name.*

"It's Fefe, Crimson, or nothing at all," I declared with animosity. My mother's discomfort could be seen even by blind eyes, and that's when she stepped her foot down.

"Let's go, mother. She needs to rest," my mother ordered in a desperate tone. If I didn't know any better, I'd think she was afraid of me.

She and my grandmother scurried out of the room, and we exchanged one last look before they walked out. As I glared into their eyes, I tried to search for any sort of clue in them. Once I was alone, I fell back onto my bed and my hands clenched the blanket so tightly my knuckles turned white. *That name, that goddamn name*, I cursed in my head. Just hearing it made my skin crawl. I've lived my entire life bearing that filthy name my mother gave me, and no matter how many aliases I go by, Phoenix would remain with me until the end of time.

In town I was simply known as Crimson, which derived from the color of my Hunter uniform, but before that I went by Fefe. I left my real name out because of the heavy stigma surrounding it, though Phoenix was indeed my real name. There's a legend out there of a woman who once attempted to overthrow The Crow decades ago; she was known as *The Phoenix.* Although the whole story and name are a but a folktale as far as we're concerned, it's still taboo, and having the same name as her can raise some suspicions. I've made countless sacrifices and have gone through hell and back to wipe that name off me- *truly hell.*

I vowed years ago to devote my life and loyalty to The Crow- the ruler of this nation; *"The one who overthrew and overcame,"* as we all like to say. He fought with us during the darkest times this nation has known and led us out of the darkness that once cast over our people. With valor and courage, he picked up the pieces of the broken country that once was and built them back up- something The Phoenix *failed* to do. So with great pride, I carried out the duty to cleanse this nation of rebels who try to defy his glorious rule.

I grew more and more drowsy as I lay in my bed looking at the same four walls I'd stared at for at least an hour. I eventually turned to check the small clock that sat on a wooden nightstand next to my bed. It read 10:36. I didn't realize it was that early; I would have thought it was midnight. The sky doesn't work around here, so we needed clocks, because time doesn't exist in a world that's always dark.

I looked out the small window beside my bed, and saw nothing but complete and utter darkness. The most notable difference between night and day was that the moon showed up during the night, and a dark void surrounded by a blinding ring of light replaced it during the day. The sun hid so much behind that dark curtain, and it was so desperate to hide itself from us; I don't blame it though, if I could, I'd hide from the world as well. During the day, the sky was painted a grayish-indigo from the dark sun faintly subduing the night's darkness with its crown of light, but the world was always dark. The only real source of light came from the thousands of lamps and torches that scattered the streets.

As I lounged in my bed, my mind began to aimlessly drift off as my body grew more and more limp. I'd imagine that anyone would quickly fall asleep after having a day like mine- everyone but me. No matter how tired my body was, my mind always did everything in its power to keep me up, and the burdens from today didn't help one bit.

I glanced down at my leg, just now realizing I was still in my uniform, but I couldn't be bothered to change. I only took my belts, protection pads, and bulletproof vest off, which in itself took a huge weight off for the night.

I took a deep breath and tried to focus on falling asleep. This weekend was going to be a busy one, so I had to be well rested. Sunday would be a day to remember- *a day that will go down in history.* As hard as I focused on sleeping, I still couldn't get myself to actually sleep, and I knew it was because of my hectic mind and the blur of emotions stirring around in my head. In this cruel world, feeling makes you weak, and weakness gets you killed. In the line of work I'm in, you can't afford that risk, but I knew I couldn't avoid my own mind forever, so just this time, I let my dreary thoughts finally cradle me to sleep.

Like most mornings in this run-down district, it was hard to open my eyes. Before I could do anything, my mind instantly bombarded me with flashbacks of yesterday's events; from the deviant escaping, to the crows burning, and that crazy encounter I had in the woods. Against my will, I found myself still trying to formulate a logical explanation to the encounter, along with the message it left with its scratchy voice. For the first time in my life, I understood what someone was saying, but didn't understand what they were trying to say.

Before I got too tangled up in a web of conspiracies, I sat up and turned to check the time. It was eight in the morning, and I was on the clock at 9:30, so I had to get going. As I sat up, I noticed my knees were still neatly wrapped in bandages. I also noticed the pain- or lack thereof. I got up and made my bed, knowing I wasn't going to sleep in it for a couple of days since I would be staying in the Executioners Cabin. The rooms there were on the smaller side and the ambience was somewhat discomforting due to the nature of our jobs, but it beat sleeping outside.

I stepped into our small bathroom and ran some water in our equally small tub. As it filled up, I took off my dirty uniform and brushed away the knots in my dark, wavy, waist-length, hair. I stepped a foot into the warmth before submerging myself in the water. I sat there idly for about five minutes before I began cleaning myself.

Taking baths more than twice a week in this town was a luxury, so I tried not to take it for granted.

A lot of things I had were probably considered luxurious to most, but that's because hard work pays off. The district mayor and his family were the most pampered, the average workers- which was everyone else- were at the bottom. Executioners and military personnel were slightly above the average person and there weren't that many of us, so it was only a thin slice of the town's demographic. The Crow firmly believed in no person being deprived of basic human necessities, nor one person within the districts being significantly richer than another, but we got a little more because of the harder roles we had to play.

D.C, the Capital city where The Crow himself resided, was evidently the richest and was the top tier of the pyramid. Despite our rather short distance to the grand city, most people could only dream of visiting D.C. The capital's demographic consists of scientists, historians, and federal workers. They're important people in this nation, but The Crow claims they have no more importance than the average citizen; their jobs just require a bit heavier surveillance.

The only times we ever saw the Capital was in the glimpses we saw on television during The Crow's speeches. It looked so modern and advanced, and they say it's the closest resemblance to what the world looked like before The Revolution, but The Crow's word was the only credible source we had left since everything was demolished after The Revolution. He claimed erasing the past was the only way to move on from it, so every book, document, and idea was erased and burned to ashes, ashes that built this new world.

When my fingers began pruning, I stood up and grabbed the towel that I placed on a chair along with a clean uniform. I dried myself and my hair off while I looked in the fogged-up mirror in front of the tub. I hadn't realized how cold it was in the bathroom until I got out of the hot water. My teeth chattered from the low early morning temperatures and cold floor beneath my bare feet as I stepped out of the tub.

I sat on the edge of the wooden tub, grabbed my thick, cotton socks from the chair, and slipped them on without wasting a second; the socks served as a barrier between my flesh and the cold floor. I wiped the condensation off the mirror and examined myself as I detangled my hair again. Despite looking like the small teenager I was, I still had quite an intimidating effect on everyone in the town. The bags under my tired, black-brown eyes really complimented my transparent skin; restless nights were my forte. My eyes went down to the purple bruise on my knee, and I smiled a little- it reminded me of the milky way.

I grabbed my black, leather jumpsuit and attempted to dress myself as quickly as I could to further shield myself from the seemingly decreasing temperatures. It was a tight but still breathable fit and it was impressively durable. I haven't ripped it to this day despite all the hazards I've encountered. It was over my lower body and I was about to pull it over my arms when I noticed a strange mark on my forearm. It looked like a burn mark at first glance- but not just any burn mark; it highly resembled a *bird*.

I leaned over to the tub which still had some water remaining and I vigorously tried to scrub it off my wrist until it turned red. No matter how hard I tried to wash it away, it refused to come off or even move. *When did I burn myself?* I wondered as I retraced everything from the past week. Before I could ponder too hard, I recalled the time and realized I had to rush out the door relatively soon.

I quickly put my arms through the jumpsuit but was careful with my wrist, which was tender to the touch from the intense scrubbing. I zipped up the suit at the chest and grabbed my bulletproof vest, and equipped it along with my ammunition belts, and my gun and sword holsters. I tied my crimson protection-pads to each of my joints including my knees, elbows, and shoulders. I made sure I grabbed one of my extra knee-pads from the closet because the one from yesterday had cracked at the impact of the fall. I took one last quick glimpse in the mirror before walking out, ready to take the day on.

The humidity of the bathroom contrasted with the dry, cold air in the rest of the house. Before walking out, I strapped my rifle onto my back, grabbed my handgun from my room, along with my sword, and slid them into the holsters tied to the crimson strap on my waist. I felt like utilizing my sword today; I was one of the most skilled swordspeople in the league, *so why not use it on this special weekend?* The clock read 9:15, meaning I had only a few minutes to get out there and start my shift.

I closed the door in my room and I made my way towards the front door, but I stopped before reaching it. My grandmother idly sitting on the worn-out couch caught my attention. She just sat there, blankly looking at the ground.

"Good morning. where's Mother?" I asked. She blinked harshly, snapping out of a deep ponder.

"Good morning, dear. I think she's out getting groceries at the market," she responded. She looked dazed and troubled, but I couldn't read her well enough to know why. I wondered if it had to do with the argument from yesterday.

"Alright, well I'm off," I said as I opened the door, instantly getting slapped with cold air.

"Are you off to work?" she asked monotonically, and then I knew something was off.

"Why wouldn't I?" I replied.

I was about to step out when she stopped me. "Are you coming home tonight at all?" she asked, almost in a desperate tone.

"I might stop by to get some stuff for tomorrow before sundown." I didn't actually plan on coming home tonight, but I felt almost compelled. I expected an "Okay honey be safe," or a "See you later baby," but instead she grimly responded with;

"I have to talk to you. I'll see you tonight."

Chapter 3

I approached the town center with all sorts of thoughts bouncing around in my conscience, all fighting for dominance over my mind. It seemed like every time I closed my eyes, I saw crows burning and their ashes crumbling. Along with that, my head was still trying to make sense of that strange apparition in the forest. I was trying to convince my brain it was just an illusion, *but how warped would my mind have to be to even come up with such a deranged distortion of reality?* And to top it all off, I had its cryptic message to think about, along with my own grandmother's bizarre behavior. I didn't know if I could take any more madness before I went utterly bonkers.

"How can you all be so blind?"

I snapped back to the present when I heard a woman yelling. Just up ahead were dozens of confused and disturbed faces; some walked right past the scene, but a few stayed and watched. I chose to be nosy and watch from a distance before interfering, so I walked extra slowly towards the commotion.

"They're controlling us! Brainwashing us into believing there is a future living under his control!" she began to spew, capturing my full attention. "The sun . . . How does no one else see it? Our own stars are telling us to open our eyes!" she exclaimed, and it sent chills traveling down my back.

She was an older woman with gray hair and pronounced wrinkles. Someone her age shouldn't be protesting like this- especially not the blasphemy she was spouting from her old lips. She was committing treason so indiscreetly, further proving that rebels were nothing more than vermin with absolutely no shame. *All deviants ever did was poison the minds of those ignorant enough to listen.*

"Our own sun is scared of what humanity has become. . . and it hides more and more from humanity as the days go on!" she yelled off the top of her lungs. The passion was evident with each strain in her voice. It made me wonder how anyone could ever be that passionate about something so *wrong.*

"The time is coming close . . . the time The Prophet will free us all- those who believe, and those who don't alike. They know mercy and salvation, and they will deliver us from this evil," she said loudly, but not necessarily yelling. "They will be the one to put an end to The Crow!" This time she screamed so loudly it rang in my ears even moments after her voice had ceased.

I didn't even realize how close I had gotten to the whole scene until I bumped into someone. I was oddly infatuated by her boldness to say such things out loud- things no one even dared think to themselves. What made me most uneasy was the undeniable parallels between what the woman was saying and what I heard last night. *Could I refute her argument with that same confidence?* I asked myself. This woman's passion made me realize how much I was truly beginning to doubt and question everything- including myself. I certainly wasn't a fan of this feeling of helpless uncertainty.

"There's an Executioner right in front of you, I'd watch what you're saying unless you want to die," someone in the crowd threatened. I was finally noticed, which meant I needed to act now before people began to suspect. *An Executioner can't have doubt; what's wrong with me?*

I approached the woman, trying my best to look as intimidating as possible. I managed to make the villagers scram and hold their breath- but not that woman. She didn't seem in the slightest bit intimidated by me, which piqued me and my pride a lot. When I was only an arm's reach away from her, she finally responded to the man's threat in the crowd.

"I don't care if I'm shot right here right now, freedom has no price. Everyone deserves to know what it's like to live a proper life," she began calmly before yelling again. "The moment we come to life, death is already waiting- and I could never die knowing I died as a slave to The Crow!"

There was so much bitterness and disdain in her voice when she spoke of The Crow. The crowd's unfiltered and raw responses were left in the air- never to be shown. Everyone was left fearful and speechless, yet it stayed that way for only a second before a hostile uproar erupted from the people. If you had asked me a week ago why they were so rowdy and confrontational, I would've answered that it was because she had just defamed and smeared The Crow's name- but not today. I knew all too well it was because she'd triggered everyone to *think*, and as a consequence- to *doubt*. The only thing they can do to kill the loud noise of doubt, is to raise their voices louder than the ones pounding in their heads.

I decided now was the time to take matters into my own hands and cease the chaos. I yanked the old woman's frail arm and held it firmly. We briefly made eye contact, and in her dark eyes, I saw a formidable resentment for The Crow and everything he stood for, including me. In just that brief moment, her gaze managed to penetrate my skin all the way down to my bones. I ignored it and resumed my frigid demeanor as I dragged the old woman away with me. I was taking her far from that crowd, because what I was about to do should not be seen by anyone's eyes.

As we went deep into the forest, I gripped the old woman's arm so tightly it would surely leave bruises. I threw her onto the forest ground; we were deep enough where there were no crows. She grunted from the impact and before she could even fully sit up, I drew my sword and pointed the blade straight at her face. I saw the same look of terror there that every rebel had on their face, and I celebrated inside knowing I'd finally managed to intimidate her. That put my pride at ease.

What kind of shocked me was that she didn't even try to fight back. I guess she knew she stood no chance against me. Though there was still something about this rebel that was different from the rest- she wasn't afraid of death, unlike the others. She knew what she'd done and was willing to suffer the consequences- she lived up to her word back there. She glared hard at the sharp point of the blade, then switched her gaze back up to me. I knew she caught onto my hesitation, and it was because I had *no* intention of killing her. Not now, not later.

"Tell me everything you know about this said 'Prophet,'" I demanded.

The look of confusion and surprise on her face was unmatched to anything I'd ever seen before. She looked at me as if I had just spoken a foreign language. The astonishment must've left her unable to speak- or maybe she just didn't have an answer.

"I don't like having to wait," I followed up spitefully while touching the blade to her chest, a small drop of blood trickling down where my sword met her skin. This was my way of reestablishing my authority; I was not to show any sort of submission to anyone, especially those as low as rebels.

"The Prophet . . . is going to be the new Phoenix. They will finish what the old Phoenix started . . . They're going to kill The Crow- It's the only way to resurrect the sun," she began, stuttering considerably along the way. "Even someone of your skill and stature will be unable to defeat them!" she blurted out to reinforce her valor, but the insult didn't faze me- I've heard much worse throughout my days.

"You're quite brave considering the fact your life depends on the pull of a trigger," I responded.

"I do not fear you . . ." she responded, "but not because you do not intimidate me, but because *I know* The Prophet is coming," she repeated so self-assuredly.

"Justice will prevail, and you murderous tools will burn in The Phoenix's flames! All of you will burn!" she choked out. Her confidence was enviable.

I found myself struggling to cut the conversation short and just kill her like I always did. I'd felt no remorse for deviants until I met this woman; she was just so hard to kill. She was the only exception . . . *but was it truly just her?* I reluctantly asked myself, really beginning to second guess everything. If I was faced with any other deviant, I'd shoot them dead with no mercy . . . so then . . . *why couldn't I do it right now?*

"Kill me now. I know I will be killed on the stage anyways, so I chose to be a silent martyr," she pleaded with a sternness in her voice which only made killing her more difficult for me.

I withdrew my sword and placed it in its scabbard. Instead, I pulled out my handgun and aimed it at her forehead as I always did with my rifle for stage executions- it was a quick and humane death. I looked her in the eyes as I hovered my finger over the trigger- death written on the bullet. Too many times I've seen a dying man pleading for another chance, only to take their life without hesitation, *so why did I hesitate with this woman? What made her so different?* I asked myself yet again, sounding like a broken record. *Could it be . . . that it was me who was different?*

When I looked at her, the image of the masked deviant flashed before me, as if they were the same person. Her tired and gray face was enveloped with such profound sorrow, not menace. I began to wonder if rebels always looked this way. My mind was going mad while flipping between what I have been told to believe and defend my entire life, and the satisfaction I was gaining from what I was beginning to unfold on my own. I couldn't take it anymore; *squeeze your eyes shut and pull the damn trigger.*

The loud roar from the gunshot echoed throughout the empty forest and I eagerly threw the gun on the ground afterward. I bent down and grabbed the woman by her tunic, pushing her against a tree that faced away from the town. She looked at me dazzled- in disbelief that she was still breathing and her heart still beating. I had shot the ground; because like I mentioned before, I had no intention of killing her.

"Listen, as soon as I let you go, you are to run as far away from here as possible. *Run and never look back*," I quietly commanded, stressing the last part. I proceeded to thrust her in the direction opposite to the town, she fell back onto the ground but got up quickly. She looked back at me, both shocked and grateful.

"GO!" I shouted, which startled her back into reality. She immediately turned her back to the town and took off into the dark depths of the forest.

I fell to my knees and held my head in my hands; *what have I just done?* I thought after considering the possible repercussions of letting yet another rebel go. I felt my body heating up again despite it only being about forty degrees outside. My mind was too preoccupied to feel anything else at that moment. *Why could I not bring myself to kill that woman? Why did I let her run away?* After everything I've done to suppress the voice in my head, *why was I letting it control me so much now?*

In order to shut my mind up, I had to remind myself of *who I really was*; The Crimson Hunter, a notorious Deviant Hunter and Executioner with the highest kill and capture count in the district, and I *refused* to let myself be influenced by such futile events. I kept that in mind on the walk back to town and kept my mind quiet for a while.

Work was a burden for the rest of the day. Besides the chaos from this morning, there wasn't much action. No deviants were caught, no chases, no unordinary behavior exhibited from people, just another gray day. The twilight sky was beginning to set, and soon everyone would go to sleep, then the night crew would surveil the town.

As much as I wanted to get home and pass the night in bed alone, I had to go to the Executioner's Cabin tonight with the rest of my squad. Since we were the main crew, we were Hunters, but also the Executioners of the town. We got to kill the rebels we caught on the public stage, and tomorrow we would execute the leaders of the most notorious rebel group, Rebellium, which was a *huge* deal. All four leaders, here today, and gone tomorrow . . . *and forever.*

I headed toward the cabin but stopped in my tracks when I remembered what my grandmother had said; *"I have to talk to you tonight."* A faint lump formed in my throat, and I grew unusually nervous. I rarely felt anxious, but I had a heavy feeling draping over me tonight. I seemed to have excessive emotions lately; *such a nuisance.* As I turned around to head back to my house, I walked straight into someone's hard chest. I didn't even realize someone was walking behind me.

"Woah there, Crimson, watch where you're going." A male voice chuckled. It was Nyrual Cadena- one of my squadmates. He was the Blue Hunter, 2nd rank in kill and capture count and exceptionally skilled with the chained blade weapon. His tanned skin, muscular build, dark hair, and sapphire eyes made him a favorite of the town- particularly among the ladies.

"Oh, it's just you," I responded blandly.

"The Cabin's this way. Where are you going?" he asked, pointing in the direction of the Cabin.

"I'm going to pick up some stuff from home, I'll be there in a second."

"Don't take too long now, we're playing cards tonight!" he responded excitedly. It was so dorky how much he and the others were amused by simple card games.

"I won't. I'll see you soon." I closed the conversation with a wave and proceeded to walk toward my house.

As I walked, I looked up at my favorite thing this world had to offer- the sky. It was mid-transition, from twilight to night. The stars began to peek through the indigo but soon-to-be black sky, and the dark sun was starting to set behind the horizon. In the distance, I heard the gentle strings of the Bardman play, even this late into the day. This view and these sounds convinced me there was no place like home. I breathed in the cold air until my lungs hurt, and the subtle pain reminded me of my humanity. So I stood still, letting the earth ground me.

In the distance and through the darkness I saw my mother; she was picking flowers- daffodils, to be exact. I have vivid memories of my mother picking those strange flowers since I was a child. She would sell them as our primary source of money, and they sold well since most flowers can't grow on our barren land anymore. Now that I was an Executioner, she really didn't need those flowers anymore, but she still grew them, even if she didn't sell any. With the night falling and only a dim streetlight nearby, it was getting really dark out, and I didn't understand how she could even see.

I sneaked toward the door, intentionally avoiding her. I didn't want her to hear me and my grandmother's conversation. I turned the knob and thankfully, it was unlocked, so I managed to get in without her even noticing me. I did a quick scan of the room, but the house was empty. The nights decreased significantly in temperature, so I walked up to the fireplace to warm my icy hands. The cold used to be tolerable, but lately, not anymore.

From a scientific standpoint it was hard to believe the world was still turning, what with the freezing temperatures we experienced all year round. Scientists in D.C. were constantly innovating new ways to support life with these dropping temperatures- *but how much longer will they be able to keep this world alive?* They grow crops with artificial light and heat, and the rest of the plants that still thrive in nature are just due to mutation and adaptation I suppose. All I've ever known are these frosty temperatures, but I guess there was a time when the days were warmer, and our bodies and vegetation alike weren't so frail and deficient.

I sat down on the warm ground near the hearth and observed the flames dancing in the pit. The bright and vibrant flames swayed back and forth like long grass in the wind. As my hypnotized eyes observed them, I asked myself, *how could something so beautiful be so destructive?* When you're near the fire, it's such a pleasant feeling, but if you come too close, your flesh will burn. Even after acknowledging that, I felt an urge to reach out for the flames . . . *and just feel them.*

"Phoenix, come quickly!" I heard my grandmother whisper-shout, and I snapped back to the present before making whatever foolish mistake I was about to make.

My hand got a bit too close to the fire and was now pink and tender. My sight was riddled with white spots from the flames' bright light, and it contrasted heavily with the darkness of the room. When my eyes finally adjusted, I saw my grandmother poking her head out of the basement trap door. We barely ever went down to the basement because there was really nothing down there. I nodded in response and climbed slowly down the ladder after her.

The first thing I noticed was that the basement was fully lit by a number of hand lanterns; I had never seen the basement this clearly or with this much light. It was bigger than I realized- about half the size of our house. I turned my attention toward my grandmother, who was digging a hole in the ground with a shovel.

"What are you doing?" I asked, completely puzzled. She ignored my question and continued to dig until the shovel hit something. She knelt down and pulled out whatever the shovel had dug up.

"What is that?" I asked, hoping to not get ignored this time.

"Something I should be killed for having," she responded eerily, and my throat got dry. From the ground, she pulled out a large wooden chest. She set it down and opened it, revealing nothing but a bunch of worn-out books.

"Why would you be killed for having books?" I asked. They weren't the most common item, but by no means were they outlawed.

Usually, the only books we saw were textbooks and other informational pieces since there was typically a fine line between literature and deviancy, but these books didn't look like anything I had seen before. She picked up one of the books and handed it to me. The title read: *The Holy Bible.* She then handed me a heavier, hard-cover book titled: *American History*- this book looked more like a standard school textbook. Lastly, she handed me a small pile of papers.

I unfolded one and it showed a map of some place called the *United States of America*. The other papers were newspapers, dating all the way back to September 18, 2028. The article was about a revolution, and I recalled that the Old-World Revolution started on that day- meaning this was the news from that very day. I was staggered by these rare primary sources, however, there was one question lingering in my head- *why did my grandmother have these and how did she get her hands on them?*

Reading my mind, she finally spoke. "You're probably wondering what these are." I nodded in response. "That article you're holding is a collection of newspapers written throughout The Old-World Revolution. From the very start, all the way till we were blasted by a nuclear bomb."

I looked at the stack and realized there were a lot of pages, and not all were from the same day. The last page was dated September 30, 2028, so I guessed the bomb fell the next day. I switched my gaze between the other books on the ground as well as the map.

"This is a map of this country, back when it used to be called 'The United States of America.' It had so many beautiful, big cities all around the country," she explained, reading my curiosity.

That also explained the big book's title, *American History*; I assumed the habitants of this land previously referred to themselves as "Americans." I scanned the map, completely baffled; there were so many dots and names of places I had never heard of. A current map of our nation in 2098 had mostly the same land outline, but a lot less dots, and the dots were concentrated toward the southeast. The west was inhabitable, barren, deserts and mountainous land, while the north was too cold for survival. The coasts of the old map extended a lot more than they did now- it's been said that the coasts were submerged overtime.

"I'm giving you these pieces of history of the world that once used to be," my grandmother offered. I looked up at her, perplexed by the offer.

Our history books started after The Old-World Revolution- after the bomb dropped- and everything before that was burned, destroyed, and forgotten, so there was no way of knowing what happened prior to the nuclear attack. Our only source of information is The Crow- and of course, we had no other alternative than to believe him. Not many are old enough to know what happened, and those who are, swear they have no recollection whatsoever. It also didn't help that pretty much every piece of history was lost in the nuclear attack. As tempting as it was to find out, *I knew I shouldn't.*

"I know you're not supposed to, honey, but you deserve to know the truth, and I'm the only one who can tell you," she uttered and stared straight into my eyes. "I don't care if you chose to kill me as a consequence, but please . . . *just listen,*" she pleaded. Making it the second time today I'd heard that plea. All I could do in the moment was nod.

She explained her entire story to me from start to finish. She was only seventeen when the war broke out. Months prior to The Revolution, there was a lot of uproar over the government's deeply rooted corruption, along with more unresolved conflicts they had within the country. The people coalesced and this brought upon a wave of rebellion, The Crow himself included. During the commotion, feuding countries took advantage of our weak state, and surprised us with a nuclear attack.

After annihilating over half the American population and rendering the country a wasteland, people, including herself at one point, were left in a weak state of confusion, hate, and unrest, which made the human mind susceptible to false prophets. The Crow rose during this time by demonstrating the immense courage and bravery the people needed in a leader, especially during those postwar times. He took the throne through his persuasive words and promises, but there was one woman who opposed him- she went by the alias, *The*

Phoenix. She saw through his lies and malicious intentions, and she fought against him right up until her last second.

"If she was actually real and not just a legend, then why does no one actually remember her?" I asked, somewhat afraid of the answer.

"The Crow captured her and burned her alive in a shack in front of only whoever was around. That was before TV broadcasting was instilled in every town, so not everyone was able to see it all go down; plus, all her followers mysteriously disappeared afterward, along with everyone's memory of her. I'm sure he brainwashed us all to forget her existence and eliminate the risk of deviating thoughts, but small glimpses of her remain everywhere, and that resurfaces vague, distant memories of her- that's how the 'legend' was born."

"How did you snap out of it and remember her?"

"Her ashes were buried in a secluded burial ground with a small, crumbling grave not too far from here. Her real name is written on that grave, so no one looks twice at it. After I saw the grave, I recalled hiding these books decades prior."

"Why does she have a burial site if she was a deviant?" I asked this because nowadays, after deviants are killed, their bodies are burnt, and their ashes are disposed of- no chance of ever receiving the honor or glory of obtaining a grave after death.

"It's a question I ask myself too. Perhaps in his twisted mind, she was slightly more significant than any other rebel was to him," she answered before continuing her story, which I thought was already over.

She explained some of the reasons scientists had to live in the Capital, one being because of the genetic mutations they performed on The Crow. During the battle against The Phoenix, The Crow had lost an eye, and so he implanted a radioactive and lab-mutated crow's eye in his vacant eye socket. After that, he is said to have gained some bizarre, non-human abilities that we have yet to witness in action.

His ultimate goal with all these mutations was to eventually find a way for him to reign over this land forever, and so after many years of tests and trials, which were performed on captured rebels, they finally managed to create a serum of immortality. Only The Crow has access to this serum, and so with his newly found immortality, along with the narrative he's painted of The Revolution, he enforced the idea that he was a *god*.

He burned all the history books, and any pre-revolution artifacts that remained, and ordered the brainwashing of all survivors of the nuclear attack to forget any memories prior to his reign. He erased history so that the past stayed in the past, and if they were to ever remember and tell anything, they'd be *eradicated*.

"We're all merely toys in his game of power, because those in power must feed off the weak," my grandma explained.

My heart was beating so hard, I could feel it pounding in my head. I couldn't even comprehend what my itching ears were hearing. I knew if I tried to talk, the sounds wouldn't come out as words, so I remained silent.

"But there is always a light in the darkness, and in this case it's a flame," she prefaced. "Before The Phoenix died, she made a promise to return decades later through the soul of another person; this person will be known as The Prophet. They will carry out her battle and put an end to the opposition's ongoing fight for freedom, and they will be the one to finally overthrow and kill The Crow. It's also been prophesied that they will be the one to resurrect the sun that died with the old Phoenix," she finished explaining, and I raised a brow in response to her mentioning the sun.

"The sun that died with her?" I repeated, surprised that words even came out of my mouth.

"Yes, darling. When she died, she truly took the sun with her. This world became so depraved and wicked, and humanity has become so vile, that even the sun hid from humanity. The sun is blacked out in a dark, permanent eclipse until overthrown by humanity's light," she answered, and I could've sworn I felt the temperature around us increase tenfold.

Everything she said paralleled with what the old deviant said, and it all seemed to connect to my encounter in the forest too. Everything lined up so perfectly, meaning this whole thing couldn't just be my grandmother bluffing. *The Phoenix, the sun, the burning crows, the burn mark on my arm,* they all had one thing in common- *fire.* My heart dropped as I pieced everything together, each time feeling it drop even lower. I couldn't understand what I was feeling, since I had never experienced shock to such a high degree.

I couldn't comprehend all of it however hard I tried, and my body began to shake as a response. I squeezed my eyes shut and covered my mouth to stop myself from screaming. I wanted to scream louder than the weight of the words that echoed in my head, but before I could, my grandmother interfered.

"When I was your age, our world was a definite disaster; corrupt, and run by what seemed like humans with no humanity; it was a world run by greed and the never-ending yearning for power, where crime-covered headlines and peoples' worth was determined by superficial traits. It was a place where dangerous diseases spread and constantly killed hundreds, all while nature was holding onto its last breath." She paused briefly and a deep melancholy glossed over her eyes. "Even with all that, the sun felt so warm against my skin- the same sun that somehow makes me feel colder now."

"Was that place . . . worth all the faults?" I asked naively.

"We had so much that we took for granted. The freedom to speak our minds, believe what we wanted to believe, and most importantly- we had the opportunity to become anything we wanted, and not have our lives chosen for us. Back then, people walked the streets without paranoia. Even in the darkness, we had hopes and dreams that no corrupt government could take from us- and yet everything was taken from us faster than we could even imagine," she answered, still melancholic.

"The Crow promised us a better world, and in all you youngsters' eyes, he fulfilled his promise- because this is all you've ever known. All the lies he's filled your heads with have made you believe he is truly a god, when in reality, he is the antichrist," she added with deep spite in her tone.

All the blood drained from my face, and I felt myself growing numb in my limbs. I sat so still, my shaky hands being the only movement. Finding out the world I lived in wasn't the world I was told of, engulfed me with utmost despair. Everything I believed, everything I defended, everything I worked for, and everything *I killed for*, was all a big lie; in other words- it was all for *nothing*.

It couldn't be true; how could this possibly be true? My mind spiraled out of control. *The woman who raised me . . . wouldn't lie to me like this . . . would she?* There was always that doubt, because I knew I wasn't thinking with my head right now; I was only convincing myself to accept the less painful version of the truth for my own sake. I've never been one to think with my heart, because rationality *always* had to stay clear of personal feelings, but there was no easy way to hear what I'd just heard.

"I know you don't want to believe me, and I know you're incredibly confused. I bet you want to scream right now, but before the truth can set you free, it will *scare* you," she comforted. "I want you to read through these tonight, and maybe you'll get some more insight." She spoke calmly, and I wondered how she could be so nonchalant after all that, then it hit me; it's because she lived through it.

After she said that, I don't know what hit me. I didn't know if it was logic finally catching up to my distressed mind, or if it was me simply refusing to accept what I'd been told, but I pulled out my gun, and held it up to her as my hand shook wildly. My head twitched as our eyes made contact. She looked at the barrel of the gun without a speck of regret or fear.

"Phoenix, are you so devoted to your cause that you'd be willing to kill the hands that helped raise you? Kill your own flesh and blood?" she asked me sternly while digging a deep gaze into my clouded eyes, making my palms sweat. "You wouldn't be the first," she added, which puzzled me. *What does she mean by that?*

"What-" I started before she cut me off.

40

"Just save your words this one time," she interrupted. She knew my reaction would be this way, because she knew the type of person I was.

She'd lived these injustices firsthand; she knew the truth and lived with it for all these years she spent in the shadows. She suffered because of people like me, and yet, she could still look me in the eyes and call me her granddaughter. I felt a stinging in my eyes and a heavy lump forming in my throat.

"I'm . . . I'm just . . . so lost," was all I could utter, even though I had so much to say to her. I couldn't even begin to explain what I was feeling; it felt everything at once, but at the same time nothing at all. Lost was the best word I could use to describe what I was feeling.

The lump in my throat grew and was accompanied by an irrational urge to scream. I admired my grandmother while thinking about how she was the strongest woman I knew. Her beautiful face was always shadowed by a sort of gloom, and now I understood why. Reminiscing on her old life was too much to bear even for someone as strong-willed as her.

I lowered the gun and shamefully looked down at my hands, the same ones that have taken scores of lives. I lifted my sleeve a bit, exposing the weird mark on my arm only to find that it had become much more prominent. The shape was a lot more distinguishable now; I was certain it was some kind of bird. Though my reaction was more or less just confusion, my grandmother's was drastically different.

She reached for my arm with desperation. "This burn mark . . . this shape," she mumbled while keenly examining the mark, "do you know what this is?" she asked me, knowing good and well I didn't.

I shook my head, and with wide eyes, she answered, "My dear . . . this is a Phoenix."

Chapter 4

Before I could even realize it, I had lost it. I screamed so loud I could've shaken the sky to the ground. I screamed aimlessly with my hand over my erupting mouth. My grandmother ran to me and threw me into her arms. I desperately covered my mouth, preventing another blood-curdling scream from escaping. I didn't understand what had gotten into me; for once in my life, I had no grip whatsoever on my mind or body. My emotions were spiraling out of control, and there was nothing I could do about it.

The more I digested everything, the further my sanity slipped. Prior to this moment, I hadn't been able to shed a single tear in years, but for the first time in years, I felt a demanding urge to cry; the kind that digs into your chest until you're suffocating. *What else can you do after finding out that you've senselessly defended a lie your whole life? I spent my days killing people over depraved propaganda. That's all there was to it.*

One tear slipped, which was followed up by two more, and before I knew it, there were streams flooding from both my eyes. The world around me went out of focus as the tears impeded my vision, making everything a big blur. I had never felt so many emotions simultaneously. I felt something within me snap, and I began to wilt and wither from the inside.

I felt my purpose in life getting ripped from me, leaving me with absolutely nothing to live for. The burden and weight of all the innocent lives I've taken fell on me all at once. All the faces of the men, women, and children that I've massacred over the years flashed before my eyes; and this time, squeezing my eyes shut didn't get rid of their faces. It incessantly twisted a knife in my heart and made my stomach turn; *so, this is what guilt feels like?* I recalled the feeling from so, so long ago.

Without noticing, I was grasping my grandmother's arm as her other hand rubbed my back tenderly; *I did not deserve a speck of her compassion.* I laid like that for minutes, wishing time would just wait for me, because now I was the one who couldn't keep up. My tears dried and I was quickly coming back down to the familiar numbness. I killed off my emotions before I could even call myself a woman; I killed them without realizing I'd killed myself in the process.

"That pain you always try to hide will be the end of you, dear. You can't hide it forever," my grandmother said, reading my mind yet again.

"I've survived this long, haven't I? You think I would've made it to where I am now if I felt remorse?" I asked in a monotone voice. She sighed loudly, knowing I was back to being a shell of a person.

"You have an important task tomorrow. You should go back to the cabin," she responded, matching my energy, "but don't forget this conversation," she added, gesturing at the books.

I sat up again and she stood. Before I could respond, my grandmother was already climbing the ladder. I glared at the mess of scattered books and newspapers on the basement's cold floor. They were begging me to open them, but I was weary of the fact that it was game over if I got caught with them. I was alone now, just me, my thoughts, and a pile of history at my feet.

Several minutes passed as I glared at the papers, yet I could not bring myself to read them, so I merely stared. The doubt in my mind remained, and it was persistent. I reached, but my hands refused to grasp the pages in front of me. *Did I truly believe all this?* I asked myself repeatedly, but I couldn't seem to come to a solid conclusion.

If anyone knew about the world pre-revolution besides The Crow himself, it would be someone like my grandmother. What she said made sense, which made this all the more confusing. There were books and articles in front of me to prove it, and yet my doubts still lingered. I couldn't think of a reason why my grandmother would make up such a complex lie, but I also couldn't bring myself to discard everything I'd been told to believe and defend my whole life. I was so afraid of believing my grandmother, *because what would happen if I did?* I refused to believe all the lives I've taken weren't justified, and that I'm nothing but a cold-blooded murderer.

After some deep reflection, it hit me that an hour or so had gone by already and I was incredibly late to get back to the Cabin. I didn't quite know what I was going to do when I got there, but I knew I was taking these books with me. I scrambled to pick up the books and papers, and quickly threw them in the chest they were stored in for who knows how long. I picked up the chest, which was quite heavy, and struggled up each step of the ladder as I carried the heavy chest in one arm, and climbed with the other.

When I finally reached the top, I threw the chest over my head through the trapdoor, landing a few feet away from the door. I climbed the remaining steps and poked my head out, scanning the room for people. I was thrown off when I saw no one, but I figured they were probably in their rooms getting ready for bed. As I sighed in relief, I could see my own breath in the cold air. My uniform was relatively resistant to weather conditions, but the windchill tonight made its way through my tissues and into my bones. It was hard to imagine there was once a time when the world didn't need fire to stay warm.

I opened the door, and it was pitch black outside, with only a few street torches and the silver moon providing a dim light. I remembered what my grandmother told me about the sun once being bright enough to light up every corner the light could reach; it was a preposterous sight to imagine. I took a deep breath of frosty air, wondering how much nuclear residue was left in it.

Still shaken up from earlier, my paranoia grew exponentially as I walked. Every small sound pounded in my eardrums, and any sort of movement made me flinch. I walked knowing crows were watching every step I took. They were all-seeing and all-knowing, but only to those who were blind. The sight of crows burning resurfaced in my head, and despite the circumstances, it was still an incredibly disturbing thought.

The faint sound of shuffling grass behind me triggered my instincts, and I immediately jolted my head in the sound's direction. I dropped the chest and grabbed my rifle from my back in the blink of an eye. It was a young man all in black, who looked mortified to see me, and I knew exactly why. He fell backward and attempted to crawl away. A wash of depravity brushed over my heart after looking into his fearful eyes. After everything I heard, I could no longer differentiate right from wrong.

"There couldn't have been a worse time for you to show up," I murmured, and my finger pulled the trigger with ease.

His body fell back from the impact, and I lowered my gun. "Fifty-seven," I mumbled as I put away my rifle.

Watching the blood pour out of his head only solidified how far gone I was. We were supposed to keep the rebels alive when we captured them, with the exception of killing them *only* if they attacked you or a civilian, *but I had no regard for the rules right now*. I didn't care who he was, what he was, or what side he was on, all I knew was that I wanted to *kill* him; I wanted to see if I still enjoyed killing innocent people.

By killing him, I cleared away any doubt of me being a good person that might've remained. Rebel or not, I understood now that this man had done nothing to deserve death, and yet I *still* killed him. I felt an internal snap, and I clenched my jaw before suddenly breaking into a fit of laughter. It started off as mere giggling, but quickly erupted to manic laughing. *This is me; this is who I really am- humanity's biggest enemy disguised as a hero.*

"What the hell happened here?" A male voice interrupted my sadistic episode. I was so dazed I didn't even notice anyone approaching.

Two older Hunters approached me, one examining the dead man with his flashlight. "Damn, young lady, that's one hell of a headshot!" praised the man examining the body.

"That's Crimson for ya!" the other man exclaimed proudly. He looked a bit older than the first man.

"I could only dream of being half as strong as her, and I'm hitting forty soon," added the younger-looking man. I just forced a smile and nodded at the pair.

I suddenly felt uneasy being commended for my killing ability, because it just didn't seem like something that should be praised. Being a Hunter and Executioner at the age of seventeen was once an accomplishment, but now it felt like a curse.

"Could you guys clean this up, please? Big day tomorrow and I'm pretty tired," I said, and they nodded. I picked up the chest I'd dropped and continued my walk back to the cabin.

"I hear she has the highest kill count- fifty-seven now and counting!" I heard one of the guards whisper to the other. I let out a deep sigh; *why was that something to be proud of?*

My hands were so cold they felt like they might get frostbite and break off from carrying this heavy chest. I was just feet away from the cozy building when it hit me that bringing in this big, suspicious chest would raise many questions. To stall from going inside, I took one last look at the sky. The other stars never stopped glowing, no matter how detestable this world became. We were insignificant to the stars; they didn't depend on us. *So why would our sun burn out?*

"Crimson! There you are! Hurry up and join us, we're about to eat dinner!" yelled the one and only Guido from the window.

Guido was known as the Yellow Hunter; 4th ranked in kill and capture count, and exceptionally talented in the shooting department-the accuracy in his aim was unmatched. He was the life of the party, the most optimistic and full-of-energy person I knew, and easily one of the kindest people to walk this earth. We'd bonded over the fact that neither of us had our fathers in our lives, but he had a younger sister and mother that loved him dearly, and that's where our similarities ended.

"You don't have to yell," scolded Nyrual. They were best friends and together they stirred up a storm, but together they were unstoppable.

I walked over and closed the door. I waited for one of them to notice the chest, but no one seemed to care, which was more than fine by me. Aurora was sitting on the couch, pillow fighting with Nyrual while Guido was pestering the cook.

"It's been forever since we've been here, I love this place!" exclaimed Aurora.

"It's only been two weeks, moron," responded Nyrual, which in turn made Guido break into laughter, and even brought a smile to my face. She responded by throwing not one, but two pillows back-to-back at his face.

"Stop Aurora! You're gonna ruin my gorgeous face!" he yelled at her. Everyone was giggling now.

"Hey, Crimson, what's in that chest? Do you really need all those clothes?" Guido asked naively, and my smile was immediately wiped off my face.

"It's nothing important," I said, and hesitated. "Like you said, just clothes."

I avoided eye contact with all of them. Everyone was staring at me now; I could feel their eyes crawling over me and the chest in my hands.

"I'm gonna go change now, excuse me." I excused myself to break the silence along with their glares.

I walked over to my bunker, which was a small room no bigger than my own bedroom at home. It had a small twin-sized bed and a small drawer with a tall mirror parallel to it. In total there are ten

Deviant Hunters in this town; the four of us in the main squad, who are also executioners, and six others in the night guard. It was hard to become a Hunter; you not only had to excel in your studies, but also be swift and skilled in combat. Only the top four make it to the main squad and become the Executioners, and I was one of the "*lucky*" ones.

I opened the drawer and grabbed one of the lounging pieces I left here. I chose a soft, comfortable sweater and some loose sweatpants to wear tonight. I felt much more comfortable now that I was fully changed. That uniform was quite restricting, not to mention the heavy bulletproof vest. After changing, I glanced at the mirror; I looked rough and drained, so no wonder the others couldn't help but stare.

I climbed into bed and lay still for a little while. I was so exhausted that if I closed my eyes, I was sure to pass out, but I didn't want to go to sleep. I didn't want tomorrow to come, and sleeping would only make tomorrow come faster. Tomorrow was a big day; the four leaders of Rebellium would be killed.

Tomorrow will be remembered for centuries, and I will go down in the books as a killer of one of the most infamous rebels. My mind drifted back to my inability to kill the woman from this morning, and then went straight to my impulsive kill just now. *I can't slip up like that tomorrow, not in front of everyone.*

I turned in my bed and hugged the pillow, then peered out a small window next to my bed. Something always drew me to the sky; I constantly stared and wondered what it would feel like to roam the skies without a worry or destination. The dim moonlight glowed through the branches of the tree that stood outside my window. Starlight and moonlight were the only non-synthetic lights left in this world, and I was convinced no one could bring the light back to earth.

"Crimson, come eat!" Aurora called lightly.

I had unintentionally isolated myself from the others in my room. I didn't realize how hungry I was until I smelled the delectable aromas coming from the kitchen. As I made my way toward the door, my foot hit something along the way; it was the chest. My heart raced at the mere sight of it. I kicked it under my bed for now and made my way out.

When I finally got to the dining area, I was so ready to devour whatever they put in front of me. Today they had chosen to sit on the bar stools, and I picked a stool next to Aurora. She was closest to me in age, so I felt most comfortable around her. I was the youngest one in the crew, and the whole league to be exact. Guido and Nyrual were twenty-two, and Aurora was nineteen. I will turn eighteen in a few weeks, but for now I am still only seventeen.

"Enjoy," said the cook. We all thanked her, and she went back into the kitchen.

Everyone dug in without saying anything, devouring our food like hounds. They were all visibly tired like me, but none of them had the look on their face that I did. For the first time ever, I was curious to know if any of them secretly harbored any disdain for The Crow somewhere in the deepest, darkest parts of their heart, *or were they also mindlessly following orders?*

"Um, Crimson, I know I'm handsome and all but why are you staring at me so intensely?" teased Guido, and I instantly snapped back to the present. "Do you like what ya see?" he asked in a humorous tone which caused everyone to laugh.

I didn't realize I was staring at him while I got lost in my train of thought. I felt my face get a bit hot from the embarrassment. In all honesty, there was a reason Guido and Nyrual were both rather popular among the ladies. Guido was tall, had curly brown hair, honey-brown eyes, and very tan skin- which was rare. Unless you were born with a tan complexion, it was virtually impossible to achieve it.

"Don't gas yourself up too much," I responded bluntly, and everyone laughed, including Guido. We finished our dinner relatively fast. Nyrual and Guido were first to make their way to the lounge area to hear the Crow's speech.

"I'm bouta have a baby," groaned Guido while patting his stomach, making everyone giggle.

"I'll be in a food coma if you guys need me," added Nyrual as he fell back onto the couch. Guido followed right behind him, leaving only me and Aurora at the table.

I must've exhibited strange behavior or had an obvious look of uncertainty on my face, because Aurora noticed something wasn't right.

She reached out for my arm and looked me in the face. "What's wrong?" she asked warmly.

For some odd reason, I felt like I couldn't lie to her, but I knew I had to. She was a Hunter, and telling her the truth would mean she'd have to detain me. I also did not want to get them involved, because no one should have to feel what I'm feeling right now. This doubt would get us all killed, and I didn't want to be responsible for more deaths.

"Let's go sit," I responded and sat on a couch in front of the TV.

Aurora's eyes never left mine until she went into her room. She came out with her violin case and sat on the floor next to the couch the boys were on, leaving me alone and in her sights. I gulped nervously, hoping I wouldn't exert any unusual behavior during his speech. Nyrual turned the TV on, and we all sat up straight, displaying the utmost respect in case a crow was watching.

"My subjects, I hope you are all faring well on this fine night. This is not so much a speech, but more of an announcement and a reminder," he began with his flamboyant tone. His ice-blue eye was so unsettling, and the eyepatch over his other eye didn't help.

"Tomorrow will be the historical executions of four leaders of the wretched rebel group that has threatened to disrupt our peace for far too long, the group who refer to themselves as 'Rebellium.' They're but a fork in the never-ending road of prosperity and freedom under my rule," he said, almost passive-aggressively. "Let their deaths serve as a reminder to every citizen of this glorious land, that deviancy will *not* be tolerated and will be punished accordingly. There is no other way to build a nation up from ashes, and don't let them convince you that there is." He emphasized that last sentence, and it made my heart drop. *It felt like it was directed straight at me.*

"Oh, and remember! I am *always* watching," he said, followed up with a grim smile. I felt my throat dry up and my palms grow sweaty.

I looked over at the others; Guido and Nyrual's faces wore the same blank expressions they usually had after his speeches, and Aurora had a peculiar smile on her face. From a surface-level perspective, her smile looked like her usual smile, but I felt like there was something off. Out of the blue she took her violin out of its case and began to play. She played a calm, soothing song which contrasted with the heavy weight in The Crow's words.

Aurora always smiled and played her violin. She was known in town to play the violin after captures, along with every time she got off the stage after an execution. I noticed she did it after every speech too, and until now, I didn't realize how strange it actually was. The boys followed up by closing their eyes and humming the tune. I gripped my spinning head tightly in hopes of keeping my grip on reality. I was starting to think I was just overanalyzing everything now, and I didn't know how much more I could take before losing my sanity.

"Crimson, what's wrong?" asked Aurora. This time she wasn't asking for an answer, she was demanding one.

"Yeah, you've been unusually distracted since you got here," Agreed Nyrual

"You know you can trust us," Guido comforted warmly.

I opened my mouth to speak, but I didn't even know what I wanted to say. *Should I do it?* This question daunted me as every possible outcome flashed before my eyes. If I told them, they could easily kill me right now and it would be justified. They were Executioners after all, and I would be just a *deviant*.

"I know you're a strong girl and you've never liked showing any vulnerability, but I wish you'd open up to us more. We work together every day, yet we barely know you," Added Aurora, and she was right, I was like a stranger to them. *Hell, they didn't even know my name.*

"We know you're insanely strong, and you probably feel like you don't need us, but it's okay to trust us," said Guido, sounding a bit upset.

"We're not just co-workers, Crimson, we're a squad, so stop trying to block us out and open up to us," Insisted Nyrual, and the others nodded.

Their words sank into me, defrosting my cold heart. No one has ever pleaded with me to tell them what's on my mind, and it was an oddly pleasant feeling. I didn't understand why they cared to know so badly, but I knew it would be unwise and dangerous to tell them. We pledged to take this job more seriously than our lives, and they would do just that. I couldn't let my guard down just because of their pleas.

"I truly appreciate your concerns, but in cases like this, ignorance is for the better, so please, stop insisting that I tell you," I pleaded, feeling slightly guilty after seeing the concern grow on their faces.

I stood up and headed to my bunker, but I was quickly stopped by Guido. He grabbed me from behind and restrained my arms to the point where I couldn't move.

"Let me go!" I demanded, while struggling to free myself from his grip.

"Not until you tell us!" he refuted as he continued to restrain me.

"I didn't wanna have to resort to force," I responded before gripping tightly onto Guido's arm and throwing him over my shoulder with all my strength. He managed to land on his feet and the room got so quiet you could hear a pin drop.

"You really want to know?" I asked angrily while panting. They looked at me with dazed eyes and nodded.

I turned around and punched the wall next to me out of frustration. I despised this horrible feeling of doubt and uncertainty. I knew the only reason this entire situation bothered me so much was because deep down, a part of me couldn't help but start to believe my grandmother, and inevitably, the deviants. If I was a hundred percent confident in what I believed, I would never have even been affected by any of this. Now, it was time I asked myself, *am I ready to abandon everything I believed and defended up until now?* And for once in my life, I truly had no idea what to do.

"Tell us now, Crismon," demanded Nyrual, a lot more sternly than anyone so far. I didn't like being bossed around, but I would let it slide just this once.

I considered the possible outcomes; either they believe what I tell them, or they don't believe a word and try to kill me, because after all, that's their job. I'm strong, but probably not strong enough to fight them all off, *and where would I even run after that?* There it was, those stupid second thoughts. Overthinking was probably a bigger enemy than The Phoenix or The Crow ever could be. My mind blanked for what seemed like several minutes, until I had an epiphany.

My grandmother, a regular civilian, provided me, an Executioner, with outlawed history and her own personal stories. She knew she ran the risk of getting incarcerated and killed, yet she told me anyway. She wasn't afraid of the repercussions, because she did it for her granddaughter, Phoenix, not the Executioner, Crimson. I swallowed hard at this realization, and suddenly, the fog of doubt began to clear.

I walked to my bunker, but not to run away this time, but to grab something. I was once again interrupted from doing so by Aurora grabbing my arm.

"Crismon, wait! Please . . . stop running from us," she implored. *Don't worry, Aurora. I wasn't going to run this time.*

"Start off by not calling me that anymore," I replied sternly, shocking everyone with my abrupt response. "My name is not Crimson," I added. Their shocked expressions slowly morphed into confusion.

"I'm not quite . . . understanding," replied Aurora, while the others just stared blankly.

"Crimson is simply an alias. My real name . . . is Phoenix," I answered confidently. It felt like a breath of fresh air to speak those words, like a heavy burden was lifted off my chest.

Confessing this would make them the only other people who knew my real name. I used my real name back when I was a little girl; the kids who knew were fine with it because we were all innocent children. It was only until their parents found out that things went downhill. Those who knew about the legend prohibited their children from being seen with someone bearing such a blasphemous name. I went by the nickname "Fefe" until I became a Hunter candidate at about twelve years old. I got the nickname "Crimson" from my training uniform, and officially became known as *The Crimson Hunter*" in town at the age of fifteen, when I was bestowed the job of Deviant Executioner and Hunter.

I lowered my gaze after revealing my name. When I looked back up, Aurora was giggling. My first instinct was to tense up and prepare for the worst- *maybe she would try and capture me.*

"Excuse my laughing," she apologized, and covered her face. "So, you're Phoenix?" she asked, and now I was just as confused as the others.

"Yes?" I answered, still unsure of where she was going with this.

"I remember you from when we were children. We used to play in that big group by the forest. They called me 'Freckles', remember?" As soon as she said that, it unlocked memories that were buried so deep that I'd almost forgot.

She was one of the older kids in the group; they called her freckles because of the very distinguishable freckles on her face. A small smile formed on my lips. It was a happy smile, but there was an underlying sadness peeking through. That whole group of kids turned on me and she knew that. Knowing that, there was still a smile on Aurora's face, though it seemed like she was holding something back.

"I don't wanna interrupt your wholesome reminiscing . . . but how the hell did you get away with being named Phoenix?" asked Guido abruptly, and Aurora hit his arm.

I only revealed my name to a few people when I was a naive child- those who even cared to ask for it. My own family didn't even use my name. The only other person who knew was the Secretary of District Four since he had specific files of the Hunters in town- every other ordinary civilian was just a number in the system- not a name. I suppose the real mystery was why *he* never said anything.

"I'm just as confused as you are. Maybe because the story of The Phoenix isn't that commonly known," was my best answer. I realized too late that a flood of questions I wouldn't be able to answer was soon to pour in.

After a moment of heavy silence, Nyrual decided to break it by addressing the elephant in the room. "This doesn't answer why you've been acting strange," he called out, and he was right. The real issue was still at hand.

I quickly ran to grab something from my bunker, hoping no one would stop me this time. I came back and their eyes went to the heavy object in my hands. I threw it on the ground, making them all jump. They switched their gaze between me and what I'd just thrown down.

"So Crim- I mean, Phoenix . . . what is that?" asked Guido.

"I'm guessing it's not just clothes then?" inquired Nyrual. I shook my head and sighed. *How could I word this without explaining for hours?*

They reached to open the chest and I slammed my hand on it. "Before you open it, I need to ask you something," I blurted out, startling them.

"What is it?" Aurora asked as everyone stared at me blankly.

"Have you guys- do you guys ever . . . doubt . . . that maybe what we're being told is just . . . a *lie*?" I managed to ask, and deafening silence followed my question.

In that moment of silence, I realized how careless I was for asking that, and my heart immediately dropped upon remembering something. I turned my head to the window directly parallel to where I was standing, and there it was, the thing I was dreading to see the most- *A crow*. Its black, beady eyes glared straight at me with a piercing gaze. I was utterly paralyzed, and I felt myself overheating with anguish. I knew it heard everything, and I knew *where* that information was going to end up.

My breathing grew irregular and my heart beat so rapidly it began to hurt. Aurora noticed my panic and shot me a confused face before turning around to see what I was seeing. Now everyone was looking at what I was looking at, only they weren't as panicked as I was since they didn't reply to my question. I felt like just falling to my knees and surrendering, but before I could do so, I looked back at the crow only to find that it had been turned into a torch.

"Uh . . . th-that's not the first time I've seen that this week," Aurora stammered nervously as she drew back. Guido and Nyrual simply stared, both astounded and horrified.

As the crow burned up, I noticed this one was different. This one didn't simply burn until it was dead, this bird was being completely incinerated. I couldn't seem to take my eyes off of it until it was rendered nothing but ashes. That sight brought my knees to the ground, and once again, my thoughts spun out of control. I wanted so badly to believe it was a mere coincidence, but I couldn't fool myself any longer. Someone or something was burning these crows with the intention of me witnessing each and every one of them.

"Who's there?" yelled Nyrual. He ran to the couch to grab his chained ax and Guido pulled out one of his handguns.

"Don't bother," I muttered, "I promise it's not a human causing this," I added, and everyone stood completely still for what felt like an eternity.

"Phoenix, about your question," started Nyrual, and the others turned their attention to him, "everyone has at least some doubt, its norm-"

"No," I cut him off, and all eyes were on me.

"Let me finish," he insisted.

"No, because I already know what you're going to say- no one will ever understand what I've gone through these past few days. This is so much more than just some little doubts!" I responded angrily.

"Phoenix, what's in the chest, and what were you doing before you got here?" Nyrual asked in a stern voice. He too changed his tone on me- it was much more hostile.

I stared into his dark blue eyes, having a mini staring contest. The depth in them reminded me of the old lady from earlier; crazy to think that happened just this morning. I didn't feel the need to reply with words, so instead I kicked the chest, hard. I watched the chest fall and open, scattering the contents out. Everyone stared at them blankly.

"Read for yourself. My grandmother told me the *real* story of this nation." I only partially answered Nyrual's question. "Now, I warn you; if any of you dare rat-out my grandmother, I promise, *you will regret it,*" I threatened, and Guido and Aurora nodded.

"It's a shame you have to resort to threats instead of simply trusting us," said Nyrual, audibly disappointed.

I felt bad for threatening them, but there wasn't a person in this world I trusted. We all stared at the books, seeing who would be brave enough to pick one up first. No one made the first move, so I decided I would.

"These are pre-Old-World Revolution history books and articles that were written during the actual Revolution. I haven't read them yet either," I explained. Everyone grabbed at least one piece. I started with the book called *American History*.

"This nation was referred to as the United States of America, but I guess they called it America for short," I explained, which took the puzzled look off their faces.

I flipped through and skimmed the pages and found myself having to re-read several phrases. I excelled in academics, and the book was written in English, but there were so many words that were foreign to me.

We skimmed through the books for hours, and I ran across a peculiar book titled *The Holy Bible*. It was a religious book and it seemed like the principles set in this book determined the morals and values of those who followed. Initially, I thought about how bizarre it was that something that can't be proven real influenced the behavior and ways of living of so many people, but then, I took a look at myself; *who was I to talk?* I supposed we humans will always be the same- always grasping onto anything that gives us a purpose.

The rustle of flipping pages was the only sound filling the solemn atmosphere. Reading these books was like reading pieces of fiction-like thoroughly thought-out fairytales. I couldn't even imagine having so much knowledge at my disposal. I couldn't fathom living in a world where I was able to use my voice- where I could choose my own destiny.

I had finally reached the stack of articles, which was probably the part I was most curious to read. It began with uproar from the citizens when their president, who I assumed was their leader, had betrayed them. He had broken the rules of their so-called *Constitution* and participated in corrupt affairs behind the people's backs. There was deep corruption within the system to the point where the citizens deemed it unfixable.

Along with that, it seemed the country had some on-going feuds with numerous countries, and even some plans to go to war. While the country faced these threats, the citizens seemingly had public plans to overthrow their leader out of their position of power. The articles toward the end discussed the possibility of nuclear warfare, and then the articles were cut off. It was safe to assume that in their state of civil unrest, they were a vulnerable target, and that's when the world decided to wipe them off the map. It was a grim thought to imagine that this nation I spent the last few hours researching was obliterated only a few hours after this final issue.

I felt a sense of satisfaction from this more in-depth information, because it verified to me that The Crow has lied to us all. We've been forced to believe a faulty story of a revolting world that once stood compared to the superior nation that stands now; it was all twisted. Pre-Revolution America was heavily flawed, and humanity had become quite despicable, but it wasn't any worse than what it is now.

People then did things at will. They had their own individual morals and beliefs, and although they too suffered great injustices-*they were free.* Now, we are all slaves to a false sense of security; we aren't individuals, nor are we people; we're a faulty nation under the supreme rule of one crooked man. We're all destined to serve him until our luck eventually runs out and our light goes out. Everyone walked around with lifeless faces, gray and dull, and with no real purpose. Under equal oppression, we all carry a mutual underlying fear that one day we'll fall victim to the Executioners' bullets.

I was so consumed in the fragments of history that I had forgotten I wasn't the only one reading. I looked up at the others' faces, expecting them to act hysterical like I had, but I was mistaken. The prevailing emotion that veiled their faces was sorrow; *why was it sorrow?*

"I- I don't really have words," murmured Guido in a disheartened voice. It tugged at my heartstrings to hear someone as lively as Guido speak in such a despondent tone. I couldn't help but feel like the one to blame.

"Don't let it get to you, man," comforted Nyrual, who even in his downcast state, never hesitated to uplift his friends.

The two of them stared at the ground, appearing almost out of their own bodies. I could see the guilt and horror slowly setting in as their faces became paler, breathing more irregular, and their eyes began to lose focus. To my absolute surprise, Aurora was the calmest out of the three. More than anything she looked disturbed, angry, and conflicted.

"Comport yourselves as damn soldiers!" I shouted, which made their necks snap in my direction. "Now, think about the *real* reasons you all became Hunters," I added. They all stared at me, then lowered their gaze again.

"My mother, she's . . ." Nyrual began and briefly paused. "I needed the money and I had the skills. Can you blame me?"

"After my father's passing, all I wanted was to make sure my little sister and sick mother never went without anything," Guido admitted.

"My father . . . I just wanted to make him proud and help him out . . . I never wanted to-" Aurora cut off as she broke into tears.

I had so much to say to them, but I could not articulate comforting words like they could. Empathy just didn't come naturally to me. Personally though, I believed silence was more desirable than words, because I knew no matter what I said, their guilt and regret would remain adamant. *I knew that better than anyone.*

"Why do you think I have the lowest capture and kill count? I see those twenty kills every night in my dreams," Guido revealed.

They all turned towards me, expecting me to give them my answer. Truth of the matter was, I had a reason- a selfish reason. I couldn't help but feel guilty for beating around the bush after they opened up their hearts to me, but I had to.

"In order to win in this cruel life, you have to fight." I paused in between sentences, taking a moment to reflect. "Unfortunately, if you have something worth protecting, it doesn't matter who you must kill to protect it."

After my vague explanation, the room got dead silent. I didn't think it was particularly because of what I'd said, but because of their own overwhelmed minds. I could feel the thick unease in the atmosphere that everyone was trying their hardest to ignore. After all, *ignorance is bliss-* the statement we all lived by. They were all nervously fidgeting, and I knew Aurora was considering reaching for her violin.

"Can you guys bring yourselves to kill them tomorrow?" I asked the big question we were all mentally avoiding, and the room stayed hushed for a while.

"All things considered, I made an oath, and my personal feelings cannot impede or interfere with my duties," Nyrual answered for everyone. We all had the same answer, but only he was brave enough to admit to their selfishness. He answered rather confidently and collected, but I knew there was so much shame behind each word.

"I think I'm gonna head to bed now," Guido announced abruptly. As soon as he stood up, Nyrual followed, then Aurora. I knew they were just trying to get out of this suffocating situation in any way possible.

I picked up the artifacts and placed them back in the chest. I peered out every window and didn't notice until now that a replacement crow never came. After the last one burned, no crow had stopped by to watch since. I still kicked the chest under my bed and put a blanket over it just to be sure. Once I finished, I crashed onto the bed. I was terribly exhausted, but knowing there was a long day waiting for me tomorrow made it difficult to close my eyes. Even worse, each time I closed them now, I saw the bloody faces of countless rebels.

As I tossed and turned with no success, the fragile sounds of a string instrument entered my ears. These entrancing sounds came from only one instrument and only one person. I got out of bed and cracked the front door open, letting in the cool breeze. Aurora was sitting on the fence outside next to a streetlamp, wearing her distinguishable cape over her nightwear. She always looked otherworldly whenever she played. The hood on her black cape was up; the one she always wore over her uniform; she says it was her late mother's. I continued to watch through the crack in the door until she suddenly stopped playing.

"You think I can't tell when someone's watching me?" she asked humorously. I fully opened the door and stepped outside. It was silly of me to think she wouldn't notice me watching her this whole time.

"You're right, it's Hunter instincts 101," I replied, and it was awkwardly silent for a while after.

"They say my mother was a rebel," Aurora said out of the blue. I had heard that rumor before as well, but she and her father never really spoke on it. "I still don't know if it's true or not, but I used the chance of it being true to mentally excuse the difficulties I faced when killing and hunting rebels," she confessed with a sad tinge to her voice.

"Aurora," I uttered, and she lifted her head toward me, "why are you awake right now?"

"Whenever I feel lost, I let music ground me," she uttered.

"Is that why you always play your violin?" I asked, leaning against the lamp post.

"No." She sighed in between. "Playing is a great distraction to stop you from crying." She paused again to look in my direction. "I play because I'm not allowed to cry after taking someone's life."

After she uttered that last sentence, all the happy songs she once played became somber. All the times she sporadically played her violin made perfect sense now. I guess we were all the same; we all had our own way to keep our emotions at bay. Tears welled in her eyes, glossy from the dim light. There weren't many instances in which I felt compelled to respond, but tonight I did.

"Maybe your music will guide them to . . . somewhere that's warm and happy." I attempted to comfort her, and I gained a smile from her. Seeing that my words were able to bring someone ease was an unusually fulfilling feeling.

"Maybe," she responded after several muted seconds. Every time we exchanged looks, it appeared like she was holding something back.

"Well, goodnight, Aurora." I dismissed myself and she nodded in response before going back into the cabin and shutting my room door.

I leaned against the door and took a deep breath. I felt queasy thinking about tomorrow, but nonetheless, it was inescapable. Whether we liked it or not, with every second that went by, we were rushing straight into tomorrow's arms.

Chapter 5

The blaring sound of the town bell's tolling forced my eyes open, signaling that the inevitable was finally here. The obnoxious bell was a standard ceremonial tradition on days of executions. As I sat up slowly, a turning feeling in my stomach, and a heavy sensation in my chest enveloped my body. I peeked out the small window, hoping to still see stars, but they were replaced by one big, dark star. The sky was grayer than its usual dark blue, and even the horizon lacked its usual pinch of orange tint. *Even the sky knew today was going to be morbid.*

The clock signaled that it was 8:15 AM, and at precisely 12 PM the circus would begin. After evading it for as long as I could, I managed to finally stand up and start this grotesque day. It was no surprise that it was freezing today, just as any other day, but today felt marginally different. Today was the kind of cold that could pierce through your bones. *If only this cold could freeze time,* I thought wistfully. I grabbed a freshly washed uniform and towel from my drawer- courtesy of the cabin's housekeepers- and made my way to the bathroom.

The bathtubs in this place were much more advanced and simpler to use because they splurged a little more on federal buildings. I laid in the hot water for what felt like only an instant before I finished; *I guess time flies by when you're inching towards a horrid event.* I looked into the foggy mirror, and I saw someone else in that reflection- someone I could no longer bear to look at. *How could anyone look at me when I can't even stand myself?*

After scrutinizing myself in the mirror, my focus switched to the burn mark on my arm. It taunted me- it knew if I was to ever get caught with this, it was game over for me. I was forced to watch myself lose my mind over it. *Oh, how I wish I could just cut it off and watch it bleed out.*

I reminded myself that there was a lot to do before the executions and therefore could not waste any more time. I picked up the towel from the chair beside the mirror and wrapped it around myself. I quickly walked back to my room and shut the door, ready to change and get ready for this dreadful day. *Who knows what today will hold,* I mused.

I shivered aggressively as I dried myself off. The room was only a pinch warmer than the temperature outside and it didn't help that I was dripping wet. I grabbed my black jumpsuit from the drawer and slipped it on as fast as I could. As soon as it was on, most of the cold was suppressed. I rummaged through my drawer for the rest of my uniform, which I quickly found, all but one piece. I looked through my entire room to recall where I had misplaced my bulletproof vest.

After scouring the entire room, the only other place it might have been was under the bed. When I bent down to search, my eyes fell on the chest covered by a thin blanket. I told myself that as soon as I finished the ceremony, I would burn it. I couldn't risk letting it fall into the wrong hands or catch attention from the wrong eyes.

As suspected, the vest was also under the bed, so I dusted it off and proceeded to equip it. I grabbed my crimson shoulder, elbow, and knee pads from the drawer and tied them on. Gearing up in all this mess was quite time consuming, but when you do it every day you just get used to it. I finished it off by tying my ammunition belts to my waist and equipping my harnesses.

After thinking I was done, I looked in the mirror and noticed I was missing my Executioner emblem pin. It was sitting right on top of my drawer. This small pin embodied my commitment and pledge to cease rebellion from proliferating in this District. I held the golden pin in the palm of my hand and admired its glimmer. I ran my thumb over the small crow engraved on the pin. Instead of making it a big deal, I just pinned it in its usual spot and sucked it up. I checked the time; 9:30, which meant it was time to go.

I walked out into the lounging area and everyone but Guido was there, though I could hear shuffling coming from his room. Aurora had her chestnut-brown hair in a loose braid and wore her black cape overtop of her Hunter uniform, as per usual. Nyrual and Guido's uniforms were the exact same as ours with, of course, the different protective pads and strap colors. Nyrual's were blue, and Guido's were yellow- fitting for his lively personality. After a while, Guido finally opened his door and stepped out. We all exchanged encouraging smiles before stepping outside, silently promising each other that everything would be okay.

We were on our way to our first morning ritual- the prayer. There was a stone path that led to the large statue of The Crow's idol. It was a crow with its wings spread on top of a cross. It was on elevated terrain so there were a series of stairs that led up to it. We were on our way up when I noticed a group of people standing idly on the path; among that group was Bryce. I thought this day couldn't get worse, but clearly it was wishful thinking. He stared me down and then grinned his detestable grin before approaching us.

"Well, if it isn't the little girl pretending to be a soldier," he taunted, but I was unbothered by his overused mocks. I rolled my eyes and tried to push past him, but he and his friends stopped me.

"You're absolutely right, Crimson . . . or should I say, Phoenix?" he added. I immediately tensed up and clenched my fists.

Telling this bastard my name was one of my biggest regrets in this world. When we were younger, we, along with other kids, played together in a group, but after their parents prohibited them from associating with me, he and a few others began ridiculing me until I never used that name again. I didn't think he remembered, nor did I think he was bold enough to ever say my name again, but I guess I greatly underestimated the extent of his hatred for me.

"Seems like you're getting desperate," I scorned, "pretty pathetic to rat me out in order to gain my position."

"Your position in the main squad was mine, but they chose you out of pity- a lowlife, starving child with a devil's name," he spat, and now he was just inches away from me.

I couldn't stand his presence any longer. After registering his words and remembering everything he'd done, I felt my bloodlust return. He laid his repulsive hands on me- and that was my last straw. I clenched my fist and threw a punch at his despicable face so hard that it knocked him off his feet. When he was finally on the ground, my fury sent such a vigorous rush of adrenaline throughout my body that I aimed my gun at his head.

He glared at me with visible rage, but just like any other unfortunate man faced with a gun, the fear they exhibited couldn't be concealed. Before I could take further action, I was restrained by two strong pairs of arms and Guido appeared in front of me, pushing my arm away from Bryce's head.

"You need to calm down, you almost shot a civilian!" Guido scolded. *Killing him would make him the least innocent person I've killed.*

Bryce's friends helped him back up on his feet and he dusted himself off. He turned to face me with a bloody nose and a look that could kill. Aurora and Nyrual finally loosened their grip on me, and I glared back.

"My gun isn't loaded," I confessed with a vengeful smirk before pushing past him and walking away from everyone. I knew this all along; *all I wanted was the pleasure of seeing him cower at my hand.*

Everyone eventually followed up behind me, all but Aurora. "Maybe there's a reason you're not wearing this uniform," she said condescendingly.

"Excuse me?" Bryce responded.

"It's very clear they made a good choice by not choosing you," she jabbed at him, and Bryce's enraged look returned.

"Shut the hell up, Aurora," he replied aggressively. It threw me off to learn that he knew her name. I didn't know they knew each other personally.

"Let's get out of here," insisted Guido, and Aurora caught up after exchanging one last glance with Bryce.

We climbed the stone steps of the prayer sight until we reached the shrine with the Crow idol- the Trojan horse of deception and cruelty. Everyone went into the praying position, and I forcefully abided. Fear and faithless prayer filled the heavy atmosphere. I glared at the statue with a hard gaze; *this "god" of deception can't tell me what is right.*

This area was heavily surveilled by crows- the shadows that never left you alone. We were forced here to pray to this miserable life on every execution day, where they constantly have us in their sights. A life where it's burned into our heads that the psalm of our great leader was the *only* truth in a world that keeps the truth disguised in lies. They've caged us and our minds like little birds and made us bite our tongues in ignorance.

After the prayer time was up, I was the first to stand and look away. It appeared as though the others were unmoved by yesterday, but it was foolish of me to expect them to act out of the ordinary. Unlike me, they know how to separate their personal feelings from their tasks at hand. It was now close to noon, so we had to get to the stage soon. As I took a last look at the statue, an intrusive thought came to my head, and I began to wonder; *how would you look completely up in flames?*

Upon reaching the bottom of the stairs, a heavy feeling of dread came over me. We began on our way to the most anticipated event in years- the execution of the four Rebellium leaders. These beacons of hope for rebels were soon to be massacred in front of every man, woman, and child's eyes without any remorse. In approximately thirty minutes, we'd be up there renewing our vows as murderers.

As we walked, I heard guitar strumming in the distance. I looked around to find the source of the music, and it was none other than the Bardman. I recalled what Aurora's reason for constantly playing was, and I wondered if he played for the same reason. He was just up ahead on our path, so I decided I would speak to him and clear the mystery once and for all.

When I finally reached the fence he was sitting on, I waited for him to stop playing, but he never did. He plucked a repetitive, simple tune which, as odd as it sounded, felt comforting to listen to. He was still covered head to toe in a long tunic, even obscuring his face with an eerie mask. I noticed he was also incredibly stiff, only his hands moving to play.

"Hello," I greeted. I waited for a response, but just got more chords. "I was just wondering if there was a reason you always played the guitar?" I asked regardless, hoping for an answer this time.

"So much noise," he uttered quietly in a breathy voice.

"Huh?" I replied in confusion.

"I don't want to hear it . . ."

"Hear what?" I asked and his hands stopped playing.

It was silent now. I didn't realize how still the town was until there was no music. The noise of the soft wind whistling and ruffling the trees was the only sound that permeated the silence while I waited for another response.

"Their screams," he stated simply. I stayed quiet to hear if he had anything else to say, but he didn't offer another word. After that brief pause, he resumed his strumming.

"Crimson, come on!" Nyrual called out for me. I was grateful that they continued to use my alias in public.

I looked ahead and they were all waving, signaling that the ceremony would start soon. I gave the Bardman one last look before running off. I considered saying goodbye, but I knew he didn't care. When I finally caught up, his answer still lingered in the back of my head.

The atmosphere was heavy all day, and not just between us. We walked on the streets covered in invisible blood as everyone was rounding up and heading toward the town center. We were near the back of the stage, and behind it I could see hundreds of gray people in the center waiting for their show. Some loyal followers were even wearing their crow masks; weird black masks with long beaks that covered the whole face, excluding the mouth.

We waited behind the stage where we would soon be called up by our names. We were actually early; the deviants hadn't even been brought up on stage. We all loaded our rifles to kill time- we generally only used them for executions. I assumed we all had chosen to ignore the morality at stake and decided our job was more important. *Fine by me.*

The temperature was around 55 degrees Fahrenheit today, which was rather warm compared to the past few days. As I stood there idly waiting for the clock to strike 12, I raised my head up to the sky. I tried to stare at the sun, even though it hurt my eyes. I didn't understand why it hurt even when it was so dark. *The least you could do is warm us up,* I thought as I struggled to stare for longer than a second.

The indigo-gray sky made me feel uneasy for some reason, and then I recalled what my grandmother told me; the sky wasn't meant to be that color. I blinked hard, and when I blinked, only for a split second, I saw a light blue horizon with a bright sky. I shut my eyes in hopes to see it again, but alas, it did not reappear. It never did.

I lowered my gaze back down to ground level and was startled to see the four deviants only a few feet away. They wore black hooded robes and masks that only showed their eyes- typical for rebels before execution. I watched them climb up the steps to the stage with the guards, and it was a haunting sight. For whatever reason, the sight of them made me so unexplainably uneasy. I have seen this routine countless times without feeling anything at all, but it's entirely different when you don't just know their reasoning, but actually understand it- when you discover *empathy*.

As I watched, I noticed one of the deviants staring in our direction, and I couldn't help but stare back. We happened to lock eyes and exchange a quick glance, and the uneasy feeling I had from before amplified itself tenfold. I heard the crowd go berserk as soon as the first leader stepped foot on stage, and I understood why. They were the leaders of the most notorious rebel association, *Rebellium*- the biggest threat to our nation. To some people out there, this will signify not only the death of four humans, but also the death of a cause, along with any hope that it will ever be fulfilled.

What added even more fuel to the fire was the fact that the main leader was thought to have been killed already around five years ago, in an ambush that massacred hundreds on both sides. The nation believed that was the end of Rebellium and deviancy as a whole, but it seems a few managed to escape and rekindle their fires. It was a shame that, after all that, they were captured and would now be killed today on the lowly town of District Four's stage by Executioners. They deserved impactful deaths, not this humiliation.

After the deviants were shackled, the mayor made his appearance- Mayor Devrim. He was the one who gave the speeches at these public executions. He wasn't gray like the others; he was quite the flamboyant character; an exceedingly passionate man who detested anyone and anything that threatened this nation- The Crow's perfect slave. His brown hair was slicked back, and today he wore a clean, off-white suit. He too walked up the steps and the crowd cheered, even if they secretly detested him. They had to at least applaud his speeches, or soon enough they'd join him up on stage.

"Thank you, my kind people. Now, please do give a warm welcome to the lovely Executioners of our District!" the mayor announced, which was our cue to start making our way to the stage.

"We'll start with The Blue Hunter," he began. He always used our nicknames in the town when being called up. Nyrual took his place on stage farthest away from the mayor. "Next up, The Golden Hunter," he continued, and Guido also took his place. "Next are our lovely ladies; The Emerald Archer," Aurora took her place next to Guido and only I was left- "and last but not least, The Crimson Hunter!" I felt no excitement as I walked up to claim my spot, only pure and utter dread.

I took my place, the spot closest to the mayor. I looked in front of me and saw hundreds of eyes watching us- all by force. Until now, it had never bothered me to see all the children in the crowd- it even used to fill me with pride. Now, I felt like I was getting a front row seat to witness their innocence being ripped from them as they watched innocent men get slain for unwarranted atonement.

"Today we assemble these deviants; The four leaders of the wretched association known as Rebellium- the biggest threat to our nation, peace, and freedom! The dangerous idea these devils try to spread is nothing more than poison to the minds of our young, and an endangerment to everything we as a nation stand for!" The mayor's loud and charismatic yelling made me jump at the first word. He was never one for a dull introduction speech. He continued his monologue.

"They plan to desolate this land, and bring this glorious nation back down to ruins, but these wretched men will pay the price in Hell! The walking plague of deviancy will be exterminated, and today we start with their pitiful leaders!" he continued, and even chuckled at the last part. The longer I listened, I grew more certain that he was a truly detestable person.

I blocked out his loud voice and instead found myself focusing on guitar strings. The Bardman played a whimsical tune on the outskirts of this bloodbath; *you're trying to block out the sound too, aren't you?* Oddly enough, my mind was pretty blank right now-essentially, I felt nothing. Every emotion I'd felt up to this point had dissipated. It was potentially a blessing, because soon enough I would have to shoot the man in front of me, and without mercy.

I lowered my gaze to meet the defenseless rebel at my feet, and there he was- a poor soul in the midst of degradation simply for fighting for what he believed. His life was soon to be taken from him, by my cold, bloody hands.

"This moment shall embark the beginning of the end of rebellion as a whole! This shall also serve to deter you all from following in the footsteps of these devils . . ." the mayor continued, but I blanked him out completely.

I found myself glaring intensely at the deviant. His eyes were closed the entire time, but the second his eyes opened, I felt a rush of cold wind fly past me and the world proceeded in slow motion. I was floating in a fragment of time with only the muffled sounds of the mayor's speech in the background to ground me to reality.

I didn't just look *at* the man's eyes, I dived *into* them. In that second, I saw something no other deviant has been able to make me see. For the first time in my three years of being an executioner, I looked at a deviant's face, and I saw a human- not a criminal. I looked into his eyes, and I saw *life*. His eyes were overflowing with humanity. . . and an overwhelming amount of *hope*.

"Hunters, arms up!" commanded the mayor; I managed to catch that part. I took out my rifle slowly whilst stuck in a daze created by this man's eyes; the shades of blue that slow-danced in his eyes.

". . . Rebellion of any kind will *not* be tolerated. DO NOT TRY AND RESIST!" I heard the mayor shout aggressively. It was the last thing I heard before completely slipping into a trance.

Time was frozen, and the world beyond him and I was nothing more than a blur. When I thought it couldn't get stranger, a rare, blue butterfly made an unexpected appearance. My eyes steadily followed the butterfly's delicate wings flutter around the scene I was trapped in. It flew past the deviant and then up into the sky. I followed the butterfly as it flew toward the sun, before losing it. Before I could begin to speculate, I took a closer look at the sun.

The eclipse- a black void surrounded by a crown of blinding light that harshly contrasted with the blue sky around it. I had never observed the sun this intricately or for this long before; it didn't even hurt my eyes this time. Suddenly, the butterfly appeared again. This time, it landed on the deviant's shoulder.

I looked into his eyes again, and this time, I couldn't break my gaze. I focused on his iris- the black void in the middle, surrounded by shades of blue that gradually diffused into blues of other shades. I made a connection that made my heart skip a beat; *this man's eyes . . . looked just like the eclipsed sky.*

"We will start with the main leader first, because why save the best for last?" the mayor announced. "He will be shot by The Crimson Hunter. Throw the first shot, soldier!" ordered the mayor.

I blinked hard and snapped out of my daze, but only enough to hear what was going on around me; I was still infatuated by the connection I'd drawn. With shaky arms and minimal control over my body, I managed to lift my rifle up to his head. I watched his gaze grow vulnerable, but the hope encapsulated in his eyes never seemed to relinquish. Even when death stared him in the face, his hope was unscathed.

I took a deep breath and closed my eyes. I felt another gust of wind blow past me, numbing me for a brief moment. He closed his eyes, but I struggled to put pressure over the trigger. I knew everyone, including the rebel in front of me, noticed my hesitation. I took a deep breath and attempted to find the courage I needed for what I was about to do, because for once, *I knew exactly what I had to do.* This time, it was my burning heart telling me what to do.

"What are you doing, girl? Quit stalling and shoot n-" ordered the mayor, but his sentence was cut short.

I aimed my gun with the absolute intention to kill as my finger pulled the trigger. When he faced me, he too had that doe-eyed look I saw before every shot. The sound of a single gunshot was heard- and it would be heard *all over the world.* That gunshot would be remembered as the bullet that set the world on fire.

The bullet that shot Mayor Devrim dead.

Chapter 6

The sound of the mayor's lifeless body hitting the hollow stage floor was followed up by the blood-curdling screams of the mortified crowd. I threw my rifle and stood there immobilized as I stared at the dead man in front of me. I could feel each pound of my heart slamming against my chest as the world fell away from me. My feelings were indescribable; I have never felt so much regret, yet so much *liberation,* in my entire life. I'd expected to feel overwhelming guilt, but not a bone in my body felt guilty.

My eyes somehow landed back on the deviant who seconds ago was designated to die by that bullet. His eyes were squeezed shut after the gunshot, which should've been the last sound he ever heard. He thought he'd never open his eyes again- but he did. His pupils dilated in disbelief as he scanned the baffling scene in front of him. The eclipse in each of his eyes doubled in size, blacking out the blue skies.

I turned to face my crewmates who were standing beside me as I went down in history. They were no exception to the look of terror as their eyes fixated on the mayor's lifeless body. Soon they would be forced to apprehend me, and if not them, then the district guards. They would be ordered to shoot their own friend, or get shot with her.

I couldn't leave this chaos to unfold; I wasn't going to stand around and wait for someone to stop me. I turned to the crowd of panicked people with horror plastered on their faces and stepped up to the podium. I clenched the hunter pin on my uniform and ripped it right off before I began speaking.

"The only enemy in this world is ignorance; it's the biggest disease on this vile planet!" I shouted into the microphone with more passion than I ever imagined I was capable of. "You are all being lied to, and you need to wake up!"

The moment of glory was short lived; the chaos in the crowd was contagious, because now I was panicking too.

"Get her!" I heard in the distance. I scanned behind the crowd and saw an army of soldiers charge towards the stage.

My heart felt like it had dropped to my stomach. In a moment of desperation, I pulled out the blade from the harness on my belt and I ran up to the deviants. Three of them tugged as hard as their shackles permitted them, but one of them just stared at me- the one I was supposed to kill.

"Extend your hands," I ordered, and they quickly obeyed.

I lifted my sword up and slashed the chains of their shackles. I was in the middle of breaking the blue-eyed deviant's shackles when the soldiers made their way up the stairs. Before they could reach me, I had managed to break the last rebel's shackles. If anyone deserved to get out of this alive, it was them, not me.

I tried to run, but a soldier managed to grab me from behind, and I dropped my sword in the process. I was now restrained and unarmed, meaning I would have to rely on my own brute strength from this point on. The soldier restraining me signaled another soldier, who had a shotgun in his possession. The soldier pointed the gun at me, and for the first time in my life- *I felt the primal fear of being the prey.*

A rush of adrenaline coursed through my veins, and with that rush, I managed to kick the shotgun out of the soldier's hands. I jumped while still in the soldier's arms, using all my weight as I dropped down. After loosening his grip, I gathered all my strength and threw the soldier over my shoulder onto the man with the gun.

After I managed to free myself, my fight-or-flight response took over and the only thing I could think to do was *run*.

As I turned to run, I got distracted by the sight of my squad members; not running, nor trying to apprehend me, but fighting off the soldiers. The part that shocked me most was the deviants in the crowd, fighting off soldiers instead of running away. I was a fool to let that distract me, because I didn't watch my step. I fell hard to the ground as I tripped over the mayor's corpse.

I tried to get up but I felt a strong hand grab my calf. I turned my head to look behind and it was the same soldier that had previously seized me. I tried to kick with my free leg, but he was too quick; he had pinned the other leg down and began to pull me toward him and a number of armed soldiers. Fear took over my body completely, but instead of fighting, my body simply froze. *I can't lose now . . . I just got started.*

My body heated up tremendously, concentrated mainly in my chest as per usual. I flipped around, squeezed my eyes shut, and threw my hand onto his face to push him away. I believed I was done for, but my body acted on its own in a moment of desperation. Expecting to hear gunshots, I instead heard agonizing screams and my eyes darted open.

You won't lose now.

There was a flash of embers emitting from where my hand and the soldier's face made contact. The man drew back immediately and my hand glowed like metal under hot flames, leaving behind a trail of embers. Racking screams filled my ears so much I thought they would bleed. All the soldiers backed away from me; now even the bravest men cowered in my presence. I sat up quickly and drew back from the man with the burning face.

I stared at my shaking hands in disbelief. *How the hell did I do that?* I questioned as I stared at my bare, human hands. My head spun like a carousel and everything around me was blurry. I turned toward the crowd, and they all looked like birds trapped in a burning cage. Even I had become afraid of myself, and I knew it would only get worse.

At least half the soldiers had run into the turbulent crowd in an attempt to control the chaos. I caught a glimpse of the blue-eyed soul in the crowd, who took down his hood, revealing his jet-black hair. We exchanged a glance, and his eyes were filled with incredulity- not fear. Our exchange was quick before he proceeded to turn around and run for his life. The remaining soldiers on stage were too afraid to step closer to me, so I took the opportunity and ran.

I ignored the slight pain from the fall I had and stood up as quickly as I could. Terrified and disoriented, I ran toward the opposite side of the stage, only to be greeted by another group of soldiers. I decided to use my intimidation to my advantage.

"Move out of my way or I'll burn this whole stage down!" I threatened, trying to stop my voice from shaking.

I was visibly shaking in overwhelming fear, and the guards knew that. They ignored my threat and got closer, holding up their guns and blades. Without warning, flames appeared from out of nowhere and engulfed the ground between us. The soldiers managed to dodge the flames, but the stage was quickly igniting. With the guards in the way there was no way of getting through, and now the only exit was blocked off by flames. I had to think of another escape route, and I had to do it fast.

I looked in front of me and realized the only other exit was in front of me; I would have to jump off the 15-foot stage. When I turned, I caught a glimpse of Nyrual, Aurora, and Guido on their knees and being held at gunpoint on the other end of the stage. My mind instantly thought back to all the kind words they gave me, the vulnerability they shared with me, how they never hesitated to accept me. I remembered the laughs we shared, all the memories, the accomplishments. I'd never truly realized how much they meant to me until I saw them on the verge of death.

A strong yearning to protect them completely drowned out the fear from before, and I dropped onto the floor and picked up a handgun. I shot one of the soldiers in the shoulder; wounding him enough to disable his movements, but not enough to kill him. I shot the other man in the hand holding the gun, jumped, and then kicked him right on the jaw as hard as I could. He too fell to the ground.

"JUMP!" I screamed at the top of my lungs.

I took a leap of faith, and they followed right behind me. I landed on my feet in a crouching position to reduce the impact, but the pain was still intense. The bones in my legs shook from the impact, causing me to lose my balance and fall forward. The adrenaline made the pain harder to feel, so I got up quickly and forced my legs to run; I had no other choice.

I ran through hundreds of people, who in turn cleared the way and ran from me. My lungs burned and my legs threatened to give out, but I couldn't allow myself to falter. I didn't know where I was headed to, but I had an idea of where I wanted to go. There was one place I wanted more than anything to watch go down in flames- even if it was the last thing I did. I ran straight toward that damned statue, *ready to set the world on fire.*

While I ran up the steps, an explosion went off somewhere in my vicinity followed up by the ground vibrating beneath my feet. I knew turning around was dangerous, so I just kept running. I ran only a short distance before a violent blast went off behind me, disintegrating the ground at my back. The explosion thrust me forward and my arm took most of the blow as I landed on it. I found myself unable to get up; this time the pain was on a larger scale than the last fall.

My arm ached considerably, but luckily my elbow pads took the majority of the blow. I lifted myself up with my other arm, begging my body to cooperate and stand. I looked to the side and watched an explosive charge at me, but I was far too weak to avoid it. I shut my eyes tightly and the sound of an explosion followed in an instant. It was deafening, and I expected it to be the last sound I heard. I was shocked when I could still hear the chaos around me.

I opened my eyes and saw pieces of an arrow fall down from the sky, along with lots of dust and smoke. I turned and saw Aurora holding her bow in the distance. She stood there fiercely while the forest burned behind her. She had shot the explosive midair, and that's why they called her The Emerald Archer.

"We meant every word, Phoenix!" shouted Aurora, referring to our conversation yesterday. I nodded in gratitude before standing up and running toward the statue. I felt a warm fuzzy feeling in my gut after hearing and seeing Aurora. *I was wrong for ever doubting them.*

A burst of chills went down my spine as soon as I reached the top. I looked up at the heinous statue one last time before reaching for a torch next to the shrine. I smashed its glass barrier into the hard ground, and I held the bare torch in my hand.

"Rise from the ashes," I whispered, and threw the blazing torch at the statue.

It instantly ignited and the flames lit up the earth around it. I watched the soft wood blacken as ruthless flames engulfed the idol. It was such a gratifying sight to watch the immaculate Crow get his wings burned off. The moment was interrupted by the ongoing chaos behind me. I turned and saw the soldiers' terrified expressions so clearly with the light from the burning statue. I examined the trail of destruction I'd left behind, and amongst the chaos was Aurora, Nyrual, and Guido fighting off soldiers, but to my surprise, they were not alone.

I caught glimpses of black-robed and masked deviants fighting too; I was both puzzled and grateful. I knew I had to join in the fight I'd caused, but I had only a handgun and a pocket dagger to defend myself with. There was also another small issue- I didn't actually want to hurt the soldiers. They were just marionettes who had no choice but to fight until someone died. It was either kill, or be killed by The Crow's hands, and that applied to the both of us. With that being said, I couldn't let my guard down out of remorse and pity; *In this cruel life, you must fight to win,* I quoted myself.

A soldier charged at me, and I reluctantly fought him off using only my strength and skills I developed during my six years of training. In the midst of battle, I heard yet more explosions, but these were different. There were multiple booms that went off back-to-back and these explosions let off a blue color. I turned my attention from my own fight to look at the source of that explosion, and it was a rebel's doing. I was confused as to where they got such weapons from, but I couldn't afford to ponder right now.

I let my guard down for only a second, and in just that second, I was pushed to the ground by a soldier who also went down with me. I kicked him off me and he immediately pulled out a handgun and fired. Luckily, I managed to roll over just in time to dodge it. I sat back up and noticed a thick chain wrapped around his neck before being dragged down the steps- clearly Nyrual's doing. I shot him a smile, but it was not reciprocated, instead his face flooded with overwhelming terror and disbelief. I looked around and everyone else was frozen with the same exact expression on their faces.

Everyone was facing me, but their eyes were not watching me. Every soldier dropped their weapons and fell to their knees while the deviants' wide eyes clouded with scorn. Aurora, Nyrual, and Guido didn't move an inch and their eyes remained glued to whatever was behind me. I looked down, and black feathers flew in the wind- crow feathers. Menacing laughter broke out behind me and every hair on my body stood up. I recognized the voice- it was awfully familiar. When I finally put two and two together, my heart fell to the pit of my stomach.

It was The Crow.

I was reluctant to look behind me, but my head involuntarily turned. He wore a sinister grin, and his blue eye was spilling with such malevolence whilst the other eye remained concealed by an eyepatch. His hair was completely gray, yet he didn't look much older than thirty-five. He wore a cape made of black feathers and a black jumpsuit like mine, with peculiar cannon-looking apparatus on his sleeves and at his hips.

"You've made quite the mess, haven't you, little girl?" he goaded.

His voice alone made my blood run cold. My heart felt like it would come out of my mouth as I stared into his singular eye, knowing he was also staring into mine. His eye was also a deep blue, but it didn't feel the same as the deviant's eyes; his gaze made me feel abundantly uneasy. Before this escalated, I turned back to warn everyone, because they deserved to get out of this alive.

"Get out of here!" I yelled in an effort to protect my friends, which only seemed to startle them out of their daze. "NOW!" I roared with everything I had, and they obeyed, quickly shuffling off and running into the depths of the forest.

The Crow let out a deep chuckle. "It's never gonna be that easy. Soldiers, after them!" The Crow ordered, and the soldiers promptly gathered themselves to chase after everyone, but I wasn't going to let them; I had such an overwhelming urge to protect, so one way or another, they would be safe.

I desperately turned to the forest. Suddenly, a fire ripped through all surrounding entrances to the forest, and it completely ignited, preventing the soldiers from going in after them. They froze in their tracks and immediately looked to The Crow for orders. I could tell this was their first time seeing him in person too. His face looked both surprised and impressed as he admired the burning forest- which was the last reaction I imagined he'd have.

"Did I tell you to stop?" he asked them with a deep, foreboding voice that covered me head to toe in chills.

The expressions on the soldiers' faces were hard to look at- despair, panic, and hopelessness. I watched them struggle to find a way to enter the forest- some of them burned up in the process, and I just couldn't bear watching any longer. As much as I pitied the poor soldiers, I wasn't in any position to feel remorse for others right now; I wasn't in a particularly desirable position either.

"I guess we can let a few bugs escape," he began, then turned to me, "after all, they're not the reason I'm here."

"Then why are you here?" I asked, knowing good and well why he was here.

"I was originally here to . . . tame the chaos," he explained, "but I think I might've found a better idea," he added. He bent down, meeting me on the ground. "I'm here to make a proposal." I felt his gaze cut me like a knife.

I swallowed hard. "A proposal?" I repeated, confused as ever.

"There's only one person that could be responsible for destruction like this- the one and only Phoenix," he mumbled to himself, ignoring my question. "I guess she does keep her promises," he finished, glaring at me as he uttered that last phrase. Even though I knew he wasn't referring to me when he said Phoenix, I still couldn't help but feel like he was directing part of that at me.

The Crow saw me struggling to understand and laughed. I took initiative and stood up and looked down at him, trying to assert myself. He quickly followed and stood, easily overpowering me in terms of size. He was around six foot three, which contrasted heavily next to my mere five three. Until we stood face to face, it hadn't fully hit me that I was standing only inches away from The Crow himself.

"You stand no chance, little girl," he whispered eerily.

"I'll stand my ground anyways . . . I'm not scared of you," I responded, demonstrating my courage. He glared at me, with only the flames to light the scene now that the sun was obscured by smoke and burning trees.

"Your courage is admirable, but nonetheless in vain," he threatened with a grin.

"Well today . . . I'm not backing down," I refuted, clenching my fists and biting my lip.

"You truly do resemble her- you're both just as foolish," he said and brought his face closer, now only inches away from mine. "Oh, and also because . . . *you will never come close to defeating me.*" He chuckled ominously after whispering the last part.

"Well then to Hell with your proposal," I spat back, without moving an inch. I began to violently shake, both out of rage, and because I had never spoken to anyone like this, especially not to such a powerful figure as The Crow himself.

I closed my eyes, and for the first time in my life- I prayed. I prayed that someone or something would lend me the power I needed to defeat this man. Almost immediately after, I felt an inexplicable feeling of warmth- like fire surging through each vein in my body.

"The only person who can determine the extent of your power, is you, but to understand the power, you must understand how far you're willing to go for it."

I heard an unfamiliar voice speak, and I shot my eyes open to verify that it wasn't just my imagination. When I looked around, there was no one else in sight. On top of that, I tried to understand what that even meant, but the stress of the situation made it far too difficult to contemplate right now.

I took a deep breath and threw my bare fist at his face. He managed to dodge my punch, deflecting with the palm of his hand, but I followed it up with a spin kick. He dodged the kick too and didn't seem in the slightest bit startled. His unbothered demeanor aggravated me.

"My turn," he said in a childish tone. He extended his arm toward me, and a barrage of hundreds of black feathers came from out of nowhere and swarmed me.

I wondered where all these feathers were coming from, then I remembered the strange contraptions from earlier; I assumed that's what they were- feather cannons. I put my arms over my face to block out the feathers as I got bombarded. They were many, but they were harmless- only serving to obscure my sight. Just when I thought they were merely innocuous feathers, I felt a sudden stinging pain, then I realized something was cutting me. First, I felt it on my thighs, then on my arms; it was like some of the feathers were actually small blades. I managed to find The Crow through the feathers; he was standing in the same spot chuckling.

My body seemed to act on its own lately, especially when I found myself in dire situations. I closed my eyes and shielded my face from the feathers, and even with my eyes closed I saw a bright light appear in front of me. A wall of bright, tall flames shielded me from the feathers, and ripped through the space between me and The Crow. Each feather burned to dust the second they touched the flames. The flood of feathers stopped all of a sudden, and then I noticed The

Crow too had disappeared. Before I could even check behind me, I felt a strong arm grab me by a chokehold.

"Maybe you shouldn't play with fire," he uttered into my ear. It was so frustrating that he was so close, and yet I was unable to do so much as kick him. I gripped his arm that was around my neck and the frustration caused my own temperature to rise; after that, I couldn't feel his arm anymore.

I fell to the ground and looked up at The Crow; the sleeve on his jumpsuit had been burned and his skin was raw and bright red; *it happened again.* More than anything he looked irritated, but not in as much pain as you'd expect after getting a burn like that. His frown slowly curved into a grin as he calmly walked toward me again. I tried to crawl away, but he was too fast. He pulled me back by the collar of my jumpsuit and flipped me over, then pinned me down with just one arm.

He glared into my eyes and his gaze was so cold it extinguished every fire within me. Up until now, all my fear was overridden by sheer determination, but right now, I felt terror hinder all my movements. I remembered the voice telling me I had control over my own power, but it just wasn't true. There were times like these where I was rendered a normal girl- times when I was deathly afraid, like every other human. I'd never flirted with death as much as I was today; now I knew what it was like to genuinely fight for my life.

"A phoenix is not a force to be reckoned with- even I'm smarter than to make you my enemy," he said calmly and gestured at the fire around us. "So, back to my proposal for you."

"Save your words," I responded aggressively as I struggled underneath him.

"I'm willing to overlook your rebellion and your attempts to attack me, but only if you cooperate and agree to come with me," he offered, and I froze.

"What?"

"I'll spare your life if you decide to join forces, darling," he elaborated. "Imagine how unstoppable a crow and a phoenix could be."

The more his words infiltrated my head, the slower time seemed to carry on. I pondered his offer, and that's when I really took in the amount of power he held in his persuasion. My eyes wandered to the forest, and I was reminded of my squadmates, the deviants I set free, my grandmother, and all the people I would be betraying if I agreed. I searched his human eye for integrity, and I couldn't find even a speck. *Even if he spared me, what would happen to everyone else?*

"I might be a lot of things, Crow, but I'm not a fool!" I yelled confidently, and I felt my fire reignite.

"Is that so?"

"How can I trust someone who's built an entire nation out of lies? How can I expect a snake to be a sheep?" I asked, and the grin on his face grew.

I tried to free myself and take my arms back, but there was no use, his grasp was way too strong. I wasn't paying attention when he grabbed a dagger from the sheath on his belt and dug it straight into my arm. I instinctively screamed as I felt a shock run through my arm, concentrating right where the blade had sliced. My brain hadn't processed the pain until he took the dagger out.

I watched my arm bleed out as a small crimson pool formed beneath. He laughed maniacally as he watched the blood drip from the blade. I stared at my arm; the phoenix mark that was once there had been shrouded by blood and a gaping wound. As the blood dripped from my arm onto the ground, I envisioned each of those droplets as falling embers.

Since my arms were far too weak right now, I targeted all my strength into one leg, and prayed it would be strong enough. I brought my knee up and hit him directly in the groin, which made him twitch. I took that opportunity to take the dagger from his hand, flip it in my own hand, and slice it through his cheek. He got up and held his hand over the small wound on his face, and I flipped myself over and stood up immediately.

"Maybe, you're the one that shouldn't play with fire," I spat out, mocking him. I watched him look down at me. He had managed to wipe off most of the blood, and despite it being a deep cut, he wasn't bleeding anymore.

"As much as I would love to kill you right here, right now- I want the rebels of the world to watch their martyr burn . . . just like they watched the last one," he said softly, and I felt the air get thinner. I didn't know if it was the smoke finally catching up to me, the loss of blood, or if it was his mere presence that was depriving me of air.

I gripped my arm, applying pressure to the wound. As hard as I tried, I couldn't seem to stop myself from falling to my knees. I was panting frantically, and The Crow noticed- making it apparent through his subtle smirk.

"So yeah, I wouldn't celebrate too soon, my dear," he added menacingly.

Before I could think of a response, something wrapped tightly around my neck and shoved me to the ground, forcefully hitting my head on the impact. There was a deviant trap around my neck, the same ones I used to use on running rebels. My arm was sore and in excruciating pain, and now I felt myself asphyxiating. I've never felt weaker than I did in this moment. My vision blurred and black splotches began obscuring my vision.

"I can't wait to watch you burn," The Crow said eerily. I managed to make out his face looking down and smiling at me, and that was the last thing I saw before the world around me blacked out.

Chapter 7

I woke up with an unbearable migraine and an intense soreness throughout my body, especially on my forearm. The ground beneath me was so cold. I fluttered my groggy eyes open, and I saw a floor made of old, deteriorating wooden planks. I tried to move my head and scan the area, but my head felt too heavy. I shifted my eyes to look down and check my arm, which had been roughly bandaged. I tried to figure out where I was and what had happened; the last thing I remembered was The Crow standing over me. That's when I recalled what he had said; he wanted everyone to watch me burn, just as The Phoenix did.

Upon remembering that, my body gained just enough strength to get back on my feet out of sheer panic. Despite sitting up slowly, I still unintentionally forced my arm too much, and the still-fresh knife wound reopened. I grunted as the white bandages quickly soiled with blood. Until now, I hadn't realized my wrists were in heavy shackles, which were attached to the ground by long chains. I scanned the room again, but there wasn't much to see. It was just an old, wooden shack.

I did however spot a small window in the shack; it was barred up, but I could still see the dark sky through it. I stood up and walked toward it until the shackles restrained me from going further, but I was close enough to see what was outside, and the sight was rather shocking. Hundreds of people gathered outside this shack, and I couldn't determine whether they were forced to be here or not. Hundreds were outside, waiting to watch me burn up in flames.

As I scanned through the familiar faces of the townsfolk, the person that struck me the most was my mother. My legs got weak at the sight of her amongst that crowd; *was she also here to watch her daughter burn?* The possibility alone made my stomach turn. To them I was just another criminal; a demon here to poison their minds and threaten their "freedom" . . . *but I never expected her to side with them.*

I willed myself to take another look outside and take a further look at my mom. She was being pushed toward the front of the crowd by guards, and it seemed like she was resisting. *Were they planning on killing her too?* is the first thought that came to my mind, and the urgency to break the chains increased tenfold. I heard muffled voices in the distance, but my ears were still popped from the explosions. They were yelling pretty loud over the crowd, so I tried to listen as best as I could with my impaired hearing.

"Cordelia Euphema- or should I say, Cordelia *Wolfe*, you will be sentenced next for the crimes you've committed and hidden from the state, which include raising a deviant in your home," a man shouted, and the revulsion on my mother's face grew more and more potent. "By order of Secretary Devrim, you are to watch the criminal you've brought up burn as part of your punishment and atonement," he added, and my blood ran cold at the last order. *She was innocent and now she had to die . . . all because of me.*

"Burn her too!" I heard someone in the crowd yell, followed up with some agreeing cheers. *They knew nothing . . . nothing.*

I clenched my fists so hard my nails pierced through my palms. I surveyed the crowd to figure out who had blurred out that comment, but instead, I found something much more shocking amongst the throng- *The Crow.* I recoiled as a rush of chills ran through my body and made me feel sick even at the mere sight of him. He was stationing a crow in the back of the crowd to get a clear view of the disaster that was about to unfold. He walked up to the front, and everyone immediately moved out of the way to clear a perfect path for him, bowing down as he passed them. He turned around and faced the crowd, and everyone who wasn't already, immediately fell to their knees and bowed down- their submission was repugnant.

"I'm afraid I'll have to cut my visit short. There's work back in the Capital that needs my attention, but don't worry, I'll be sure to watch with you all from the eyes of this crow, who will also broadcast this nation-wide for those who couldn't make it here today." He paused briefly, "Trust me, I wouldn't miss this for anything." His voice lowered as he muttered the last part. The crowd stayed down without making a sound; *what a circus.*

I couldn't help but feel like something was off about the way he spoke this time; his typical, powerful aura had a tinge of weakness. It could've been all the hits I took to my head recently, but he looked almost *sad.*

"Now my people, feast your eyes upon the brilliant sight . . . of a burning phoenix," he announced- which was more of a command since it was coming from him, so everyone stood up on the spot.

"Long live, *The Prophet,*" he announced casually before walking away, and all the blood immediately drained from my face. My breath got caught in my throat, as I tried to digest the name he just called me by.

"Phoenix Euphema, by order from our gracious leader, The Crow himself, you are to burn in the public eye for treason, affiliations with rebellion, spreading ideas of rebellion, and the aiding of rebels," the announcer read off a page. "This shall mark the beginning of the extinction of deviancy that threatens this nation!" he finished. Some people in the crowd applauded, but most remained quiet.

I tried to look for The Crow again, but there wasn't a single trace of him anywhere. I slowly drew back from the window; I couldn't bear to see all the familiar faces in the crowd watching me burn down to ashes. My eyes happened to fall on my mother, protesting the men restraining her, right before I backed away from the window. I could hear the heart-wrenching hysteria in every one of her screams so clearly from here, and those sounds would haunt me even in the afterlife. The sight of her resisting and her crying face would be the last thing I ever saw. *Why? Why did it have to be you?*

"NOW!" the speaker commanded, and just like that, *he threw the first stone.*

The shack ignited rapidly as more and more torches bombarded the small structure. In just a few short seconds, the air around me thickened considerably, and the temperature increased drastically. A large piece of the roof collapsed behind me, and it shook the shed. I tried to cover my nose with my arm to avoid inhaling the smoke, but it was getting harder to breathe as the seconds went by.

It didn't take long until I fell to my knees; my legs had become too weak to stand from the lack of oxygen. Debilitated, I weakly pulled on my shackles in an attempt to free myself even though I knew it was an utterly futile effort. I coughed as more smoke filled the small shack which inevitably would soon enough collapse on me- and then burn us as a unit. Never in my life had I been so close, and so encompassed by so much fire before, and yet- *it didn't feel as scary as I would have thought.*

Right when I felt myself about to surrender, I took one last look at the world, and although my groggy eyes could not discern what they were seeing from how rapidly my vision was slipping from me, it looked like someone was standing right in front of me. They wore the same mask as the deviant I saw in the forest, and a familiar burnt, white robe. It made perfect sense that I would hallucinate right now, but I just wanted to die with a clear, empty conscience.

"Why can't you just let me die in peace?" I managed to ask in between coughs.

"I'm here to change the course of this longitudinal battle," she responded, ignoring my question.

"How'd you get in here?" I asked, wasting my last few remaining breaths to talk to a mirage.

"You shall serve as my vessel." She ignored my question again and began to approach me. "We will share the same soul and therefore the same memories, but the memories you are about to witness may discomfort you," she warned. As much as I wished I could be confused by what I was seeing and hearing, nothing really made sense to me anymore anyways.

She proceeded to place her hand on my head, and I was under the impression that I was just hallucinating all of this, until I felt an actual touch on my head. I flinched by instinct, and her touch was warm at first, but as the seconds went by it quickly began to *burn*. I flinched again at the pain, but she firmly held my head in place. She warned me of unpleasant thoughts, but there were none yet. Another burning plank fell behind me, but this time I couldn't even react. The world blacked out and at first, I thought I had passed out, but that's when I began to see the visions she talked about.

Multiple images flashed rapidly through my head. There were visions of war zones, desolated sites, large gas masks, and streets filled with blood and countless corpses. One that caught my attention was a man who looked like a younger version of The Crow, accompanied by a woman. Her face was blocked by the angle, but she was injured and laying on the ground. The Crow stood above her with a blade drawn, but he didn't finish her off. It looked to me that he couldn't bring himself to do it- which was the only time I saw an ounce of humanity in him.

After several more disturbing war sights, the memories took a turn. There were multiple scenes of people getting shot and captured like animals, children being pulled away from their dying parents, shackled rebels desperately praying in their last moments- all for them to get their brains blown out. My heart clenched as they all flashed; something about these last few hit differently. *Why were they all in first person?*

In the last scene, a rebel falling to the ground with a bullet hole through his head quickly flashed, and then appeared again but from a different angle. In the background I saw the killer was wearing an executioner uniform- *a black and crimson one*. They held a gun in one hand, and a sword in the other. That person was me; *these were my memories.*

I wanted nothing more than to stop watching, but I couldn't stop looking by closing my eyes- they were already closed. It was like a nightmare you couldn't wake up from, because you were never asleep to begin with. Hot tears slid down my face- liquid regret. There was a suffocating pressure on my heart as I felt it corroding. Unfortunately for me, that wasn't where the memories stopped; there were plenty more murders to follow that one up.

After about twenty more memories filled with blood and bullets flashed rapidly, there was one final memory. It was the inside of a burning building, and muffled yelling and fire cracking was all I could hear. The view panned upward, and through the smoke, a large hole in the ceiling revealed an unusual-looking sky. It was so bright I almost didn't recognize it. It was a light shade of blue- not indigo, not gray- and the sun . . . it wasn't a *void*; It looked like an enormous flame lighting up the sky. A hand reached for the sun before the ceiling collapsed, then the scene went completely black. I only got to see that sky for about three seconds, but it was a sight I would never forget; *I want to see it forever.*

I fluttered my eyes open, only to find myself alone in a dark, burning shed with no bright blue sky or burning sun to look up to. In front of me were only four walls of a burning shed which was currently crumbling and would soon collapse on me.

"Are you afraid of burning?" came a woman's voice. I looked around, but this time there was no one there. The masked deviant was gone, and no one else was in sight.

"What?" I asked, essentially speaking into the atmosphere.

I stared into the empty, smoldering room and wondered if the lack of oxygen had just been messing with my head this whole time. The flames danced in front of me, and it hurt my eyes if I stared too long- just like the sun. As I listened to them crack, I caught my hand subconsciously reaching for it. *I've officially lost my mind, haven't I?* I thought as the heat was in dangerous proximity to my flesh.

"To feel safe in the fire, you can't run from it," came the voice again.

On the other side of the flames, I could've sworn I saw the masked rebel, beckoning me to walk toward her. I focused my eyes back on the flames, and the woman disappeared again. My hand extended slowly into the glowing fire; *am I afraid of burning?* I asked myself. After the atrocities I'd committed, death was righteous, *So no, Phoenix. I am not.*

A piece of the wall collapsed, causing the flames to blow toward me, and before I knew it, I was on fire. It was an inexplicable feeling; I knew I was on fire, and I was supposed to be dying, but I had never felt more *alive* than being this close to death. The flames wrapped around me, and I could feel them igniting every cell in my body. The insane heat spread from my fingertips all the way down to my very soul; that's when something within me kindled and went off like a bomb. I opened my eyes and I felt as if the flames had infiltrated my bloodwork.

Put an end to this carnage, and resurrect the sun, echoed in my head.

A surge of determination ran through me. I lifted and yanked on my shackles with all my force, and the chains on the handcuffs snapped. I slammed my handcuffs on the ground, and the cuffs that once bound me to death were useless metal now. I was free again, *like a bird.*

There was a large cracking sound before the ceiling collapsed, and the rest of the shed followed shortly after. I was trapped and unable to move under all the heavy rubble, but despite the considerable weight of several burning planks, my body felt no pain, and my heart knew no fear. While I remained buried under the ruins, I heard some selfish cheering in the crowd, but immediately after followed a fair share of eerie silence- complete, bitter *silence.*

I closed my eyes and momentarily imagined a world where humanity was free. My thoughts immediately went to a bird, soaring the skies with no direction. Before opening my eyes, I envisioned myself also soaring through the sky, heading straight toward the sun with a pair of crimson wings. I wondered if there would ever be a day when I could reach that same level of freedom. *Maybe one day, I'll fly too.*

I opened my eyes and my hand reached for the dark, ash-clouded sky, and I jumped and pushed through the loads of rubble, and before I could fall, I soared. I was feet above the ground, looking down at the dazzled crowd with my pair of crimson wings. Their reactions were priceless; many of their mouths hung open and some people even fell to the ground. I made my way down gently like a weightless ember, and I landed on top of the ruins that once held me captive.

"You can't put a Phoenix in a bird cage," I proclaimed confidently.

Their wide eyes were fixated on me, and the look of bafflement and terror was present in every single one of them. The wind blew and scattered embers and ash around the scene; it was bitter cold, but I felt no chill. At the front of the crowd, I found my mother, who was on the ground with her shaky hand over her mouth, and her emerald eyes wider than anyone else's. She had a million words on her tongue but was unable to utter even a single sound.

I looked at the guards that once harassed her, and I shot them a look that could kill. The intimidation seemed to work, since they flinched and backed away immediately. I switched my focus from them back over the entire crowd. I stared at the crow in the back, straight into its eyes, or should I say- cameras. I took a deep breath of thick, polluted air before speaking.

"I am Phoenix Euphema, and I don't care if I have to burn this world to the ground to rise again, because a phoenix *always* rises from the ashes," I declared proudly, now all the eyes in this nation were on me, and all ears were listening. "As The Prophet, this is my vow *to resurrect the sun!*" I declared, and with that, the promise was set in stone.

Stunned looks filled the crowd- too shocked to even panic. I glanced at my mother and saw tears slipping from her weary eyes.

Through the tears, she still managed to smile, and it reminded me that she had the most beautiful smile. There was so much pride in her face, and between the tears and the look she was giving me, I got a strange nostalgic feeling. There was a crowd of people behind us, but at that moment, I felt like it was only her and I.

"That's my Phoenix," She muttered softly, but I still managed to hear it. "Set this damned world on fire."

It felt like ripping my heart out of my chest by leaving her behind like this, but I had some ease knowing the guards would probably just hold her until the next execution, and I know I'll be back before then. *I won't let them kill you, momma.* As hard as it was to turn away and run, I had no other choice- unlike her, they wouldn't wait for me. I took one final look at my mother and took off, and didn't look back.

I scanned the perimeter; we were in a forest behind the town. All the fires had extinguished, and the district was once more dark and gray. I flew into the woods and got through a decent chunk before my wings disbursed into embers. I ran the rest of the way toward the Executioner cabin; I needed to grab some things before fleeing for good.

I reached the back of the cabin and broke in through my bedroom window to avoid wasting extra time on doors. I geared up into a fresh uniform as swiftly as possible and filled up on ammunition and grenades from the emergency stash. I also stole a portable lantern from the cabin too, because light is scarce and never promised in this world. Before heading out, I would do one final thing I'd been meaning to do since this morning. I reached under the bed and grabbed the chest full of books. I gave the place one last look, before burning it down, along with the chest.

As I ran out of the cabin, which was quickly igniting, a thought sparked in my head that made my heart stop; *wasn't something missing?* I asked myself, then, when all I had to do was look behind me, shame weighed over me as I admitted to myself that even after everything they'd done for me, my squadmates' whereabouts and safety had slipped my mind. The building we created our fondest memories in was now going down in flames, and the longer I looked at it, the more I began to regret everything.

Before getting any more distracted, I pushed and kept moving forward no matter how hard I wanted to turn back around. I ran toward the battle ground from earlier where once stood the statue of The Crow, and then turned into the woods beside it, which had been heavily damaged from the fire. The ground was covered in holes from the explosions, and everything was blackened from the flames, leaving the place unrecognizable.

I ran aimlessly through the dark forest for a good while and burned each and every crow I ran into without remorse. This time, the sight of a burning crow did not frighten me, but actually brought me a sense of satisfaction. The forest felt endless as I ran through the darkness without a destination in mind or any idea of where I was. My lungs were out of breath and gasping for air, but I was too afraid to stop in case someone was to catch up to me.

I was extra careful as I ran to avoid stepping on any landmines- a common trap deviants set out to stop us from following them. I was trained to avoid them and taught how to react if one accidentally sets off, but I had never actually run into one myself. It proved to be a rather difficult task with the given circumstances that the forest was almost pitch black, and I only had a small lantern to light my surroundings. While looking out for traps, I ran into some unfortunate sights scattered around the path- many of the soldiers from yesterday, either killed by the traps, or burnt from the fire.

I found a solid path that looked to have been walked on before and hoped there wouldn't be many traps on it. A pungent smell, aside from decaying corpses and burnt vegetation, lingered in the air, as well as various glimmery, shiny objects hanging from the trees- crow repellents I assumed- which explained a big reason these forests were generally crow-free. Deviants were a lot more cunning than I had imagined, because all these traps were set so strategically, and they definitely got the job done, because I never attempt to chase them through here. I couldn't imagine having to go through this horrific forest blindly, just for the slim chance of obtaining a better life living in freedom of rebellion- and yet, here I was, doing just that.

Despite the major boost of adrenaline, my body was bound to stop running eventually. I leaned and slid down a large tree, dropping to the cold earth to catch my breath. Until now, I hadn't had even a pocket of time to process anything that had happened today. It was so much easier to think in here- the silence in the forest was almost uncanny; the only sound I could hear was my obnoxious panting for air. It was also incredibly dark, with no torches or lights in sight.

I didn't think about how long I was inside that shed for; so long that the sun would go down shortly, and the pages would soon turn. Today, however, would go down in history for ages and eons to come. I thought back to the eyes of that rebel and how much hope hid inside them; *maybe the sun also hides hope for us behind the eclipse?* I inquired. While stuck on my train of thought, I was caught completely off guard by a hand covering my mouth.

Panic shot through me and my body temperature exponentially rose.

"Ow!" a man grunted as he let go. I drew away as quickly as I could.

"Wait, please!" the man pleaded.

He was unarmed, carrying only an oil lantern. Through his lantern's faint light, I recognized his face vaguely as one of the four leaders, but I was certain of it once I saw the black execution robe which was now covered in burn marks. He had a dark complexion, a tall figure, and an equally apprehensive expression on his face. He also had a distinct scar right on his eyebrow.

Before I could say anything, he ran up to me and covered my mouth again. "Don't make too much noise, and please don't burn anything . . . or me for that matter," he pleaded, and I felt a bit embarrassed. "We are going to the Rebellium quarters; you and your friends will be safe there, but we need to be discreet," he explained, and I felt a massive weight lifted off my shoulders. My heart fluttered with relief and excitement, two things I haven't felt in a while.

Whether I trusted him or not, I didn't have many other options, so I just nodded and played along. He took his hands off me and motioned me to follow him. He moved swiftly and managed to do so with minimal noise; it was clear they did this often. It's no wonder we were never able to catch them until recently.

"I'm Daxon by the way, pleasure to make your acquaintance," he introduced himself quietly as he ran.

"I'm Cri-" I paused to correct myself, ". . . Phoenix," I responded as quietly as I could. It was my first time introducing myself with my real name in years, and although it was still foreign to me, it felt liberating.

"Lovely name," he commented. It was also my first time getting a compliment on my name, which also felt unusual.

We ran for a few more minutes until finally coming to a halt. "There's a hole in the gate that leads to the outside of this District- we just have to find it," he explained.

I had never been this far out from the town, let alone outside of the gates. Anything beyond a mile of the town was an exclusion zone- so ninety percent of the forest encompassing the town. Ordinary civilians never dared come out here, because these areas were not only prohibited, but they were also dangerous, and most importantly- unguarded; which today I learned was mostly the rebel's doing. Between the complete absence of light, all the traps- both for crows and humans- I found it almost impossible to make it far into the forest alive- even rebels, too.

"I found it, c'mon." He motioned me toward a small hole in the wall, which had been camouflaged well by leaves and twigs.

"After you," I said, motioning with my head. Even though I didn't have much to lose, I didn't trust this man or the rebels just yet, so I let him go first.

He nodded and crawled in, but after a few seconds, I followed right behind him to not lose track. It was a small crevice in the wall, but wide enough to fit at least one person at a time. It wasn't until I crawled through it that I realized just how thick the gate walls actually were- at least fifteen feet wide.

When we finally reached the end, the scenery was completely different to that within the walls. I took in my surroundings, which looked exactly as I expected a desert to look like- deserted and empty. It was never-ending barren plains as far as the eye could see. The indigo and deep orange sunset drew a clear line with the ground, with no trees or buildings to obscure the skyline. On the fading horizon, the black sun had begun to go down, slowly hiding behind it.

"Phoenix!" I heard a familiar voice from behind me and my breath caught in my chest. I turned around immediately, and my eyes met with Aurora's. She was wrapped in a blanket, alongside Guido and Nyrual. They boys lay motionless on the ground and the blood completely drained from my face. I ran toward them and kneeled beside them.

"Guys, what's wrong? Answer me!" I exclaimed. I listened closer, and to my not-so-surprising surprise, I heard faint snoring. Daxon and Aurora couldn't contain their laughter.

"Don't worry, they're just real tired," Daxon said and chuckled, and I felt my face heat up with embarrassment. I looked at both of them and I slapped them across their sleeping faces, immediately waking them up.

"What the hell was that for?" asked Nyrual in a raspy voice, still trying to open his eyes. Guido rubbed his eyes open.

"For making me believe you were dead!" I explained.

"It's not my fault you're stup-" Guido began while rubbing his eyes, then the boys both looked up at me, and their eyes lit up. "You're alive!" Guido exclaimed, and they both sat up and hugged me. Aurora also joined in on the group hug.

Holding them felt relieving to such an immeasurable degree. It temporarily ceased all the angst and worries from this dreadful day. As much as I wanted this moment to last forever, I knew I had to break it off.

"So, Daxon, where are we headed?" I asked.

"Follow me, it's closer than you think," he answered. I stood up first then everyone followed.

"Lead the way, big guy," said Guido.

With that, we followed him blindly to the infamous Rebellium hideout that was so sought out; *I suppose yesterday's enemies are today's allies after all.* We wandered aimlessly through the desert for what felt like an eternity, with only two lanterns and the moon's glimmer to light our path, although the moon did feel much brighter out here. We walked for miles on end until we finally caught a glimpse of something besides dry, cracked land in the distance.

"How do you know how to get there when everything looks the exact same for miles?" Aurora asked Daxon.

"We follow the sun and the moon. They will always guide us home," he responded with a glimmer in his eyes and a smile on his lips.

As we got closer, the large silhouette we were seeing was becoming clear. It was a ghost town; the walls around it were practically torn down, and the buildings inside which I spotted through the large holes were falling apart, if not already destroyed.

"What is this place?" I asked while examining the abandoned city of ruins.

"It was once a small industrial district- the most this place had to offer was either acres of empty plains, or the huge mansion which once belonged to a powerful mayor and his family. The city lost to rebel rioting, which erupted into a full-blown battle about eighteen years ago. Now all that's left is ruins," he explained.

We easily made our way in since the gates were practically rubble. It surprised me that this place wasn't surveilled by even a single crow, but I suppose ghost towns didn't really need protection.

"Where do you all hide?" Nyrual asked.

"Underneath this big mess. There's a large cellar beneath the mansion, though we do occupy the mansion too, we just make sure to avoid windows," Daxon explained, which made sense. They couldn't exactly be out in the open.

As we walked through the town, I felt an odd familiarity and nostalgia with the town despite it being my first time even being outside of the confines of District Four. I recalled The Phoenix's memories that she shared with me, which included some desolated sites and ghost towns, so I came to the conclusion that it was most likely the reason this burnt town would even strike me as familiar. These ruined streets resembled the ones in her memories, which were now also my memories. Everything here was black and gray, even the mansion, which was blackened by flames and soot. Whatever happened here, it must've been *bad* for the whole town to go down.

We approached the mansion, and a heavy surge of unease and guilt came over me as I fully processed that every single person in there was going to be deviant, the same people I've mercilessly hunted for years. I never gave them a second chance, or even a chance to speak, yet they were willing to forgive me, and give me the chances I hadn't given them. Images of dead rebels resurfaced in my brain, and I began to wonder, *how many of their friends and family members have I taken from them?* With that in mind, I couldn't bring myself to keep walking, which caught Daxon's attention.

"What's wrong?" he asked. I couldn't even look him in the eyes as my face burned in shame.

"I can't go in," I blurted, earning a puzzled look from Daxon.

"Why? We've already come this far-" Daxon started, but I cut him off.

"How can you even look at me right now?" I asked, as my knees gave out, and I fell to the ground. I was dancing on the edge of a mental breakdown.

There was a cold silence, but I didn't even know if I wanted to hear his response. After a while he sighed loudly, then kneeled to meet me on the ground.

"You either grow and move on from the past, or let it catch up to you, because time isn't gonna wait for you," he answered sternly. "We're making the decision to trust you, so whether you decide to break our trust is completely up to you."

"Why would you even trust me to begin with?" I asked, genuinely not understanding why. I wasn't sure what answer or reaction I was expecting to receive, but a *smile* was definitely not it.

"Come on, freedom won't come on its own," he answered with that same glimmer of hope in his eyes as the blue-eyed deviant's. *I suppose that was enough of an answer.*

I stood back up, swallowing the heavy lump in my throat as we walked into the scorched building. There was some evidence of life in the interior, which I would not have expected after seeing the crumbling exterior. Glasses, sleeping bags, pillows, even children's toys were all scattered around. There was a trapdoor in the corner of the room we were currently in, which we all made our way toward. Daxon climbed down first, and we followed, me being the last to step down. My stomach turned, and my face was hot and ridden with shame as I threw myself into the deep end, feeding myself to the wolves.

Chapter 8

Upon reaching the bottom, I expected a heavy, mournful atmosphere- but it was quite the opposite. In fact, I had never seen a room so vibrant, with people so spontaneous and full of life. Never before had I seen so much spirit, so much . . . *life*. They all had smiles on their faces which they exchanged with each other, and unlike the gray people back home, they behaved like actual living beings- not machines.

I didn't quite pay attention to how many people were actually in here, but there were at least a hundred in this massive room alone. As I scanned the room, there was one person who stood out to me over all the hundred plus people here- a tall man with a lit cigarette in his mouth, sitting on top of the bar table at the opposite end of the room parallel to where I stood. His hair was raven black and styled in a messy undercut, roughly complementing his lightly tanned skin, which was covered in tattoos on both his arms and neck. His facial structure was chiseled perfectly, sculpted like a work of art. He wore a straight face while he mingled with a small group of people who looked at him with incredible admiration; *I wonder if they see what I'm seeing?*

Just as I looked away, I felt a glare pierce into me. I slowly shifted my eyes back to the man, who was now staring me down too. My breath was taken away for an instant as the air thickened. My heart raced and I felt every beat against my chest as the surroundings beyond him and I faded. I studied the very eyes that were the culprit to this unusual reaction, and there was no mistake- it was *him*- the eyes with hope burned into every corner and crevice. The dark sun was encompassed by swirling shades of blue; *the man with the sky in his eyes.*

Unfortunately for me, he didn't stop at just a glance, he stood up and slowly began making his way toward me. I felt my body stiffen considerably as he approached me for what felt like an eternity. Everyone's eyes followed him, until he finally stood only inches away from me. His presence was demanding, and I struggled to keep eye contact.

"Phoenix Euphema, or should I say- The Prophet," he uttered in a deep, husky voice, breaking the silence that formed the second he stood up.

For years, I've been the one who intimidated everyone into submission, but this time, it was me being intimidated just by someone's presence alone. His voice was deep and faintly raspy; it was my first time hearing him talk, but his voice matched what I had expected a leader like him to sound like. I had completely blanked out on what he said just now; *he was talking to me,* I finally processed.

"Th-that is me," I replied, stuttering.

"Also an Executioner and self-righteous murderer," he added with a bizarre tone. I would expect it to be disdain or disgust, *but it wasn't either of the two.*

I swallowed hard and looked down in shame, because deep down, I knew he was right. My heart dropped heavily as my initial fear was unfolding into a reality right in front of me.

"I-" I tried to defend myself, or at least respond in some sort of way, but my tongue got caught in my mouth. Either way- he didn't seem like he wanted a response or was done talking.

"Now it's your turn to look down when being faced with the bastard sons of society," he spat out, this time animosity riding on each word. He raised an arm to the wall behind me and leaned even closer to me. "Tell me, *princess*, how does it feel being on the bottom?" he mocked.

A heavy lump formed in my throat and my mouth was too dry to swallow it. Guido stepped in before I could respond; *not like I was going to anyways.*

"Okay man, she saved you and your friends, the least you could do is show a bit of respect," Guido protested.

For once I didn't feel the urge to defend myself, and I didn't want anyone to defend me either. The man was considerably taller than me, and even a few inches taller than Guido, so his mere presence alone asserted considerable dominance. We clearly weren't a threat to him right now.

"You've all known respect or at least experienced basic human decency your entire lives on your high horses," he began to refute, "so, brat, I ask again- how does it feel to be on the bottom?" he retorted with a smirk.

His question echoed in my head, and I felt my shame be overridden with anger. I looked up at him with fury in my eyes, and surprise flashed through his stern face before dissipating almost immediately.

"Let's get this straight, I had to work like a dog to gain that so-called 'respect'- and never in my life have I been respected- people were only *afraid*, and there's a distinct difference between being feared and being respected," I answered sternly without once breaking eye contact.

I bit my lip and dug my nails into my palms to avoid getting overly emotional; *all emotions ever do is get in the way,* I reminded myself. Silence echoed throughout the room and I knew every single person was watching. The man stared back with a virtually emotionless look, but I managed to find some sort of sympathy in his eyes before turning his back toward me.

"Daxon, make sure they get taken care of, then make sure they speak with The White Raven," he ordered. Daxon nodded, surprised by his lack of reaction.

"Come with me," Daxon said, and we followed. I took one last look at the man, who was walking back to his original spot while blowing smoke from his mouth.

"This isn't a funeral, no need for such silence; raise another glass!" he exclaimed without raising his voice much; somehow it still reached every corner of the room. Everyone cheered loudly and glasses flew up in the sky. He had an undeniable gift of being able to raise the atmosphere so effortlessly. *This was someone who was truly respected, not feared.*

Daxon led us to a room that unexpectedly had several people in it. It was a kitchen by the looks of it; there were at least four cooks at work, and two guys leaned against the wall talking. Their presence also felt strong, reminding me of a more subdued version of the man back there.

"Khalon, Fremont, come here," called Daxon, and the two men looked toward us, sticking their eyebrows up in confusion. One of the guys had straight dirty-blond hair, light brown eyes and was about five inches shorter than the other. The other man had dark brown curls, coffee-brown monolid eyes, and a tan complexion.

"So, you made it back with all of them. Good job, Daxon," praised the taller man as he approached us. "I'm Khalon."

"And I'm Fremont," the blond followed up. "Word has it you're The Prophet, miss?" he asked me.

"Now we're cooking with gas," added Khalon as he rubbed his hands together. They examined me, and for the first time in my life, right now and earlier, I felt self-conscious about my current appearance, realizing I was probably covered in dirt and ashes.

"She seems to vaguely fit the description in the books," explained Daxon, "not just any ordinary person can spawn fire out of thin air. Whether she's the Prophet or not, she's a significant piece to finding them," Daxon continued.

"I am The Prophet," I clarified, and they all got quiet and looked at me, surprised by my level of certainty. "She told me."

"The Phoenix spoke to you? How and when?" asked Khalon; everyone was desperately waiting for me to answer, and even the cooks had begun to stare.

"She and I are one now. She merged her soul with mine, I guess." I placed my hand on my chest. "She told me when I was supposed to burn in the shed- like her."

"Someone call The White Raven A.S.A.P!" ordered Daxon, seemingly overwhelmed by the information.

"I'm on it," replied Fremont before rushing out of the room.

"Angie, make them something to eat; if I was them, I'd be starving right about now," stated Daxon. A young, pale girl with slick black hair nodded and immediately got to work. The truth was, I wasn't even hungry. After all the events from today, my appetite was non-existent.

Soon enough we were sitting at a small table and were given some sort of hot stew. Everyone dug in except me; I simply stirred it around in the bowl. I looked up and saw a woman, who looked to be around my grandmother's age, walking in with Fremont. She had a strong pacifistic aura around her, and you could tell she too was very wise and respected around here.

"My, this is a sight you don't see too often, rebel slayers and rebels sharing a meal," she said with such a golden smile it made the air feel lighter.

"You can have my seat ma'am," Nyrual offered as he stood up.

"Why, thank you, handsome gentleman," she jested and took the seat as everyone chuckled.

She stared at me, then she stared *into* me. I felt her eyes searching inside me for *her*. She looked at me like she had just seen an old friend.

"You remind me so much of her," she said, smiling from ear to ear. I didn't know why, I couldn't help but smile back. "It only takes a pair of eyes to know you're The Prophet," she continued, and then placed a worn-out page on the table.

"But why would she choose me- the one who's killed scores of deviants? I'm the last person to deserve that title." I expressed my shame and her smile fell, but not completely. She sighed loudly and looked down at the book.

"Though there are elements of truth to what you say," she began, and everyone watched and listened intently, "and while being The Prophet is indeed an honor, it's also a massive misfortune, my dear. You will carry the weight of the world on your shoulders along with a heavy fate," she explained vaguely.

She fiddled with the edges of the yellowed paper. "The Phoenix wrote this poem days before she died. She knew from the beginning that she would lose the battle, but she left this to remind us that the battle was far from over," she prefaced, and handed me the page. Everyone huddled around me, trying to read as well.

"Though I have lost the battle, the battle is never fully lost. Though I burn to ash, a revolution will rise from the ash. Though the sun won't shine today, it will dry our tears one day. Though I, Astrid Eleodoro, will not return- The Phoenix will. They will wield the power of the sun itself, for humanity- no matter how strong- will never be stronger than the sun," it read. I flipped it over and this is where the real mystery began. Everything I had read up until now had already happened; now I had to learn my fate as The Prophet.

"Malevolence and corruption cannot be killed by a blade alone, and that is the enemy we are dealing with here. Only the sun can burn the darkness; she will overthrow and kill the darkness. . ." I hesitated to read the last few words, but in the end, I knew I had to, so with dread I lowered my eyes, *". . . but will burn The Phoenix along with it,"* It finished, as bluntly as that.

Everyone looked at each other awkwardly, holding their words and reactions in their mouths. I stared at the words written on that page and all I could do was blankly stare and reread them. I heard whispers around me but didn't listen to the words. I should probably be hysterical, or at the very least upset. . . *but I'm not in the slightest.*

"This didn't answer my question," I said nonchalantly. Everyone was thrown off by that being all I had to say.

I looked at the woman for a possible answer. "She was a close friend of mine. She was the strongest woman I ever knew, with a strong heart, admirable courage, and burning determination," she shared with a big smile; the way she talked about her was beautiful. "Whether it was something good, or bad, she saw something that caught her attention, and only she knows what it was. So please, refrain from calling yourself unworthy, my dear," she explained as she cupped my cheeks with her cold hands. For a second I imagined that she was my grandmother, and that I was back home. I smiled, genuinely.

"Hey everyone, Asier is about to give a speech, you guys need to hear this!" a young boy with dark, olive skin and dark features abruptly announced. He looked to be about eight years old. *Who was Asier?* I questioned. He nudged on Khalon's leg, and he smiled down at him.

"Lamie, don't barge in like that!" A young woman came running behind him and scolded. "Sorry, corporal," she apologized to Khalon. She was a few inches taller than me, slender but still rather muscular, and had shoulder-length black hair with a wispy fringe that reached her eyebrows. She had a curious look in her eyes as she glanced at each one of us.

"We'll be out there in a few, Nila," said Fremont.

"Sure thing. I apologize for the interruption." She excused herself and took the little boy's hand as they exited back to the main room. All eyes turned back to me.

"Does your fate not bother you?" The White Raven asked. I didn't have a definite answer, but I had a response.

"I don't know," I said, keeping everyone in suspense. Everyone was puzzled by my response, myself included.

"Well on that note, everyone, follow me," Khalon directed, and motioned everyone to an empty table for us to sit at, but there weren't enough chairs for all of us, so I decided to stand.

I looked toward the bar out of curiosity and saw the man again. I figured he was the Asier guy they were talking about; it was a stunning name. Despite the man's coldness, I was still eager to hear him speak- I needed to hear what he had to say. He stood on top of the bar table even though he was already quite tall to begin with, and he wore so much pride on his face- but not the bad pride, it was the good kind. Everyone watched him like a movie; the admiration in the crowd's glossy eyes was evident in every gaze- I had never seen anything like it.

"Ladies and gentlemen, today I would like to celebrate a couple of things. The first one, of course, being that we're all still alive," he began and everyone was already cheering. "As you guys know, we were in death's hands today, but I knew that even if we died, this fight would not, because I rest assured knowing that if one day the end were to befall us, the rest of you would still feel the sun one day," he explained- his words hitting me like a brick wall. That's when I had an epiphany.

All these people I saw before me, fight day after day for their freedom, knowing they could easily meet death at any moment, and yet . . . that didn't stop them from fighting. They didn't just fight for themselves, but also for the future generations. They fought so one day they would feel the sunlight on their skin; so that no one had to die on that stage again, and so no one would ever have to hide to stay alive. There was not a speck of selfishness in these people.

"Remember, we are Rebellium- the ones who resist when the world tries to restrain us, and we won't stop resisting until our shackles break," he continued, and people had already begun to cheer and whistle. "So raise your fists, and hold your heads high as we defy the throne- BECAUSE WE ARE HERE TO TAKE BACK THE WORLD THAT ONCE WAS OURS!" he shouted proudly, finishing off his grand speech with a bang. His energy was infectious- everyone went ballistic as they threw their hats and raised their drinks.

Daxon, Khalon, and Fremont raised a glass and then walked to the front. The people cheered for them as they placed themselves next to the table Asier stood upon. They were all leaders, but it seemed as if Asier truly held the hearts of the people; there was just something about him.

"Can't seem to take your eyes off him, huh?" the woman bantered, and I felt my face involuntarily heat up for what felt like the millionth time today. "His name's Asier. He is the one who founded Rebellium- that's why everyone here follows and respects him so much as the leader and commander," she explained as her eyes admired him too.

I switched my gaze from her back to him, and once again, he reminded me of the sky- holding countless mysteries, with the answers so distant. Every time I looked at him, I was reminded of the choice I made- the choice to be free. He was the start of a new beginning for not only me, but the entire world. He instigated the rebirth of a nation and personified the immortality of humanity's wish to be free.

"To establish an entire rebel association, he must have a very strong reason to revolt," I suggested. "Am I wrong to assume so?"

"Every person you see here does, dear," she replied.

I looked over at him again and he was conversing with the other leaders. I assumed my name was brought up in the conversation, because they kept staring back at me. I felt my anxiety spike and my face heat up whenever I caught him looking at me. I heard a chuckle from the woman as she watched my body language expose the tension I was feeling.

"Don't fret, you look beautiful," she teased, and I felt my pride stir so much I forgot I was even nervous.

"As if I care about something so trivial," I refuted like a bratty teenager. She giggled at my response. I just sighed in defeat.

"I forgot you're still a young girl, figuring out her emotions," she said.

"All they ever do is get in the way," I replied, and there was a brief moment of silence.

"To understand the power one holds we must first begin by understanding ourselves," she preached, and I turned to face her. "You and Asier aren't too different there, you know?" she added out of the blue. "He can front all he wants, but there's always another show going on behind the curtains."

I tilted my head while trying to comprehend what she meant by that. I looked over at Asier again, and unexpectedly, he looked back at me, only this time I didn't look away. I searched the skies embedded in his eyes, and then I understood what she meant. There was a hint of deep melancholy buried under all that hope, making it more than clear that he had been through his fair share of hardships; he was just another human being after all.

I looked away before creeping him out, but then snuck in a quick glance a few seconds later. He was raising his hand to quiet the crowd, smiling as he was about to speak. *How'd you teach yourself how to smile in a world where your dreams were so far beyond your reach?* I wondered as I studied his every move. *Who are you really, Asier?*

"As you all know, The Revolution began with a woman known as The Phoenix, who prophesied she would aid our victory through a 'Prophet,'" he briefly explained. "Well, I believe we've found her- the 'new Phoenix'- The Prophet," he announced somewhat hesitantly, but everyone still clapped. My heartbeat spiked as soon as I realized they were talking about me.

"I believe she should be given the opportunity to introduce herself formally," he suggested as he jumped down from the table. *Was I supposed to go up there?* I panicked, my head spinning. I felt my heart bang against my chest as Daxon beckoned me to stand up there.

I froze up, realizing I had to face all these rebels and their main leader- who evidently hated my guts. Slowly but surely, I made my way to the front, and the cheers understandably diminished. Everyone moved out of the way, making a clear path for me. I had never experienced anxiety at such a degree as I did during the walk up to the bar.

When I finally reached the table, two strong arms picked me up as Khalon placed me on top of the table. I looked around and so many eyes were watching me, but my head was spinning too much to make out their expressions and figure out what they were thinking. I searched the crowd for a familiar face, and my eyes automatically landed on Aurora, Guido, and Nyrual; the second I saw their smiling faces, my heart rate slowed down and my anxiety began dissipating. I inhaled sharply before opening my mouth to speak.

"My name is Phoenix Euphema, and I am no longer afraid to say that." I took another deep breath before continuing. "Today, I was set to kill the man who just stood up here, but for once, I was unable to pull the trigger, because today, in his eyes I saw something I had seen countless times, but in a way I had never seen before," I said and it was so silent you could hear a pin drop.

"For the first time, I looked a deviant in the eyes, and I saw a human being. I saw adamant, unwavering hope even in the face of death, and in those same eyes, I saw the sky- the same dark void in a sea of blue that I see every time I look up, and I felt the desire to change that sky," I explained, looking over at Asier, who returned his usual cold glare. I knew he was at least a little surprised behind that stagnant demeanor.

"One day when this war is over and won, simply existing freely in this world will no longer be a dream, but a reality. I vow to resurrect the sun for those standing here, and those who died trying. This is the least I can do to atone for all the blood I've shed," I promised, and the room was still deathly silent; no enthusiastic cheers like the ones Asier received- just bitter silence.

I couldn't blame them; their enemy was standing in front of them, suddenly claiming to be their salvation. Right when I was about to get down and just accept that the only response I would receive was silence, something strange happened. Everyone got down on one knee, brought their fists to their chest, and threw the other in the air. The leaders were the only ones exempt from saluting, but the crowd was more than enough for me. *They were saluting . . . me.*

I scanned the room full of saluting people and mimicked them. I lifted my fist to my heart and fiercely shot the other in the air; solidifying my promise to fight with them. The room remained silent for the duration of the salute, but it felt like silent cheering. I jumped down, and Aurora, Nyrual, and Guido all approached me with proud looks on their faces- The White Raven also followed behind them with an impressed smirk.

Several minutes had passed since my monologue and everyone was enjoying the remainder of the night- everyone but me. I may be in the most crowded room, but I always felt alone. That was usually the case with me; I've never exactly been the most approachable or sociable. I scanned the room and apparently, I wasn't the only lonely wolf in the pack- Asier sat alone only a few empty bar stools away from me. He was zoned out, smoking a cigarette, and staring blankly at the wall, away in his own distant world.

My observation was interrupted by a man who slammed his hand down next to me. I turned my head slightly and from the corners of my eyes, I caught the furious expression painted on his face. His face was red, and his eyebrows scrunched. He was tall, strong, and appeared angry enough to break me in half at any given moment.

"I don't know who you think you're fooling; you could be The Phoenix herself but nothing you do will *ever* atone for all our innocent people you've slaughtered," he spat out and gripped my arm tightly, making me tense up. I knew I was probably capable of beating this man to the ground, but I didn't want to spoil my reputation even more than it already was.

"Don't touch me," I responded as calmly as I could and simply retracted my arm. I knew everyone around us was staring heavily- I could feel their glares burning holes into my back.

"Don't you dare tell me what to do, murderous bitch," he responded more aggressively.

Rather than defending myself, I fought against myself to stay quiet for my own good. As provoked as I was, I knew he probably wasn't the only one thinking that- hell, even I was thinking that- only he was brave enough to actually say it. Before he could do anything else, Nyrual emerged from the crowd and stepped in between us. He shoved the man slightly, enough to where he was a safe distance away.

"What are you gonna do man, hit me?" the man asked, and I saw a vein pop out on Nyural's face. He was extremely protective of the people he cared about, particularly the women in his life. His mother had raised him well.

I backed up before things got more heated, and I didn't notice just how much I had backed up until Asier was practically right behind me. The man shoved Nyrual to the side and began to inch toward me, but before either me or Nyrual could do anything, he froze in place. Asier stood up from his stool behind me, and simply glared at the man. The man looked back at him- furious, yet still submissive. All Asier had to do was glare and all the man's words got caught on his tongue; I suppose he thought there was a chance Nyrual and I could lose, but he *knew* Asier wouldn't lose.

The man surrendered and walked away with his tail between his legs, his face pouring with frustration. Asier waited for him to leave the premises before sitting back down again and sighing. I exchanged a smile with Nyrual, and he returned to the crowd once the man was gone. I turned to Asier, who was once again facing away from the crowd as he blew smoke from his flushed lips. I wanted to thank him, but quite frankly he intimidated me too, especially when I remembered how our last encounter ended. Despite the confrontational tension, I decided that for once I had to swallow my pride.

"Thank you," I uttered, fidgeting with my fingers to suppress the awkwardness.

"You don't have to thank me," he replied coldly without even looking in my direction.

"I didn't have to, but I did."

"Stupid, little girl," he taunted. As much as I felt like saying something back, I turned my back and just walked away. I had to learn that having the last word didn't mean I won.

I quickly grew bored of just idly standing and it didn't seem like Asier wanted much company either, so I decided to walk around and explore the place I would be staying in for God knows how long. I wandered all over the place until I somehow ended up in a narrow hallway. There was a bookshelf at the end of the hall, stacked with various books and newspapers. Out of curiosity I decided to open one of them; I chose a book titled *"The Lone Wolf."*

I skimmed through the pages, and it seemed to be a fiction piece, which was incredibly rare these days. Literature was an easy and effective way to subliminally spread ideas- particularly deviant ideas- and reading and understanding literature also required a level of critical thinking, which is why most literature was outlawed. The Crow likes us to use our brains as little as possible, but so do we. We're all just in love with the bliss that comes with utter ignorance.

As I flipped to the last page, a folded piece of paper fell out of the book. I picked up the page from the ground and unfolded it, revealing a handwritten note. I was conflicted on reading the note, in case it turned out to be something personal, but curiosity got the better of me.

Although it pains me, I have to go. I've finally made up my mind- I know what I want to do and what I have to do, so don't try to come find me. The sun has set on this, dear Asier. Goodbye forever.

I hope one day you can forgive me.
-Valerie.

I reread the words over and over again, but I couldn't quite grasp the weight they carried. By putting two and two together, I concluded that Valerie was someone important to Asier, but had seemingly abandoned him somewhere along the road. After comprehending that simple fact, the weight of every single one of those words began to fall on me. I felt a wound in my heart that had been numb for so long open up and start to sting again. Without knowing either of them, or the situation, my heart sympathized with Asier, because I knew exactly what he must've felt as he read those words- abandoned and betrayed. *I knew the feeling all too well, but at least he got an explanation and a farewell.*

Before tucking the note back in the book and closing it, I read the last page of the novel.

In the pack, all the wolves are one. The wolf who betrays the pack will walk alone for the remainder of their days. The lone wolf is bound to walk alone forever—for solitude is the greatest punishment.

Though it was only a short segment, it was definitely food for thought. I wondered if it was a coincidence or not that this note was tucked away on this specific passage. I reread the last phrase, "*Solitude is the greatest punishment,*" repeatedly. *Is solitude really the greatest punishment?* I pondered, *even when it's all I've ever known?*

I thought about returning to the main room, but I had the worst sense of direction and couldn't remember how to get back. I had never been in such a large building, and this was only the underground portion. While trying to retrace my steps, a cold hand placed itself on my shoulder, which startled me a great deal considering the surrounding area was vacant mere seconds also. Considering my last encounter was with an angry rebel who wanted nothing more than to smash my face, I reminded myself I always had to stay alert, because in this world *no one* was ever safe.

Chapter 9

I swung my fist as I turned, and I only had a split second to see who it was before it was too late. The person behind was no other than the black-haired girl from earlier, though I had already forgotten her name. She withdrew her hand from my shoulder and dodged my fist almost instinctively. I tried to mask the pulsating pain in my wounded arm after the missed swing, praying it wouldn't open back up yet.

"You have impressively quick instincts," she praised playfully to dissolve the awkward situation.

"I could say the same for you," I said, returning the praise.

"My apologies, I shouldn't have startled you like that," she acknowledged.

"No, don't be sorry. I shouldn't have swung like that either. I guess it's just-"

"Instinct?" she finished for me.

"Something like that."

"Miss Phoenix?" I heard a voice behind us. The girl turned and her face lit up when she saw The White Raven, but there was also a man beside her who seemed to catch her attention.

"Oh- hello again," I responded, relieved to see a familiar face.

"Did you get lost, dear?" she asked, giggling. I was a bit embarrassed to admit it even though it was more than obvious.

"Kinda . . . yeah," I admitted. She chuckled and rubbed my head playfully. Her gesture reminded me of my grandmother again, and it gave me a fuzzy feeling.

"All of you come to my room," she said, and we all headed into the room at the end of the hall.

I took a closer look at the man who accompanied The White Raven; he had messy brown hair, brown eyes, and a scar across the bridge of his nose. He was tall, rugged, and strong like most of the men around here, but there was a different aura to him- he radiated a more refined type of strength. The girl gave off a similar vibe to that of the leaders, and I could tell she was much stronger than she appeared just based on how effortlessly she dodged my swing. Despite the man's intimidating features, he radiated warmth, as did the girl- they were strange people indeed.

"I don't think I've properly introduced myself. I'm Nila, and this is Markus," the girl said, introducing both of them. Markus smiled and waved.

"Finally, someone your age, Nila," teased Markus. "She and her friends all look about your age."

"I doubt they're all eighteen," Nila started. "How old are you, Phoenix?" she asked. I would've never guessed she was that young, but the more I looked at her, the more I believed her.

"I'll be eighteen this month," I answered, and they all looked at me surprised.

"Ah, what a beautiful coincidence. It's no surprise you're a Leo, the zodiac sign of the sun," The White Raven replied, though I didn't understand what she was talking about. She was practically speaking a different language.

"What's a zodiac sign, and what's a Leo?" I inquired, once again embarrassed by my own ignorance.

"We humans are creatures full of desire, particularly the desire to understand the things we have no answer to," she prefaced, and even Nila and Markus were listening. "A concept known as astrology was born out of that desire; beyond this world lies an infinite number of stars- a sky full of mysteries."

"What's astrology?" I asked, especially invested because the stars were my favorite things this universe had to offer.

"There are twelve signs with different characteristics, and one is assigned to each person depending on the month they were born."

"So, what does mine mean?"

"Leo is a fire sign ruled by the sun; Leos dedicate their burning hearts into everything they do. They're very determined and loyal, but also known to be quite stubborn and prideful," she explained with ease.

"Fitting for a phoenix," Nila commented with a smile. Her comment reminded me of a question I'd been meaning to ask.

"Hey, why do people call you The White Raven?" I asked and the woman looked up at me as a grin crept onto her face.

"White ravens are traditionally believed to be messengers of the gods and were once associated with prophecies. The name was fitting since I was entrusted with delivering the Prophecy to The Phoenix's future Prophet if they were to ever come in my lifetime," she explained, and it began to make a lot more sense.

"Why did you agree to be entrusted with it? That's a huge responsibility," I said, hoping I wasn't wearing her out with all my questions.

There was a long pause before her answer, but eventually her lips curled and she responded, "Because I loved her," she said with a glow in her golden eyes that told me it was more than just simple admiration or fondness.

It was not what I expected her to say. As far as I know Rebellium has been around for only a little over a decade. This association was fairly young, but she has been a deviant all her life, meaning that for most of her life, she hid from society *alone*.

"You lived your whole life as a deviant . . . just because you loved her?" I asked.

"People do crazy things out of love, my dear. *Always* remember that," she replied, emphasizing the last part.

"I wouldn't know," I replied. She frowned at my response.

"Let me tell you a little story, Phoenix," she said out of the blue. "There were once two young lovers, Astrid and Lanon. The two were completely infatuated with each other, so much so that they'd do anything for each other." She began to tell what sounded like a love story. "Astrid wanted a future with him, but Lanon had bigger ambitions calling to him. However, she loved him so much that she'd support him even if it wasn't what she wanted." She paused, but I wasn't grasping the moral of this story.

"And?" I asked.

"She quickly realized he was going down the wrong path when his noble cause had turned into spiteful greed, which was rapidly growing out of proportion. She had to make a choice between the world, and him." She sighed before concluding her story. "But the truth is, she never had to decide; the answer would always be him. She promised to always be there to ground him back to the earth, *no matter the cost.*"

"What am I supposed to get out of that?" I asked cluelessly. I was growing frustrated at my inability to comprehend.

"That promise has caused an ongoing feud that's lasted to this day," she explained, and that's when the lightbulb finally went off in my head.

"Astrid and Lanon . . . are they The Crow and The Phoenix?" I asked in disbelief, and she smiled.

"You're a smart girl, Phoenix," she replied, but I couldn't wrap my head around the idea that these two mortal enemies were once lovers- and that this war could have concluded much sooner.

"How selfish can she be?" I blurted out. "Doesn't she realize the destruction that could've been avoided had she just killed him sooner?" I asked, and I hadn't realized how much I had raised my voice until I saw Nila flinch.

"Let me ask you a question I've been meaning to ask you, Phoenix. What's *your* motive for killing The Crow?" she asked me, ignoring my question. My face fell at the thought of the answer.

"It's my responsibility now. She chose me for whatever reason, and it's my duty to go through with it," I answered vaguely, knowing it's not the answer she wanted.

"Is that it?" She kept pushing. I knew I couldn't lie to her; she wasn't easy to fool. Especially because I had a feeling she already knew.

I sighed deeply. "I should've burned in that shack and then in Hell for all eternity, but death would've been the easy way out, and I don't deserve that. I must atone for all the innocents I've massacred, and that's the least I can do for them," I responded hesitantly. It made my face burn with guilt and my stomach turn just talking about it.

"So, your motivation . . . is punishment?" Her voice was so calm and serene.

"I suppose," I answered shamefully.

Nila and Markus stared at me, their brows furrowed and their faces full of concern. The White Raven only smiled and let out a deep breath. She began to stand from her chair, and I looked up at her; *is that it?* I asked myself. I was still so curious, and I knew she had more to say. I stood up from my seat as well as she began to walk toward the door.

"Wait, why did you tell me that story? And why'd you ask me that? I'm still not understanding anything," I uttered desperately.

"One day, you'll find a true motive, Phoenix, then it will all become easy," she replied, "and one day, you'll understand Astrid's motive too; the beauty behind the madness that is The Phoenix." She gave me a reassuring smile and walked out of the room. I stood there, trying to understand what she was attempting to tell me.

"Do you want us to help you get back to the main room?" Nila offered.

"I'd appreciate it," I responded flatly.

As we walked down the halls, I felt oddly apprehensive around Nila and Markus. They were quiet the entire way as we walked, but didn't seem very bothered by it.

"Let's get you cleaned up and ready for bed. You've had a long day," Nila suggested. I felt my face turn red; I forgot I still looked like a dirty mess.

"You don't have to be nice to me out of pity, you know," I said to Nila.

"I have no obligation to be nice, nor any reason to pity you," she responded casually with a genuine smile on her lips.

"Then why are you being nice?"

"Does kindness need a motive?"

"No one is ever kind purely for the sake of being nice- it's always out of pity."

"Then if that were true, do you believe your squad followed you and gave up their freedom solely out of pity?" She'd asked a big question, looking directly at me this time.

The question hung in the air for a while, but I avoided thinking of the answer. A random memory briefly resurfaced of a hand extending out to me. I was on the ground, and someone was offering to help me up, but I couldn't quite put a face or time frame on it. This memory felt awfully familiar, so it had to be my own and not The Phoenix's. While trying to figure out who the person was, I hadn't been paying attention and I walked straight into someone.

I looked and it was The White Raven, who had a tense look on her face. The ceiling shook, which was followed by a loud eruption of yells and screams. I turned to Nila and Markus, who exchanged looks that suggested they were ready to dive headfirst into the danger. A woman came running up to us, her face plastered with fear; I knew that look all too well.

"One of The Crow's armies managed to find the base and our soldiers are outside hunting them down," the young woman panted. She was a pretty, young woman- seemingly in her early twenties. She wore a bow in her wavy brown hair and an apron over her light blue dress.

"We can't risk them giving away our location!" exclaimed Nila.

"We can't let a single soldier escape!" Markus added.

"I'll chase them down, where are they?" I asked, courage pouring out of me.

"Get a head start." The woman motioned to Nila and Markus.

"Got it, Lana!" Nila shouted and they both immediately took off without hesitation. I assumed Lana was her name.

"Please take cover until this passes," she insisted to The White Raven.

"Not gonna happen Lana, I'm grabbing something and I'll meet you two up there," she responded and hurried back to her room. Her stubbornness worried me since she was about as old as my grandmother.

"Follow me, please," Lana said as she grabbed my arm, and we ran through a narrow hall leading to a ladder.

Pain shot through my arm as she was gripping it. I had forgotten about that stab wound until now. I tried not to wince, but the pain was hard to ignore, especially while climbing up the ladder. When we reached the top, we ended up in an empty and rather fire-damaged room. *I wonder what this place looked like when it was inhabited?*

We ran through multiple blackened halls and rooms until we reached a door that led to the outdoors. It was extremely dark outside now- the only light coming from the moon. The mansion was conveniently situated on the edge of town, so the walk to the gate was short. The fighting was taking place outside the town in the desert, but luckily the gate in this town was riddled by cannon holes, making it easy to get in and out.

As soon as we were on the other side of the gate, I followed the sound of Lana's footsteps and the very vague outline of her body through the dark desert. There was utter silence for a split second, but it was immediately followed up by the roaring boom of an explosion. We ran in that direction, and right behind that explosion, a chain of blue-colored explosions followed. I had seen that same, blue-tinted explosion chain before back in the battle at the shrine. The chain of blue explosions reminded me of lightning cracking in a dark sky; I could never have imagined something so destructive being so beautiful.

Adrenaline pumped through my body, and I was prepared to fight, but this time, for the right thing. The adrenaline was potent, but short-lived as soon as I reached for my sword, and I felt nothing-even my sheath was gone. My heart dropped to my stomach, and I broke into a sweat after realizing I only had a handgun with which to defend myself, and it was probably on its last few bullets. I preferred a sword in combat like this, but I had lost my sword somewhere along the way.

In the distance, the scattered flames expelled from the explosion lit up the area a bit more, and the first person I recognized was Asier. He was being chased by a soldier, but he didn't hesitate to pull out a small handgun and shoot the soldier down. Without a second to spare, he proceeded to slice down two soldiers that crossed his path with just one swing. It was evident that along with being a great leader, Asier was also an extremely skilled shooter and swordsman.

My eyes crawled around the battlefield as I watched the people I once sided with get shot down by the people I once swore to exterminate. I was once one of those soldiers- fighting for the wrong, selfish reasons. Dozens of injured and dead soldiers scattered the ground, but the thing that took me by surprise was that almost all of the soldiers I saw were Crow soldiers.

As I examined the battleground, I spotted a small boy being chased down by a Crow soldier. Although it was difficult to see with the limited amount of light, I knew he looked familiar. I did a quick scan of his surroundings, and there was no one in sight who could save this boy. I looked at him again and finally recognized him from the kitchen- he was the little boy who had barged in. I remembered his innocent face and all his excitement, which was now replaced by horror and torment. He was just a little boy who had a whole life ahead of him; *I would not let him die in this dirty war.*

An appalling scream came from the boy's direction, and it triggered a flood of adrenaline, causing me to blindly dash toward the boy as fast as I could. I had no sword, and no guarantee that I could protect us this time, but I had determination- and the urge to protect this child. When I got close enough, I threw myself at the boy, hoping I was close enough. I reached for him and wrapped my arms around his small frame, shielding him as we hit the cold, desert ground.

I watched the soldier chasing him fall to the ground from the momentum of his failed swing. I kept the boy in my arms as the man got up in what felt like the blink of an eye. The man charged at us at an alarming speed which gave me no time to reach for my gun. Panic rushed through me, and I extended my arm like it was second nature to me. I hugged the child closer to my chest and shut my eyes as a blinding light shone through my closed lids.

I opened them back up to the man, who was now burning mercilessly on the ground. Soon the fire would eventually burn out, along with his life, and there would be no one left to tell his family the story of his "heroic" death. To stray away from that grim thought, I looked down to the boy in my arms, who stared at me with a look on his face that was new to me. It wasn't fear like I had anticipated, it looked more like admiration. It reminded me of the way people looked at Asier.

He sat up then wrapped his small arms around me. I didn't know how to react; no one had ever done that to me before- and no one had ever hugged me like this before.

"You're my hero," he said, muffled as his face was pressed against me. I didn't know what else to do, so I rubbed his back and I felt a strange warmth in my heart, and it wasn't fire this time- it felt warmer than any fire.

Our beautiful moment was cut short when I caught a glimpse of another soldier charging at us from the corner of my eye. I reacted instinctively and picked up the boy tightly with one arm and began to run. An excruciating pain pulsed through my arm; the kind of pain that demanded to be felt with every breath. I picked him up and carried most of his weight on my wounded arm, which applied way too much force and pressure to it. I lowered my eyes to my arm, and blood was staining through my sleeve where the wound had reopened. I involuntarily let out a cry of pain.

"Miss, are you okay?" the boy asked, concerned.

"Don't worry about me," I insisted, my voice strained from trying to mask the pain.

The man was getting closer to us, and I began to panic. I didn't know how much longer I could keep up this pace with the boy in my hands.

"Phoenix!" I heard someone call in the distance and I turned in that direction.

There was a crowd of people holding torches, and the flames from explosions lit up the area, so I was able to see that it was The White Raven. She was holding something in her arms- something that looked like a sword sheath. She drew a sword from its sheath and held it up, looking as though she was about to throw it.

"Be wielded by your Prophet's hand!" she yelled and threw the sword as hard as she could, reaching a surprisingly far distance.

It pierced the barren ground like a knife through butter as it landed not too far from me. I picked up the pace and ran toward it; it called to my hand like a moth to a flame. I pushed my lungs and my legs to run just a little further until I finally reached the sword. I extended my hand for the handle, and as I effortlessly pulled the sword out of the ground, a burst of embers emitted from the contact between my hand and the pommel.

It fit so perfectly in my hand as I gripped the handle tightly, holding it at an angle while lightly raising my arm. I stopped running and turned my body around as fast as I could, swinging my sword as I spun. I put all my force into the swing and sliced right through the soldier's chest. It was too dark to see any blood or wounds, but I knew I had pierced deeply into his flesh. I made sure the boy's eyes were covered from the gruesome scene that just occurred in front of him, even though I was aware that by being a rebel and living in the frontlines of this war, he must've seen dozens of sights like this and maybe even worse. Hell, by simply existing in this world we grow desensitized to the sight of a dead man.

I set the boy down gently and stood up. Ahead of me were scores of soldiers; they moved like mindless robots, which was unusual and ominous. The truth was, I didn't want to kill them. I didn't want to kill anyone anymore, but I couldn't let them escape and give this place away, so once again I found myself obligated to kill.

"Lambegus, come here!" Lana yelled from the crowd, using his full name I presumed. He looked at me one last time and flashed his hopeful smile before running toward the others, and to safety.

A soldier ran around the man I had just sliced down and charged after me; these soldiers had not a speck of humanity in their faces. I ran toward him and when I got close enough, I swung my sword- the blade glowing like it had been in flames. I saw an explosion in the distance that was tinted blue- it was Asier. He had taken down a number of soldiers as well; together we could probably take down an entire army.

The battlefield was completely still, flooded with the echoing silence that remained after every bloodbath. I looked around and several black-caped rebels scattered the field, putting away their weapons with slight affliction on their faces. Among the soldiers I saw Nila zoning out as she dazed at the dead men on the field. She was frowning, but not as disturbed as one would expect from such a young soldier. Markus also stood beside her, looking even less affected than Nila.

I finally faced the aftermath once I was sure there were no more soldiers left. I stood speechless as I scanned the carnage before me. My hands were covered in blood that only I could see; for the first time since I could remember, the idea of killing actually felt disturbing. A lot of their bodies were either on fire or concealed by the darkness, so I wouldn't have to stare at the numerous lives we just took. People threw torches at some of the bodies to incinerate their remains, which was unsettling, but I knew it was better than just letting their corpses rot in the middle of the desert.

I looked around and there was one soldier still standing. Before I could even react, I watched a bullet go straight through him, followed by his body falling to the ground. My breath was caught in my throat and my body felt unable to physically react, aside from just staring. *Since when did it feel this heavy?*

"He's not dead. I'll let you finish him off," came a familiar deep voice from behind me. I turned around and it was Asier, who approached me with a small handgun in each hand. The surroundings were dead silent, so I knew all eyes were on us; I knew he did this on purpose.

I glanced back at the dying man on the ground, who was trying to crawl away from us- away from his inevitable death. The sight haunted me; yet again I was faced with a dying man, pleading for one more chance. He kept on crawling without saying a word, not even sparing a look in my direction. *These soldiers were so distinct, as if they had no humanity whatsoever.*

"What's wrong? You've killed countless people before, why can't you suddenly kill now?" Asier was taunting me, which was the last thing I needed right now. I took a deep breath and remained calm, not letting his remarks faze me. I tightened my fists and closed my eyes to try and block him out.

"Kill him like you killed my comrades."

Chapter 10

My rage and guilt grew out of proportion, and it completely clouded my judgment. All I could see was red, and all I wanted was to see him *covered in red*. I gripped the handle of my sword so tightly I thought it would snap. In the blink of an eye, I remorselessly jabbed my sword into the soldier's back without even flinching. After finishing him off, I pulled the sword out, and held it up to Asier's neck. He alternated his glance between my sword and my blazing eyes.

There were a million things I wanted to say, but my head could not form the right words. I breathed heavily to regain control with my sword still up to his face. I didn't realize the severity of what I was doing until I saw him motion to the others to stand down. I was locked in a gaze with him, and not once did he break eye contact; the confidence this man exerted was commendable.

"Don't play with fire, commander," I threatened, and his lips slightly curved at the corners, which irked me even more.

He lifted his hand and lowered the blade from his face so calmly. "Look down," he said, and I hesitantly obeyed. "That's no man- none of these are real men," he explained. I examined the motionless body, trying to figure out what he meant by that.

"No blood, and no humanity- just bunches of feathers programmed to kill," he explained as he kicked the soldier's body, flipping it on its back. Needless to say, feathers began to escape his wound, not blood.

I felt a raindrop on my face, which was then followed by many more. I looked around the battlefield, and piles of burnt feathers scattered the site from the flames that had begun diminishing. Watching the rain wash away the remains from the battle and the flames I created truly brought me back down to earth. It served as a reminder that no matter how powerful we may become, we're only as powerful as the earth around us.

"Everyone, get back inside!" demanded Asier. He put his guns in their designated holsters on his belt and began to walk back to the mansion with everyone, but I remained put.

"You coming, brat?" asked Asier.

"I'm not going anywhere with you," I replied coldly. It didn't matter how high he stood, he was still a cold and arrogant individual.

There was a near-silent pause where the only gentle sounds were the raindrops splattering as they hit the ground. I got no reply before he proceeded to walk away. For an instant, I felt a tinge of regret, and I wanted to take back what I said, but then I remembered every spiteful word he'd spat at me from the minute I got here, *and it's not like he actually cared if I went back inside, it was merely his duty to guard me,* I reminded myself. He only despised me just as much as I despised myself, *so I suppose the feeling was mutual.*

I looked up at the sky, squinting my eyes to shield them from the rain. Today there were no stars, and only the moon's faint glow managed to peek through the thick clouds of smoke. *Not even the stars can guide me home today,* I thought, feeling a little homesick. I brushed that thought aside and took a deep breath before making my way back to the mansion. *There's no use crying about it.*

This had to be the longest day ever, and I just wanted it to be over. So much history was made on this day that started off just like any other Sunday. I wanted to pinch myself and find out it was just a wild dream, but unfortunately, this was real life. My reality had become stranger than my dreams.

I finally reached the back entrance of the mansion and I saw the outline of a person sitting on the porch by the door. I focused my eyes through the dark and rain until I managed to discern that it was Asier- smoking in solitude as usual. Just seeing him by the entrance told me this long day was not over yet. I thought about sneaking past him to hopefully avoid him noticing me, but it was a futile effort, because he was staring straight at me.

"Why aren't you inside?" I asked reluctantly. I didn't want to talk, but it was better than having another awkward staring contest.

"Couldn't just leave you out there unguarded. What if The Prophet decides to run away?" he responded with a mocking tone.

There was another moment of awkward silence. Tension filled the air and it was very uncomfortable. He was illuminated by the subtle light of a few lanterns on the porch, and the light outlined the muscles on his tattooed arms perfectly.

"Take a seat, little girl," he said to break the silence and I reluctantly sat down. I sat near him, but far away enough so the tension wasn't as potent.

"I have a name you know," I replied in annoyance.

"I know, Phoenix," he responded while looking off to the side to blow the smoke out, showing off his defined jawline.

"Then why don't you just call me that instead of 'little girl'? Just how old are you anyways?" I asked.

"Hi, my name's Asier Jovano, I'm twenty-four years old, and I'm a runaway criminal- anything else the princess wants to know?" he answered sarcastically, once again in a mocking manner.

"No, I'm leaving." I stood up and began to walk away. The truth was I had a million questions, but my pride decided it was not worth my time.

He leaned forward and grabbed my wrist, stopping me from leaving. "Hold on, brat." He pulled me to sit back down, and I felt a burning pain shoot through my forearm, and I retracted my arm with a grimace.

"Careful!" I exclaimed and clutched my wounded arm, trying to ignore the pain by squeezing my eyes shut.

"Oh shit. Lana, bring the first aid kit!" Asier yelled, looking down at his hand which now had my blood on it. I sat back down where I had originally.

"Let me see," said Asier. *Why was he suddenly acting concerned? I wondered.*

He sighed and shook his head before scooting up closer to me. He was now inches away from me and I felt my face warm up. I quickly wiped that weird flush off my face and looked away; *why did that always happen at the most inconvenient times?* I asked myself. He lifted my sleeve, revealing a poorly applied bandage that was not only saturated in blood, but was also beginning to unravel.

Asier whistled at the sight of the wound. "What happened here?" he asked as he undid the bandages.

"I got stabbed during my fight with The Crow," I explained as briefly as I could.

Lana came through the door with the first aid kit and handed it to him. "Do you need help with that?' she offered to help.

"Nope." He dug through the kit, wasting no time. She nodded and went back inside without another word. *I guess coming home with wounds like this isn't unusual for them.*

Asier began to clean my wound, which burned insanely, but I made sure to remain quiet and keep a straight face on. To distract from the pain, I attempted to focus on something else, and my eyes landed on the bloody bandages on the ground. As I looked at the soiled bandages, I began to wonder; *who dressed my wound the first time?* I looked back at my wound, which was now almost completely clean. I hadn't noticed the severity of it until now, when it wasn't obscured by blood.

"Why are you doing this? Don't you hate me?" I asked him. He chuckled as he wrapped my arm.

He let out a sigh before answering. "I don't hate you. I don't like you- but I think maybe we're both a bit too hard on you."

"What do you mean?" I asked.

"You're too hard on yourself. If your only motive is to punish yourself and repay us for the folks you've killed, then you're being too hard on yourself and it won't get us very far," he answered, and it reminded me of the conversation The White Raven and I had about motives.

"Well, that's the only motive I have, I don't care if it fits your standards or not," I responded coldly.

Asier rolled his eyes. "I can tell you're still a kid."

"I'm almost eighteen."

"Damn, I couldn't tell," he replied sarcastically. Now I rolled my eyes at him.

After he finished bandaging my arm, I decided to ask him the real question I've been wondering since I first saw him speak.

"Can I ask you something?" I said reluctantly, and he looked at me. "What's *your* motive? Like . . . for everything?"

Before I got an answer, there was silence again. The raindrops and our breathing were the only sounds that filled the air.

"Freedom, obviously," he stated, but I needed more.

"Start from the beginning," I requested. "Where did it all start?"

There was still silence for an uncomfortable amount of time until I gave up on the possibility of getting an answer. His eyes watched the rain and he seemed to be in a zone that I was unable to take him out of. I sighed and looked down at my freshly bandaged arm. *I suppose that was enough of an ice breaker for today.*

"My dad was executed when I was about five years old; the state killed him for simply expressing his opinion on one of The Crow's policies he was not too fond of. That was the day I first realized man would never be free unless we were dead." He paused after prefacing. "I grew to hate The Crow and the cage we were all forced to live in more and more as the days went by. My mother tried to convince me otherwise because she didn't want me to end up like my father," he continued, putting the cigarette to his lips and exhaling the smoke before finishing, "so I ran away."

There was another short pause before he proceeded. "I was only thirteen, but if I wanted to leave that cage alive, I had to run for my life; that's when I ran into this ghost town and founded Rebellium." He looked me in the eyes. "I silently promised the world I'd lead us to salvation, despite being just a man."

After finishing, he stared off into the distance, back in his zone. I didn't know what to say or even where to start, as I was truly at a loss for words. I realized thanking him would be the most appropriate response, but I cringed at the idea of thanking *him*. As hesitant as I was, I knew I had to; after all, he didn't have to share that with me, but he had anyway.

"Thanks for sharing that with me," I said, then swallowed my pride.

"I mean, you asked," he replied, once again without facing me. There was a long silence after that, and we were both lost in thought.

"Did you do it for your dad?" I asked.

Asier chuckled and looked down, then back at me. "I did this for me, and for my freedom. I barely even remember the man," he responded. "My reasons are simple. I was tired of being a slave to The Crow. The world wasn't meant to be like this, and I knew that from the start."

"How did you keep pushing all this time?" I asked, but his face told me he was going to give me the vaguest rendition of his real answer.

"I started from nothing, a thirteen-year-old without a pot to piss in or anyone to catch me when I fall, but I made a promise . . . to one day paint the sky *blue*," he finished and looked up at the starless sky. I watched him like that for a while.

"Can you help me understand something?" I asked and he turned to face me now. "Why does The Phoenix hunt down The Crow even to this day?" I asked impulsively. "And I'm not talking about the obvious reasons," I added, not realizing how stupid I probably sounded. I immediately regretted asking him when I felt him staring at me.

"Did The White Raven tell you the story?" he asked, slightly squinting.

"She did," I replied

"People do crazy things out of love." He imitated The White Raven as he crossed his arms above his head and leaned back on the wall.

"Yep, that's exactly what she said," I replied.

"Love can make or break people," he said flatly. I saw affliction brush over his tired eyes for an instant.

"I wouldn't know. That's why I'm asking," I replied, and Asier shifted his eyes to look at me. His gaze reminded me of the one The White Raven gave me when I said the same thing.

Every time I said that people stared at me like I have three eyes. I don't understand why it was so hard to fathom. I don't understand love, and I don't think I ever will, especially now that my days are numbered. It didn't bother me though, since I didn't even know what I was missing out on to begin with.

"Love seems like any other emotion, and emotions just get in the way," I added to my previous statement.

"You sound like The Crow now, which is probably why he killed Astrid; to kill the love of his life along with the obstacles that 'useless emotion' posed, isn't that right, Phoenix?" he asked, though I didn't know what he was getting at.

"He killed her because she tried to oppose him. How could people who supposedly loved each other so much grow to hate each other this much?" I asked bluntly. There was a momentary silence.

"There's a fine line between love and hate, Phoenix," he said bluntly. It sounded as if he spoke from experience.

A look of melancholy brushed over his pale face, not just his eyes this time. As I watched Asier, I noticed more how he always seemed lost in his head. He was never quite grounded down on earth-never fully in the present. I lost track of how long I had been staring at him until I saw his eyes look back at me. I quickly looked away.

"Here's a question for you, Phoenix, and I need you to answer with the truth," he said, so I faced him and nodded. "What was your reason for becoming an Executioner?"

As soon as he asked the question I gulped, almost choking on my spit. I felt a layer of sweat form, and my heart began to race. Memories I suppressed for years began to creep back as the secrets I've fought so hard to keep threatened to slip out. Before the panic grew out of proportion, I grounded myself and thought logically; *I was a deviant now, the worst that could happen has already happened, so what do I have to lose?* I asked myself, and with that in mind, I exposed the secret that's kept me and my family alive to this day.

"I did it to save someone," I uttered.

"Save who?" he asked, looking at me while I avoided meeting his gaze.

I took a deep breath. "My mother."

"From what?"

"Me."

"Can you elaborate?"

"They found out about my real name, and they found me. They told me they'd spare me and my mother if I worked for them as a Hunter and Executioner- it was a way of repenting for our blasphemy."

"But then, how did you get away with it for so long?"

"I came to the realization that something was wrong with my name when I was just a little girl. The other kids avoided me as soon as their parents told them what having my name meant for me; they knew one day I'd be the next to walk the stage and have my head blown off, and they wanted no association to me," I explained, "so I went by my nickname, Fefe, for the next couple years until I was recognized as Crimson for the color of my trainer's uniform, which eventually became my Hunter uniform."

"How did The Crow or even the mayor not catch on sooner?"

"In official resident files, we aren't referred to by our names, we are all just a number that we were given at birth in the government's eyes, but word spreads like wildfire in District Four, so word of my name was bound to reach them eventually. It's a mystery to me as to why they gave us a second chance and didn't just kill us from the start," I answered while hugging my knees to my chest. "I remember every sleepless night I spent watching the door, afraid they would come in and take us away at any moment."

"Seems like you've been living as a deviant longer than you think," Asier responded with his gaze planted on me.

"I guess so," I answered, and there followed more heavy silence.

I practically admitted my selfish reasoning behind every comrade of his that I'd murdered; it was essentially a case of my life or theirs. I expected him to seem mad, disappointed, or even just upset, but his face showed none of those. He seemed almost hopeful, which didn't surprise me, since this was the man whose overwhelming hope drew me to rebel.

"Well, I guess I should get going now," I said, and excused myself. I didn't want to make this situation any more awkward or painful for the two of us. As I stood up, Asier said one last thing.

"Love can be disguised as anything, Phoenix. Keep that in mind," he advised, blowing smoke from his cigarette.

"Then maybe love can be disguised as hate," I responded naively.

He smiled and closed his eyes. "Maybe," he responded, "just maybe."

After that heavy discussion between us I went back into the mansion and Asier stayed outside to finish his cigarette. I looked for the rest of my squad, because I recalled not seeing them out there during the battle. Among all the deviants that were preparing their blankets and pillows for the night, the only familiar face I saw was Nila's. She had a smile on her face while she talked to Markus, who wore a sheepish flush on his face. Nila turned in my direction, and I saw her say goodbye to Markus before approaching me. A look of disappointment washed across Markus's face as she walked away.

"Phoenix! Just who I was looking for," she exclaimed. "I wanted to let you know your friends are sleeping in a room up here and we didn't want to wake them for something we could handle ourselves."

"They should've woken themselves; they should be more alert for these types of things," I responded, but the more I thought about it, the more I understood them. I realized how tired they must've been- today had been a heavy day for all of us.

"I also wanted to apologize . . . on behalf of Asier," she began, twiddling her fingers.

"Don't worry about it, we talked," I informed her before having another awkward tangent.

"Oh, I'm glad to hear that!" she exclaimed. "He might come off as cold and arrogant, but underneath that tough exterior, he has one of the biggest hearts I know," she continued, and I saw the flush I'd seen on Markus earlier appear on her cheeks.

"Are you two close?"

"Yes! Markus and Asier have trained me during my entire time here. I train to one day become a leader too. Asier even said if I keep going, soon enough I'll surpass him, but I think he was just being humble."

The way she spoke about him- she spoke so highly of him, but in a way different than the rest did. It seemed like admiration, but there was more- like a sort of attraction.

"So, Markus and Asier have been your only trainers? That's hard to believe considering how good you are."

"Yeah, well, I've been training with them since I was thirteen- them and another woman, but she's not here anymore," she answered, and I watched as her smile fell a bit at the last part. Guilt immediately crept up on me for asking, because my first thought was to assume that she was killed.

"If you don't mind me asking, who?" I needed to feed my curiosity and hopefully ease my guilt a bit.

"A traitor," she answered bitterly, "she's the reason the leaders got caught," she added, and the note inside the book on the shelf kept popping into my head.

"I'm sorry to hear that," is all I could really say, so I decided to change the subject instead. "So why is Markus all geared up still? Aren't you guys going to bed?"

"Markus and Asier are going to clear the surroundings tonight to make sure the Crow soldiers didn't call for backup."

"I see."

"I can only hope to one day be as strong-willed as our leader, he just keeps fighting through the hurdles thrown at him," she said with a glisten in her eyes- *hope*.

"You guys have the same look in your eyes, so I'd say you're on the right track," I complimented, and she smiled, the apple of her cheeks blushing with it, "but for the meantime, let's get to bed."

Chapter 11

I woke up in the middle of the night for probably the fifth time. Every time I woke up, my heart sank as I realized yesterday wasn't just a bad dream. Everything that's happened these last few days made sure I had enough to think about before I slept. I was so exhausted, and my head was in overdrive. My body ached and I couldn't close my eyes; I was too scared of what I would see in my sleep.

Aurora, Nyrual, and Guido were all still sound asleep. We all slept in a small room on the upper floor of the mansion with sleeping bags and pillows. We had the choice to sleep downstairs or up here, but we wanted to be able to run outside easily if we had to.

As I lay in an old sleeping bag on the cold, burnt floor, my mind drifted in a dismal direction. Once again, I began to think about my mother and grandmother, and I wondered if the rest of the town was soundly sleeping tonight. I looked through a small window, and the stars were visible again. It comforted me to know that if momma and grandma looked up, they would be seeing the same sky.

The room was dimly lit by the moon coming in through the window. I turned my gaze back to the ground; Guido and Aurora were cuddled together to fight off the cold from the dark August nights, and Nyrual slept close to them as well, making me the only outcast. I could tell they missed their loved ones too- they would've never wanted to leave them behind. *I still couldn't understand why they had.*

I carefully stood up as to not wake anyone. I decided to take a short walk, in hopes of clearing my mind. I opened the door and there was only a small lantern lighting the narrow hallway. I tried to minimize the sound of my footsteps, but this old building creaked at even the slightest movements. I made my way toward the deck behind the mansion where me and Asier talked last night. It still surprised me how well that conversation went last night, I guess I could even say we don't despise each other anymore.

I hadn't realized how cold it was until I opened the back door and the wind poured in, so I quickly closed the door after stepping outside to stop sand and cold air from getting in, since windy air tended to carry sand with it. The climate was so bizarre that there could be a fully-fledged sandstorm and rainstorm on the same day- all in a desert, might I add. Most of the deserted land in the nation was not natural though, it was a result of the nuclear explosions decades ago. The radiation from those bombs was also like no other; over time it gave the barren land abnormal qualities- like the ability to grow vegetation. The horrendous state of the earth and the sun blacking out has created strange biomes- it was the Earth's last effort to stay alive.

I sensed that a sandstorm would brush over soon, so I decided it would be better to go back inside and just try to sleep again. Right as I was about to open the door, I heard a loud noise, and a subtle vibration on the ground. It was definitely an explosion, and it was somewhere in the near distance; I recalled what Nila had said last night about Asier and Markus, so I just hoped they were inside by now. I picked up a lantern on the porch, looked down to avoid the sand, and sprinted in the direction of the noise. Even though I was facing the ground, I still saw dozens of black feathers flying past me as they were carried away by the wind.

The wind got increasingly stronger, and it was beginning to hurt my skin. I kept looking down since the sandstorm had officially arrived and it was *intense-* my eyes were barely open at this point. I didn't have my uniform right now, so I was unarmed and unprotected. Though I did prefer if they were inside safe, I really hoped it was just Asier and Markus killing off a few more soldiers, and that it wasn't anything serious.

Shortly after exiting the gates, the velocity of the wind picked up even more and ended up knocking me to the ground, where there were black feathers scattered all over, with even more blowing in the wind. I tried to control my breathing through the suffocating wind, but it was becoming almost impossible. In a moment of desperation, a pair of large, crimson wings extended from my back, shielding me from the voracious winds and burning every feather that touched the flaming wings. *This was the power the wings of a phoenix held.*

The wind whistled, but besides that, it was awfully silent as I ran aimlessly into the desert. I hadn't heard any noise after that boom, and it was filling me with paranoia, because I had gotten to the point in my life where silence had become more threatening than noise. Just as I wondered why it was so quiet, I heard a distant scream coming from the same direction I'd heard the explosion. The scream sent chills down my spine, because it was a masculine scream; *please don't be Asier or Markus.*

I lifted my head a little and I saw something unusual shoot up into the sky. It looked like a canister as it went up, but then blue powder came out as it went off in the air. *A smoke gun? Who shot it?* I wondered. Generally, the smoke bombs we used as Hunters were red and were only fired when we needed urgent back up, but this one was blue. I thought harder while attempting to remain calm; *the color blue . . .*

It hit me as soon as I repeated the color in my head; the color rebels used was often *blue,* the sky was supposed to be *blue,* the color blue . . . *Asier.* I cursed under my breath- *Asier and Markus were definitely in danger.* I dashed through the storm again, and I did that for a while until I stopped to catch my breath, though the wind and sand made it almost impossible.

"Hello!" I shouted, but got no response. "Asier! Markus!" I yelled at the top of my lungs, but the storm roared louder than me, and carried the sound of my voice away. I used my arm to block out some of the sand and continued to keep moving forward.

Minutes of more aimless running and walking passed, hoping I would run into something. The longer I spent alone, the more my anxiety grew, though I didn't understand why I was so bothered by the notion of being alone when my entire life- I've practically spent alone. I've never needed anyone; I've fended for myself for as long as I can remember. My mother was distant and was never there to comfort me when I cried, and I never had a father to run to when something scared me at night. I never even had friends to play with as a child, or a hand to hold when I was lonely. I've never had anyone to lean on or trust, but for whatever reason, the solitude tonight felt . . . *different.*

I was completely alone this time, with nothing but my own demons trying to pull me to my grave. I was alone and unarmed in a hazardous sandstorm, but somehow, my head and its irrational fears felt like an even bigger threat. Distracted by my thoughts, I tripped on something, once again falling to the ground, only this time, I stayed down. I couldn't even stand up, and I couldn't explain why. Perhaps I tried to open a window to cool off, but it seems like only more heat had poured in.

I sat up and hung my head in defeat, aware that Asier and Markus were probably long gone now; I was surely too late. My eyes burned, though not from the sand, but from the tears that began to form. I'd failed Rebellium and I hadn't even had the chance to prove myself to them yet. I wanted to prove my worth as their Prophet- as the new Phoenix, but I couldn't even prove myself as a soldier. I let their leader and beloved comrade slip away from me.

But there's no use crying about it.

It felt as though a strong wave of fire surged through my body, and every bit of doubt, self-pity, and despair all got caught in the fire.

I opened my eyes to the now orange-tinted darkness in front of me. A large beam of light shone through the thick sand, and I instinctively stood up and began running toward it with no explanation as to why. My crimson wings from earlier reappeared and acted as a shield to block out the sand as I ran against the storm and toward the beam. I had no clue where this determination came from, but the beam was drawing me in like a moth to a flame.

I approached the light and reached out for it, extending my hand toward it. Each step I got closer, the more I felt my body temperature increase- particularly my chest. Right before I could reach the light, the heat became too much to bear, and my limbs grew weak. The wind blew strong enough to push me around until I finally fell to my knees again. I clenched my heart, which felt like someone had poured lava on it. It was just like before, but much worse.

I dragged myself through the remaining distance whilst simultaneously trying to ignore the pain, which proved to be much more difficult than anticipated; I couldn't help but shut my eyes and utter a scream. All of a sudden, the storm around me stopped for an instance, and when I opened my eyes, I saw the light I had been pursuing up close. It wasn't a beam of light- it was a person. They wore a bird mask, mouth cover, and a burnt white robe, but most importantly- they were on fire. After encountering her so many times, I could confidently say that this time, it was The Phoenix.

She held a hand up, and the flames that engulfed her body collected in the palm of her hand, emitting a blinding light. She then brought her hand down and began to walk away without a word. The burning sensation in my chest dissipated the further away she walked.

"Wait, please," I begged, but she did not look back, "don't leave me!" I implored, reaching out to grab her hand.

"I'm always with you," she stated before vanishing into thin air, followed up by a blinding light, which made my vision go completely white for a split second.

I covered my eyes with my hands and grunted, but it was over quicker than it could hurt. I sat there alone again and looked around, noticing that the storm had almost completely abated. I squinted my eyes to decipher what was in front of me, and then I realized where I was. Before me was no other than The Phoenix's grave; I focused hard on the old tomb, and it read, *"Astrid Eleodoro, 'The Phoenix' 2007-"* but the death year had been scratched off. I ran my fingers over the scratched off date, which should presumably say 2029, but it had been scratched off by someone. I'm guessing that someone was The Phoenix herself.

She is trying to tell everyone she's not done; Astrid might be dead, but The Phoenix was still burning. She led me here so I could see this; *is this her strange way of motivating me?* I wasn't sure, but one thing I did know was that I needed to act now. The time was not near, it's *here.*

I got up as fast as I could and ran back to the mansion with a small flame in my hand to light my path. I ran through the weakened sandstorm while trying to come up with the words to explain the situation to everyone once I returned. When I finally reached the front door, I charged inside without even looking around me. I barged into the room where I left my uniform, and immediately undressed. I equipped my intricate Hunter uniform as fast as I could, but there were just so many pieces to it. I was aware that I was making a ton of noise, but it didn't matter, because I needed to be out of here as fast as possible.

"Phoenix, what are you doing?" Aurora asked as she stood by the door. I saw the boys behind her, everyone equally as confused.

"Markus and Asier- I have to avenge them and everyone else. I'm the only one who can," I hastily explained as I slipped my boots on.

"Woah, woah, woah, slow down there," Aurora responded, visibly puzzled.

"It's three A.M, where are you coming from this late?" Guido asked from behind Aurora.

"What's with the sudden burst of motivation?" Nyrual asked as he walked in, attempting to stop my hand from picking up my sword sheath. I slapped his hand out of the way and he backed off.

146

"I can't just wait here; we have to kill The Crow now!" I exclaimed without worrying about making any sense. They all had distinct looks of concern on their faces and looked at each other for understanding.

"Well then we're coming with you," insisted Guido with a grin. Nyrual and Aurora looked at him like he was crazy. "It's gonna take a lot more than just some middle-of-the-night determination to kill him; you need all the backup you can get."

"Yeah, Phoenix, we need to have a plan ready for the rebels if you want to pull this off, and that would take weeks," Aurora elaborated logically, but quite frankly, their opinions were the last things I cared to hear right now.

"What's going on?" Nila asked, who chimed in from the hallway.

"She just barged in here, loud as hell, claiming she's ready to single handedly kill The Crow," Guido explained. Nila tilted her head in confusion.

"He killed-" I began to explain, but I held back, because I didn't want to break the tragic news to Nila so abruptly like that. "Why are you all even awake right now?" I asked to change the conversation.

"The Crow has abducted Asier and Markus," an older woman said as she too walked into the crowded room. She was tall, looked to be in her forties, with glasses, and medium- length gray hair. She had a strange device in her hand and a stern look on her face.

"I was wondering why they were taking so long," added The White Raven, who I didn't notice had walked in behind the other woman.

"Where are they? Odile, can you track them?" Nila asked, a lot more calmly than I expected. *Was I the only one freaking out right now?*

"They're all in The Capital now," she answered with a frown, "but at least they're alive." When she said the last part, a heavy weight was lifted off my chest- a combination of grief and guilt.

"Nila, go tell Daxon, Fremont, and Khalon . . . we'll decide what to do from there," The White Raven commanded.

Nila nodded and ran out the door to fetch the leaders. Guido, Aurora, and Nyrual looked at each other with shared concern. The White Raven had a focused look, but there was not a trace of fear.

"Are you guys not scared? Or even worried?" I asked.

"I've watched those boys mature into the soldiers they are today, and I trust that they're smart and strong enough to take on predicaments like this. Besides, this isn't really Asier's first rodeo," The White Raven explained.

"And what's that device you guys have?" I asked the woman who Nila had addressed by the name Odile.

"It's a tracking device; each of the leaders has a piece embedded into their uniforms, and with this, I can track their locations at all times. Asier also shot his smoke gun, which besides being an alert for everyone nearby, also sends a signal back to this device when it's shot," she explained, and we all stared at her, dazzled. Technology like that was only found in The Capital and was used by high standing Crow armies.

"How do you have such technology?" asked Nyrual.

"I worked as a developer for The Crow. We were the ones who created such technologies to track each other and others who worked directly under The Crow, so I figured out how to work around them, along with how to replicate them completely before I deviated."

"You were one of the science workers? How was that?" Aurora asked enthusiastically.

"It had its benefits; a more luxurious life, life in The Capital, even immortality," she began, "but the downsides were greater. We were heavily guarded, overworked, exploited, and had not a pinch of freedom," she added.

I acknowledged that we were all equally slaves to The Crow, but I was also aware that the people who worked in The Capital had even less freedom, despite what the rumors of "the great Capital life" insinuated. They were too important and useful to be put in any danger, or let die, for that matter, so they were injected with the same immortality injection they were forced to create, just so that they could live this nightmare for all eternity. I could only imagine the security in The Capital, but I guess Odile still somehow managed to escape.

"I saw the smoke signal go off, and I tried to run to them and help them, but I was too late. I couldn't even save them," I scolded myself.

"You mustn't be so hard on yourself anymore, child," The White Raven responded. I looked her in the eyes, and I knew she could see how lost mine were.

"That sword you hold was The Phoenix's. She used it and told us to pass it down *only* to The Prophet. She named it 'The Phoenix Feather,'" she explained. It was a fitting name. "You'll understand everything sooner than you think. You'll discover many things soon, darling," she added, and then walked out of the room without further explanation.

The room cleared shortly after to hear what the leaders had to say. I sat there alone with my head in my hands, trying to figure out what to do. *When will this nightmare end?* I wondered, but then I remembered; once this nightmare ended, so would my life.

"Miss . . ." came a small voice. I lifted my head and saw the little boy from last night standing at the door frame. I looked at him, unable to offer him a smile.

"Don't doubt yourself, miss. You're a hero, remember?" he assured me while wearing a sweet smile on his small face. I couldn't explain the way his words touched my heart, but it was so comforting.

I stood up and kneeled in front of him, looking him in the eyes. "I might not be the Prophet you all hoped for, but I promise to give you my life, so you can see the sun one day," I promised. He responded by throwing himself into my arms, and I took the embrace without hesitation. All the stress I had was suppressed for at least an instant.

"Please save him. He's not a mean man . . . he's just hurting," he pleaded, referring to Asier. "He puts on a cold act, but I know he's hurting; I can hear his heart crying. He cries without making a sound, or shedding any tears," he explained.

"How do you know?" I asked.

"I might be partially blind, but when you lose one sense, you rely on the others. I *hear* his broken heart, and I *feel* his pain," he answered. I was unaware that he was vision-impaired until now, and it shocked me to learn how mature he was for his young age.

He was the third person to tell me this, so there had to be some truth behind it besides everyone just trying to excuse his behavior. I still didn't know much about Asier, but from the bit I did know, I knew that he must've gone through some unimaginable hardships. Asier might be the strongest soldier, a leader, a commander, and the founder of Rebellium, but he was also human, and no human was immune to pain- not even the great Asier.

"I promise, I will," I vowed, and I intended to keep that promise.

Before he could respond, the leaders, Odile, The White Raven, and Nila barged inside the room, armed and ready. They had a look on their faces- determination like no other. It stunned me how hopeful and determined everyone remained even in the darkest of times. It ignited the fire within me, and I hoped it would last long enough to rage through this storm.

"You do realize what you're getting yourself and all of us into?" Daxon inquired, and although the question wasn't meant to, it made me feel a bit defensive.

"Yes. But I know we can do it," I assured. This wasn't the time for second thoughts.

We walked to the large room where Daxon had rounded up all the rebels; they broke into groups- the soldiers who would fight with us, and the ones who would stay behind. It was surprising how many rebels were willing to put their lives on the line for this mission without a second thought, even with no guarantee that any of them would come home again. Everyone on the other side of the room was visibly disheartened and perturbed knowing this would be the last time seeing some of their friends alive. I climbed onto the bar table where I once stood for my introduction speech and scanned everyone in the room, particularly the side that would fight with us, which was a little over half the room.

"Tonight, we storm the capital, retrieve Asier and Markus, and destroy The Crow's empire once and for all," I explained loudly. "Like your leader once said, we'll take back the world that once was ours," I announced, and it echoed throughout the room.

The room was back to complete silence, and then everyone put a fist to their chests and threw the other in the air. Aurora, Nyrual, and Guido stood beside me along with the leaders and Nila. When I looked at my squadmates, it brought me a sense of tranquility. I could pretend we were back home again, going on another mission like any other.

They gathered a few horses they kept in an abandoned cabin, along with four large wagons to serve as our transportation. The Capital was only a few short miles away; it surprised me how short the distance between all the districts was, yet we were never really allowed outside of our own. We all stood outside the town's gates and confidently looked ahead- staring the storm in the eyes. We prepared to run in the direction of the wind; we didn't know what was waiting behind the storm, but we were ready to face it.

I had a heavy responsibility on my shoulders, because they decided to entrust the duty of commander to me. I insisted that Daxon, Khalon, or Fremont take the role, but they were persistent about The Prophet being the one to lead the force. Although it wasn't preferable, commanding and leading the army was the only way my plan would be allowed to go through, so I hesitantly took on the role despite my inexperience and extreme unease in doing so. I just hoped I would make the right choices, because like Daxon said earlier, it wasn't just my life on the line now- it was at least a hundred.

Our plan was to storm the city; a scheme they already had in the works for months, but did not plan to do so soon. The goal was to destroy The Crow's empire little by little, beginning at the heart- The Capital. During the night, all the civilians were on the other side of the city, which was enclosed by another gate within the capital; that side would remain unharmed to minimize civilian casualties. The main goal was to retrieve Asier and Markus whilst destroying The Crow's golden city, but killing The Crow once and for all was on *my* agenda. If I had to burn the city to the ground to do it-

Then I'd be prepared to set the whole world on fire.

Chapter 12

"Well, boys, here we go again," said Khalon as we all sat anxiously in the wagon.

"Why is it that we're always running headfirst into the most dangerous situations imaginable?" questioned Fremont.

"Because we always end up putting the craziest people in charge," replied Khalon to lighten the mood.

"Well at least this time we have four more experienced soldiers on our side," Daxon responded.

Their lightheartedness was a much-needed speck of light in this grim situation, but nothing could wipe the heavy feeling off my chest. It felt like guilt, but I didn't necessarily have a reason to feel that way. My unease was visible to anyone with eyes, and I could tell Nila had caught on. She looked at me with her eyes wide and her eyebrows furrowed as she sat next to me.

"How are you all so calm?" I asked, turning toward Nila and looking into her big, dark eyes.

"Maybe I just believe in us too much, but I just know Rebellium can do this. I trust all my comrades and I trust that Markus and Asier are strong enough to hold off until we get there," she answered with a soft, innocent smile.

"You're not worried about Markus at all?"

"He used to be a guard at the capital- if anyone knows how to navigate that place, it's him," she began. "Asier and Markus worked together to come up with an outline of the city and the plan to storm it for months. It may have happened sooner than expected, but we're well prepared."

"What about you, are you not scared?"

"Not necessarily. Once again, I trust we're all strong enough to persevere," she briefly explained, "and I'll never be afraid to fight for the right thing, Phoenix."

From the minute I walked into the Rebellium mansion, I admired the rebels' exceptional optimism, but no one's faith, bravery, and optimism compared to Nila's. She was like a lion; courageous and brave, with an unbreakable faith in her comrades. As much as I admired it, I was afraid that I was confusing her bravery and optimism with naiveté and inexperience, but I was sure that wasn't the case. I just hoped that the fire in her never burned out.

I dozed off on the way there until multiple gasps from the rebels on board brought me back to reality. I looked forward to see the cause of the commotion, and felt a knot grow in my stomach at the sight ahead of us; a mob of hundreds of Crow soldiers guarding the gates- ready to kill any and every unfortunate soul they ran across. We were still far enough to disguise ourselves in the darkness, so they hadn't noticed us yet. The gates themselves had built-in lights, so I could only imagine what the inside looked like. Looking at all those soldiers seemed like a suicide mission, but I clenched my fists and held my head high; I was their commander, so I needed to act like it.

"Stop the wagons here!" I ordered and the people maneuvering the horses immediately stopped. "Stay a safe distance away from the gates- the rest of us are going in," I continued, and everyone looked at each other, confused and alarmed by my bold statement.

"I'm sorry, Phoenix, but what the hell?" Nyrual asked the question that was on everyone's mind.

"I'm not concerned about taking down these weak soldiers," I began explaining, "not while there's a time-sensitive mission on the other side of those gates."

"How are we supposed to get in with all those soldiers surrounding the gates? They might look weak, but they outnumber us by plenty, and we don't even know how many are inside yet!" Khalon expressed his concern.

"Nothing's impossible for Rebellium- your resolve has proven to be your strongest weapon," I began, and everyone's expressions softened, "or am I wrong to trust in all of you?"

They all stood still as the wind whistled. They were conflicted, but slowly it turned into determination- the look I was used to seeing on them. They all reached in their pockets, and I reached for my belt- they understood the plan without me even having to say a word.

"Throw the first stone," I ordered in a low voice, and hundreds of grenades flew over my head and straight toward the gate.

I reached for my biggest and deadliest bomb and threw it in with the rest. The smaller grenades went off first, which caused considerable damage to the wall along with the Crow's unit. Some soldiers managed to dodge the grenades, but they'd never be able to dodge mine. The large bomb went off and blew out a large chunk of the lower wall, causing the rest to collapse. Smoke and dust obscured the atmosphere, and we all took that as our signal.

"REBELLIUM, COMMENCE THE STORM!" I shouted off the top of my lungs and we all hopped off the wagons, storming straight into the city.

Hundreds of black-caped rebels poured into the gates; most of them weren't even trained soldiers, just ordinary people willing to fight for their freedom. Perhaps they weren't professional soldiers, but they were *fighters*.

"CHARGE!" shouted Khalon as he waved his hand toward a fleet of Crow soldiers waiting inside the gates.

Khalon and Daxon would take charge of the units and hold off the Crow soldiers, while Nila and I searched for Asier, Markus, and hopefully, The Crow. Odile had given Nila the tracker which had both Markus and Asier's locations on it. Fremont, Odile, Aurora, Nyrual, and Guido would all fight with the rest of the rebels, which gave them a huge advantage over the artificial Crow soldiers. Everyone split into their units and began the attack on the barrage of soldiers.

Bullets and grenades flew, and weapons began to swing. Nila and I ran through the battlefield to head deeper into the city and track down Asier and Markus. We were aware that we were practically charging straight into The Crow's trap, but we were prepared to take on any obstacles. Explosions went off behind us as we ran, which produced tons of dangerous debris we had to doge.

I looked up for a second as I ran, and time seemed to pause for that brief moment. I took in the view; all the carefully constructed skyscrapers, buildings, and the bright lights that lit up every corner of the city. For the first and last time, I witnessed the undeniable beauty of the capital- which was soon to be demolished.

A large boulder flew and landed in front of me, but I managed to draw back just before it could crush me. Although I somehow avoided it, unfortunately I couldn't say the same for others. Arms and legs poked out from under the blood-splattered boulder, but despite the incredibly disturbing sight, I had to stay focused. I pulled Nila aside and we hid behind the huge boulder to shield us from the remaining debris. I looked over at her, and her face was much paler than usual.

I scanned the big, luxurious city from everyone's wildest dreams, which was now covered in rubble, blood, feathers, and corpses. The same people I saw on the wagon only minutes ago were now bleeding out on the city's smooth pavements; some covered in bullet holes, others were missing limbs, and yet more were crushed by debris. These horrendous sights, no matter how many times you see them, never get easier to witness because no one, no matter how twisted, ever gets used to the sight of *war.*

I looked over and saw Aurora shoot down a couple soldiers with her arrows, and on the other side I saw both Guido and Nyrual bring down a few more with their rifles. I wanted to join in and help, but I knew they would be fine; after all, they were the strongest people I knew. I glanced at them and waited, but this time they didn't look back, nor did they flash me the reassuring smile they always gave me. I didn't want to get up and run into the big city alone, but I knew The Crow was hiding somewhere inside, so I forced myself to keep going no matter what.

I jumped out of the hiding spot and dragged Nila with me, sprinting as fast as we could away from danger. A few soldiers tried to get in the way, and I pulled out my sword and sliced them down. I looked at Nila and she did the same without hesitation. She pulled out her rifle, knelt down, and shot a few more soldiers in the direction we were headed in. She looked a lot more on edge than usual, but she was still standing brave.

I motioned her to get up and follow me and we ran a bit further until a bomb flew in our direction. Nila took initiative and pulled me aside and we hid behind another pile of rubble. We were breathing heavily, and our eyes met; hers still contained that glimmer of hope, so I knew we were still going strong. I gave her a nod and she returned it before standing up and jumping back in.

"Follow them!" I heard Daxon yell from a distance.

I looked over and a group of about ten rebels ran towards us to aid us in battle until we reached either Asier, Markus, or The Crow. We all ran, killing enemies as they crossed our path until we reached a much quieter area. By the time we reached it, we were all covered in black feathers and minimal blood; most of the soldiers were artificial, which we were all secretly grateful for. *I didn't want more unnecessary blood on my hands.*

"Would you like us to follow you the rest of the way?" asked a young man.

"I think twelve is better than two," Nila answered for me, running her hands through her silky black hair, now covered in dust.

A woman with her hood up pulled out a map and scanned it. "If this map is correct, we're still a few miles away from the center where Asier and Markus are-" she began to explain, but suddenly stopped after the ear-popping sound of a *gunshot.*

Her eyes widened before completely closing, then she fell to the ground. As she hit the floor, a pool of blood formed beneath her chest, staining the map she carried. The other rebels were stunned after watching their comrade get shot, and all they could do was watch her as she bled on the ground. Only a few seconds passed before ten more gunshots followed behind the last and five more rebels fell to the ground. The blood of one of them splattered on Nila as she stood immobilized and filled with *terror.*

I quickly looked in the direction of the gunshots, and there I found the man behind the bullets. Under the flickering streetlights in the distance stood a tall, strong man, and unlike the other soldiers, this man seemed more animate and conscious. He wasn't just a mindless pile of feathers; he was a *human.* He had a large, golden pin on his bulletproof vest which told me he was more than just a soldier- he was part of The Capital's main league- which were people who worked directly in The Crow's unit. He was loading his rifle again, which meant he was going to fire soon.

"Get a grip, you guys!" I yelled to snap them back to reality, and we ran to hide behind a building.

With all the city's lights going out from the explosion, the darkness made it extremely hard to see, especially to spot any soldiers. I heard a bomb go off above us and bits of rocks and dust fell onto our heads. I heard a cracking noise from above and noticed the entire top of a building was coming down. My heart dropped to the pit of my stomach, but my instincts kicked in fast enough.

"EVERYONE RUN!" I screamed and ran as fast as I could.

As I ran, I heard screaming behind me, and I knew exactly what those screams meant- *they didn't make it.* A loud rumbling followed the building as it fell behind me and I pushed my legs to run faster, which still wasn't fast enough. I caught a glimpse of Nila running beside me, and for an instant, I felt a small rush of relief. I knew it was pointless to try and outrun gravity, so in a moment of desperation, I threw myself at her. We landed roughly and rolled on the ground until we hit a pile of rubble, which worked in our favor to shield us from the cloud of smoke and flying debris.

My heart banged against my chest, and my arms ached from hitting the rough, cemented surface. I sat up and hugged Nila tightly while the dust cleared. I opened my eyes as it gradually dissipated, and briefly caught a glimpse of someone on top of a roof a few buildings away, though I couldn't make out any features. I looked over at Nila, and for a second she seemed almost unrecognizable. Her brave, cheerful demeanor was completely overshadowed by horror. She was frozen and staring straight ahead, blankly, until suddenly her mouth twitched, and her eyes grew.

"Markus!" she called loudly. I looked ahead and was beyond surprised to see Markus there, standing on top of the building next to us. *Was he the person I saw just now?*

"Nila!" he called from the edge of the rather unstable looking building.

A brief smile flashed on Nila's face and the glimmer in her eyes momentarily returned. She reached her hand out for him, as did Markus, but I noticed something drop right in front of him. Before I could even process what it was, my question was answered by a loud blast and blinding light. I squeezed my eyes shut and hugged Nila tightly.

"MARKUS!" she screamed at the top of her lungs. It was a blood-curdling scream that forced my eyes open. Her face was plastered with affliction and horror; a look that permanently burned itself into my brain. She yanked my arms off of her and ran into the building to find Markus- or whatever was left of him.

"Nila!" I called out and reached for her arm, but she was too far.

I got up and jogged after her. We went up countless flights of unstable stairs, and she didn't once stop for a breath. After my twelfth flight, I had to stop for a breath, which burned my icy lungs. Though

I stopped, Nila kept going, until she reached the thirteenth floor, and then finally, the roof.

"Nila, please wait!" I called for her from the stairs and began running again until I too reached the roof, which still had a thin cloud of dust obscuring the surroundings.

Once I reached the top, Nila was almost at edge where Markus had last stood. I ran after her, until I heard the same cracking noise from before, only this time, it was much louder. I immediately stopped, looked ahead, and saw a large crack on the ground that Nila stood over. Nila was too focused on finding Markus to even notice that the ground beneath her had begun to crumble. It was a split-second decision, and I was conflicted on what to do, but deep down, I knew I had no choice but to stop chasing her.

"NILA, RETREAT QUICKLY!" I shouted so loud that my voice cracked. "NILA, NOW!" I called once more, and she finally turned back.

The look on her face in that split second, which seemed to stretch out for hours, would forever remain etched into my brain; the absence of all the hope, optimism, and courage that was typically present in Nila's eyes. A heart-wrenching whimper escaped her mouth right before a loud crash, as the ground beneath her collapsed. I instinctively reached my hand out as if I could still catch her fall, and what hurt the most, was that as her feet disconnected from the ground, she stretched her arm back. A single tear slipped from each of her dark eyes as the wind carried them away. She didn't even try to fight her fate; she simply let herself fall.

I fell to my knees with my arm outstretched, and once my eyes lost sight of her, and my ears heard the final crash, my heart dropped to the pit of my stomach, and I involuntarily shut my eyes, because I knew exactly what that meant for Nila. I wanted to keep them shut forever, because I knew the havoc that awaited behind them. When I finally willed myself to open them, I saw something from the corner of my eye. I looked up and saw a woman with short, raven-black hair, wearing a uniform and pin like the soldier from before. She held explosives in her hands, which told me everything I needed to know. In that moment, I felt a fury like no other; my vision went red, and my body acted of its own volition. I pulled my rifle out, loaded it as fast as I could, then aimed it straight at her head.

I pulled the trigger, but the noise gave her a warning and enough time to move just before it could hit her head. After barely dodging the bullet, she spotted me and just glared. To my surprise, instead of throwing another bomb or attacking me, she just continued our little staring contest. It stayed that way for a few seconds until she eventually ran away. Although I was thrown off by her reaction, I knew there was no use in wasting time overthinking it. I reminded myself of the simple fact that despite everything I saw, no one in this world really wanted to kill, *but even angels had blood on their hands.*

I took a deep breath and gathered enough courage to climb down and face the dreaded aftermath. A deep anguish brewed up inside me and the air around me became drastically harder to breathe. I swallowed the heavy lump in my throat and gently climbed down piles of ruins until I reached the ground with one final jump. I took small steps toward the fresh ruble, which was still encompassed by a thick cloud of dust. Besides rocks and dust crunching under my feet, the area was eerily quiet and still.

Amongst the pile of concrete and steel from the collapsed building, I saw Nila sticking out of it. Her legs and the bottom half of her torso were crushed underneath a large, heavy piece of debris and only her upper half was poking out. Her spine was snapped, causing her head to be abnormally tilted upward, with her eyes still slightly open. Blood dripped from her mouth and down her forehead from a deep crack on top of her head which was well disguised by her black hair. Her left arm was broken and folded in an unnatural angle while the other was extended above her, *still reaching.*

Once again, I found myself watching the most hopeful, determined, and brave soldiers being crushed under the weight of this war. I remembered the light in Nila's eyes wherever she talked about becoming a leader, and it made my heart feel unbearably heavy. I wanted that light to burn forever, but unfortunately, I was reminded that no flame was eternal. She was single-handedly the bravest, most determined soldier I would ever have the pleasure of meeting, and I wished I could say that courage stuck with her even in her final moments, but that would be a lie. Even the brightest flames were eventually extinguished by the brutal winds of war.

I inched closer to her and knelt down. "You lived up to your word- you died trying," I lamented as I closed her eyes fully with my thumbs. "It was a pleasure meeting you, Nila. Now rest," I concluded. *I hope the sun shines wherever you're headed.*

I couldn't bear to look at her lifeless face for any longer, so I stood up and turned away. I scanned the perimeter briefly with my eyes, and on the ground, I spotted a singular arm. I closed my eyes and turned away immediately, biting my tongue to avoid a reaction. I recognized that arm, the same hand that once shook mine. I had seen some of the vilest sights in my eighteen years of life, but the sight of Markus's arm on the ground made my skin crawl like no other.

An intense blur of emotions whirled in my brain, but I held back from letting them interfere with such an important mission. In instances like this, I would usually block out my heart's voice, but it didn't feel right to do that following their deaths. For the first time in years, I allowed myself to feel the anger, grief, anguish, and sorrow following a loss, but instead of letting them debilitate me, I let them set me free. I found a sense of peace when I imagined the two of them smiling, reunited somewhere with sunshine and light, because that's where they belonged for an eternity- with each other.

"I'm surprised you made it this far, birdie, but sadly, this is where your journey ends," I heard The Crow's voice echo around me, and every hair on my body stood up. I looked in every direction to try and figure out the source of his words. Just hearing it made me nauseous.

"Show yourself, coward!" I threatened and pulled out my sword. I kept my guard up to avoid a surprise attack.

"You're all talk, little Phoenix. Just look at what you've done; so many of your beloved comrades have already perished under your weak command- the same ones that trusted you with their lives," The Crow refuted, and my arms involuntarily lowered my sword. "With no reason to fight, you'll never be worthy enough to wield that power of yours," he mocked.

"You'll burn in this desolate city, killed by your own doubt and failure. Such a sad way to go-"

"SHUT UP!" I roared and covered my ears with my aching hands. I wanted to rip my ears off and block out his rancorous voice.

Before he could continue, I decided to do what I did best- run. I quickly realized he was talking through the thousands of speakers scattered around the city, so running was useless, but I was determined to run through the cursed city and find Asier with the last bit of determination I had left. The Crow's words echoed in my head, tattooed on my mind. He knew my biggest weakness- my own head. He knew he could easily exploit my guilt and doubt.

"You're just trying to wash the blood off your hands. You can't stand yourself, so you're trying to become a hope these poor fools can hold onto," he continued condescendingly. I covered my ears to block it out, but it was futile, as they had already heard his words.

I stopped running to catch my breath and that's when I saw a large, worn-down poster stuck onto a building. The letters were starting to fade but I saw *DISTRICT FOUR* written as the headline, so my attention was caught. It was covered in dust, and the dark didn't make it easier to read, but I managed.

ALL THE REBELS AROUND THE NATION TO BE ROUNDED UP AND SENTENCED TO DEATH BEGINNING AUGUST 15 IN DISTRICT FOUR TO INITIATE THE CROW'S "7 DAYS OF CLEANSING" ORDER. WE SHALL WIPE OUT REBELLION FROM OUR GLORIOUS NATION ONCE AND FOR ALL.

"By the way, has anyone ever told you that you and your mother are so similar?" he asked from out of nowhere. I paused my reading and listened.

"Cordelia Euphema- such a beautiful and clever woman, but even she couldn't hide the truth forever," he began.

"What are you talking about?" I asked, not caring if I sounded desperate.

"Like mother, like daughter. You both gave up everything to pursue a fruitless cause- so much so that you were willing to kill your own *blood* for it," he explained, but my confusion only grew.

"What?" I asked once again.

"Oh! I forgot, you probably don't know. Maybe you should read the back," he whispered. I ripped the poster off the wall and read it carefully.

BREAKING NEWS: CORDEILA WOLFE FOUND ALIVE IN DISTRICT FOUR; PUBLICLY CONFESSED TO THE MURDER OF MAYOR WOLFE DURING SIEGE OF DISTRICT FIVE EIGHTEEN YEARS AGO.

CORDELIA'S DAUGHTER AND RUNAWAY REBEL, PHOENIX EUPHEMA, GONE MISSING: WANTED **ALIVE** FOR REBELLION, TREASON, AND MURDER OF MAYOR DEVRIM OF DISTRICT FOUR.

I stopped reading because my brain could not process all the information at once. *My mother killed the mayor of District Five?* I tried to wrap my head around it, but it would not add up. I also failed to understand the second part of his claim; *I never killed anyone in my bloodline . . . did I?*

"She mercilessly murdered her father, Mayor Wolfe, eighteen years ago, and now you, Phoenix, followed in her footsteps."

"Who . . . did I kill?" I asked, and I instantly regretted asking.

"Surely it won't faze you considering how many lives you've taken, but the bullet that killed *your father* was shot by *your* hand yesterday," he explained, "You killed your father, Phoenix, Mayor Devrim of District Four."

His explanation went in through one ear and then out the other, then it went back in ten times as impactful. Upon processing his words, I dropped to the ground and sat there, eyes wide and completely speechless.

I brought my hands up to my face and covered my mouth to stop myself from screaming. My world was closing in on me as I lost a grip of my surroundings. I was immediately bombarded with a barrage of memories of me as a naive child, constantly wondering who my father was and why he never searched for me the way I searched for him. Although I no longer had any desire to meet him, I never imagined I would be the one to take his life.

I felt a sharp pain jabbing into my chest. I clenched my heart, but the pain wouldn't stop. I squeezed my eyes shut and grunted, then slowly opened one eye back up. There I saw a bright, flaming butterfly floating in front of me; *has the truth driven me into madness?* As fast as it appeared, a swarm of black feathers engulfed it and trapped it. As soon as that happened, my surroundings became significantly hotter, and that's when I realized everything around me was *burning*. Ordinary humans burned in fire, meaning I was now rendered an ordinary human.

Has Astrid also given up on me? But then why did she ever save me? She should've just let me die back there. The Crow managed to cut off The Phoenix's wings, *and now this phoenix was burning out.*

"Just give it up, Phoenix. You've already lost," The Crow persuaded.

I didn't respond, instead I stared blankly into the flames. I remembered once walking through them without burning; *was this time going to be different? Would I actually burn this time?* I wondered; *would it feel like walking into the sun?* As the flames scorched everything they touched, I saw a butterfly dancing among them. I followed it with my eyes and only for an instant, and I could've sworn it was *blue*.

A blue butterfly . . .

Would it feel like walking into the sun? I repeated the question in my head. *No, because the sun doesn't shine back- and it never has. There is no sun to look up to, and there never will be unless I stand up now. Even if I wasn't worth saving, everyone else fighting for their lives tonight was, and I made them a promise.* I slowly began to stand, ignoring the scorching heat surrounding me. I looked ahead, and there was a burning road that led deeper into the city.

"Even if it's not enough- this is all I've got . . . so give me all you've got, Crow!" I shouted into the atmosphere and began to dash.

"It seems like your only weapon is your mouth, young lady. You're really going to run straight into the flames without The Phoenix's protection?" he asked, clearly scheming something.

"I don't need it," I shouted back.

I ran without looking back. *Fear is only in my mind,* I repeated to myself. *Don't turn around, and don't give in,* I told myself as I ran for mine and everyone else's lives. I wasn't sure whether the flames would spare me this time, but I had no other choice. I wasn't scared of the fire, *because to feel safe in the fire, you can't run from it.*

I ran far enough until I hit a dead end. There was a large gate wall blocking the way, the wall that separated the industrial side of the Capital from the civilians' homes. The only entrance was on fire, and I couldn't even fly over it because right now, I was virtually a regular girl.

"I'll tell you a little secret, Phoenix; your commander is somewhere behind that wall," he hinted, "which means your only option is to go through the fire and hope you survive."

I knew he was just trying to lure me into burning myself, so I refuted. "I'll just blow up this wall."

"That's also an option, but maybe there's something you should know first," . . . he paused and laughed maniacally . . . "there are hundreds of innocent civilians, and a handful of living, human soldiers just on the other side of that wall- so if that wall falls, so do they."

As soon as he said that my heart dropped. Once again, the decision was kill or be killed. This building falling meant that I could reach Asier and we'd both come out alive, but a large number of people wouldn't. There were innocent civilians and human soldiers on the other side. I felt the heat creeping closer as my skin began to sweat profusely. I closed my eyes, took a deep breath, and reminded myself of the phrase I was always told back home; stop at *nothing* to complete your mission.

Nothing at all.

With that in mind, I reached for my belt, and threw the entire thing into one of the windows on the wall. I ran as far as the fire permitted me, and I ducked, waiting for the deafening sound of my decision. The bombs went off like fireworks, and my ears rang with every blow. The large wall cracked and punctured, until it eventually began to tilt back. I closed my eyes and swallowed hard, blocking out the sound of my heart's cries as always.

The wall collapsed onto the civilian's side, and I heard screaming and chaos coming from the other side. Without waiting for the dust or debris to clear, I ran as fast as I could through a large opening as stray bombs went off around me. *Since when did I care about doing the right thing? Never. In this world, "the right thing" is not about doing what's morally correct, it's about doing what it takes to survive in this depraved, wicked world.*

"You thought I wouldn't blow it up just because there're people on the other side? Do you have any idea of how many people I've already killed?" I shouted as I dashed through the destruction.

I relentlessly ran without looking back, losing more of my humanity the further I ran. All I could feel was frustration; *why did it always have to be me who had the blood on her hands? Why did I always have to choose who lived or not?* My brain flooded with questions until I passed someone who was concealed behind the clouds of smoke. I came to a halt and froze in place.

"And you call yourself a hero?" The Crow spat out behind me, sounding amused with a pinch of disgust.

I let the question sit in the air for a while before responding. "I'm humanity's biggest enemy disguised as a hero."

I turned around and The Crow was gone. I stared blankly at the ground for a while before I continued running. I didn't want to waste time standing idly- I had a world to save. I no longer had the tracker or a map, so I would have to run through the city blindly, searching for Asier. I ran until I ran out of breath, then leaned against a wall that still stood amid a collapsed building. It was incredibly dark since all the streetlights around had been destroyed, but I saw a lot more light deeper into the untouched part of the city.

As I leaned against the wall, I heard someone walking in the distance and my heart immediately started racing. I hovered my hand over the rifle on my back and prepared to shoot as soon as I spotted a figure to aim at.

"Calm down, brat. It's just me," a familiar voice shouted, and it brought me more relief than I'd like to admit.

"Asier?" I called in a hushed voice. My lungs wouldn't allow me to speak louder.

"Idiot, why did you come after me! You should've all stayed back!" Asier shouted upon seeing me. I could only see his dimly lit outline in the darkness.

"Wow, nice to see you too, commander," I responded sarcastically. "Your people need you, and I wasn't going to let you die."

"They don't need me any more than they need you, Phoenix," he refuted. The tinge of disappointment in his tone stung a little.

"Just shut up and let me save you," is all I could respond with. His annoyed expression fell and became almost concerned. I think he could sense that I was suppressing a lot, and that any wrong words could set me off.

"Where is he?" Asier asked, referring to The Crow.

"I saw him a little bit ago, but then he just vanished."

"Phoenix . . ." he paused . . . "Why did you listen to him?"

The silence between his question and my response felt like an eternity. He looked me in the eyes, almost asking me to break down. I knew exactly what he meant without him even explaining. *He heard everything.*

"Where were you?" I asked with a shaky voice, fighting hard to keep my composure.

"Right behind the wall. I escaped just before the whole thing collapsed."

After hearing his answer, I struggled to breathe, let alone respond. I could feel all the guilt I was suppressing begin to drown me.

"He was trying to get you to kill me. Don't expect a liar not to cheat at his own game."

Before I could break down, he grabbed my wrist and started to run without warning, pulling me with him. "He has to be looking for us now, we have to run."

"Let him find us then, so I can finish him off once and for all!" I shouted back at Asier, who didn't react.

"Don't forget what your mission at hand is; don't bite off more than you can chew," he answered calmly. Instead of responding, I stayed quiet and considered what he was saying instead. He was right; the main goal was to retrieve him and Markus, and although we couldn't kill The Crow or save Markus, we at least managed to save Asier, and that should be enough.

As we ran, we passed by dozens of bodies- civilians, rebels, and Crow soldiers. Asier ran past them without looking back or even looking their way, which threw me off completely. I looked ahead, and the ruined street we ran through looked awfully familiar, then it hit me. I held my breath once I realized we were approaching the bodies of Nila and Markus. I ran right behind Asier, and in front of him I could see the large chunk of debris that had crushed Nila. I mentally prepared myself to pass by her body again, and I subconsciously searched Asier's face for a reaction.

Prior to Nila, he hadn't looked back for anyone, but I guess even Asier had a breaking point. He turned his head ever so slightly and his eyes looked as far back as they could. A shadow lay over his face, and I could tell by the look in his squinting eyes that he was grieving more than words could describe. I could see all the memories he and

Nila shared flashing before his eyes as he stared at her lifeless body. The girl, who admired him more than anyone, lay dead in front of his face; I knew he too was crushed by the fact that the sweetest, bravest girl he knew was killed by the same war that had ripped hundreds of his comrades from him. *If only you heard the way she talked about you, and the look on her face whenever she did.*

His eyes lowered to the arm on the ground as we passed it, and the same look he had for Nila, he retained for the arm. It was impossible to tell whose it was unless you were there, but something told me he knew anyway. Another one of his strongest and most knowledgeable soldiers was torn from his side, and he couldn't do anything to prevent it. It must've been tearing him up on the inside, but he kept his composure regardless.

"Goodbye, you two," he muttered under his breath as we ran forward.

We ran for a while longer, until I felt a sharp pain suddenly rip through my thigh. I grunted and was forced to the ground. An arrow with crow feathers stuck out of my leg as blood dripped out of the wound. The sensation reminded me of the stab wound in my arm, as the pain pulsated throughout my entire leg. The arrow was still embedded in my thigh, so the real pain hadn't even happened yet.

"Shit!" Asier cursed under his breath as he ran back to me.

I saw something get thrown at us from a distance, and my instincts responded like a match when it touched gasoline. I jumped onto Asier and two flaming wings extended from my back, carrying us into the sky as the ground below us was obliterated. I was unaware of when my power returned to me, but it was well received. We tumbled onto the roof of a tall building, and I grunted at the pain in my thigh.

"Phoenix, make a run for it!" Asier yelled.

"Are you stupid?" I responded between grunts.

"Phoenix, run. That's an order," he commanded sternly. A million thoughts swirled in my head but running was not one of them.

I sat up, pulled out the arrow, and threw it off the side of the building. To ignore the pulsating pain on my thigh, I looked to the building across from us and there I saw the woman from before again. She was crouching behind a water tank, ready to throw another bomb. I panicked- I didn't know if I could get up in time to dodge another explosion. I looked over at Asier, whose eyes were wide and glued on the woman. The expression on his face was like nothing I had seen on him before; it looked like *betrayal*.

He stood frozen in place, his piercing gaze stuck on her. I knew she saw him too from the look on her face; for a second her expression appeared conflicted, but she immediately snapped back to normal. The woman stood back up, and without a second to spare, she threw another bomb. I tried to get up, but the pain in my leg didn't let me stand. The bomb landed next to me, and all I could do was shut my eyes.

Please . . . I'm not done yet.

Chapter 13

I shut my eyes and prepared to never open them up again, but before my life could flash before my eyes, I heard Asier pick up the bomb. I opened my eyes, and his face was plastered with resentment and rage, outlined with the betrayal from before. He chucked the bomb straight back at the woman, but it managed to blow up mid-air in between the two buildings. He threw himself to the ground next to me as the bomb went off.

The force from the explosion had blown off part of the building we were on, and I could feel the top of the structure beginning to fall, with us on it. I rolled over to Asier, grabbed onto him tightly, and hoped that The Phoenix would lend me her power again. I pushed my aching legs to jump, and we flew into the sky again with my wings, but the panic and fear debilitated my control over my still weak flames, and we rapidly plummeted back toward the ground. I felt Asier tighten his grip on me and put his strong arm over my head to protect it. I knew now was not the time to be moved by gestures, but despite the circumstances, I couldn't help but feel like I was *safe*.

I managed to get my wings under control again, which softened the fall considerably, though we still hit the ground roughly. We fell onto a pile of rubble and Asier let go from the impact. I rolled down the pile, hitting myself on rough debris until eventually I crashed into a huge piece of rubble and stopped. My body ached in several places, but was concentrated on my thigh, which was still bleeding.

"Phoenix!" he called out and stood up.

I sat up and he began to walk toward me, when suddenly someone walked up behind him. Too quick for Asier to even react, The Crow grabbed Asier by a chokehold and pointed a blade straight at his neck. The blood drained from my face at the sight.

I wasted no time to react and stood up immediately despite the burning in my leg. I crawl-climbed the pile to avoid straining my leg too much. The pain in my thigh went numb for a moment, but before I could feel relief, I felt another shockwave of pain run through my body, and it hurt *immensely*. I froze in place and lowered my head slowly down to my torso, where a piece of metal had pierced into me a little above my hip. I watched blood drip from that wound as well.

My body weakened at the sight, and I involuntarily let go. I rolled back down to the bottom, and I couldn't move. I lay on the ground, that was ice cold but burning at the same time. It felt like waves were coming down, and I couldn't breathe, nor could I come up for air.

"Phoenix!" I heard a muffled yell. "Get up and fight, brat!" I heard them call again.

"Remember! You have to remember!" It was Asier shouting. *What was I supposed to remember?* "Remember why you looked up at the sky that day!" he shouted from above.

I let his words sink into my skin. *Remember, remember, remember,* I repeated. I closed my eyes and saw the eclipsed sun waiting behind them, then, a pair of blue eyes and the never-fading hope that filled them. Lastly, I saw the sun again, but this time it wasn't eclipsed- it was so bright my eyes hurt- *So, so bright.*

I shot my eyes open and realized there was fire surrounding me- *so bright.* I tried to regulate my breathing in a way that didn't cause any more pain. It felt like I couldn't move without screaming, and it hurt to even breathe. Asier was still attempting to free himself from The Crow's grasp, but he was no match against The Crow's artificially enhanced strength.

"I'm always with you," Astrid's words repeated in my head, and that's when I finally understood; I was never powerless, just sabotaged by my own fear and doubt. I sat up and bit my sleeve to stop myself from crying out in pain.

"I take it you choose to die with him?" asked The Crow.

"No. I choose to live," I responded and flew straight at him. I used all my force, and put everything I had into it.

I wanted to get him as far away from Asier as I could, before I performed the final touch- *the* bomb. I had one last bomb I kept for an emergency, and I pulled it out with my free hand while the other grabbed The Crow by the neck. As I flew, I set off the bomb, and placed it on his chest. I let go of him before it could explode, though I knew I would get caught up in the explosion no matter what. I closed my eyes and waited for the bomb to go off, and when it finally did, the impact threw me into the sky again.

I let the world fall with me in slow motion. I caught a glimpse of the sky as I fell; the dark sun was finally coming up. As I approached the ground, I shut my eyes and let go. I enjoyed the temporary, blissful feeling of being carried by the wind while the world slipped away from me.

I don't remember hitting the ground. Surely it was daytime now, but it was hard to tell since it was still dark, and since it was still dark, *I knew I had lost.* The ground under me was cold and rough against my skin, and my body was sore and throbbing with pain. I didn't even want to open my eyes, I just wanted to lay here, pathetically defeated until I disappeared. I led an entire army to their deaths, and it was all in vain. *As this nation fades away, can I not even stand up?*

A phoenix was made to burn the heavens to the ground, a power I should've known was too strong for me to handle. Now I've lost; burned out and left with no reason to continue. My entire life I've fought with my eyes closed to reality, and now that I've finally opened them, I was blinded by its *darkness.* Now I'm left here in my last moments wondering, *was the blood and sweat I sacrificed . . . really all for nothing?*

174

I heard the gravel crunching under someone's footsteps before I felt them hover over me. They kneeled down and lifted my head, laying it gently on what I presumed to be their leg. I slowly opened my groggy eyes to Asier, his black hair hung from his face and his blue eyes stared into mine. There was a look on his face that I couldn't decipher- he was always so hard to read.

I looked past him with my sore eyes and saw that the sun was coming up. I extended my arm and reached for the black sun, but my arm gave out. I closed my eyes, hoping he would just leave me there to rot, but he didn't. Instead, I felt myself being lifted off the ground, carried bridal-style as we began our walk through the desolate city.

"If you're too busy looking behind you, how can you ever move forward?" he asked, I hoped he didn't expect an answer. "You can't fight for the future if you're stuck in the past," he added as he continued to walk.

"Over and over, I find myself in a battlefield kneeling over my dead comrades, but through every single one, I keep moving forward without looking behind me, because it's up to us- the living- to keep them, and their sacrifice, alive," he explained passionately. "Sometimes we have to crawl to fight a war . . . but we *always* keep moving forward. We can't waste our time on tragedies when there's an entire lifetime ahead of us."

"Don't you get it? I'm not fit to be a savior. Not when I'm standing over a mountain of bodies," I uttered.

"Being a commander comes with the responsibility of carrying the weight of a hundred lives on your shoulders, but at the end of the day, you're just that- a commander. You're only leading them, whether or not they choose to follow your lead is on them," he began. "We're both standing over a mountain of bodies, Phoenix, and we both share a common goal; to not let those bodies drag us down to hell before we make something out of their deaths."

"What kind of commander would I be if I didn't die with my army?" I refuted sarcastically.

It was an uncomfortably silent pause before Asier asked, "Tell me, Phoenix, can you say you've lived your life to the fullest? Are you satisfied with someone telling the story of your life as it is now?"

Every word that came out of his mouth left my mind thinking. *Was I satisfied?* I began to ponder the question as we walked toward the horizon, but I was interrupted by a sound so familiar to my ears and my heart alike. I looked behind us in anticipation, and my heart skipped a beat as soon as I saw just who I wanted to see; Aurora- and behind her were Guido and Nyrual, followed by Daxon, Khalon, and Fremont. The surviving rebels began pouring in from all over, emerging out of the ruins.

Aurora's eyes were closed as she put her soul into every stroke of that bow. She danced and swayed as she played each note. The song she played started off desolate and lost, but then turned so hopeful and full of determination- just like Rebellium. The rebels gathered in a crowd around us, and with the music, it seemed almost like a parade.

"We always fall down," Asier began, "but we'll always stand back up."

"Always!" everyone shouted. Aurora's violin played while everyone chanted, and it sounded like the most beautiful song.

Asier kneeled and set me down on the ground. I sat and watched the horizon; no matter how dark and flawed the sun was, it never failed to astonish me. *I would tear the dark curtain it hid behind one day,* I thought as I watched the sky behind the sun faintly change colors. *If the sky can change colors in one day, so can I.*

"A phoenix is the most powerful creature in this universe, and a heart that waivers won't be able to tame it," Asier said as words of encouragement. I gave him a smile, but before I could respond, we were interrupted.

"Asier! More Crow troops are coming in from the south!" said a panicked Fremont. Everyone pulled out their weapons in response.

"But we just fought so many of them!" Aurora reacted.

"Damn, can we ever get a break?" Daxon complained.

Asier raised his hand to get everyone's attention. That's when I noticed the back of his jacket, which read: *SUPREME COMMANDER AND LEADER ASIER* in rustic white paint.

"Okay everyone, get in formation. I'm aware that there's not too many of us left, but it'll have to do," Asier began. "The plan is to ward them off while I get Phoenix and the rest of the injured to safety," he explained, and everyone agreed without a complaint.

The soldiers were visible in the distance as they marched toward us. Everyone stood their ground and drew their weapons. Asier looked at the enemy unit with an intense glare.

"Are you good to fight?" Khalon asked Asier. I had almost forgotten- Asier had been through a fair share of damage too, and no one really knew what happened to him after The Crow captured him.

"Don't worry about me," he replied in his usual indifferent tone. He raised his arm up. "REBELLIUM, CHARGE!" he shouted and brought his arm down. Everyone charged at the fleet of Crow soldiers.

I tried to stand up and fight, but I ended up pathetically falling to the ground. My wounds were still fresh, and the pain remained intense.

"Don't even try it, brat, you're in bad condition," ordered Asier. As much as I wanted to protest, I couldn't.

An older rebel man volunteered to carry me while Asier warded off the soldiers that tried to interfere. Asier used a sword, and it was surprising to see that he was actually quite skilled at close combat. He chopped down three soldiers in a row with one swing using a unique spin technique. I heard it was common in northern districts to use that technique, so that gave me a clue as to where he could be from.

Being carried across a battlefield and watching everyone else except you fight felt oddly humiliating, and I hated every second of it. I was so weak, and I could feel myself coating the man that was carrying me with blood from my wounds. *This is bad.* I cursed the pain and the circumstances, and felt so helpless and useless in such a desperate situation.

A few rebels situated the wagons closer to the now demolished gates so everyone could jump on easily, and we could take off as soon as possible. When we finally reached the wagons, the man laid me down gently on an empty wagon, and immediately ran to help the rest in charge of gathering the remaining injured. I looked to the side and saw that one of the wagons was filled to the brim, but they were all abnormally still. I stared for a while until I finally caught on, and when I did, my heart sank. That wasn't a wagon full of injured soldiers; it was a wagon full of *dead* soldiers.

No matter how injured they thought I was, I couldn't stand being away from the action and just sitting there idly. I pushed my tender arms to get me off the wagon and crawled until I regained enough strength to stand. Unfortunately, I only managed to crawl a few feet from the wagon before my body gave up. I was sore all over and the pain concentrated heavily at my wounds, making it painful even when I breathed. I looked around and caught a glimpse of Asier.

I noticed him struggling and I focused my blurry eyes to see why. I crawled closer and saw that the soldier he was fighting was not an ordinary soldier- it was The Crow himself. My heart stopped upon seeing The Crow. I pushed my body to crawl more and assist him, but I was just far too weak, so I pushed until I couldn't anymore.

I flopped onto the ground and raised my head to see Asier get thrown to the ground closer to me. His sword was far from his reach and The Crow was about to release a swarm of sharp feathers while Asier was defenseless. I gathered every ounce of energy I had in my body to go help Asier.

"Shut up and let me save you," echoed in my head. I remembered saying those exact words to him, and it sparked something within me. *I'll save us all.*

I don't really know how, but I stood up, ignoring the debilitating pain that followed as I darted toward Asier. He had closed his eyes and placed his arms in front of his face for defense. I jumped in front of him, and I swung my arm up, creating a shield of tall flames. The feathers incinerated the second they touched the flames. I held my hands in front of me to keep the shield strong, but I felt my body threatening to give out on me as I began to shake. I noticed The Crow had a scratch on his face and his uniform was a bit torn and roughened up; *I guess my bomb did at least some damage.*

"What the hell are you doing?" exclaimed Asier.

I looked back and saw his baffled expression, and I felt a small rush of relief seeing that he was safe. My flame was beginning to give out along with my strength, and a few of the sharp feathers managed to get past me and scratch my cheek, arms, and legs. My legs gave out, but Asier caught me in his arms before I hit the ground completely.

"Phoenix!" he uttered in concern. He grabbed me and threw himself onto the ground with me in his arms to avoid the remaining feathers. A bit of my blood managed to get on his face.

"Stubborn brat, I told you to lay low!" Asier scolded. A Crow soldier was approaching us with a sword and was ready to swing. Without a second to spare, Asier reached for his sword and blocked the soldier's swing just in time before it could strike either of us. I used so much strength that my body had virtually none left. The Crow walked up to me, and I began to panic. My stomach twisted and my palms grew sweaty as I lifted my head to his menacing face.

"You're coming with me," he said before picking me up by the collar of my uniform. I was now face to face with him.

With the last bit of fight left in me, I grabbed a small dagger from my belt and grasped it tightly. As quickly as I could, I lifted my hand up to his face and slashed him. He grunted and held his eye in pain, then threw me back on the ground. I attempted to crawl away but he pulled me back by my hair then held me in a chokehold. I turned my eyes and saw that his eyepatch had ripped off, revealing a grayish-blue eye with a large pupil in the center. It was speculated that he hid an actual crow's eye behind his eyepatch, but actually seeing it made my skin crawl.

"You like my new scar?" he asked, and that's when I noticed there was no blood on his face. The gash I had cut healed instantaneously and left only a red scar. "I wouldn't get too used to it though."

"How?" I accidentally uttered.

"Mutated regeneration- and that's only the start of it, honey," he explained with a nasty grin.

"Phoenix!" Asier shouted as he ran toward us.

"No no, you're coming with me, baby bird," The Crow declared ominously and jumped up before Asier could reach us.

He jumped unusually high, until I realized we were *flying*. The Crow had extended his own wings which were always concealed behind his cape. They were large and looked exactly like a crow's wings. It was slightly disturbing to witness all his modifications firsthand. *He's a lot less human than I imagined.*

From below, I saw hundreds of eyes looking up at us in the sky; Crow allies, rebels, and even citizens on the other side of the gate who were awakened by the noise. Without warning, his grip around me loosened, until he let go completely. My heart dropped and my scream got caught in my throat as I plummeted to the ground at an alarmingly fast speed. I was too afraid and panicked to focus on trying to fly, so I just closed my eyes and hoped for a quick and painless death.

"*You give up too easily,*" criticized a faint, female voice.

Before I could even open my eyes to see who it was, a blunt force hit my back midair and sent me flying parallel until I collided with a hard surface. The initial hit, along with the second one, knocked the air right out of my lungs and made me extremely nauseous. The pain pulsated throughout my body, and I thought I would suffocate from the lack of air. I opened my eyes since they were the only thing I could move, and everything was blurry and spinning. Despite my impeded vision and disorientation, I still managed to make out my surroundings somewhat.

I was inside a large metal cage, but through the bars I could still see the sky. A tall, dark figure with large black wings stood at the small door of the cage . . . *a fallen angel?* He approached me and reached his hand out toward me, and I instinctively reached my own toward him.

I didn't even have enough energy to move, nor did I know who or what he was, but for some reason reaching out felt like the right thing to do. There was a delay in his response; he stopped his hand and withdrew a bit; I could tell the gesture confused him. My weak arm dropped and I shut my eyes because the spinning sky only made me more nauseous.

I felt something wrap around me, while simultaneously being lifted off the ground. It was like ropes were wrapped around my arms and legs, and they were uncomfortably tight. I opened my eyes, and I was hanging from the top of the cage by the ropes tied to different bars on the top. I looked closely at the rope and noticed one last detail- they were made of *black feathers*. I tugged and struggled to free myself, but it was futile as they were too durable.

"Don't try and fight it or it'll be worse for you," threatened a voice that chilled my blood. I must've hit my head hard when I was thrown in here, because I couldn't make anything out. "The ol' bird is finally in her bird cage."

Once more, I tugged as hard as I could in my weak state, but I was unable to break free. "I told you to stay still," the man warned menacingly. He snapped his fingers and the rope that wrapped around my arms and thighs dug even further into my skin. A small cry escaped my mouth as every wound in my body reopened. "If you don't die on your own, I'll just finish you off," he whispered in my ear.

A warm liquid dripped down my arms and legs, and the ropes darkened as they stained red. My body went limp, and the pain was so intense I almost didn't feel it anymore. My mind began to stray further away from reality, and my eyes began to shut. The sound of gunshots, screaming, and explosions in the distance rang in my ears as I took my last breath.

Chapter 14

It was dark all over. The darkness that surrounded me was blinding, with not even a speck of light in the abyss. *Was I dead?* I wondered. The absence of noise was so potent that I could hear my thoughts so clearly, almost like they were being spoken out loud. *What am I doing here? How do I get out?* I wondered.

A small light appeared in the distance, but it was enough to dazzle me. I always heard people say that when you die, you see a light in the darkness, and that you would have to walk towards it, but I didn't want to believe that I died, or that this was the end. I didn't want to go out like this, but the glimmer gradually got bigger- or closer. It expanded until the darkness was completely consumed by *light.*

"They say when someone is on the verge of death, their life essentially flashes before their eyes as their mind digs through memories to find something that could save them," a familiar voice echoed in this empty abyss. "Surviving is a lot harder when you have no real desire to live."

She was right. With enough determination, I could've probably woken up by now, but the truth was, I really didn't care if I died- I never really had. Life has been a game of survival up until now, with only the pride of not losing that game being the only thing keeping me alive. In my mind I deserved to die after all I'd done, *so why would I wake up?*

"So, am I dead?" I asked, surprised I was able to speak.

"No. You're searching for a reason to live, and I'm going to help you," came the voice, and I was finally able to recognize that it was Astrid- The Phoenix.

The light faded into the real world again, but I couldn't move anymore- I was merely a spectator now. I was in a burning town, where what seemed like rebels and civilians wearing Crow masks were fighting on the streets. Riots had broken out, and blood was splattered all over the tarmac. This vision was brief before it switched to a big mansion, which looked awfully familiar. It hadn't been scathed by the riots yet. I took a closer look only to realize- it was the Rebellium mansion, and the burning town was the ghost town.

"These aren't my memories. I don't remember this," I called out.

"They're my memories. We share memories, remember?" Astrid responded. These must've been sights she witnessed after her passing- when she was spectating as The Phoenix.

It faded into another memory, which appeared to take place in the mansion's cellar, except it was dark and empty here. It was odd to think that I walked through those same halls now years later. It caught me off guard when I heard a blood-curdling scream after a long period of silence. A bunch of nurses and doctors surrounded a table, and on the table lay a young woman with long, dark hair; it was none other than Cordelia Euphema, my mother. She was the one screaming- she was in the middle of labor giving birth . . . *to me.*

It was rather disturbing to listen to, especially because she looked younger than I did. She was sixteen when she had me, but she hasn't visibly aged much since then. I understood that there was a war raging outside, and that it wasn't particularly ideal to be in town, *but why was she giving birth in the cellar of this mansion? Does she live here?* The memory switched after a while, which I was kind of grateful for.

One of the nurses carried the baby upstairs and placed it in a luxurious crib inside one of the rooms. As soon as she set the baby down, she reached in her pocket for a syringe with an oddly colored fluid inside, and without a second to waste she injected it into the baby's arm. An older, gray-haired man in a beige suit entered the room with a panicked look on his face. The syringe was nowhere to be seen.

"Where's my daughter? Has the cub been born yet?" he asked in a demanding voice.

"She's in the cellar sir, I think you should let her res-"

"There's no time for that! The district has fallen into disarray!" he yelled; the nurse flinched at his loud tone. He sighed. "You should get going too, run as far as you can. Don't let the flames catch up to you," he said, more softly this time. She nodded and bowed slightly.

"Mayor Wolfe, I wish you and your family good health." She reached for her coat and looked back at him. "And best of luck," she added before running off.

After connecting the dots, I concluded that this was all happening in District Five, this man was the mayor of District Five, and my mother was his daughter. I couldn't even wrap my head around the mind-blowing similarities. The scene switched back to my mother, and now she was alone in the cellar wrapped in a blanket with tears in her eyes. She was trying to keep warm while the town above her burned to the ground.

There was something about watching her cry that made me feel like I shouldn't be watching. She wiped her tears fast, stood up, and began changing in a rush. She didn't even seem like she had just given birth. She wore a fancy, burgundy dress, and draped a long black coat over it. She began to climb the ladder right before the memory switched. It was still of my mother, but there was an older woman with her this time. They were in a room that slowly began to engulf in flames.

"Run, I'll catch up later. I have to save my daughter!" my mother shouted at the woman.

I recognized the woman- it was my grandmother. My mother pushed her out of a door that led outside and shut it immediately. My grandmother banged on the door, but mother fearlessly ran back into the burning mansion. The look on her face was aflame with determination- something I've never seen on her. She ran through the fire without stopping, that was until she ran into the mayor- her father.

"Cordelia, we have to get out of here- just leave the cub behind!" he shouted.

"No! She's my daughter!" she yelled back and tried to run past him into the room where the crib was. He grabbed her arm and held her back.

"You didn't even want the kid to begin with! Just have another heir later on."

"How can you speak of her like she's just some object? She's my blood- my new reason to live!" she barked with a furious look on her face.

"You idiot! You'll die trying to save that brat!" he yelled, his face red from rage.

"I don't care, because now I have something more important than my life. I'd run through fire for her- now and a thousand more times- and I'll do it again, and again, and again if I have to," she said with stimulating courage in her voice.

If I could cry right now, I probably would. As her words replayed in my head, I couldn't help but wonder, *does she still mean that?*

"The wretched rebels are burning this place down- everything in that room is probably ashes by now. If those devils find us here, they will kill us!" He tightened his grip on my mother's arm. "All this killing and destruction over a hopeless cause. I've never seen such foolishness," he added, repulsed.

"They're fighting for freedom," she corrected him with venom in her voice. The man gasped and let go of her hand.

"Don't tell me you agree with those fools . . . You're the daughter of a government official!" he scolded, his eyes wide and his gaze burning more than any fire.

"I never was your daughter, nor did I ever consider myself another blind eye to that tyrant's senseless slavery!" she asserted and pulled out a blade from her black coat.

She tightened her grip on it before plunging the blade straight into his chest. He let out a loud, piercing scream and then she withdrew the blade before stabbing it back in, deeper this time.

"Co-Cordelia . . ." he gasped.

"I was never either one," she uttered quietly, and drew the blade out for the last time. The mayor fell to the ground, and breathed his last breath. She threw the blade into the fire, along with her blood-stained coat, and looked down at the dead man on the floor one last time. "Long live, Mayor Wolfe."

She barged into the room in search of the infant and saw that the room was indeed engulfed in flames. She began to silently weep as she frantically scanned the room until finally locating the crib. She immediately ran to it, completely ignoring the fire. The newborn, despite being in a room full of fire, was miraculously untouched by the flames. She picked up her baby and held her close as she cried. She gazed at her new purpose, and smiled through the tears.

"The flames of rebellion didn't kill you, they protected you," she whispered to the baby in her hands. "Your name . . . will be *Phoenix*," she said to her softly before dashing out of the room with the baby in her hands.

She ran and ran through the burning, crumbling building until she reached the back door- the same door I ran out of. She ran without stopping until she reached the back of the gates where her mother was. Together, all three of us ran from the burning district, and ran toward a new life.

". . . And the lone 'Wolfe' ran from her wolf pack," narrated Astrid before everything went dark again.

"She loved me then . . . so why did she stop?" I asked.

"You still believe you aren't loved?" asked Astrid.

Before I could answer, another memory appeared in front of me, but this one was nothing like the others. It felt oddly familiar, everything about it. It was like my brain had dug for memories that had almost completely faded. I was probably about five years old; my eyes were watery and I was on the ground. I was alone, the way I always remembered it, and in the distance a few kids were looking back at me.

"What's wrong with you?" taunted one of the boys.

"You're a freak!" a little girl shouted.

"You're one of those devils!" yelled another. "You're going to get killed and you deserve it!" he added, and his voice in particular struck a nerve.

I remembered this moment, his name, his words, and how hard I tried to forget them all- Bryce. He and all the kids around him ran away from me because their parents wouldn't allow them to be associated with a kid named Phoenix. I remember always wondering, *why did my mom give me that stupid name anyways?* Up until this day, I cannot understand why. I wonder if she knew I was going to be The Prophet.

The memory switched before I could ponder much longer. It was still me, but now I was walking home, alone and with tears in my eyes and cuts on my knees. I was on the hill, looking up at the sun; *even back then huh?* I looked back down and saw my small house. My mother was in the yard, growing and picking the small yellow flowers she would sell for our income.

I finally reached her, and she looked at me, her eyes immediately landing on my watery eyes. I thought I knew what would happen next; she'd turn away like she always did, but to my surprise, she didn't. She reached out for me and held me in her arms. *But I have absolutely no recollection of this whatsoever.*

"Momma, why did you give me this name? Why's everyone afraid of me?" I asked innocently in her arms.

"The world is afraid of those who are different," she responded before letting out a deep sigh. "I'm sorry, Phoenix."

"Why, Momma?" I asked again.

She pulled away from the hug and faced me, giving me a reassuring smile. She reached to the ground, picked a flower, and placed it in my small hand.

"Your name means resurrection- that's what you did to me when you were born."

"What does resurrection mean?"

"You'll find out one day, my love."

I didn't recall this conversation ever happening; *all I ever knew was being alone and rejected.* A new memory surfaced; it was me again- same age, sitting on the ground, alone again. I remembered the constant feeling of being an outcast- so alone, and so hurt. That's when I saw a hand reach out to me. I looked up, and it was another little girl, but she was slightly older. She had light brown hair, a freckled face, and the greenest eyes I had ever seen besides my mother's. She held her hand out to me and I reluctantly took it.

"Hi, I'm Aurora! What's your name?" she asked happily.

"I'm Phoenix," I replied, and she pulled me up.

"Come on, let's go!" She pulled my hand, and we ran off, *together.*

As the memory faded to black, my mind went back to the night before the execution. We were in the cabin, and she had mentioned something about us when we were younger; she remembered this moment after all these years.

"Your mind only remembers what you deem as convenient for you to remember," Astrid explained. "You've convinced your mind to block all of that out for the sake of desensitizing yourself, losing the good moments of your life in the process."

"I did it because I had to . . . or else I'd lose everything," I defended.

"As a result of teaching yourself to suppress your emotions, you're convinced nobody loves you, because you can't recall any of the memories of you feeling loved."

I let her words sink in and into my skull; *she was spot on.* This world was cruel, and the path I chose had no room for weakness, and it taught me that having emotions was the worst obstacle in surviving this world.

"Your mother distanced herself because she felt guilty. She thought it was all her fault that you lived the life you did, so much so that she even began to regret deviating. Eventually, once you became one of the strongest Hunters, she inevitably grew afraid of you, seeing as both she and her mother were deviants on the run," she explained.

It hurt to hear that my own mother grew afraid of me. I've always been feared, but I never wanted her to fear me as well. *If only she knew why I did it.*

"One thing that guilt and fear have never been able to change is that she never stopped loving you, Phoenix." Astrid paused, then said, "To this day, she would still run through the fire for you."

As soon as she finished, memories of me and my crew members flashed before me. All of our memories together, all the wins and the losses, all the laughs and the pain. *How could I have been so blind?*

"They risked their lives for you by accompanying you on this journey; they ran from their comfort and left their homes behind for you. They've cared about you from the day you became a squadmate and haven't stopped since then."

They believed in me when I didn't even believe in myself. I was loved from the very beginning, but I was blind, because all I had to do was look at the world waiting in front of me. Right now, while I'm sleeping, they're on the battlefield fighting for their lives.

"Your mother needs you now, and your friends do too," she continued, and I felt myself freeze completely. "This time, why don't you run through the fire for them?"

I thought back to all the times I looked up at the sun, and a flood of memories flashed in front of me again; memories of every time I reached up to the sun. I am The Phoenix, the one that rose from the ashes and protected the sun. From the second I took my first breath, I was destined to resurrect the sun, and it always called my name, because *I am the sun.*

I looked in front of me and this time, I actually saw my body- I was me again. Aurora, Nyrual, and Guido were in front of me, levitating a few feet from the ground. They extended their hands at me, smiling as always. I took their hands and jumped, spreading my blazing wings as big as I could, and took off to face the darkness.

I zipped through the dark sky like a torch in the night, lighting the way as I flew. The world as I knew it emerged from the darkness and I spun around and dashed through the familiar sky, setting the world behind me on fire. I flew until the world disappeared and it was dark again. Above me, I saw my current self in the third person, hanging from the cage, completely unconscious.

"Wake up, Phoenix," a voice pleaded; it was my mother's. She was up there with me, floating in front of me. She held my face, her hands on each cheek.

"Wake up, Phoenix," another voice called out, and this time it was my grandmother. She held my face the same way mother had, in the same spot my mother just was.

"Wake up, Phoenix!" Yet another voice spoke, and it was Aurora now. She too held my face the same way and in the same spot.

"Wake up, Phoenix." It was Nyrual now.

"Wake up, Phoenix." Now Guido.

"Wake up, miss." Lamie's turn.

"Wake up, *Prophet.*" Lastly, it was Asier.

"All these people are depending on you, and they all believe in you. Let them be your motive- to protect them and set them free," The Phoenix said as she appeared in front of me, still in her robe and mask. "Now, it's time for you to wake up, and protect the ones you love, Phoenix," she concluded.

I closed my eyes, and once more remembered every time I'd looked up and seen no light. I recalled the cold air laced with the smell of war that always left me shivering, with no sun to warm my skin. I wanted to change that so badly . . . *and I can still make it happen. Who will be there to catch my fall? No one will.* As much as I wanted to fall and give up, I couldn't. I have no choice but to win, because they need their Prophet.

"Wake up, Phoenix," I called out to myself. *It was my turn this time.*

Chapter 15

My eyes shot wide open. I inhaled sharply and it felt like taking the first breath after nearly drowning. Every vein in my body flooded with scorching fire and my strength increased tenfold. I tugged at the ropes restraining my arms and legs, but I quickly realized how futile it was, so instead I just closed my eyes. I imagined a bird breaking free from its cage, and then the cage going down in flames. Soon enough, the ropes turned to ash, and I was finally free.

I imagined that same bird that had just broken free, but this time, I imagined it burning along with the cage, and I let that thought sit for a while. The bird which just burned, soon resurrected and rose from its ashes, and from those ashes, a phoenix arose, spreading her crimson wings made from the sun's hottest fires. I looked down at the battlefield through the cage's bars, and there were no signs of The Crow anywhere. The number of Crow soldiers was greatly outnumbering the rebels, and they were visibly struggling.

I gripped the metal bars tightly and focused all my energy on my hands. The metal around my hands began to glow as their temperature increased significantly. I did this until the heat made the bars malleable enough to bend, and using all my strength, I pushed an opening large enough to slip out of the cage. I stood over the edge and let myself free fall. I looked above me, pulled out my handgun, which was somehow still strapped to my belt, and I aimed it at the blimp which carried the cage. I fired, hoping the wind would work in my favor, and the blimp immediately began to go down as the bullet pierced it.

I turned back around, and as I plummeted down, the freezing wind felt like icicles cutting my face as it pushed against my skin. I fell for a while longer before catching my fall with my wings. As I got closer to the ground, I noticed heads turning and eyes following me. I extended my arms and flew slightly above the ground, and as I sped through the battlefield, I burned everything I came across. I avoided rebels and civilians, and targeted large groups of Crow soldiers along with remaining buildings.

I landed on a tall pile of rubble and looked to the horizon as the city burned behind me. I pulled my sword out and held it in my hand as I stared directly at the man who once again failed to burn me out. A look of annoyance riddled his face as he lowered himself down with his own synthetic wings.

"How many times do I have to remind you? You can't put a phoenix in a bird cage," I mocked proudly. His face scrunched even more.

"Back for more?" he asked bitterly.

"I will be until I free the world, because that's what I promised," I replied as ashes and pieces of burnt feathers from the cage fell around us. As I spoke that sentence, I felt as if it was more than just me speaking.

"Let's say you manage to do as you say . . . are you prepared to die for it, little Phoenix?" he asked, trying to intimidate me.

"Yeah, I might die today, but I'm gonna die anyway," I affirmed. "Someone once told me they didn't mind dying if it meant dying for the right cause," I added, in homage to Nila.

I didn't give him time to respond, and immediately swung at him with my sword. He quickly pulled out his own blade and blocked my swing; his agility was remarkable. I noticed the similarities in our blades; mine had a gold handle and was adorned with crimson

193

feathers, and his sword had a silver handle and black crow feathers. The sound of the two blades hitting was music to my ears.

"You have no idea what you're dying for, Phoenix. You don't understand how wicked the means truly are," he claimed. *Too bad that wasn't going to work anymore.*

"I no longer care what you say," I responded, our faces only inches away from each other. His crow eye was even more baffling up close. "I'm not scared of you anymore," I uttered before kicking him with all my force, knocking him back a lot. He was winded and holding the spot where I kicked him.

"An insolent child like you would never understand the complexity of the situation. You're just fighting out of pity for the rebels and a naive desire to see the sun; you don't know even half of what you're trying to bring back," he shouted angrily. His voice sounded almost desperate.

"Someone once told me of a world where the sun shone on every inch of this world; they spoke of a world where the light wasn't shrouded by darkness- in that world, everyone was free." I paused to take a deep breath. "But I'm no longer looking to bring that world back," I added, and he furrowed his eyebrows in confusion.

"A world that fell for a reason should not be salvaged, but a new one should rise from its fall," I finished.

"Is that why you woke up?" he asked, but for some reason, it didn't feel like a question for me.

"I have something to live for, and I won't surrender to you. I've set my sights to save this world, and I *never* go back on a promise," I answered anyway. Once again, I felt like it wasn't just me choosing the words I spoke.

"Well then, you should've just stayed asleep," he answered with a sinister tone that sent chills down my spine. Not a hint of his usual sarcasm or taunting demeanor. "This world isn't about hopes and dreams, sweetheart, it's about *survival*, and whoever's strong enough to be on top, decides the fate of the world and the people in it."

"I can't wait until the day I watch you burn," I said in a vindictive tone.

"If that's the case, I can't wait to watch you burn with me," he responded with a chilling grin.

We briefly locked eyes before he released an abundance of feathers from the small cannons hidden behind his cape. They caught me off guard, but I managed to draw back and burn the feathers as they approached me. The barrage was thick and I couldn't see beyond them, and once the feathers had finally stopped, The Crow had already fled.

I fell to my knees and punched the ground so hard I cracked a piece of rock from a building. I was furious that he had managed to escape yet again. I let out a deep sigh and flew back down to the ground where an army of rebels awaited me; I was greeted by the smiling faces of those I promised to protect. I smiled back, but the smile was quickly wiped off my face. All at once, the excruciating pain from my injuries once again ran throughout my body.

I cried out in pain and fell to the ground, watching small drops of blood stain the cracked concrete. Muffled voices called my name and it all sounded like one big blur of noise. My vision began to blur as well and every time I blinked, I was unsure if I'd open my eyes again. *Not again, not again.* I didn't want to black out again, but it was evidently beyond my control. My body began numbing one limb at a time, and it did that until I was once again consumed by the darkness.

"It was definitely her. She clearly has no shame since she was the one that gave away our old hideout, she was literally there when we were caught!" I heard Khalon speak with rancor in his voice.

"Why would she go as far as to do that?" asked Daxon.

"I don't know. I don't care either," answered Asier, bitterly. I felt a vibration every time he spoke.

"Don't worry, we'll help protect this hideout," assured Guido, positive as always.

"Your uniform color fits you," I heard a familiar voice say, but I couldn't put a name on it.

"So I've been told," I heard Guido respond, and then chuckle.

I heard everyone speaking around me, but my eyes were still closed. I felt wind brushing against my face, but I wasn't walking. I wasn't moving, but I was on top of someone who was moving. My body was pressed against someone else's while my arms wrapped around their neck and legs, secured by someone's arms. I was being carried piggyback style . . . *by Asier.*

I came to this conclusion because each time he spoke, I felt the vibration of his voice. I could also faintly smell his distinct smell of mint and cigarette smoke behind all the gunpowder from the battle. I yelped slightly before leaning back, letting go of my arms that were wrapped around his neck. I fell to the ground and landed on my tailbone, which hurt more than I imagined.

"Well, it looks like the brat is awake. Good, now you can carry yourself," Asier said in his monotone voice.

"Don't be such an ass, Asier," scolded Lana. It was her voice I heard earlier. She kneeled down to meet me on the ground, her wavy brown hair blowing slightly in the wind.

"You're wounded, let him carry you back," she insisted.

"It's fine, I'll just walk it off," I insisted in return, and pridefully. I tried to stand up, but froze upon intense pain shooting throughout my body. I bit my lip to stop myself from screaming and just sat there, motionless. I heard Asier sigh in response.

"You're hopeless, just let me carry you and stop protesting." This time Asier insisted as he kneeled with his back toward me.

"No-" I refused but was cut off when I felt him grab my arms and wrap them around his neck.

"You better hold on or you'll fall again," he advised as he slowly stood up. I reluctantly grabbed on, and he picked up my legs. I felt my face heat up when I realized everyone was watching this. I heard soft chuckles coming from beside us.

"What are you morons gawking at?" Asier asked in a menacing tone while looking straight at Khalon and Fremont.

"Oh nothing," Khalon replied before bursting out in laughter. Everyone around us followed right behind him. I knew if I could see my face, it would be bright red.

"Imbeciles. Keep laughing and it's supply-run duty for all of you," threatened Asier. Everyone quickly ceased their laughter. As we walked, my arms slid closer to his neck.

"You're choking me, brat," Asier grunted.

"You brought this upon yourself, so endure it," I responded, though I did move my arms. Everyone began to laugh again.

I turned around and saw the remaining rebels, though I had to strain my eyes to see them since they all wore black hooded capes to conceal themselves. Some were engaged in small conversations, but most of them just walked. I could tell they were worn out, both mentally and physically.

I looked behind them and saw only three of the wagons we'd originally brought. They were filled with people; some were moving, while others were not. One of the wagons was filled to the brim with heavy duffle bags which I assumed were corpses, and it was incredibly disturbing to see the amount. The other two were crammed with injured soldiers and a few duffle bags as well. *Why wasn't I there? Why am I being carried by Asier instead?* I wondered.

As he walked, I tried to avoid his neck so I wouldn't choke him again. Without realizing, I ended up landing my hands on his chest in an effort to avoid his neck. I could feel his heart beating behind his defined chest. I quickly moved my arms once I realized I was unwittingly stroking his chest. My face burned with embarrassment more than any fire in this universe ever could.

"You're slow," I taunted him to diffuse the awkwardness.

"Well maybe if you'd stop feeling me up, we'd get there faster," Asier bit back. I turned bright red in extreme embarrassment, and heard chuckles from the others.

"Who wouldn't wanna feel up such a strong beast like Asier?" teased Khalon in a feminine voice.

Asier let go of one of my legs to shove him. They all broke into more laughter. It was embarrassing of course, but it was refreshing to see everyone could joke around with each other like that, especially after such a heavy battle.

"You're on toilet duty for a week. I want to see my reflection in that shit," threatened Asier, making everyone laugh again.

"Oh stop. You know you love the flattery," Lana teased.

"You're begging for toilet duty too," Asier responded.

"Well, it's a break from kitchen duty."

"Yeah, maybe you'll meet your dream gentleman when he's dying to take a dump while you scrub the bathroom floor," teased Asier. Everyone erupted in laughter once again. Guido and Aurora could barely contain themselves anymore.

"Very funny," responded Lana as she crossed her arms.

"What would your dream bathroom man be like, Lana?" asked Daxon, obviously teasing her.

"I don't think she needs the bathroom to find him," Khalon teased while elbowing Guido's arm. He blushed and turned away.

"Well, what about you, big guy, what's your dream girl like?" Guido asked Khalon while playfully shoving him.

"Not sure, but she'd probably have green eyes, cute freckles, play the violin, and fight like a badass," he explained, making it as obvious as possible that he was describing Aurora. Everyone began to whistle and make "*oooh*" sounds.

I looked over at Aurora and her pink cheeks were visible even from afar. "Corporal!" she exclaimed timidly then pulled down her cape's hood to cover her face.

"Does everyone here just confess their love to each other like it's nothing?" asked Nyrual, eliciting a round of chuckles.

"Ugh, all of you, get a room," said Asier, faking his disgust. They all laughed and the slight awkward tension ceased.

"What about your dream girl, Asier? Don't think we forgot about you," teased Daxon.

"The opposite of all of you," he answered in his usual unconcerned voice, making it even funnier.

After the laughs faded, we all walked in silence for a while. I think everyone remembered the issues at hand. It stayed that way for a while before someone broke the silence with a not so lighthearted comment.

"So, what are we going to do about the intrusions? If we're positive it was her who gave out the location, should we go after her next time?" asked Daxon.

"That's basically suicide. She was already strong as hell and now that she's allied with The Crow, it means she's even stronger and better equipped," answered Khalon.

"Plus, she was always a clever girl, she'd never let herself get caught so easily," Added Fremont. Asier remained silent.

"I still refuse to believe she would do that," Lana added, and you could hear the hurt in her voice. I was lost, but I was too scared to ask questions. Afterall, it might not be any of my business.

"So, one of your old allies is revealing your locations? What would she gain out of that?" asked Guido.

"No one really knows. We were nothing but kind to her," Answered Fremont, brushing over his dirty-blond hair.

"I still don't think it was her-" Daxon began.

"She was there when we were captured, and today I saw her blowing up our comrades. She killed Nila and Markus with no remorse, and then tried to kill me and Phoenix. If you still don't think she'd do it, you're absolutely delusional," Asier interrupted bluntly. Animosity burned in his voice.

"Who killed them?" I broke my silence, but nobody answered. "Answer me! Who killed Nila and Markus?"

"Val-" Fremont began to utter a name.

"I'll explain . . . the *situation* to her," Asier cut him off. Everyone just remained quiet. "Daxon, lead the squad for a bit," Asier ordered. Daxon nodded without question.

With that Asier and I deviated from the group, walking far enough to where his words were unheard by the others, but close enough to where we could still see the group. I wondered why he had gone so far.

"What's wrong?" I asked. He looked essentially the same; his face remained aloof, but his heartbeat felt irregular.

"This lone wolf we speak of, it's a hard story," he responded.

"Who?"

"We refer to this . . . woman, as the lone wolf. A lone wolf runs from their pack, acting independently," he explained. I recalled that was the nickname Astrid had given my mother too.

"Did you really have to take us this far to tell me that?"

"No. The reason we are this far is because I am going to tell you something, and I don't want the others to be around," he explained, and I felt his heartbeat speed up each time he mentioned it.

"Her name is Valerie. She was a very close member of Rebellium." He took a deep breath before continuing. "Every bone in her body was that of a rebel, but one day, she just . . . disappeared," he said. I thought back to the note I saw in his room, and I remembered it was signed by that name.

"We initially thought maybe she wandered off on her own and went back to live in the districts when I found a note she wrote, but we soon realized we were too optimistic," he continued, but once again paused. I could tell it was hard for him.

"Where did she go?" I asked.

"We originally had two locations; the main location is where we stay, and the second one was a cave where we kept a lot of materials, a lot of our plans, and housed a few rebels that lived further from the capital," he explained and sighed. "That place is now gone. It was obliterated completely."

"What happened?"

"Fremont, Daxon, Khalon, and I went one day to continue to write out our plan to invade the capital, and that day, a storm of Crow soldiers invaded our hideout instead. Valerie was among them, and the soldiers were going to her for instructions, meaning she's the one who led the invasion. That's the day we were caught and sent to the closest District for execution- District Four."

I could hear the grit in his voice when he talked about her. You could tell her name left a bitter taste in his mouth, but there was also a profound amount of hurt behind each word. I recalled what Asier said last night about love turning into hate, and how he seemed to be speaking from experience- I think Valerie was that experience. The note I read in the book, and the woman I saw on the top of the building, *that was all Valerie?*

"Why don't you want the others to hear? Is Valerie more significant than you're making her out to be?" I asked, possibly pushing the limit. He stayed quiet for a bit.

"She was . . . a lot more than what I've made her out to be," he answered, his voice laced with a deep melancholy, and I immediately regretted asking him.

"So that dark haired woman we saw . . . that was her?" I asked.

"In the flesh," he said, followed up by a deep sigh.

Even I was baffled by her actions and I had only just learned about her today. I didn't know Valerie, but hearing about her and seeing what she'd done firsthand made me feel sick to my stomach. It didn't matter whatever her reasons may have been, she turned on her comrades in the worst ways possible, and it was absolutely vile.

"She used to help Markus and I train Nila," he said, which added even more salt to the wound.

"I'm no saint, I know I'm in no place to judge someone else's sins . . . but that's just . . . *despicable!*" I could barely even find words to describe how appalled I was.

I remembered the look of relief on Markus's face when he first saw Nila in the distance, and then the terrified look on Nila's face right before she fell. To think Valerie was capable of killing such amazing people whom she had such a strong connection with made my blood boil. I remembered Nila's arm and how it was extended when she died, and Markus's leftover arm; *they were reaching for each other.*

"I'll rip her apart," I accidentally mumbled out. I didn't realize I had said that out loud due to how furious I was.

"Slow down, sunshine. We all have a bone to pick with her, but we have to stay focused on the real mission," he responded. It always amazed me how much self-control he had over his emotions.

"You're right. We have a world to save," I said, trying to add a little humor.

"Is that why you slept in that cage for half the battle?" he retorted with sarcasm.

"The Crow was right, I should've stayed asleep, you ungrateful loser."

"What could you possibly be dreaming about that's better than real life?" he asked, once again, humorously sarcastic.

"Well, while I was asleep, I had several visions while The Phoenix spoke to me. It was my subconscious searching for reasons to wake up."

"Like what?"

"One of the visions was my mother running away from a burning town after she killed her father," I explained as briefly as I could.

"Ah, so your mother lived in that ghost town?"

"Yeah, her father was actually the mayor. She rebelled and killed him before running away with me and my grandmother after giving birth," I answered, in disbelief of the words that were coming out of my own mouth.

"So, your grandfather is Mayor Wolfe?"

"Guess so."

"And your mother is Cordelia Wolfe?" he asked, a bit stunned by the revelation.

"Yes?" I responded unsurely, because that surname would always throw me off.

"That crook and his weird wolf obsession; he and his family were called the Wolf Pack. There were rumors his wife and his daughter might've managed to flee to a nearby district since they never found their remnants. Everyone is under the impression that a random deviant had killed the mayor though."

"Well, I think the truth is out. I saw on a poster in The Capital that she was found and is being tried for multiple crimes, killing her father included. She and every remaining deviant will be executed sometime before the end of this month," I explained, trying to hide my sadness.

"We'll get to her before they do, don't worry," Asier reassured me, and I couldn't help but smile.

"My entire life I told myself my mother didn't care about me, since she always seemed to avoid me. I was under the impression that she hated me for ruining her life, since she was forced to have me at such a young age, but I found out the truth inside that cage. She's always loved me, she just felt guilty, and grew afraid of me. She knew her daughter wouldn't hesitate to kill her if I found out she was a deviant," I explained. I didn't realize I had begun to ramble. Asier was probably uninterested.

"I'm sorry, I'm just rambling now, I'm sure you have enough on your mind-"

"I don't mind. Keep talking," he said to cut me off, his voice still monotone, but somehow, I knew he was being sincere.

"It's nice to know someone loves you, even when you can't love yourself," I said. "How did she not get caught sooner though? How did you guys go this long without being discovered in your father's district?"

"It's a really long story, if you're willing to listen," I said, "one I've briefly told you before."

"I'm listening."

"Well, one day Mayor Devrim's brother, Secretary Devrim, heard of a woman named *Cordelia* with a daughter who went by the name *Phoenix*, so he decided to do his own private investigation."

"What'd he do?"

"I was about eleven years old, and I was at school when suddenly I was called out of class by Secretary Devrim. He told me he knew everything; he knew what my mother had done, and he told me he knew the affiliation behind my real name. At the time I didn't know what my mother had done; I was under the impression that her only crime was naming me after The Phoenix, but now I know he knew more than just that." I paused and took a deep breath. "I pleaded for my life and hers, and he proposed the deal I explained before."

"Refresh my memory."

"He told me to sign up to be a Hunter trainee, and to train and become the strongest candidate. He told me to become the strongest Hunter, and eventually an Executioner. He said if I worked for the state, it would be my way of repenting, and would reestablish my loyalty for The Crow," I said and paused briefly, before adding, "and so I did. I promised I would do it all, and that day, I traded my humanity for our lives." I felt tears threatening to escape my eyes, but I quickly pushed them back. The story I relived constantly in my head hit differently after knowing everything I know now.

"I trained every single second of the day, I worked for the best grades in the class, and did everything I had to do to be the top trainee. Once I was thirteen, I was declared a candidate, and I kept proving myself worthy until I was elected to be a Hunter and Executioner at the age of fifteen, the youngest to do it in District Four."

"So, you've been at it for a while then?"

"I still remember my first kill. No child should have to kill someone at the age of eleven," I began. "I remember the night that followed as well; I'd jump at the slightest of sounds and could swear the hallways echoed with rebel screams. My room was awake with shadows, but it wasn't something I could hide from under the covers. Every single night, my paranoia would keep me up. I'd look out the window and cry, thinking they'd come for me and my mom at any minute." I allowed a moment of silence to let my words settle.

"I couldn't live in peace while holding that secret, but I had no other choice. The rest of my life was destined to be a game of kill or be killed, but no one should get to decide their life is more important than someone else's," I concluded.

"Those who kill should be ready to be killed at any moment, I learned that at a young age too," Asier replied. "We'll save your mother and the rest of the rebels before the Executioners lay a finger on them. No child should have to watch their parents be killed," he reassured, speaking from his own experience.

"Watching your father be killed couldn't have been easy," I said ironically. As soon as I realized the irony, I felt a knot grow in my stomach.

"What about your father, Phoenix?"

"My . . . father?" I swallowed hard, trying to not make my discomfort obvious. Asier sensed the hesitation.

"You don't have to answer that."

"No, it's fine." I gathered my thoughts before explaining. "I never *really* met him. When I was young, I always wondered who he was, but the more I grew up, the less I cared. I told myself he lived far away and that we would never cross paths, but the truth was . . . a lot different." I bit my lip to avoid getting emotional.

"How so?"

"I just found out my father was the mayor of my district. The man I shot dead yesterday."

"Holy shit. I guess history does repeat itself," Asier responded. "It makes more sense why they didn't just kill you then."

"But Mayor Devrim never knew about any of this, only Secretary Devrim and I, or else he would've figured out he was my dad, which he didn't."

"That's quite the mystery then."

It was silent then, but it wasn't an awkward silence, it was comforting. I never talked about my reasoning for becoming a deviant until these past few days, and it was really a heavy weight lifted off my chest. My mind was still scrambled from all the revelations, but talking about it really helped put my thoughts in order.

"I'm sorry for assuming life has been easy on you, it's clearly been just as much of a nightmare for you as it has been for the rest of us. Also, thanks for saving us all back there, especially me." Asier had apologized and even thanked me, which came as a shock to me.

"I guess we both had the wrong impressions of each other." I responded.

"You're still a brat though," he teased. I playfully hit his head.

While still on Asier's back, I looked up at the sky and once more admired the sun. The bright ring around the eclipse refueled my hope that one day the whole sun would shine that brightly. I smiled as I began to daydream; me, mother, grandmother, and all my friends, all running around back home without shackles, and with the sun on our skin. Although I knew that dream could never become *my* reality, it could for them, and for that reason I would live-

And for that reason, I would die.

Chapter 16

When we regrouped, we briefly stopped for the leaders to discuss something, though I imagined it probably wasn't the safest idea to stay out in the open for too long. While we remained stationary, Lana attempted to bandage my wounds to the best of her abilities with the few resources we had at that moment. My uniform had definitely seen better days; it had rips throughout the thighs and biceps, along with two large holes where the arrows had pierced through. I flinched when I felt a burning sensation coming from my cheek.

"I'm sorry, darling! I should've warned you," Lana apologized.

"It's okay, it doesn't really hurt, it just caught me off guard," I insisted.

"You're so pretty, Phoenix. It's hard to believe this face could be such a dangerous and fierce opponent," Lana commented, and I felt myself blush a bit. People rarely complimented me.

"Isn't she just the cutest?" added Nyrual as he pinched my nose, and I slapped his hand in annoyance. "So, what's up with you and the commander, big girl?" Nyrual teased, shoving me slightly.

"Oh, I want to know too!" Lana exclaimed.

"Me too!" Aurora and Guido chimed in. I turned to face them, shooting them a death glare. Everyone just laughed.

"Nothing, you fools," I replied coldly to try and scare them away, though it was not successful.

"Aww, she's adapting his mannerisms and attitude too!" teased Lana, making the others laugh. I tried to hide my face with my messy hair in case the slight embarrassment translated onto my face in a red tint.

"Alright everyone, listen up!" Asier shouted from the front, and all conversation ceased. "We're going to lay our comrades to rest, so head to the pit instead of heading straight to the mansion."

Everyone quickly stood up, and with the help of Lana I followed slowly, being careful to not force my wounds again. I leaned on her as we walked, and it didn't hurt as bad as I thought it would.

"What exactly are we going to do?" Aurora asked Lana. "I don't like the sound of 'a pit.'"

"For the bodies we were able to retain, we're going to cremate them in our usual ceremony," she explained vaguely, making us both widen our eyes. I know me and Aurora both thought the same thing.

I hadn't even thought about how many times they've watched their comrades leave, just to never see them again, not even their dead bodies. On top of that, they lacked the luxury of burying them, and had no other choice than to cremate them. It had been a big battle too, and we lost over half the hundred-man army that followed us. I know that the wagon was not all of them, as we surely weren't able to retain all the bodies.

We were finally back inside the gates of the ghost town, and now that I knew what this town meant for me, I couldn't look at it the same. I recalled the brief visions I saw of this town, and how beautiful it looked when it was engulfed in flames. We walked to what appeared to be a giant pit with large logs on the bottom and gallons of gasoline scattered around the rim. I turned around and watched people unload the bodies of their comrades, stuffed inside black bags.

"How many were we able to salvage?" asked Asier, still seemingly nonchalant.

"I believe twenty," answered Fremont.

It was almost hard to believe how composed and collected everyone was. I had witnessed many deaths in my day, and none had ever touched me, but that was because those people never meant anything to me. These people, however, were friends, allies, comrades, even family to each other, so their reactions surprised me. There was definitely a mournful attitude, but no one was even crying, which was much different to most reactions I've seen.

As I contemplated, I was handed a small piece of blank paper and a pen. I accepted it with a clueless expression on my face, making the woman who handed it to me chuckle.

"We write a promise on these sheets of paper, and when the fire is lit, we throw them in," she explained briefly after noting my confusion.

"A promise?" asked Guido, who I hadn't noticed was listening.

"Yes, a promise or a wish related to our overall battle."

I looked down at the small paper, and my mind immediately went to the vow I made, then I knew exactly what to write. I put the pen to the paper and wrote each word with my heart at the end of the black pen. Once I finished, I passed the pen to the next person and delicately folded my small paper. Everyone crowded around the pit, and I stood right in the front.

Once all the bodies were lowered in, they began to pour gasoline all over the corpses and into the pit itself. Following that, there were people holding torches the entire time to light our surroundings, but now it was time to throw them in, instantly igniting everything in the pit. The fire spread faster than I could even blink, and it glowed so beautifully. Such a destructive element- one of nature's most dangerous, yet beautiful gifts. This fire felt different though; it wasn't destructive; if anything, it felt like *creation*.

"Time for the slips," announced Asier, and we all threw in our vows and wishes.

I held onto mine for the longest and was one of the last few to throw their slip in. Everyone began to cheer once they were all in. Unlike any funeral I've ever seen, this one was full of life, not death.

I reread my promise in my head as I watched the paper blacken and shrivel against the flames.

I promise your deaths won't be in vain. You too will rise from the ashes and live out your glory.

I looked to the opposite side of the pit and saw Asier, his face perfectly lit by the bright fire he stood before, and as per usual, he looked deep in his zone. His feet were grounded, but his head was up in the clouds. Once the cheering concluded, everyone around me put their fists to their hearts, and threw the other in the air with their faces still glued to the flames; a hope in them burned brighter than the fire in front of us. Their comrades' deaths had been swallowed up by *life*.

I walked around the crowd and made my way toward Asier. I guess he sensed me coming closer because he looked my way. He glanced at me then turned his attention back to the fire, the warm light extenuating his facial structure. Once I was next to him, I too turned my eyes back to the fire. I had so much I wanted to say, but simultaneously, nothing to say.

"What did you promise?" I asked to initiate conversation.

"The same promise I always make."

"Which is?"

"I promise my comrades their deaths will not be in vain," he elaborated, and my eyes widened at the realization that our promise was virtually the same.

"It's a really nice way of honoring your comrades, but isn't this hard for you guys? Doesn't it make you feel sad?" I asked in regard to the lack of grief.

"There's no use crying about it, because like I said before, we can't waste our time on tragedies. If we die, we will rise from our ashes and live out our glory." He brought his gaze back to me and explained. "We can't let our spirits be burned out by death, you just have to keep pushing forward without ever looking back."

He turned back to the pit and closed his eyes. I looked around and felt a deep respect for every person my eyes landed on. They all knew that they could easily end up in that pit one day, but they didn't let that stop them. Like Asier said, they kept fighting without looking back, and I knew it had to be hard- living in the shadows, and constantly fighting to stay alive.

"Do you ever miss it? I asked, catching his attention. "Do you miss not having to constantly fight and hide to stay alive?"

He sighed at the question, and his eyes traveled up to the dark sky. "All we can do is hope we don't ever regret making the choice to fight for our freedom."

"Even at the cost of your life?" I asked while staring directly at him. He turned back, and his piercing eyes latched onto mine.

"If something costs you your freedom, then it's already too expensive."

I looked into the fire and let his words sink in. He might be young, but his life experience and knowledge were profound. The feelings of disdain I harbored from our first few interactions have completely vanished and have all been replaced with respect. I just hope he feels the same about me.

"You see, no one ever really knows the outcome of this war any more than any other battle we've fought. We can choose to believe in The Prophecy, or we can choose to believe in ourselves, but no matter which one we chose, we must remember that our destiny is ours for the taking," he said as he glared into my eyes.

It took me a second to figure out why he was telling me this, but then I remembered what The Prophecy promised. It assured victory, but at the expense of my life. *Was this his way of encouraging me with hope of the possibility of my survival?* I wondered, then smiled at his gesture, but I'd let him know it was not needed.

"I'm not afraid of death, Asier. If it means saving the rest of the world, and ensuring that the sun will shine again, then I'm not afraid to die," I assured him before looking back up at the eclipsed sun, which was starting to set.

"You're growing up, brat," he teased and shot me a brief smile.

He reached for something in his pocket and handed it to me. I looked down at the palm of his calloused hand and saw a thin, gold bracelet with small pinkish-orange stones engraved throughout the delicate chain. It looked somewhat familiar, but I couldn't pinpoint where I exactly recognized it from.

"It's the bracelet Nila always wore. We weren't able to salvage her body, but we managed to retrieve this from her as a memento," he explained, and my heart seemed to skip a beat. As much as I wanted to take it, it felt selfish to do so.

"I can't . . . it's too much," I refused immediately. "Someone like you should keep it, I know you guys were a lot closer."

Asier rolled his eyes, placed it in my palm, and closed my hand. "It's a sunstone- it represents personal power and freedom. I know she would've wanted you to keep it," he insisted. I looked him in the eyes as he handed it to me, and for just a brief second, I saw a glimpse of all the pain and countless tears he's been holding back.

"Thank you," I uttered quietly. I held it in my hand and closed my eyes, and there I saw her soft, reassuring smile one last time.

A couple hours had passed since the fire, and we were all back inside the mansion. I changed into loose clothing to allow my bandaged wounds to breathe while my uniform was being stitched up. We were in the cellar again, eating dinner as a group. We sat on the ground in a small circle that consisted of three of the leaders, Aurora, Guido, Nyrual, and Lana. Asier was doing paperwork in his room, so he wasn't with us.

The hospitality of this place still amazed me. Everyone talked and smiled as they ate, which was so different to life back home, where everyone was always so *gray*. Lana and the leaders had quickly become good friends of ours. Those four along with Asier and The White Raven were all early members of Rebellium and had basically become a family.

I thought back to my own family. My mother and my grandmother were all I had. After that vision I had in the cage, I contemplated my relationship with the two of them. I realized Astrid was right, I had gotten so good at blocking out the memories that made me feel any sort of way to the point where I had practically forgotten the majority of my life. The bitter truth was, they always tried their best for me, and I was the one who blocked them out- even from my own memory.

The daffodils in my mother's garden, the house over the hill, the sound of the Bardman's guitar- District Four, that was my home. I wondered how the town was doing tonight; hopefully they were no longer on fire. Whatever was going on over there right now, I just hoped they slept well tonight. *Close your eyes tonight, but don't dream too deep; I don't want you to see me in your sleep.*

"Phoenix!" Aurora's voice snapped me out of my thoughts and brought me back to the present. "I've said your name like five times already! What's on your mind?" she asked.

"Home," I responded bluntly. Her face fell briefly before curving into a smile.

"You wonder how they're doing too?" she asked and I nodded. Guido and Nyrual looked down.

"I miss my dad too," she said while placing her hand in mine, "we all miss what we left behind."

"I wonder about my mother too. I hope she's feeling okay right now," added Nyrual. His mother had been ill for a while, and he was the one who cared for her.

"Yeah, I think about my girls too. I hope they are doing alright," Guido added. I felt tears threaten to well up, but I fought them off successfully.

"I haven't found the right moment to tell you this yet, but thank you for leaving everything behind to follow me, for which I'll be eternally grateful. I promise you'll be able to hug them again soon, under the warmth of the sun this time." I had a thousand words on my tongue, but this was the best I could say.

They all stood up and we fell into a group embrace. The warmth from the hug was not only external, but internal. I thought back to the list of things that defined home to me, and scrapped what I said previously; District Four wasn't my home, home was in every person I loved. *Aurora, Nyrual, and Guido were my home.*

"You know, sometimes I miss my parents too. I always wonder where they are now that it's been eight whole years," said Lana.

"My parents were killed eight years ago, so I can't completely relate to you guys on this one," Khalon added, fixing his curly hair, "but for that, I fight to avenge them every single day."

"It's been ten years, but I still hold my parents and my siblings near and dear to my heart. I just hope they'll hold on till the end of this battle with me," Daxon said quietly.

"I'll always hold onto the hope that I'll hug my mom and grandpa again," Fremont said, finishing the chain

It was comforting to know others could relate with me for once, and that we were all in the same boat. It warmed my heart to know they also did it and continued to do it for the ones they loved. An odd rush of relief brushed over me as they shared that vulnerability with me, and it felt good to know they were beginning to trust me.

"I'm sure Asier misses his mom too. He can act tough, but he's a real softie," added Daxon as if he'd read my mind. I was just thinking, *If only Asier were here, I'd love to know more about him as well.*

"Why do you think he liked Val so much? She cured his mommy issues-" Khalon was cut off by Lana, Daxon, and Fremont covering his mouth.

"Was Valerie someone he loved?" I asked, and everyone paused and looked at me, perplexed by my straightforward question.

"I guess one could say that," Lana responded as she scratched her head awkwardly.

"I can tell she was important to him," I concluded. Everyone just stared at me, dumbfounded by my boldness. "But it's also apparent he's not the only one hurt by her betrayal." Everyone nodded.

"We really cared for her, so when she did that to us, it was like a kick right to the teeth," Lana answered.

"Especially Asier. Man, he was gutted when he saw her leading the squad that captured us," Khalon added, and Lana gave him the death glare. "He's honestly still not over it. I swear every time we bring her up it's like Hell unleashes on his face. They do say a dog never forgets his first owner-" Khalon was cut off again by Daxon hitting his head.

"Do you ever think before you speak, man?" Daxon scolded. Guido and Nyrual visibly fought to contain their laughter.

My hunch was correct this entire time- she was someone truly important to him, and that's why he hesitated to kill her- making her the only person I've seen Asier hold back on before going in for the kill. His words, *"Love can turn into hate,"* were certainly from experience, when his love for her forcefully morphed into disdain. The situation sounded awfully familiar, and that's when I began connecting dots. Lanon and Astrid- Valerie and Asier. *I'd keep that similarity in mind.*

"It's like The Crow and The Phoenix. Two people in love, forced to fight each other," I said abruptly, mostly just speaking out loud at this point. Once again, everyone just stared at me and my commentary.

"Maybe?" Lana responded unsurely.

"Never mind, just forget it. Sorry for the random questions," I apologized, just now realizing how awkward it was getting.

"Looks like we have a love expert over here," teased Nyrual.

I watched everyone giggle, and as embarrassing as it was, I wouldn't trade it for anything. Although my pride ripped me to shreds, I had to learn the value of just living with it. Sometimes what was left unsaid was a greater response. Either way, my mind was so serene as I watched the smiling faces of my friends, both the old and the new.

Later that night before going to bed, I stumbled into a group of people crowding around something. My curiosity wouldn't let me just walk past it, so I tried to peer through everyone to see what had caught their attention. In the center was a small television, and it seemed to be on the news channel, then I remembered it was time for The Crow's scheduled nightly speech. The camera was panning over the desolated and ravaged capital that once shone brighter than the sun itself.

The leveled city with the blacked-out sun in the background really showcased how far gone from the light this world had become. It was a chilling sight, but it wasn't nearly as impactful as witnessing it firsthand. Most of the fire had been extinguished, and you could see the charred bodies and feathers that scattered the streets a lot more clearly. It's insane to think how desensitized we've all become to death and the gruesome visuals that accompanied war, so much that a sight like that would not make even a child flinch.

The camera angle switched over to The Crow, but instead of being in his usual, lavish office, he was standing on a pile of ruins clearly trying to make a statement. There was a look in his eyes that reminded me of a snake's deceitful glare.

"The rebels have truly crossed the line today. They demolished the heart of this nation, destroying laboratories, government buildings, homes, and killing hundreds of innocent citizens and important workers in this country. If you even had a speck of hope in these barbaric bastards being the *'hope for humanity'* they claim they are, maybe this will change your mind." He paused, menacingly, then continued. "I've seen the rate of deviancy gravely increasing this weekend, and all I can say is this; beware of false prophets that come to you in sheep's clothing. *Nothing* is ever as good as it seems," he warned in a threatening voice that never failed to chill me to the bone.

"All the rebels will be rounded up in the lovely District Four since it's the closest to The Capital and will be dealt with *accordingly*. Every single one will be eradicated by the end of August; the plague of rebellion will be wiped out once and for all," he announced, and I remembered seeing this information on the posters in The Capital. "So, before you think of deviating, remember the consequences that come with defying our laws . . ." he said before reaching down to grab something from the ground.

He picked up a middle-aged man with gray hair and a horrified look on his face. His wrists were tied, and The Crow picked him up by the hair effortlessly. He pulled out a handgun from his belt and aimed it at the man's head. The man pleaded and whimpered, but The Crow didn't even flinch, or care to pay him any mind. Without a second's pause, he pulled the trigger with no hesitation, and no reaction.

Everyone around me looked away, but I idiotically kept my eyes on the screen. Blood splattered all over the rubble behind them, and a bit even got on The Crow's face and eyepatch which he replaced from the one I ripped off. He threw the dead man on the ground as if his body were a piece of cloth, and casually dusted himself off. He wiped his cheek with sleeve, never once breaking eye contact with the camera, and began to undo his eyepatch.

". . . And let this serve you as a reminder . . . *of who's in control*," he finished, fostering a foreboding atmosphere, and debuting his grim crow eye on national television.

The TV momentarily went static before returning to the usual news broadcast. For years now, I've been the person behind the trigger, but seeing someone else do it for a change was a completely different experience. I've seen a fair share of killing in my time, but his lack of reaction that accompanied the shot made me feel sick. Never before have I seen someone appear so human, yet simultaneously lack every single speck of their humanity. Now I realized what we were up against- the physical embodiment of malevolence. We were no longer up against a human being-

We were up against a monster.

Chapter 17

August 4th- the day everything broke out was now but a haunting memory. Today was August 16th, and twelve uneventful and concerningly peaceful days had passed since then. For us, the days were filled with training, strategizing, and learning. The entirety of Rebellium was preparing, some for battle, some for sideline tasks like nursing. The energy was just as contagious as when we first arrived, and hope still filled every corner of the mansion, even after losing so much. In these twelve days, I got to know everyone better, and they began to trust in me as not only their Prophet, but also their comrade.

One person in particular I got to connect with more personally was the commander himself. Me being The Prophet and him the lead commander, we spent a great deal of time together with the rest group carefully strategizing our next move. He was still quite the enigma, but I could feel a small bond forming between us. It was a bond I had never felt before, one that could seemingly break through both our stubborn shells. He was still particularly aloof and distant, but at least now I was confident that he no longer hated me, and that was good enough for me.

It was the break of dawn, and I could already hear everyone up and running. I rubbed my eyes and did a quick scan of the room, and to my great surprise, there were no signs of Aurora, Nyrual, or Guido, who all usually slept in here with me. I rubbed my eyes again and took a closer look, but there was definitely no one around. It was unusual for all of them to be up and gone, since we generally all got up at the same time and spent most of our day together.

I got up to look around the mansion for them, but after checking all the places they would typically be in, I came to the conclusion that they were not here. I frowned at the idea of them leaving me behind without even informing me of their whereabouts, especially since we were all hot targets right now. My initial instinct was to panic, as most people would given our circumstances, but I tried my best to remain calm. I had a history of overreacting when I wasn't certain of where something or someone was, and that clearly didn't turn out so well last time. Instead of searching underneath rocks and scanning the entire surface of the earth, I decided on something much more simple- to just go back to sleep.

Without them I couldn't do much, and I knew if I stayed awake I'd just end up running around to search for them. I assumed if they were in any sort of danger, the rest of Rebellium would not be this calm. I walked inside an empty room with a small window, and a comfortable plush chair against the wall. I sat down and closed my eyes as the faint glow of the dawning sky crept in. *They wouldn't leave me . . . right?* I reassured myself as I drifted back to sleep for just a little while longer.

Pink petals fell around me from a cherry tree I found myself sleeping under, and they tickled my cheeks as they landed on my face. Light beamed down through the branches, and my eyes squinted from the intense brightness as I tried to fully open them. The grass beneath me was bright green, and the air felt warm- but not hot. While I laid, my head rested on somebody's lap as they stroked and played with my wavy hair.

I looked up, and the woman stroking my head was no other than my dear mother. Her long, glossy hair fell to the side as she looked down at me. She had such a look of serenity on her face, like there wasn't a worry in the world for either of us. I was certainly dreaming.

"May there always be light to guide you each step of the way," she said softly into my ear as she caressed my head, "and may the fire keep you safe from all harm."

Her dark hair swayed as a warm gust of wind blew right through us. I didn't want this dream to end, but I knew all too well it had to, so I cherished each imaginary second that passed in this rose-colored dream. I gazed into her emerald eyes, which looked so drained. They've seen a lot, and she's suffered a lot, *but it'll all be over soon, Momma.* I continued to stare into her captivating eyes, never once breaking contact as the dream faded and burned like a melting film.

I gasped as I awoke, forcefully brought back to reality. Ironically, reality had become stranger than my dreams. I woke up uncomfortably positioned on the chair, leaning against one of the arms. *How long had I dozed off for?* I wondered as I looked out the window, though I wasn't quite sure what I was looking for; the sky didn't indicate time very well.

My back was sore, and my arms were asleep, so I stretched before standing up completely. As I stretched my arms, something on my back slid down. I turned around and there was a blanket, which had a vaguely familiar scent on it. *I didn't grab a blanket before falling asleep,* I thought as I scanned the still, empty room. I stood up and folded the mysterious blanket, neatly placing it on the chair in case that person returned to retrieve it.

There was a lot more noise compared to the last time I was awake; *figures, it was noon after all.* I headed toward the training area outside hoping to get some fresh air. I stepped out the door and immediately got slapped by the bitter cold; it must've been around forty degrees; *maybe I should've kept that blanket.* Everyone outside was either sparring with each other, or working to improve their aim with firearms.

As I looked around, I saw a familiar face- Daxon. He was usually present during the training since he was the second in command. He was the only person I had seen all day that I was actually close with. As I approached him, he turned and smiled at me.

220

"Good afternoon, Phoenix," he greeted.

"Hey, you wouldn't happen to know where everyone went?" I asked, hoping they at least told someone here where they had gone.

"I believe they ventured to District Six this morning for supplies since we we're running low. I stayed behind in case of an attack, that's why they left you behind as well," he explained. It made perfect sense, but I felt somewhat upset that they hadn't explained that to me directly, especially since sneaking in and out of a District was such an incredibly risky move.

"So, they didn't feel the need to inform me of such a risky and last-minute mission?" I asked, not concealing the annoyance in my voice very well.

"We've been doing this for years, so it's not that serious to us anymore," he clarified. "They'll be back soon- especially since they have your friends accompanying them this time. Just spar with me until they're unoccupied."

The whole situation sounded strange to me; *why didn't they tell me at the very least?* I wondered. Instead of poking more at the subject and getting nowhere, I just nodded at Daxon and agreed to spar; he was being kind enough to explain, plus, it's not like it was his fault. I got myself in a sparring position with my fists close to my face and he did the same. Daxon was actually quite brawny and skilled at hand-to-hand combat; unlike most people I sparred with here, I actually had to keep my guard up and push myself a lot more with him.

He threw the first punch, and I dodged it effortlessly. I dodged a few more swings and I saw sweat drip down on his dark skin, which made me feel confident. We swung and dodged for quite a while until I caught one of his punches with my fist; after that we took a break, which I definitely needed after that match.

"Damn, little lady, here I was thinking I'd have to go easy on you." He praised me with a fist bump, making me grin a little.

"Well, you're no easy opponent either," I commended while catching my breath.

"What do they teach y'all over in District Four- goddamn!" Daxon added, making me and a spectator chuckle.

"Good thing she's on our side now," the spectator added, making people around us chuckle.

Each day I felt more and more comfortable living with the rebels, so much more than I ever had back home. Although living in constant hiding to stay alive was not preferable, it didn't feel much different than living in the districts. Here in Rebellium, happiness was genuine and stemmed from genuine hope, not like the false sense of fulfillment that the people back home constantly gloated over. Back home, they prayed to stay alive, not realizing how dead they already were.

My attention was fully caught when I saw a giant bug charging toward me; unfortunately for me, I had an irrational phobia of even the most harmless insects. I panicked as it got closer, and I instinctively shut my eyes and held my hands over my face. I heard a quiet sizzle, and slowly opened my eyes, lowering my hands too. I heard chuckles from all around me as small ashes sprinkled onto the ground.

"I forgot I could do that," I said while rubbing my neck, mildly embarrassed of my childish fears.

"Well at least you know the fire still has your back in moments of great danger," Daxon jested. Everyone laughed, including me; *who knew smiling could be so easy?* "Anyways, you ready for round two, Phoenix?" asked Daxon, this time getting in position for sword fighting. I nodded and pulled out my sword.

"Actually Daxon, I'll take it from here," came a deep voice from behind me. *Oh boy.*

I turned around and saw Asier, who was also holding a sword. He wasn't wearing his usual white tank and black jacket, instead he wore a loose, long-sleeved, black V-neck, tight, black pants, and still had his black cape over his shoulders. I was surprised to see him here, since everyone was gone.

"Don't you have better things to do?" I asked, purposely sounding petty.

"I think training is pretty important," he answered as he removed his cape and threw it to the side.

Everyone around us dropped everything they were doing to watch the show we were about to put on. They were all intrigued to see the victor between their commander- their strongest soldier, and their Prophet, previously known as the strongest Hunter. I had never fought or really even sparred with Asier, so I wasn't sure what to expect. All I knew for sure was that he was easily going to be the strongest *human* opponent I've ever faced.

"All you," Daxon said with his hands up, moving away for Asier to take his spot. He flashed me a quick wink as he backed away.

"Give me your best, brat," Asier said as he stared me down.

I wasn't quite sure how to approach him, but I knew for sure I wasn't going to hold back, because I knew he certainly wasn't going to either. I gripped the handle of my sword, and went for the first swing, which he blocked with ease. He immediately swung back, which I quickly blocked, and we repeated that pattern for what felt like forever. I knew he was strong, but man was he not giving me a chance to breathe.

Along with his great agility, dodging his swings was difficult because he didn't have a specific pattern, it was completely spontaneous. He did however have a style, and I caught on fast. He often defaulted to a spin-swing, which carried a lot of force and momentum. In real battles it was tremendously effective, but when it was against only one person that you weren't even actually trying to kill, it was too strenuous, and he would tire quickly.

As each second went by, it got much harder and harder. His attacks were hard to block on their own, and with added fatigue, it wasn't looking so hot for me. I noticed his breathing was getting much heavier as well, and that brought me some sort of reassurance. His attacks, however, were not subsiding like I imagined they would by this point, and I began to wonder if this man was actually trying to kill me.

Right as I had that thought, I felt my sword slip right out of my hand; Asier had successfully swung my weapon out of my grip. It landed not too far from me, but in Hunter training I was taught that it was dangerous to go after your weapon, and that apprehending them was more effective, especially if your opponent was close in distance. I assumed maybe Asier would go easier on me since I had no weapon, but I was quite wrong to assume. He swung at me as if I were still fully armed and I ducked as fast as I could. *Yep, he's definitely trying to kill me.*

Asier was at least a whole foot taller than me and therefore would not be easy to apprehend, but I *always* knew a way. While in a ducking position, I charged at Asier from below and threw myself onto him. I knew it probably wouldn't knock him down since he was bigger than me, but that wasn't my intention. He flipped me around and wrapped his arm around me, restricting my own arm movement. He held his sword up to my face and in his and everyone's eyes I was defeated, *but not for long.*

I managed to free my arms enough to wrap them around his, then I proceeded to jump up as high as I could under his restraint. I dropped all my weight down in that jump, which threw off his balance. I gripped his arm tightly and bent over, pulling his arm with all my force. I used all my strength to lift him off the ground and toss him onto the ground over my shoulder, though I only managed to throw him aside rather than completely over me. He rolled over and landed face up, and I quickly put my foot on his chest, pinning him down.

I grabbed my sword from the ground and held it up to his eyes, shoving my victory in his face. Everyone clapped and whistled as I smiled, while sweating and panting like a dog. I took my foot off his chest and put my sword back into its scabbard. He shot me a grin as he sat up, not seemingly bothered by his defeat.

"Aren't you supposed to go easy on me since I'm just a little girl?" I teased.

"That move was a little reckless, don't you think?" Asier teased back.

"In a real situation, I would never surrender," I refuted, making Asier grin and shake his head.

He stood up and put his sword back in his sheath. He picked up his cape from the ground and threw it over his shoulder. He gave me one last look before walking back inside. The look he shot me was full of praise, and it made me feel proud, accomplished, and oddly fuzzy inside. *Did he really only come out just to test my combat skills?*

"Uh, are you okay, Phoenix?" Daxon asked and waved his hand in my face.

I blinked repeatedly. "Sorry, I must've zoned out."

"You know, you're the first person to ever beat him in combat," whispered Daxon from behind me.

I raised an eyebrow. "Damn, I must be pretty strong then."

"Yup, you sure know how to humble a commander," Daxon said, referring to himself and Asier. I giggled a bit.

"If he's back I assume everyone else is too, so I'm gonna go find the others. I'll see you around." I dismissed myself, and Daxon nodded and waved.

I headed back into the building and decided to have a quick rinse before looking for everyone, since I was now sweaty and dirty. I wasn't sure how, but Rebellium somehow managed to keep water running in this place. The cool thing about this building was also the fact that it had showers, not just tubs of water like most places. It was pretty standard for more luxurious homes, but for many people, showers were rare to have in their homes.

As I stood under the running water, I looked down at my arms, which had red marks wrapping around my biceps and a distinguishable scar from the original stab wound on my forearm. The strange mark that was previously there was now covered by the healing scar. My other wounds had also healed considerably; they weren't completely healed, but they healed a lot faster than human wounds typically healed. The rapid healing was due to an injection serum one of our comrades found amongst the ruins in the capital; it's the same one The Crow uses for his superhuman healing, but in a significantly lower concentration. *Being a little superhuman sure felt good.*

When I was finally done showering, I tried to get out as quickly as possible. The worst part of bathing or showering was getting out because the freezing temperature felt ten times colder. I grabbed a towel with my shivering arm and wrapped it around myself as fast as I could. The cold air didn't really bother me anymore, but there was just something about being soaking wet that made it intolerable, even as a walking ball of fire.

Today's wardrobe was warm and comfortable; it was a loose, red sweater, and some black leggings. I put them on as quickly as possible before I began to freeze, and when I was finally dressed, I looked in the mirror on the wall and brushed through the stubborn knots in my wet hair. I'd never noticed how long it had gotten until now; it was down to my waist. I studied my face as I brushed, and for the first time I was able to distinguish which genes were my mothers, and now that I knew my father, I could distinguish which were his as well.

When I was finished, I made my way toward the kitchen, hoping I'd at least be able to see Lana and Lamie. I figured everyone was still "*busy*" since I hadn't even seen any of them. Before I could even reach the kitchen, I was stopped by someone grabbing my arm. I turned around and it was Guido. I was relieved to see they were safe, but also irritated since they had left me behind without a word.

"You should come with me," Guido insisted, sounding rushed.

"Where was my invite when you guys left this morning? And why have you been avoiding me?" I asked, audibly peeved.

"Come with me and you'll see," he replied, and without warning, he threw me over his shoulder.

"Let go!" I exclaimed as I punched his back. I could hear him giggle in response which only irritated me more.

We headed into the big main room and made our way toward the bar, which apparently seemed to double as a stage. He finally set me down on top of the bar table, and only then I noticed the large number of people in the room- probably all of Rebellium.

"What's going on?" I asked.

Guido playfully rolled his eyes and sighed. "You ask a lot of questions," he complained.

I looked around and saw The White raven sitting at a table with Lamie, and Asier stood right beside them. His arms were crossed and looking off into the distance as always. Khalon, Daxon, and Fremont were next to them too, but I couldn't seem to find Lana, Aurora, or Nyrual. As I scanned the room, my vision was suddenly blocked by a blindfold being tied around my head.

"What are you doing?" I asked whoever was blindfolding me.

"Blindfolding you, duh," answered Guido. *That damn Guido.*

I was so confused, and I couldn't draw any sort of proper conclusion. Whatever it was, it must be a big deal since almost everyone was in here, and whatever it was- it included me.

"You can look now," I heard Aurora say behind me after what felt like an eternity of me being blindfolded.

I untied the blindfold, and everyone immediately cheered- incredibly loud, I must add. I looked forward and saw Aurora, Nyrual, Guido, Lana, Asier, Khalon, Daxon, and Fremont all gathering around a table with a big cake. Confetti fell all around the room filled with dozens of smiling people.

"Happy Birthday, Phoenix!" The group cheered. *That's right, it was August 16th- my 18th birthday.*

I covered my mouth with my hands to avoid showing my embarrassing reaction. *I had forgotten my own birthday, but . . . they hadn't;* The thought made my heart feel really warm and fuzzy. I wanted to cry, but not out of sadness, but out of *joy*- something I had never felt in my entire life. Arms wrapped around me, and my face felt warmer than usual as everyone pulled me into a group hug.

227

"Thank you . . . thank you guys so much." I could barely speak with my shaky voice.

As soon as we pulled out of the hug everyone cheered again. I switched my attention to the cake, which was easily big enough to feed everyone here. I hadn't seen a cake in years, and I've never seen one this big. It had white frosting and letters that read *"Happy birthday"* on the top.

"That's why some of us "went to town" A.K.A we were stuck in the kitchen all day." Guido had finally answered my question.

"Hey, some of us actually went to town!" Nyrual clarified.

"We got you a present too!" added Aurora as she handed me a box.

I took the small box in my hands and looked at everyone's faces before opening it; it was obvious they'd been anticipating this moment all day. I undid the small ribbon and lifted the top slowly, creating more suspense for everyone. Inside was a delicate gold pendant, and in the center was the imprint of a phoenix which had been delicately engraved.

"Luckily, an undercover rebel in District six is a jewelry maker and has some mad skills, so we asked him to make this," added Aurora.

I clenched the pendant, and my eyes began to water. *Is this what genuine happiness felt like?* I thought as I fought back tears.

"I love it. This is more than I could've ever wished for," I replied, my voice still shaky.

"Well, what are we waiting for? Let's cut that beauty and celebrate!" exclaimed Daxon. Everyone cheered and people slowly began coming up to the table.

In my eighteen years of life, I celebrated my birthday with just my grandmother and mother. We couldn't really celebrate big because we couldn't afford to, but after becoming a Hunter, we had a nice dinner and a small cake whenever it was any of our birthdays. There were never really presents though, or much of a celebration, so this was more than I could've ever asked for. *This might be my last birthday, but it was most definitely the best.*

Hours had passed and it was nighttime now. Most people were still in the main room, conversing and eating, but I decided to go upstairs and get some fresh air. I clutched the pendant in my hand as it hung from my neck. I sat down on the small deck behind the mansion, hoping the view of the sky was at least better than the one from the windows inside, but it was just as obscured by rubble and chunks of the remaining wall around the district. I frowned because if I wanted a clear look at the stars, I would have to go outside the gates, but that was far too risky. I settled for the view I got from here, until I heard someone open the door.

"Running away from the party, birthday girl?" I didn't have to turn to know it was Asier. I'd recognize his voice anywhere.

"No, I just wanted to come outside for a bit."

"Are you not freezing?" he asked as he sat next to me. His breath was visible in the frosty air when he talked.

"You're just normal," I joked, gaining a small chuckle from him.

He went mute for a moment and looked reluctant. "I actually have something for you," he finally said and I turned to face him.

He reached for something beside him and handed it to me- a yellow flower I would recognize anywhere; the flower that denoted home in my heart. My mind went blank, and the same fuzzy feeling from before I felt again in my chest. The more I looked at it, the more I thought for the hundredth time today that I might cry.

"Aurora mentioned that you liked these or something. Anyways, I managed to find one in town this morning and just hoped it survived the trip- it's a daffodil I think," he explained as I took it from his hand. The gesture left me speechless, but I knew I had to at least express my gratitude.

"Thank you, Asier . . . I hope you didn't go through too much trouble for this," I responded, unable to hide that I was blushing.

"Don't worry about it," he responded in simple words as per usual.

He slouched and extended his legs in front of him, facing down at the ground with his eyes closed. *Those blue eyes.*

"You remind me of the color blue," I admitted from out of nowhere, practically thinking out loud. He looked up with a curious look on his face.

"Oh? And why is that?" he asked, raising an eyebrow.

"Blue is the color of the sky."

"Is that so?" Asier teased, and I could see his pupils dilate in response. I didn't answer straight away in an attempt to find a way to say what I wanted to say without sounding too awkward, but I decided to just say what was on my mind, no matter how dumb it sounded.

"I can see the sky in your eyes . . ." I paused briefly to look him in the eyes. "You hold the blue sky inside of you."

I watched a smile creep up from the corners of his lips before looking back down at the ground, and he wore that smile for a while. It was quiet, but I didn't mind, I just watched the stars like I always did. Watching the sky always reminded me of the considerable distance between me and the stars I watched, and it always compelled me to feel grounded to the earth. The stars made me feel like an ordinary girl, even if it was just for a little while. After minutes of silent watching, my concentration was broken when I felt Asier's eyes on me.

"You like stargazing, right?" he asked abruptly, and I nodded in response. "Follow me. Birthday present number two," he said as he stood up. He held out his hand for me, and I eagerly took it. *That was oddly sweet.*

He helped me up and I picked up my daffodil before following him. I had no clue where he was taking me, but wherever it was, it was deep into the town. He picked up the pace and began to jog, so I followed right behind him. I giggled a bit and he smirked as we jogged carelessly. After a handful of minutes of jogging, he stopped and I stopped too. We spent another minute catching our breath before he said anything.

"Cover your eyes, I'll lead you the rest of the way," he instructed in his husky voice.

I did as he asked without question and closed my eyes, also putting my hands over my eyes. He took my hands and led the way, and my face involuntarily warmed up from that small, stupid gesture. He walked slowly to avoid us tripping on something, because there were plenty of things to trip on around here. While we walked, I also noticed Asier's hands were rough and calloused, but also incredibly warm- *just like him.*

"There're some steps here, so watch your step," he warned, and I cautiously continued up each step.

After what felt like a million steps, we stopped, and he lowered my hand. "We're here, you can look now," I heard him say.

We were on top of a wide, grass hill which had marble stairs built in that led up to the top. Judging from the amount of effort put into this structure and the large pile of ashes, I assumed this was once the town's designated prayer spot and Crow shrine. It was incredibly dark, but the mansion was the only building here with light, and you could see the dim glow through the windows from this height; I knew it wasn't too far considering how small the town was, and the short distance we'd trotted. This hill was leaning against the wall and was almost exactly the same height, so we could literally climb onto the gate wall.

"Besides the mansion and the stables, there's no light around here, and in this direction, there aren't any Districts or pollution to obscure the skyline," explained Asier, "but the real view is after we climb over this," he added, and I felt my excitement grow.

We exchanged smiles before gripping onto the wall like bugs and racing to the top. The walls were roughly ten feet wide so there was plenty of room to walk up there. I closed my eyes right before reaching the top and opened them as soon as I was on the wall. I'd opened my eyes, but nothing could prepare me for what they were about to see.

The biggest smile crept on my face, and I could barely contain my excitement. I was standing underneath possibly the most beautiful and unobstructed view of the stars in the entire country. Millions- no, *billions* of stars decorated the black sheet above us, and I gawked at it in absolute awe. The milky way tore through the darkness of the night, and it was absolutely stunning. If I hadn't felt the ground at my feet, I would be convinced we were somewhere in the sky.

"You like it? It's the clearest view of the night sky around here," stated Asier, and I turned to him, smiling like an idiot.

"This is unbelievable, I love it!" I exclaimed like a total child, but he grinned at my excitement.

As I looked up, I could feel Asier's gaze on me again; *there were a million stars in front of us tonight, so why would he look at me?* I slowly turned my head to face him, and I managed to catch a glimpse of his face before he looked away and up toward the sky. In that brief moment, I saw a smile on his face, and it wasn't just a smirk or a grin, it was a *genuine smile.* There was a look in his eyes that made me feel some type of way. *Is this what people meant . . . when they said they felt their heart skip a beat?*

"So many fireflies," he muttered, and I tilted my head in confusion. "Oh . . . that's what my mother used to call them," he explained bashfully. "When you're a kid, you'll believe anything adults tell you; like when they say the stars are just millions of fireflies." There was a smile on his face, but sorrow in his voice.

"Do you ever miss her?" I asked, hoping I wasn't pushing the limits.

"If there's anything in this world I'll allow myself to miss, it's her. Every man's first love is their mother," he replied with a melancholic gleam in his eyes. He always tried to hide the pain behind his cold, stern disposition, but right now, I felt like I was finally peeking behind the curtains.

"She chose conformity, and you were left with no choice but to run alone, so now you unknowingly hold a grudge," I prefaced, "but even with that grudge, in the deepest depths of your heart, you still

232

miss her arms around you." I chose my words carefully so this description could also apply to someone *other* than his mother.

"My mother wanted what was best for me, not for the world, and in a sense, that's what your mother wanted too," he responded, pausing briefly before continuing. "She didn't want you to carry the weight of the truth on your shoulders, and she's a good mother for that."

"She's been selling the idea of rebellion my whole life through those daffodils," I explained while looking at the fireflies in the sky. "I didn't realize how much I had forgotten; she once told me those daffodils and I were the same, because we both stood for rebirth," I said as I twirled the daffodil between my fingers.

"What a coincidence," he said, then chuckled.

"I just wanna hug her one more time before I go," I mumbled, failing to hide the hurt through my voice.

"You will. I promise," Asier replied softly while still keeping his eyes locked on me. I was seeing a new side of Asier, and I liked it- a lot.

We sat under the starry night for a while yet, both mesmerized by the universe's art. It felt good knowing we related to each other in more ways than we imagined, and that we could be vulnerable with each other in this lonely world. Every once in a while, I would sneak a glance at Asier, and I could tell he was thinking about something like always, but this time, there seemed to be a sense of peace in his face.

As I fiddled with the daffodil he gave me, a feeling I hadn't felt before crept in. I looked at him again, and this time it was me who thought, *there were a million stars in the sky tonight, yet I could look at you all night.* It felt similar to unease and anxiety- like that feeling of butterflies fluttering inside me. I shook my head and pushed that thought away. *Stop it, Phoenix.*

After a while, we jumped off the wall and landed back on the grass. I sat down upon landing and Asier followed. The cold outside didn't bother me too much since it wasn't significantly colder than the mansion. The only difference was the wind, which usually made a huge difference, but tonight, the winds were subdued. I laid down and closed my eyes for a second, and it wasn't until now that I realized how tired I actually was. I knew if I kept my eyes closed, I would probably sleep right here, so I sat up and decided it's better if we headed back.

Before I could even say anything, I felt an arm wrap around me and pull me back to the ground. It remained that way, which meant Asier was essentially cuddling me. I was so glad it was pitch black outside, because my face was probably about as red as a tomato.

"W-what are you doing?" I asked, trying my best to keep my composure. I could feel him breathing against my neck, covering me in goosebumps.

"It's freezing out here and the body temperature of a phoenix is just so warm," he teased. I turned around to face him, and his arm was still loosely around me.

"Well, aren't you full of jokes?" I responded in an irritated voice. "Let's go back inside so you're not so cold then."

"I have crippling insomnia and for once I'm actually falling asleep. I cannot let this opportunity pass," he mumbled.

His eyes were closed as he spoke and held me, and what made this even stranger, was that his tone and expression were both as indifferent as always. I didn't notice how hard I had been staring at him until he opened his eyes, but I didn't turn away. There was something in his stare that felt different, and I didn't know what it was, but it wasn't there before. It felt really unusual being this close to anyone; I had definitely never been this close to anyone's face, and Asier was the last person I imagined myself in this situation with. We searched each other's eyes for a few seconds before he closed them again and pulled his arm back.

"Goodnight, brat," he said as he rolled over and turned the other way.

I grunted as a reply to his comment. I was trying to make the impression that I was relieved he'd let go, but deep down, *I didn't want him to.* I shook that weird thought away and I sat up. His body was turned away from me, but I could tell he wasn't asleep yet. *If he planned on sleeping here regardless, why did it matter if I stayed or not?*

"Why do you want me to stay?" I asked. It was silent for so long, I began to believe he'd actually fallen asleep.

"You reminded me of some people . . . who used to help me fall asleep," is all he said, and with that simple sentence, I felt my heart sink a little.

I had a feeling I knew who he was talking about, and for some reason, it hurt a little to hear. I knew one of the people had to be his mother, but the other could only be one person; his heart belonged to her after all, *and it would never belong to anyone but her,* I thought as I looked at him. *What was wrong with me?* I wanted to punch myself for thinking these strange thoughts. I had no business feeling this way for anyone- especially not Asier.

I gathered some sticks and wooden planks in the area and started a small fire. We'd inevitably be cold, but this should be enough to scare the frost away. I laid back down after starting the fire, because I couldn't bring myself to leave him here alone, and he didn't seem like he was going to walk back tonight.

I turned to my side and saw the daffodil Asier gave me; it always surprised me how some flowers could still bloom and survive in this cold, barren world. I held it close to me along with my pendant as I dozed off beneath a blanket of a million stars.

Chapter 18

I opened my eyes randomly in the middle of the night and found myself all alone. With the moon being the only light source, I tried to adjust my eyes to the darkness before sitting up. The fire had been put out, and Asier was gone with no trace. *Had he gone back to the mansion and left me behind?* My heart sank a bit, and I felt a tinge of anger at the thought of that possibility.

Whatever the reason was, I deemed it as unimportant, because I had to go back regardless. I pushed my body to get up, except . . . *I couldn't*; I tried to move my arms, then my legs, but I had no luck- like I was paralyzed. I was stranded out in the open, alone and unable to move; *of course this would happen to me.* To prevent myself from panicking, I tried to keep my breathing under control, and focused solely on moving each muscle one by one. After a while, I managed to wiggle my fingers and eventually make a full fist, then I did the same with my feet.

I felt something poking the side of my neck, and then the dots connected. I pushed every muscle in my arm to remove the tranquilizing arrow planted in my neck, which continued to pump the sedative into my bloodstream. I was sweating from how much I was forcing my body along with the anxiety of it all, but I continued to push for what felt like hours. I finally lifted my arm enough to draw the thin dart out, and I immediately felt a rush of relief flow throughout my body, and it gradually became easier to move.

I dragged myself to the stairs at first, but I eventually transitioned into crawling. I went down the stairs one by one whilst still sitting down, which I knew would take forever, so I stood up and to my surprise, was somewhat able to stand on my weak legs. I leaned against a railing that felt like it would break at any moment, and searched for the mansion through the darkness, but rather than finding the mansion, I spotted a warm light accompanied by the smell of smoke in the distance; something was definitely on fire. Did *The Crow or his army find us?* I panicked.

Between being tranquilized, and seeing something burning in the distance, I knew we were in for some big trouble. Right as I was about to rush down the remainder of the steps, I remembered that I'd left behind my daffodil. It was ridiculous and I knew it, but regardless, I went back to grab it and hid it under my shirt. The adrenaline and panic must've helped me regain my strength, because I reached the bottom in no time.

I made a small fire in the palm of my hand to light my surroundings, and I turned around to unexpectedly see a Crow soldier hiding in the shadows. My heart dropped to my stomach from the jump scare, and that's also when I had the unfortunate realization that I didn't have my gear or any weapons on me. The soldier recklessly charged at me with a blade, but I was able to dodge it. I roundhouse-kicked him in the face, then set the bunch of feathers on fire with a punch. He quickly disintegrated and dropped his sword, which I didn't hesitate to take for myself.

The fire was a lot closer than I'd imagined, but it felt like a further walk since I was still trying to overcome the sedative's effect. There was a plain field of grass that led to a large stage identical to the one in District Four, and I took a closer look and saw Asier on one end of the worn-down stage, although his usual apathetic expression was replaced by *agony*. I couldn't see any visible wounds, so I assumed something he saw must've perturbed him to such an extent.

"Asier!" I shouted as I got closer, using the sword as a cane.

Once I climbed up the stairs and was only a few steps away from Asier, I quickly realized we were not alone. Someone walked up the stairs behind me and joined us up on top. I turned around to an absolutely stunning woman; she had slick, black, shoulder-length hair which framed her face like a perfect curtain, and deep, almost violet-colored eyes. She wore a uniform like mine; a tight, black, long-sleeve jumpsuit with a gold Crow pin, meaning she was part of The Crow's main army. She loaded her handgun and aimed it straight at Asier's head, and that's when it hit me that she looked *awfully familiar*.

She averted her attention toward me, and a puzzled look formed on her face, which quickly turned hostile. She aimed her gun at me and looked me dead in the eyes, like we were having the most high-stakes staring contest. The blood inside me turned ice cold as soon the grim realization hit me; *this was Nila and Markus's murderer, and the woman who tried to blow me and Asier up.*

"Phoenix!" Asier yelled before dashing towards me. There was the ripping sound of a gunshot, but the flood of emotions immobilized me - fear, grief, and potent *loathing*.

No pain followed up the gunshot; instead, I felt my body get pulled then thrown like a ragdoll, followed by the impact of hitting the ground. I lifted my head and saw Asier, crouching on the ground, holding his arm which was dripping a considerable amount of blood. He had managed to throw me all the way back to the edge of the stage near the stairs, but he didn't get so lucky. My breath got stuck in my throat at the sight of his wound, and I could feel the woman's piercing glare tearing me more apart by the second.

"Valerie . . . you damn traitor," Asier yelled as his voice cracked. My eyes widened at the sound of that damned name.

Valerie.

There was so much affliction straining Asier's voice, and it wasn't solely from the physical pain. Valerie's face was visibly conflicted every second she looked at him, especially after what he said. I started to sit up, but someone kicked me back down and pinned me to the floor with their foot on my back. I grunted and turned my head as far as I could, looked up, and saw another Crow soldier. I looked back to where I was standing before Asier had pushed me and spotted my sword, but it was too far for me to reach now. Right beside my sword I spotted my daffodil on the ground, which also must've fallen when Asier pushed me.

As I brainstormed a strategy to free myself and Asier, I caught Valerie's eyes drifting down to the flower. She suspensefully approached it, and once she reached it, she looked down at me.

"Salvation cannot be achieved through one person alone," she professed coldly. Her voice was unexpectedly deep and sophisticated, but it matched her demeanor perfectly. "Just who do you think you are, anyway?"

I had no answer for her, and she didn't intend on waiting for one. She looked down at the delicate flower on the ground and proceeded to remorselessly crush it. The dainty petals ripped apart as she stomped on it, and I held my breath the entire time it happened. As soon as she finished, she approached Asier, and held the gun to his head, though she was bad at hiding her reluctance to do so.

Asier stared her down with bitterness and rancor in his eyes. "Run . . . and never come back," he painfully threatened. "Run like you know best, coward."

"Why should I?" she replied snarkily.

"This time I won't hesitate to rip you apart," he growled.

I couldn't stand watching anymore. I knew so little about this woman, but I knew one thing for sure; I wasn't going to let her torment Rebellium or the people in it any longer. She was a threat, and all threats needed to be eliminated *no matter what*. An immense fury sparked throughout my body, rage like I had never felt before.

A sudden surge of strength raced through me, and I flipped around under the soldier's foot and reached high enough to grab his sword. I stabbed the sword deep into the soldier's leg and quickly withdrew it. He jerked his leg back from my chest and crouched a bit from the injury, so I took this opportunity to sit up, and lunge the sword straight into his chest. He grunted and fell to the ground as I extracted the blade.

I promptly turned around to go after Valerie, until something peculiar caught my attention from the corner of my eye. I looked down at the sword in my hand, and noticed that it wasn't clean this time, and human blood was dripping from the blade onto the ground. My eyes widened, and I gripped the handle of the sword tightly as I looked down at the bleeding man on the ground. My stomach turned at the thought of me killing yet another human being. It was another case of the classic kill-or-be-killed, *but that didn't make it righteous.*

Before I could get too distracted, I gripped my sword and reminded myself of the task at hand; *it's a violent world, Phoenix, and you shouldn't be shocked that people die- be surprised you're still alive,* I reminded myself. I've had to give myself this speech countless times before; it's what I used to convince myself that my killing was self-righteous. Six years from my first kill and I'm still having to repeat it.

I charged at Valerie without another second to spare. I didn't get very far before three soldiers stepped in front of her and came after me. *You can't afford to care about the enemy in this violent world,* I thought as I mercilessly swung my sword; *this world is too cruel to care about what's right or wrong,* I added as I felt warm blood splatter my face. Their bodies hit the ground and I lowered my sword while breathing heavily. I recalled the bittersweet thrill of killing, and just how exhilarating it felt to eliminate your *obstacles.* I never wanted to feel that rush again, yet here I was, replaying the same old song.

I looked over briefly and saw Asier staring at me with staggered eyes. I couldn't bear to look at him after he witnessed me killing with such little mental exertion, and I certainly didn't want to see his face when I killed Valerie. I threw the bloody sword aside with disgust as an attempt to grip onto my sanity, but immediately reached down and took a gun from one of the lifeless men on the ground. I heard another soldier approach me from behind, and I pulled the trigger without even turning to look at his face.

My eyes met Valerie's, and her face was now filled with panic she was trying hard to subdue. I charged and jumped straight onto her, taking us both down to the ground. We tumbled down the steps on the side of the stage and I landed on top of her. I straddled her and held my gun to her head as I panted like a dog, all while images of dead men and blood clouded my mind- *the harsh side effects of guilt.*

I turned briefly to look at Asier. "Asier, run back to the mansion!"

Valerie took advantage of my wandering eyes and kicked me off her; now the tables were turned, and she was holding her own gun to my head. She was on her knees, and I was sitting with my legs free, so I easily kicked the gun out of her hand, and then kicked her in the face as hard as I could. I stood up to go after her, but then my arms were restrained by a soldier. She stood up and slowly drew back, holding her hand up to her bleeding face. I looked behind her and noticed dozens of soldiers surrounding us; some were human, some were feathers, but at this moment, *they were all the same to me.*

I looked at Valerie in her violet eyes and focused. Suddenly, the soldier who restrained me went up in flames, and I heard agonizing screams accompanied by the putrid smell of burning flesh behind me. Valerie watched the scene behind me, and she was completely aghast. Her eyes had the distinct look I have seen too many times for my own good; the doe-eyed look humans have once they realize they're in danger.

"I'm salvation delivered in the form of destruction," I answered her question from earlier.

I closed my eyes and imagined a raging fire incinerating the area around us. *I'm sorry . . . but I have no choice,* I thought before opening my eyes, and fire immediately engulfed the entire area around us along with every soldier in its path. The perimeter burned violently, and I quivered at who I was in this moment. Nonetheless, I held my ground against Valerie, and she was trapped in the fire with me- she had nowhere to run.

I picked another gun off the floor, then clenched my jaw and approached her slowly as I loaded the gun. She tried to back away but tripped on something and fell back. Her small nose was dripping blood, and her bottom lip was busted, which all complimented her horrified eyes perfectly.

I grabbed her by the collar of her suit, and once again, looked her in the eyes before finishing my answer to the question she asked back on the stage. "I am The Phoenix," I asserted, "but who are you?"

I lifted my gun to her head but this time, she didn't fight back. Her eyes reflected something other than horror and resentment, though I couldn't quite put a name to it yet. It was a look I'd seen before, something I constantly saw in myself.

"Phoenix, retreat now, that's an order!" I just barely heard Asier call out in the far distance, but it was clear enough to snap me out of the zone I'd trapped myself in. I turned in the direction of his voice, and Valerie did too. Through the flames I could vaguely see a shed which wasn't too far from here, and I assumed that was where Asier was hiding.

"Phoenix . . . *please* just come here," he pleaded, and this time his voice broke. *I've never heard Asier plead for anything.*

Before pulling the trigger, I recalled the reason I was even hunting her and all those soldiers down in the first place. Ultimately, it was really all to protect us, not for revenge. I lowered the gun and threw Valerie to the ground before tossing the gun into the flames. I watched her crawl away, and the look on her face kept reminding me of a feeling that I used to know.

"You're trapped and unarmed- there's no point in killing you, since you'll probably die here regardless," I explained. "If you do somehow manage to escape, then good for you, but if the flames catch up to you, at least I can sleep at night knowing I didn't have to kill you directly," I snarled as she crawled as far away from me as possible, coughing her lungs out from the heavy smoke.

For whatever reason, when it came down to it, I couldn't bring myself to kill her. Maybe it was because I knew the impact her death would have on the people of Rebellium, regardless of what she did to them. I knew deep down she still meant a lot to them- I could see it in their eyes when they talked about her. Even after everything she'd done, those sins were not mine to forgive, they were theirs. Ultimately though, I'd spare Valerie- not for her, Asier, or Rebellium's sake, but for my own.

I knew the flames could sense my internal turmoil, because they grew considerably. I walked through the fire like it was water and headed toward the shed I saw. Once I reached the door, I noticed fire was spreading dangerously close to the shed.

"Don't come any closer!" I shouted before running inside and slamming the door. I probably sounded insane shouting at a raging fire, but I knew it was ultimately me who decided *what* it burned and *how* it burned. *This fire is a lot stronger than it usually is though,* I thought as I stared at the swirling flames through a broken window in the shed.

I looked down at the wooden floor and was relieved once I saw Asier in the corner, leaning against the wall, holding his wounded arm. His head was turned away, and his eyes avoided mine, but I could still see the visible pain in his face from his open wound. I kneeled down to meet him on the ground, and the best thing I could hope for was that his opinion of me hadn't changed too negatively.

"I'm sorry . . . you had to see all that," I apologized while looking down in shame. I was never good at apologizing, because I've never really had a reason or felt the need to directly apologize to anyone for anything.

My clothes were stained with blood from different people, and I knew my face was covered in it too; I did not want to see myself right now. My hands had been metaphorically covered in blood for years now, but right now, it was actually visible. It bothered me more than ever this time, because someone who had put their life on the line to have faith in me, could see it too.

"Don't worry about it," he answered apathetically. His reply was so generic and not the most reassuring, but the fact that he even responded meant it was genuine, because Asier wasn't the type to bluff for the sake of making someone feel better. A sense of relief brushed over me, but even if he forgave me, I still couldn't completely forgive myself.

"We're in a war, and in war, blood is guaranteed. It was a necessary move, they would've run back to The Crow and ratted us out if you had let them escape."

"I let her escape though," I confessed- unsure of what his reaction would be.

He paused for longer than usual before eventually responding. "It's whatever."

"I knew you would've never forgiven me if I killed her . . . that's why you called me back here after all."

Asier simply looked down at the ground, and it was silent again for a minute. I didn't need a response though; his actions and his face told me enough. I switched my focus back to his arm, which would not stop bleeding. I ripped off a piece of my sweater sleeve with my teeth and tied it around his arm, roughly serving as a tourniquet. I was no physician, but I knew how to stop bleeding one way or another.

I created a small flame on the tip of my finger and proceeded to carefully cauterize his wound. He flinched, but he took the pain way better than I expected. I supposed his head had enough to think about rather than focus on the external pain.

"No . . . it wasn't that," he abruptly responded to the comment I had made earlier.

"Then?" I asked, looking up from his wound to his eyes.

He turned his head away again, still facing the ground before hesitantly answering. "You two would've ended up killing each other, and I don't want to lose anything more to her. I've already lost so much progress, along with many comrades, and obviously I lost her long ago . . . but not you too, Phoenix."

I wasn't sure how to respond. *Someone's worried about losing me?* That simple fact momentarily debilitated all the dreadful feelings I had built up. The warm feeling from last night returned, and that's when I was starting to admit to myself that I might've begun to feel something for Asier- something I had never quite felt for anyone else. I didn't know how to respond to him in words, so instead of replying, I scooted up next to him, and leaned against the wall too, extending my legs forward.

"It wasn't the bullet that hurt, but the person behind the gun," he admitted with a strain in his usually hollow voice. "Seeing her is much more painful than getting shot."

Once again, I found myself unable to respond, and I hated the fact that I couldn't help him, or even offer him any solace; *I wish I could understand the feelings ravaging your heart right now,* I thought. My general lack of empathy, paired with never experiencing the pain of betrayal, left me unable to sympathize with him. The only situation I could think of where I'd remotely felt betrayal, was the whole situation with my mother, but even then, it was still better to feel like strangers around someone you once cherished, rather than sworn enemies.

"Well, no one can hurt you anymore." I offered him a small smile. "You're safe now." I managed to get a brief grin from him, and it felt good to even just temporarily bring some sort of ease to his aching heart. "The fire is still raging. We should stay here until it's safe," I suggested.

After saying that, he scooted closer to me and unexpectedly laid his head down on my lap. Heat crept up on my face along with a definite shade of pink, but thankfully he was facing away from me. Strands of his black hair obscured his pale face and his closed eyes. His vulnerability in this moment really reestablished his humanity; it was just Asier Jovano, not the great leader and commander of Rebellium, not a deviant or a soldier, just an ordinary human man with soul and a heartbeat.

"Are you just gonna keep staring at me until I fall asleep, creep?" he teased, and my face burned red with embarrassment.

"You're the one that laid on me, you weirdo!" I refuted, audibly vexed. I assumed he was somewhat back to normal since he still had room to joke around, and that admittedly brought me a deep sense of relief.

He didn't respond, and he didn't move away. It felt weird having someone use my leg as a pillow, but I just let it happen. As I watched him fall asleep, I noticed his vulnerability elicited an inexplicable sense of protectiveness over him, which explained everything that happened back there. I listened to his mellow breathing which harmonized well with the cracking fire outside, and I began to say all the things I wanted to say to him in my head; *just close your eyes and sleep for now, the sun will soon come up and dry your eyes.*

Several minutes had passed, and it was safe to assume Asier was asleep by now. I recalled the dream of me on my mother's lap under the tree, and this moment reminded me of it so much. With that dream in mind, I gathered up enough courage and carefully stroked his head, brushing aside the strands of hair from his face. I was obviously rather inexperienced in showing affection, but small gestures like this felt like a good start. His face looked so serene when he slept, like all his anguish had just been vanquished; *I hope it remains that way even once you wake up.*

My eyes were starting to feel heavy as well now. My legs were falling asleep from the weight of Asier's head, but I didn't mind it. I rested one hand on his arm, making sure to avoid the wound, and put the other down beside me. My eyes traced the black-ink tattoos on his arms until they grew more and more tired, and eventually closed for good. I hoped that the unique art on his arm wouldn't be ruined by the bullet wound.

I didn't expect a dreamless night, but I wasn't sure what to expect tonight. I was back in the mansion, and Asier was leaning against the doorframe, arms crossed and looking outside. In front of him, Valerie was sitting on the porch, looking at the sky. She had much longer hair, but besides that, she looked virtually the same. She was so beautiful; it was no wonder Asier fell for her.

"I know you're there, so why don't you just join me?" she offered. Asier remained put for a solid minute before reluctantly joining her. He sat next to her, and they looked at the desolate town of ruins in front of them with the night sky as a backdrop.

"Can't sleep tonight?" she asked.

"If I sleep, I'll see them," he uttered in his gravelly voice. You could see their breath as they spoke in the frosty air.

"Well, maybe some skywatching might ward off our insomnia," she suggested, but Asier didn't respond. "One day you'll paint that sky blue, right?" she added, and then she began to fade. I assume that was one of their first interactions with each other.

Now, it was only Asier on the porch with just the ruined town and the moon in front of him; there were no stars in the sky tonight. He was alone, sitting with his knees up to his chest, holding a note in his shaky hands while fighting back tears- something I never thought I'd see him do. While it was heart-wrenching seeing him like that, it was also somewhat comforting to know that even someone as strong as Asier could be brought to tears. *What makes the strongest man want to cry? Love does.*

I fluttered my eyes open, and I was back inside the shed. I looked around, and it was significantly darker and colder in here. All the flames had been extinguished, and the only remaining light was from the faint, dawning sky. Asier was still asleep on my lap, and after that dream I had, the whole night made a lot more sense.

Last night on the hill, he wanted to sleep out there together, because that was the only way he would sleep peacefully; that's what he would do with Valerie. *Is that why he slept so soundly last night? Did he manipulate his mind into thinking I was her?* I wondered. Whatever the reason was, I was just glad he got proper rest, even if it was only for a few hours.

My musing was interrupted as soon as I heard shuffling outside. I carefully grabbed Asier's head while simultaneously removing my legs from under him. When I successfully managed to move him without waking him, I stood up as quietly as I could, which proved to be quite difficult with the old shed's creaking floor. I grabbed

Asier's sword from its sheath for defense, and slowly creaked the door open.

The air was alarmingly thick with smoke and the area still felt a few degrees warmer. I scanned my surroundings with the blade in my hands, prepared to attack if I needed to. I heard more shuffling coming from behind me, and I immediately turned.

"Phoenix?" The smoke and the darkness made it hard to see, but I recognized the voice to be Lana's.

Lana and Aurora emerged from the smoke and a look of relief flushed over them. I realized me and Asier never really told anyone where we were going last night, and we didn't make it better by not returning. They were probably incredibly worried, and I don't blame them; their leader and Prophet had suddenly disappeared without a word.

"Where the hell have you been? Where's the commander? And why are you covered in blood?" Aurora asked a barrage of questions while looking me up and down.

"Look, I promise I'll explain later, but Asier is injured so please take him back to the mansion immediately," I ordered the girls. "It was too dangerous to go back to the mansion last night, so I wrapped a tourniquet around his arm and cauterized his wound to the best of my abilities, but it definitely still requires proper care."

"What? Where is he?" Lana exclaimed.

"Right behind you," Asier announced behind the girls, emerging from the smoke.

"Asier! Your arm!" Lana panicked like a worried mother.

"You're awake?" I asked, for some reason unable to look him in the eyes.

"You'd think after all these years, my reflexes would respond to obvious noise and movement."

"Well then, I'll catch up to you guys later," I said before turning around and running off without another word.

"Wait, Phoenix!" I heard Aurora call out, but I didn't stop. I heard them start to chase after me, but I out-ran them, and the smoke stopped them from finding me.

I needed to make sure there were absolutely no survivors; I would not risk this location being given away- even if I had to slaughter another army. I ran through the rubble and fresh ashes until I heard coughing in the distance. My heart began racing and I gripped the sword while inching closer to the area the sound came from. The cough sounded feminine, and I had a feeling I knew who it was. Half of me wanted to find Valerie alive, but the other half of me didn't, because then I had to decide what to do with her. *If put in that situation, will I actually be able to kill her this time?*

I stopped as soon as I saw someone leaning against a burnt tree; just as I had guessed, Valerie had survived, and it was her coughing. She was so weak she could barely lift her slender arm enough to cover her mouth and nose, which were both still bloody. Her eyes were red and puffy, and I could tell she had been crying all night. She reluctantly looked up at me with intense enmity in her glare.

"Have you come to finish me off?" she asked boldly. "The Crow mentioned you'd hesitate to kill soldiers if you knew they were human, but I guess even that isn't enough to stop you."

"After all the people I've had to kill, what made him believe it would be different this time?" I asked as if she knew the answer, or even remotely cared.

"Well, I suppose it's my turn now," she said, turning her head to the side, "so what are you waiting for?"

"Why do you work for him?" I asked impulsively, and there was total silence.

"What does it matter to you?" she responded coldly.

"We're not so different, Valerie."

It was true. She was once a rebel who became a Crow Soldier, and I was once an Executioner who became a rebel. We were more similar than different, and that's when I figured it out; the look I kept seeing in her eyes was the same look I saw whenever I looked in the mirror- *regret*.

"I got tired of waiting . . . for *you*," she mumbled, but I still managed to hear it.

A strange feeling crept over me the second she said that, because there was no room for dishonesty when a human repents during their final moments. The dried tears on her face were the guilt and regret that had been eating her alive, so much so that she's now *pleading* for death. With that being said, I could not bring myself to kill her anymore.

"I won't kill you."

"Don't be foolish. Don't let your pity get in the way," she insisted as I approached her.

"I don't have to take any orders from you," I responded before kneeling down in front of her. "Death is the easy way out. Face your consequences head-on like a soldier."

I turned around and motioned her to get on my back. She shook her head and looked at me like I had grown an extra skull.

"What the hell are you doing?" she asked, then broke out in a cough.

"Get on before I drag you all the way there," I said as apathetically as I could, "I think you owe the rebels something."

She hesitated, but I made it clear I didn't intend on moving. Eventually I felt her wrap her arms around my neck, then I stood up slowly and I held onto her legs; she might've been taller than me, but she was so light. I began walking with her on my back, and it was dead silent as I carried her. I was going to take her back to the mansion, and as awful as that idea sounded, something told me it was the right thing to do.

"Why didn't you kill me?" she asked, finally breaking the silence.

I didn't answer immediately, because I had to think of the answer myself; *why am I sparing this traitor's life?* I knew why, but I didn't quite know how to word it. I left her without an answer for so long that it was probably foolish to even answer anymore, but I did anyway.

"I'm not very smart with emotions, but I do recognize one well, and that emotion is regret," I began, and her silence told me she was listening. "You have the same look on your face that I did, and trust me when I tell you, I know better than anyone the feeling of wanting to do right after doing wrong your whole life," I finished, and she remained completely silent.

"Plus, I think we both know someone who would be devastated if you died," I added, and the atmosphere tensed up when she realized who I was referring to.

"But after all I've done . . . do I even deserve a second chance?" she uttered, sounding a lot like me.

"Someone once told me, no matter how far down the wrong path you've walked, it's *never* too late to turn around."

Chapter 19

When we arrived at the mansion, I set Valerie down. She stood slowly and leaned on the wall to hold herself up as she looked around, probably reminiscing of the time she'd spent here. The first people we encountered were Daxon and Fremont, who immediately froze in place the moment they laid their eyes on the dark-haired woman.

"V-Valerie . . .?" Daxon stuttered. Fremont was left utterly speechless.

"What the hell is she doing here?" Khalon asked coldly upon walking in. He immediately pulled his gun out and aimed it at her head.

"Valerie?" Lana exclaimed from a distance, then covered her mouth in disbelief.

Everyone was approaching us now, and I could tell it was going to be hard to explain this one. Just when I thought it couldn't get worse, I saw the last person I wanted to see walk in- Asier. His arm was bandaged but he moved and looked like nothing was even injured. The vulnerability I saw from him last night was gone, and he stared at Valerie with the same apathetic look he gave everyone, only much colder.

"She has something to say," I explained, and everyone's eyes were on me now. "More importantly, I think she could be of use to us in our mission."

"We don't need help from a traitor," Daxon spat with scorn in his voice.

"Let me explain-" I began but was cut off by Valerie's coughing. She fell to her knees as she coughed her lungs out.

She coughed so hard her nose began to bleed again from the kick I had given her. Asier scrunched his eyebrows and there was potent rancor in his eyes. He knelt down and grabbed Valerie by the collar, making everyone gasp.

"Some guts you have to show yourself here," he said spitefully. You could see the overload of emotions in Valerie's mortified expression.

"A-Asier," she uttered out loud, but was too shocked to speak cohesive sentences.

"That day . . . who called the shots?" Asier asked. I assumed he was referring to the day they were caught.

Her eyes were wide and glossy with tears. You could tell her emotional state was unhinged; she was unrecognizable from the relentless soldier we saw back at the capital, and even the one from last night. Affliction held her by a chokehold, and you could tell her answers were going to hurt. She took a long time to answer, but eventually got herself together enough to speak.

"The Crow was getting suspicious of this place, and he originally planned to send troops here, so I jumped in and gave away the other location," she explained, trying to hold back tears. "I had no clue you would be there that day."

"What about now?" he asked. "Why did you and the other troops show up and try to ambush us?"

Everyone in the crowd was stunned by the news, as they didn't know any details of the events from last night yet. Valerie swallowed hard; you could tell she didn't want to answer. Whatever the answer was, she knew it was never going to be good enough for Asier. Her silence was loud enough for Asier, and in response, he threw her onto the ground with no remorse, causing Valerie to whimper. Everyone's eyes were still glued to them- I don't think they were even blinking.

Asier pulled out his dagger. "Maybe this will make you talk."

"My plan was to sedate The Prophet and capture you all while she was asleep!" she confessed in panic at the sight of the dagger. "Once you were all captured, I'd take her back to The Capital with me, and there we'd kill The Crow together before he could do anything to anyone."

"And you thought capturing us was a better alternative?" yelled Daxon.

"Better than having you all die on a battlefield!" she tried yelling back, but it came out as more of a croak.

"Now, what if your plan failed, and you got us all captured, and didn't manage to kill him before it was too late for all of us?" Asier abruptly chimed in.

"I was willing to take that chance," she admitted selfishly, and you could hear everyone's dismay.

"You were?" Asier asked with clear disappointment in his face.

"You know better than anyone, Asier . . . the ends *always* justify the means."

After Valerie's brutal honesty, it became so silent you could hear a pin drop. Asier's fury slowly morphed into hurt, which his face reflected perfectly. Rage, deception, betrayal, disappointment, and pity- all simultaneously coexisted on his face.

"Why did you run in the first place?" Lana asked as she came to the front of the crowd, her voice shaking.

"Asier, you always told me destiny was in our hands," she began whilst looking up at Asier, who's eyes avoided looking at her, ". . . and so I tried to change it," she continued, and Asier caved in, returning the eye contact. "I didn't want to keep idly waiting for salvation until every last one of us was caught and killed like animals- so I ran away. I changed my identity and worked for The Crow in hopes that one day I could kill him myself."

Everyone's faces reflected their uncertainty of whether or not she was being truthful. Asier maintained their eye contact for several seconds, until he finally looked away and closed his eyes. He seemed to be trying to process all of it at once, and I could see it was ripping him apart from the inside.

"The ends justify the means, Valerie, but there was always *one* exception, and that exception was abandoning your humanity, because then you become equivalent to your enemy," Asier explained and knelt down to Valerie's level, glaring into her eyes. "You betrayed us in the worst way possible and killed scores of our comrades- the same ones who once considered you family."

Tears welled up in Valerie's eyes. "Asier-" she uttered, but Asier cut her off immediately.

"If there's one thing I hate more than being a prisoner, it's people who've *abandoned* their humanity," he scoffed, and with that, he stood up, turned, and walked away without saying another word.

Valerie stayed down and her eyes followed Asier as he walked out. The amount of anguish and grief in her eyes was immeasurable. The tears she fought so hard to contain escaped all at once, and she made no noise, nor did she move an inch as tears streamed down her pale face. Everyone around her gave her a look, but it wasn't sympathy, it was pity. I couldn't even blame them; after everything she'd done, I too would be weary and distrustful of her.

Everyone followed and walked out in silence, and only myself, Daxon, Khalon, and Fremont were left. Daxon handcuffed Valerie as a safety measure, and she did not try to fight against it. Her face was drained, and if heartbreak had a look, I assumed it would look like that. The three leaders escorted her out, and I was left in the room alone. I took a deep breath before heading to the room I stayed in.

I saw Guido standing by the door with a troubled look on his face. I approached him, but it was like he didn't even see me.

"You alright?" I asked him, snapping him back to the present.

"Oh, you're back. Thank goodness, we were all so worried," he said after finally noticing me. "That uh . . . sure is a lot of blood on your shirt," he added to distract from his abundantly anxious behavior, which was unusual for him.

"What's wrong?" I cut straight to the point.

He sighed heavily with a frown and shook his head. "It's bad back home, Phoenix. It's so bad," he explained while jittering. "It's a warzone back there. I watched his speech last night on the television downstairs; so many people have coalesced against The Crow and people are getting captured left and right- some are even being killed on the spot."

"We have until the last week of August before he kills all the captured deviants," I tried to reassure him, but it only seemed to worsen his anxiety.

"He said they're almost done rounding up all the rebels, so they're gonna start the executions tomorrow." He held his head. "My little sister is in that town for fuck's sake! She hasn't done anything. She doesn't deserve to be stuck in the heart of all that."

His eyes glossed up from the tears that threatened to escape. Once again, I found a slight comfort in seeing others putting their vulnerability on display. Throughout these two weeks living as a deviant, I've seen even some of the most dedicated and strong soldiers fill up with doubt and fear. It reminded me that despite my status as The Prophet, The Phoenix, or whatever you wanted to call it, *I was still just another bird*. We were all human, and sometimes you have to break just to know you're human.

I put my hand on my heart and kneeled down on one knee. "With my heart in my hand, I promised to give my life to save this nation," I said to him while staring into his eyes, "and I don't intend on ever going back on that promise."

The smile we all loved painted on his face again. "You're right. *We* will take back this nation," he agreed, emphasizing the word *we*.

"Perhaps sooner than we expected, but nonetheless, we're prepared," I added.

Guido furrowed an eyebrow, and I walked past him and began searching for my uniform in the room. It's been a while since I've worn it since it was being sewn, so I didn't quite know its whereabouts. When I finally found it, I held the jumpsuit in my hands, but couldn't bring myself to do anything beyond that. I felt the leathery texture of the material in my fingers, and I couldn't help but think that this was possibly the last time I'd equip this suit.

I let the situation really sink in and I immediately felt uneasy. Recognizing that this was one of my last counted days on this earth felt suffocating. It was a bitter pill to swallow, but nonetheless, it was my inevitable reality. Once again, I felt an unusual fondness for life that I had never possessed before.

"Why are you changing into that?" Guido asked while standing at the door.

"I think I'm gonna get a head start," I answered, realizing how ridiculous the idea was.

"Phoenix, are you crazy? You can't go alone! Just wait until we all accompany you!" he pleaded.

"I won't let this world lie in the palm of his hand a single day longer," I answered, trying to assert my courage. "I'll die before I lose that choice."

"Phoenix, District Four isn't home anymore, it's a *battlefield*. There's going to be people that weigh their lives on your victory, but there are equally as many that will do anything to see you dead."

Hearing that reminded me of how self-righteous the human race believed itself to be. What I've gathered from history, is that all we've ever done is fight over our differences, whether it's the god we worship or the color of our skin. Now, even in the face of total oppression, humans will still continue to disagree and fight one another.

I didn't turn to face Guido, but I hoped my silence was enough of an answer. I heard him close the door and walk away; I assumed he knew my stubbornness and pride was far too strong for him to change my mind, so he'd find someone who would be able to convince me. I gripped my jumpsuit again, but instead of just staring at it, I took off my bloodstained clothes and began to slip it on. I immediately threw the clothes on the ground, because I couldn't stand the strong, metallic smell of human blood anymore. I reached for my black boots and slipped them on, then carefully tied my bright, crimson shoulder, knee, and elbow pads on.

I went back and forth on whether I should wear the bulletproof vest or not, but I decided against it. I tied my crimson belt and my ammunition belts around me and attached my sword sheath and gun holsters. I didn't have my Hunter trench coat anymore to put over this, but instead, I now had a black cape, like the rest of the rebels wore. When I was finally done, I walked up to a tall mirror that leaned against the corner of the room and stared myself down.

I couldn't recognize the face before me anymore; *she looks so unfamiliar.* I constantly put on the act of a courageous soldier who would honorably die to free mankind and resurrect our sun, so much so that even I'd begun to believe it. To the rebels, I was The Prophet, The Phoenix, a savior, and to the rest, I was the enemy, the antichrist, but the truth was, I was just a lost girl, from now until the end of time. *How can I still see myself through this disguise?* I thought as I gazed at my reflection.

I heard muffled voices in the distance, and one of the voices sounded like Valerie. She sounded distressed, and then I noticed there was a deep voice accompanying hers- I figured it was Asier. I focused my attention on their voices to see if I could decipher what they were saying. Even though I brought her here, I couldn't bring myself to one hundred percent trust her.

"I knew I would lose you, but if I knew it would be this hard, I would've never-"

"Don't finish that sentence." Valerie was cut off by Asier's stern voice.

It was brutally silent afterward. I had no context of the conversation, but it clearly wasn't a pleasant one. I fiddled with the pendant I was gifted as I waited for them to speak again, but there wasn't a single word exchanged. Instead of voices, I heard footsteps walking toward me. They got louder and louder until the door opened behind me and I saw Asier's reflection in the mirror. It was evident that he was trying to wipe the troubled look off his face and return to his typical poker-face.

"Mind explaining a few things to me?" he asked while raising an eyebrow.

I looked down then looked back up at his reflection in the mirror. "Ask away."

"Let's start with the elephant in the room- why the hell did you bring her here?"

"She was weak and dying."

"Really funny. I'm serious, brat."

"I am too. Personal feelings aside, she's beneficial for the mission; she knows more than we do," I retorted before finally facing him. "She poses no threat, she's too weak to try anything, and simply killing her is the easy way out. We wouldn't benefit from her death in any way," I answered, which didn't wipe the annoyed look off his face.

"I don't know what's more ridiculous, you bringing Valerie back, or this idea I'm hearing of you single-handedly storming District Four," he responded. I figured Asier was the first person Guido would run to in order to knock some sense into me.

"I don't see the problem with killing him before he wipes out half the population. Isn't that the whole point of my existence?" I inquired, and Asier dragged his face with his palm.

Asier's response was delayed after hearing my answer. "It's not that simple, Phoenix, and you know it. Going in there without backup is practically suicide, and I hope you're aware that once you're out there, there's *no* turning back."

"Look, I'm not gonna sit back and watch the carnage that's about to unfold from afar any longer than I already have. I don't intend to let hundreds of innocent people get slaughtered- my mom included. This war ends now, Asier."

Silence filled the air after my insistent response. Asier had nothing left to say, because deep down, I know part of him agreed with me. He stood at the door frame, staring straight at me as I returned the gaze.

"You're out of line, soldier," is all he could say. *Soldier? Not even using my name now?*

"Oh, is that how it's gonna be, commander?" I replied, piqued by his response. "And in case you forgot, I'm *The Prophet*, which in case you forgot, means I'll stop at *nothing* to fulfill my vow," I retaliated.

"Just The Prophet?" he asked with a weird smirk on his face.

"That's all."

"I don't know, the girl from yesterday was much more than just The Prophet," he said, and my heart felt like it skipped a beat. His words hung in the air, allowing them to sink in before saying anything else. "Don't rush to your death, Phoenix. Just hold till dawn and we'll be there to fight with you." He paused as he walked up to me and placed his cold hand on my shoulder. "We're all in this battle together, so we'll fight together till the bitter end." he added, and I felt the tension around us slowly dissolving.

"Meet us in the main room in ten. We'll kick our battle off with a celebration, then we'll decide how we go from there," he said before walking out and closing the door behind him.

That confrontational encounter quickly took an unexpected turn. It didn't take much convincing to get me to hold off on storming District Four until tomorrow. I suppose as a commander, he obviously cared about the mission's success, and as a comrade and human, the lives of his comrades were above everything. Like me, he didn't want to wait around much longer, but he knew if we took the time to strategize a plan tonight, it would decrease the number of casualties and increase the chances of victory; he truly was an admirable commander.

After a while, I finally made my way to the main room to meet everyone for possibly our final celebration as Rebellium. I stood at the doorway and scanned the room to find a familiar face until I saw

Lana sitting at a table. I walked up to her, and I noticed she was alone, and looked to have a lot on her mind.

"This seat taken?" I asked and she smiled before shaking her head and motioning me to sit. "You okay?" I asked.

She sighed and smiled. "This might sound weird . . . but it's almost as if I didn't want this to end." She paused to find my gaze before explaining. "I just have so many fond memories of this place; this is my home, and they are my family. Rebellium is a permanent part of me," she explained with a woeful expression.

"Do you know what you're going to do after the war?" I asked.

"I guess I'll start by going back to my district and seeing if my parents are still alive, then I'll go from there."

"How did you end up here anyways, Lana?" Her face became shadowed with light sorrow. A smile still managed to break through, implying that it was more or less a bittersweet story.

"When I was a child, I adored fairy tales; my sister would often tell me stories, and I always listened. They always had happy endings, until one day, she told me a story that didn't- the story of the star-crossed lovers, *Lanon and Astrid*," she began, and a few chills ran through my skin. "I remember asking her if our stories would have happy endings, and she answered, 'no matter what hardships we face, once The Phoenix comes back, this life would have a happy ending,'" she quoted, and her smile had fallen by this point.

"How'd she know?"

"To this day, I'm not sure how she got a hold of that story, but she told me everything from The Crow and The Phoenix, all the way to the alleged prophecy," she explained, "but we were far too careless, and a crow heard the whole thing."

"Is that when you ran away, after you were caught?" I asked and she shook her head.

"A day later, deviant hunters came to our house and forcefully took my sister away from us. At the time I didn't know what they were going to do with her, but the next time I would see her, her blood would paint the stage in front of our whole town," she said grimly. "After that, I would always ask my parents why our lives were so unfair, but they would say nothing, all out of fear; they continued to be slaves even after their daughter was slaughtered," she added with a sour taste in her mouth.

She paused to recollect her thoughts, and unexpectedly, a smile appeared on her face again. "But one night, I remembered what my sister had told me about The Phoenix, the prophecy, and the rebels, so I ran away and searched for it- for that happy ending."

I smiled at the conclusion. "Thank you for sharing that with me." I expressed my gratitude, and she returned the smile.

"Thanks to you, I can say I will finally reach that happy ending in my lifetime."

"I'm a pathetic pick for a Prophet, but at least I can die knowing I helped at least one person," I responded with a forced chuckle.

"You're saving this world, Phoenix. You're honorable, and not in any way pathetic."

"But why would she choose me to be The Prophet? I still don't understand."

She was silent for a while, trying to articulate a response. "Maybe because unlike all of us- you harbor no real hatred towards The Crow," she theorized. "At the end of the day, I doubt *her* love for him has vanished completely."

I raised a brow at her response. *I've never thought of it that way.* I broke out of that thought and became aware that I was blankly staring at Lana without even blinking.

"That's a wonderful theory, Lana." A voice startled me from behind us- The White Raven.

"Good to see you," Lana greeted. She gave us a smile and we exchanged it.

She pulled up a seat across from us and sat down before continuing. "The world has erupted into hate and unrest, but this bleak world will be no more once you, Phoenix, burn a light bright enough to eliminate the darkness for good." She paused briefly to thoroughly peer into my eyes. "But tell me, Phoenix, are you truly ready to return to ashes?" She always searched for something in my weary eyes, and she finally found it.

A heavy feeling in my chest and stomach followed her question, and I suddenly became aware of my own heartbeat. The road I'd wandered for many years left me alone and deprived of life, and now I was soon to hit a dead end I wasn't ready for. Until now, the idea of dying had never presented itself to me accompanied by fear.

"Your reaction is more than enough of an answer to me. You've undergone a radical change of heart, young woman. You're no longer the same lost child that wandered into this place two weeks ago," she declared.

"I've always watched death all around me without even flinching, but now, it seems as though I've developed some sort of attachment to life at the most inconvenient time possible," I explained, unable to look either of them in the eyes.

Lana and The White Raven both looked at me with pitiful looks on their faces as I struggled with myself. I despised pity more than anything, and I hated thinking about my own dilemmas- I preferred to just act like they didn't exist.

"Phoen-" Lana barely uttered part of my name before I cut her off.

"Oh well, I'm just putting off the inevitable. Yeah, I might die tomorrow, but I'm gonna die anyways, right? The ground is calling my name, so who am I to keep it waiting?" I added in a laid-back tone, trying to disguise my newly found fear.

"But until then, let's enjoy our last few moments as deviant fugitives, because soon enough, we'll be ordinary human beings," The White Raven added to diffuse the tension and rose from her seat.

"Amen to that!" Lana responded enthusiastically.

After The White Raven walked off, I scanned the room that still somehow frolicked with life and enthusiasm. People with remarkable amounts of hope rejoiced with their loved ones in this room, and I was blessed enough to be a part of their celebration. However, in the corner I saw something that made me tense up- Valerie and Asier sitting together. I didn't know why the sight of them bothered me, but it did.

I felt an arm wrap around me, and it was none other than Guido. "Hey girls, come celebrate with the rest of us!"

I saw a blush creep up on Lana's face, along with a shy smile. She was usually so bold that it was weird seeing her act so timid. Guido was no exception; a hint of pink brushed over his face too; the chemistry between them was undeniable.

"I think I'll leave you two lovebirds alone," I teased, and the pink on their faces amplified. I grinned at them before walking away.

I walked aimlessly, then turned my attention back to Asier and Valerie; neither of them were talking, they just sat with each other, occasionally exchanging looks. I tried to make my glare discreet so they wouldn't look my way. As a consequence of my distraction, I didn't watch where I was going, and I accidentally walked straight into someone's chest. I lifted my head a bit and saw a dirty-blond-haired boy smiling at me.

"Hello, Miss Phoenix," he said as he slightly bowed with his hand on his heart.

"Uh, no need to be so proper, Fremont." I giggled and he nodded.

"I apologize, I should've paid more attention to where I was walking," he said, and I quickly shook my head.

"No, it's completely my fault. I was the distracted one."

"If you say so, Miss." It was quiet for a little too long so I decided to break some ice.

"So, Fremont, what's your plan after the war ends?" I asked curiously. Connecting with my teammates was long overdue, but I suppose it was better late than never.

A bright, optimistic smile formed on his face. "Well, I'm going back to my district to finally see my family again," he began, and I saw a glimmer in his eyes. "I'm also thinking of becoming a history teacher, so the new generations can learn real, uncensored history, and grow from the past's mistakes instead of repeating them like we did."

His optimism was like a breath of fresh air, and quite frankly, I hadn't expected such a thorough response from Fremont. "I wish you nothing but the best, Fremont. A bright future awaits you and your future students," I replied, returning the smile. A small blush appeared on his smiling face, really showing off his young age.

A small, dark-haired boy crept up behind Fremont and flashed his pure smile at us. "Is it true? Are we really gonna see the sun tomorrow, miss?" Lamie asked exuberantly; his enthusiasm was ever so contagious.

"If not tomorrow, definitely sooner than later," I answered optimistically. Fremont smiled at my response.

"Will I finally get to play in the sun?" he asked just as eagerly.

I knelt and laid my hands on his shoulders. "You'll never have to play in the dark again," I answered quietly, and he smiled before throwing himself into my arms and bobbing up and down. Fremont giggled and placed his hands on our backs.

"Resurrect the sun! Resurrect the light! Resurrect humanity!" The room had erupted into a repeating chant.

Everyone had their fists up, but behind them, I could see Asier preparing to make a speech in the same spot I first saw him. His low, growly-toned voice was easily distinguished from the rest of the crowd, and he too threw his fist in the air.

"Time is slipping away, and oppression has no deadline. Our efforts have not been in vain; after biting their tongues for so long, people are finally beginning to open their eyes and resist," he began to explain in a much calmer tone than expected. "Tomorrow, we storm District Four, free all the captured, then we overthrow the tyrant. We must prepare to fight the biggest, hardest battle we've ever fought, but it's a small price to pay for our future!" As he preached, everyone cheered.

Their hope was infectious, and I too had a lot to say, but I let my words remain unsaid; I knew Asier would deliver the message much better anyways. I got back on my feet and decided it was my turn to listen. For a second, I allowed myself to feel the hope that emanated from Asier's speech as if I were any other rebel.

It always amazed me how valiant and courageous these people were; the possibility of death did not dim their light. Asier turned his gaze toward me and a smirk appeared on his face. Once again, becoming aware of my heartbeat, I smiled back. I clenched my pendant in my hands and smiled back. *For all of you, I am not afraid to die.*

It was late now, and I had gone outside to get some fresh air as usual. The mansion was getting a bit too rowdy for me, and I needed some time to breathe and process what was in store for tomorrow. I looked up at the stars and my heart grew heavy upon realizing this would probably be the last time I'd ever look at the night sky with such serenity.

"If you fly high enough, you'll touch the stars- even during the day," came a deep voice from behind me. I quickly turned around to find Asier, who was leaning against the doorframe. I gave him a quick smile before nodding and turning back to look at the sky.

"You start to appreciate the little things when you know you're inching closer to your death," I scoffed. "My deadline is approaching, and I'm starting to feel like I'm not ready to let go- it's so pathetic."

Asier sat down next to me. "Nothing wrong with having an attachment to life," he reassured, "it's only human nature."

"Like you once told me, one can only pray we won't regret our choices down the line," I said, resting my chin on my knees.

"I've never prayed a moment in my life," he replied, "and I'll never look up to the sky and say a faithless prayer; it's like spraying shit with perfume," he added as he ironically looked up to the sky. I giggled at his analogy.

I didn't believe there was a person in this nation that has never prayed- that's never believed for even a second all the lies they're being fed were *true*. Worshiping The Crow was forced, but since

Asier's disdain dated way back, it would make sense that he'd probably only ever feigned his prayers.

"Maybe that's why I was awarded the life I was given- I prayed and devoted my life to the wrong salvation," I said as I tucked my face further into my knees. "Thinking about it, maybe ending it sooner than later is probably the best option- I don't need to live in this hell for any longer."

It was silent for a while, and only the muffled noise from downstairs and the cold wind blowing around us could be heard. I let my words sit in the air before continuing.

"Half my happiness was created in my head, and I've never felt a genuine appreciation for life until now- maybe that's why I'm so afraid to go," I pondered out loud. "But somebody like me doesn't deserve that happiness."

Asier let out a deep sigh. "So you have plenty of blood on your hands, brat- don't we all?" he firmly replied. "We can't take back the things we've done or bring back the lives we've taken, but you also can't live as a prisoner to your decisions, Phoenix." I was always dumbfounded by his philosophies, and I could only hope that one day I'd eventually listen.

"You have two options when it comes to the past; you either run from it, or you learn from it, and right now you're running from it," he lectured. "You have to release those demons in order to be human; rid yourself of the past that's held you down for so long, because you can't fly when the weight of your past is weighing you down."

I smiled at him as a response, aware that I probably wouldn't get one back. I knew that although I didn't fully understand him right now, I had hope that I would eventually. I felt a warmth in my core knowing he would be able to see me as a person by the end of this journey, and not a monster.

"Without my past I have nothing else to me, because I have no future to look forward to," I replied. "I sure can't wait to die," I added ironically.

Asier rolled his eyes. "Think about your life back home- your mother and your grandmother - are you ready to leave that all behind?"

"What's the difference when I have to beg for love?" I responded pessimistically. "I have nothing left for me to come home to."

"I know what it feels like to shake the hand of despair. I too have been down that road one too many times," he comforted and placed his hand on my shoulder.

"I guess behind every strong soldier, there's always a painful story," I said.

"You and I can both attest to it," he added, which made me grow more curious.

The conversation brought light to another question; *how did he get to become the way he is?* I wondered. Like the sun above, Asier was always such a mystery, and I just wanted to look behind that dark veil. A small smile formed in the corners of my lips and I turned to face him. As soon as my eyes met his, something completely unexpected happened. The world around me disappeared, and in the blink of an eye, I was in a completely different place.

I assumed it was another weird vision of the past, but this one involved Asier. He appeared a little younger- maybe around my age. He was leaning against the wall of an empty, dimly lit room, sitting on the ground and hugging his knees with a cigarette in between his fingers. I had never seen a man look so miserable and empty.

Whatever scene I was witnessing had drifted to a little boy who sat in the exact same position as Asier, only without the cigarette. He was in a moonlit room with a small window to his right; the moonlight reflected off the tears streaming down this boy's face. It took me a second to figure out that this boy was Asier as a child. He turned around and placed his hand out the window, reaching out for the sky.

That same boy was now running in the desert on the outskirts of a district; he ran without once looking back. Then that drifted back into the version of Asier from the first memory, still running, only this scene was a lot more gruesome. Hundreds of dead soldiers and rebels scattered the path behind him as he ran through a trail of bodies, black feathers, and blood. Once again, *he ran without once looking back.*

He sliced down Crow soldiers with vengeance as he ran; feathers poured out of some, while blood poured out of others and stained Asier's young face. He grabbed his pistols and shot down a few more before switching back to a sword. After cutting down the last Crow soldier, no one was left standing on the field. He stood there catching his breath, looking down at the ground, his blood-covered face hollow and gutted. A darkness rested on him as he fell to his knees.

That was the last thing I saw before I returned to the present, once again, in just the blink of an eye. *What the hell was that?* I internally screamed. From what I already knew and by the looks of it, I presumed it was a flashback of the Rebellium ambush that was believed to have killed *all* the rebels, leaders included. I imagined it was another one of The Phoenix's memories; she was always there in the background like a fly on the wall. I felt shivers crawl down my spine as I processed those visions. I suppose that was just a glimpse into the answer to my question.

"Hey, brat, you there?" Asier asked while waving a hand in my face. I blinked a couple times, and I noticed I was still staring into his eyes.

"Yeah, yeah. I'm fine," I responded, awfully unconvincing.

"Yeah, okay. Why did you just blankly stare into my soul for a second there?" *It was only for a second?* I thought. It felt much longer than just a second.

I remembered the distraught look on his face before falling to his knees. If anything, those memories served as a reminder that even the strongest soldier was still just a human; even he once broke down and thought he'd lost it all. *We all have to break to know we're human.*

"There you go again," Asier added. His hand was still on my shoulder, and I raised my hand to his. Heavy tears welled up in my eyes at the thought of everything Asier had probably gone through.

"Hey, what's wrong?" he asked, concerned as much as he was confused.

"I'm sorry, Asier," I began, still fighting to hold back the tears, "I promise you'll have a happy ending," I added, referencing the story Lana told me.

He raised an eyebrow in response. He was obviously confused, but he must've decided it was probably easier to just drop it. He grinned slightly and patted my head as if I were a child; *I suppose that's one way of showing affection.* The tears in my eyes were beginning to dry.

"You make it sound as if I'm gonna die tomorrow," he teased.

"No, but I am."

"You're so annoying, brat."

"I'm just being honest."

"Look, if it wasn't already obvious enough, I've never been one to believe everything I'm told- especially not from a book, so in my eyes, a book doesn't establish your destiny, *you* do." He paused briefly, then said, "Phoenix, you hold your fate in your own hands."

He didn't look up from the ground, and strands of his straight, raven-black hair fell on his face from his messy undercut. His arms rested on each knee with his sleeves rolled up despite the freezing weather; I could still see the bandages on his upper arm under his sleeve from the bullet wound. I hadn't noticed that behind the loose strands of hair, his eyes were watching me as I stared down his every feature. I also hadn't noticed that a grin managed to make its way onto my face.

I raised my head up and broke the silence. "Hey, Asier?" I asked without moving my gaze from the sky. He turned to face me, but my eyes remained on the stars.

"Tomorrow . . . will we finally paint the sky blue?"

Chapter 20

Sharing a soul with The Phoenix had an effect on my memories and dreams alike. I hadn't had a dreamless night since the day I ran away, but tonight's dream was something else. Occasionally, I would get a taste of her memories, and tonight was one of those nights.

I was in a world that wasn't completely gray- it had color and life thriving all over. The grass was green, and the sunset was a swirl of orange and crimson with the blinding sun adorning the sky so perfectly. There was a young girl sitting under that sun on the vivid green grass. Her skin was a medium shade and olive-toned, and her dark, curly hair framed her smiling face. Her beauty was radiant- like the sun itself.

A young man approached her, who appeared slightly older than her. His hair was dark and his familiar eyes were a stellar blue that glowed when they landed on her. They sat beside each other, exchanged smiles, and laughed at the world around them. You could see in their eyes that they wanted that moment to last forever.

"Lanon?" asked the girl.

"Astrid?" he asked back.

"I'll *always* lead you out of the dark and guide you back into the *light*- even when you don't want me to," she said as she hooked her pinky around his and lifted their hands, "I promise you this," she vowed with sincerity before the scenery changed.

It was now a city where everything the eye could see was either dead or reduced to rubble; this looked a lot more familiar. Desolation had encompassed this land, and bodies with gas masks covered in bullet holes and bloody wounds scattered the barren ground, because like I said before, even in the bleakest moments of humanity- humans continued to fight each other. Ashes of the old world piled on the ground like snow- but somehow this nightmare still appeared brighter than the present. That's because there was still light here, and amongst that light lay the remaining shred of hope for humanity.

Our world had lost to hate- and this was the price we paid. Nobody won that war all those decades ago, and now we're here, living as the victims of a nuclear game of Russian roulette between corrupt leaders. Amid the aftermath's unrest, the power rested on those who were strong enough to carry our future on their shoulders as they led us out of the dark. Lanon Koraki- better known as *The Crow*- happened to be that person for many . . . until *she* came along; Astrid Eleodoro- or should I say, *The Phoenix*.

She stood on the edge of the underworld, with her head always looking up to the sun. She burned like fire yet was nothing more than a mortal woman. She wore her heart on her sword with an oath to protect the nation from falling into his corruption; but not just the nation, him as well. She swore to protect him from falling into the darkness-

And that's just what she's doing all these years later.

The mansion had been up and running since the break of dawn- and I was no exception. Asier had announced and explained the plan last night and everyone wasted no time following it. The physicians, elders, and children gathered medical supplies and water to aid the injured. Everyone else was going to fight on the front lines, so they loaded up on ammunition, weapons, gunpowder, explosives, and other miscellaneous battle materials. Whether we were preparing to aid the injured or fight on the battlefield, we were all prepared to fight with our lives on the line. I hadn't known such a dreadful feeling existed until this morning- concurrently feeling exhilaration and dread.

I changed into my uniform with the thought of it being the last time lingering in my mind. I had finally gotten to the point of not pushing the thought away and embracing it instead; it was foolish of me to ignore the inevitable. I looked at myself properly one last time before heading out and helping the others. My long wavy hair hid behind the hood of my black Rebellium cape, and it created a shadow over my face. *The prophet is ready*, I said to myself as I took one last look in the tall mirror.

I walked the empty halls of the mansion one last time and headed outside where almost everyone was gathered. I took in all the irreplaceable friendships and memories I had made within these walls as I slowly made my way to the door. When I finally reached the door, I went to open it, but my body unexpectedly froze up. My head began to spin, and I put my palm on my forehead as I closed my eyes. When I saw what waited inside my head- I regretted ever shutting them.

I saw a glimpse of my mother running out of a burning building with infant me in her arms; she held me close to her heart as she valiantly fought off the flames. I fluttered my eyes and snapped out of that weird flashback; *why did you come up just now?* I wondered before a cold hand touched my shoulder, startling me even more. I turned around and it was Asier; I seemed to be running into him a lot lately.

"Chill out, brat, it's just me," he clarified in his usual tone.

"What do you need?" I asked, audibly irritated.

"I want to confirm the plan. You're going in first to distract everyone as we storm the south entrance closest to the prison; how long of a delay should there be between your entrance and ours?" He got straight to the point.

"I'm flying, so I'll be there in no time. I'd say ten minutes is probably enough, seeing as the trip on foot for you guys might take up some time." I subconsciously avoided eye contact for some odd reason. For whatever reason, I felt myself unable to face him right now, and I think he caught on.

"Won't even look at me now?" he asked as he lowered his head to my face.

"Don't make this harder . . ." I mumbled under my breath, because the truth was, I didn't want to get any closer to him or anyone for that matter. Soon I was going to die, and he would continue his life the way he planned before he ever met me. There was no room for me in his future.

"What was that?" he asked.

"I'm gonna die soon, so what does it matter?" I yelled irritably. The only response I got from him was laughter, which irked me.

"Mind explaining what's so funny?"

"You."

"Excuse me?"

"You never learn, do you? You never listen. You just choose to let the weight of the world crush you."

"I -" I couldn't even utter a word out before Asier cut me off.

"That's what you think, Phoenix, but have you ever bothered to wonder what everyone else thinks?"

I knew what he was trying to say but I didn't want to hear it. Instead of waiting for my smart mouth to reply, he did the most unexpected thing; he pulled out his gun and aimed it straight at my head.

"If I were to pull this trigger right now, you'd die," he said nonchalantly. "Now tell me, Phoenix, are you afraid to die?" I was startled by his suddenness, but I was comforted by knowing he would never dare to pull it.

I stared him down before lowering the gun's aim to the ground with my hand, asserting my valiant nature. "Don't aim a gun unless you intend to kill, Asier," is all I responded with before walking away.

"It's less significant to die for the ones you love than it is to live for them," he added, which stopped me in my tracks. "Live for your loved ones, Phoenix . . . don't feel pressured to die for them," he advised, and my breath caught in my throat.

The vision of Asier standing above a battlefield filled with his dead comrades came to mind, and I immediately understood the weight behind that advice. I'm sure he wanted to drop dead with them at that moment, but instead, he stayed alive for them, and every single time he'd fallen down, he'd gotten back up for them.

"I wish I had a choice," I admitted quietly, unable to disguise my voice's quiver. *I don't want to die, but who really does?*

As soon as I opened the door, I saw hundreds of rebels in black capes preparing for the battle of their lives. Amongst the swarm, I saw Lamie sitting on a crate, looking down at the ground. It was a discomforting sight to see children scattered throughout the army, especially because I could sense the unease radiating from Lamie. As I observed him, I caught Valerie approaching him; she had a nervous but sincere smile on her face.

"Hey Lamie, how have you been?" I heard her say in a sweet voice as she knelt down in front of him, but his eyes refused to meet hers. "Lamie?" she asked again, but there was only silence on his part. I watched her as every second of silence tore her up.

"I'm so sorry, Lamie, I left you and consequently broke our bond. I missed out on watching you grow and being there for you for those long years, and now I come back with no excuse for you," she apologized, and there was a deep sorrow in both her words and her face. It reminded me of the way she looked at Asier.

"I promise you when this is all over, we'll play together just like the old times. Just you and me, under the warm sun."

After her disheartening apology, she remained in that spot for a while longer, still unable to make him face her. After a long minute of not getting a response, she sat up in defeat. "I'm sorry, Lamie. I hope one day you can forgive me," is the last thing she said before walking away.

I knew she'd had those words hanging on her tongue and that guilt building up in her heart since the day she left. I felt bad eavesdropping, seeing as it was a personal conversation between the two of them, but I couldn't help but feel for Valerie. If she was telling the truth, she sacrificed everything and carried the cross to work toward freeing the ones she loved. She wore the crown of thorns and made herself out to be the villain in hopes of one day saving the world; *she deserved the title of The Prophet more than I did.*

I decided to approach Lamie, who was trembling now. I assumed it was a hybrid of both Valerie's words and the pre-battle anxiety building up. I saw a small tear run down his face.

"What's wrong, soldier?" I asked in an attempt to lift his spirits.

"I'm scared, miss. I'm so scared," he admitted, and it ripped my heart apart. I knew how he felt, because I felt exactly the same, only I had become a master at suppressing it.

"It's okay to be afraid, Lamie. It took me a while to master it, but you just have to learn to turn your fear into courage," I said to him as I knelt down in front of him the same way Valerie had just moments ago.

I wanted to stray the conversation toward something more lighthearted and unrelated to the war, so I brainstormed on the spot until finally coming to a hopefully more cheerful topic. "I always wondered, Lamie, what does your name mean?"

"They gave me that strange name," he answered, referring to the leaders. "My full name, Lambegus, apparently means 'a land with a promised bright future' or something."

"How fitting," I responded with a smile which he returned. I was happy to see his smile again.

"The world will remember your name, miss. Heaven will hear them cheer your name." He surprised me with his response and made me feel a warmth inside my chest.

"Thank you, Lamie," I responded. *A land with a promised bright future, huh? I'll make it more than just your name.*

I approached the crowd, and everyone opened up a path for me. They all kneeled and put their fists to their chest; a fire within me ignited as I walked through everyone. Just as I had advised Lamie, I turned my fear into courage. When I got to the front of the kneeling crowd, everyone shot their fist up in the air.

"The storm commences today, and the end of this tormentous war starts today. I will ensure that the sun above shines on your future if it's the last thing I do," I vowed with my fist to my heart too. I lifted my other fist in the air, and everyone cheered. The faces in that crowd were filled with that same infectious hope as always.

"I will initiate the attack; you will then proceed with the plan to free the deviants in the prison tower. We will fight any soldiers who get in our way, so we must be prepared for anything," I declared, repeating the plan to everyone, and I caught several nods in the crowd.

Aurora, Nyrual, and Guido made their way toward the front. They had brave smiles on their faces, but I could tell they were just as anxious as everyone else.

"You're doing it, big shot," said Nyrual as he patted me on the head.

"Soon home will finally feel like home again," added Aurora.

"We're so proud of you, Phoenix. The universe couldn't have chosen a better Prophet," Guido added on behalf of the group, and it made me feel fuzzy inside.

"I'll see you guys on the battlefield to kick some ass," I said to them, and they smiled. *The faces back home will smile like that again too.*

I pulled my cape's hood up, which had "*THE PROPHET*" embroidered on the back; I wanted to keep a low profile as I walked through the town, so I planned to wear it inside out once I arrived. Once I finally gathered the courage to turn around and run, I heard voices call my name. It was a mixture of Lana, Valerie, The White Raven, and the four leaders. They made their way to the front like everyone else.

Lana and The White Raven were in nursing attire, and Valerie kept her Crow uniform on for practicality. The four leaders wore black tank tops, black pants with ammunition straps going around them, and belts to hold their weapons. They all had bulletproof vests, black jackets, and their signature black capes, which also had their titles embroidered on the back. Fremont's cape read *"SECONDARY CORPORAL,"* Khalon's read *"LEAD CORPORAL,"* Daxon's read *"SECONDARY COMMANDER,"* and Asier's read *"LEAD COMMANDER."*

"Best of luck to you, miss Phoenix," said Fremont. *Always with the unnecessary formality.* I giggled.

"We will follow up ten minutes after your departure. Stay alive until we get there, okay?" Asier reassured me. He was trying to be nice in his own way, but I was still a bit stirred up from our conversation from earlier. I nodded in response to both of them.

"We will meet again, champ," added Daxon.

"Show em' who's boss," stated Khalon.

"Promise me this isn't the last time you'll see us," pleaded Lana and my heart sank a little at her words.

The hopeful attitudes of everyone here had almost made me forget that this would be the last time I saw a lot of them, and that thought made my stomach turn. Following that thought, Asier's words, *"Our destiny is in our hands,"* replayed in my head. *Could I really . . . change my destiny?*

"I promise," I answered. I didn't quite know what I had just gotten myself into, but I made a promise, and now there was no turning back on my word. "I wish you all the best of luck, and I will join you in battle at some point," I began, but paused to gather the strength to utter the next part. "I ask just one favor of you all, please . . . *stay alive for me.*" I was the one pleading now.

I pleaded to the whole crowd but aimed it especially at my friends. I just wanted to know that when I died, as many people as possible would live out the victory. I didn't wait for a reply, instead, I just turned around, closed my eyes, and ignited the fire. I manifested the fire onto my back, creating a set of glowing wings. I looked back one more time, and everyone stared at me in awe; *they were staring at a Phoenix.*

I forced my legs to run and told myself there was no going back now. I ran a few feet before spreading my blazing wings and dashing into the dark, gray sky, leaving behind a trail of embers. As I flew higher into the sky, I felt like a real phoenix- the mythical bird that symbolized resurrection. Fire and determination coursed through my veins as I lit up the dark sky. This time I had something to fight for, and I wouldn't surrender.

Even if I die, I have no choice but to win.

After a while, in the far distance, the gray district was finally visible on the dark horizon. Soon enough, I reached the tall gates, and I landed on top of the thick walls that confined the district. Withering forests encompassed the small town in the center which reached all the way to the gate walls. Observing the view from here and seeing how miniscule everything was from above, reminded me of how insignificant we all truly were in the great scheme of things.

I was finally back home again, but this time, home wasn't there when I returned. I breathed in the familiar air and took in the view of the mundane town that raised me. The view took me back to the town of ruins from The Phoenix's memories. It vastly resembled the ruined nation of ashes that it was back then; only now, the ashes were cold, and every ember had burned out. In addition, just like The Phoenix- in this world filled with people who hated me, I would prevail.

I balanced myself on the edge of the gate, preparing to play Russian roulette with life. I put all my weight forward, and without a second thought, I let myself freefall. It felt like flying, but with my life on a tightrope. I closed my eyes for a second and envisioned myself as a bird's feather, simply drifting through the wind. I stretched out that mere second of serenity for as long as I could before opening my eyes.

Before I could hit the ground, I re-spread my wings, curved my fall, and flew straight toward the town beyond the forest. *Oh, how I loved playing with fire.* The possibility of my power not responding was thrilling, and everyone knows I lived for a good thrill. I used to constantly put myself in perilous situations back when almost dying was the only thing that made me feel alive. Back then, the only thing I had to lose was my insignificant life, but now, I carried the fate of the entire world.

The ten minutes had passed, meaning Rebellium would probably be on their way any time soon. I flew until I was in close proximity to the outskirts of the town, then I continued the rest of the way on foot. As I walked through the quiet forest, the silence was broken by a muffled male voice in the distance. I froze in place to eavesdrop, and the voice- much to my disdain- sounded incredibly familiar. I approached the source of the voice to hear what was being said.

"They definitely won't be prepared for this one. We stationed all the troops the way he asked us to, so they'll have no way in- they'll probably die before they even get close!" the man said.

I discreetly inched closer, disguising myself with the trees to avoid exposure. I pulled my hood up as I peeked from behind a tree; my jaw dropped upon seeing the person behind the voice. The man speaking was none other than Bryce. I wanted to vomit when I saw him dressed in a Hunter uniform as he spoke into a Hunter communicator. I tried to push away my disdain and focus on what he said; *he's talking about troops being stationed somewhere, but where?*

I've hated this man for as long as I could remember, but he knew something that could risk the success of this mission, along with many lives. I couldn't hide from him like I did when I was a little girl; I was The Phoenix now, *so act like it,* I reminded myself. I emerged from the forest and cracked my knuckles menacingly as I began to approach him; *I am going to have fun getting the truth out of you, Bryce Miller.*

"Who's there?" he asked with a threatening glare. I pulled down my hood in response, and his eyes widened.

"How does it feel to be in the presence of The Phoenix, Bryce?" I asked mockingly, and his face grew furious.

"You sure have some serious guts showing your face here again, especially to a Hunter," he snarled, his hand hovering above his pistol.

"I'm so scared," I responded sarcastically as I walked closer to him.

"Stay away, bitch!" he exclaimed and drew his gun. I swiftly kicked the gun out of his grasp and apprehended him by throwing him against a tree, pinning his arms behind his back.

"There's a reason I was picked to be a Hunter and not you," I taunted, and I could hear him curse under his breath. "You never compared in agility or skill."

"Burn in hell," he snarled.

"I plan to, but I have some stuff to do before then, and you're going to help me."

"You're more delusional than I thought if you think I'm going to help you with anything."

I ignored his remark and asked my question. "Where are the troops stationed? And while you're at it, tell me where The Crow is hiding too."

"Are you deaf? I said I'm not gonna help-" he began, and I cut him off by twisting his arm, making him yelp.

"Watch that tongue or I'll rip it from your mouth," I threatened, and flipped him around to face me, holding him up by the collar of his shirt. "Now, answer me while you still have it."

"You must think you're some sort of savior now, huh? Well, you're about to cause a war in which hundreds are going to die. How can you call yourself a hero?" he shouted. To both of our surprises, his words didn't faze me in the slightest.

"Oh yeah, the guilt is practically tearing me apart," I responded sarcastically as I shoved him back onto the tree and held up my fist, which was engulfed in flames up to his face. Upon seeing the flames in my hand, he had the doe-eyed look in his own eyes, only this time, it brought me real satisfaction.

"Th-the troops . . . they're surrounding the gates- every corner of them! They're planning an ambush!" He finally gave in as the heat of my fire got closer to his repulsive face.

"And The Crow?" I insisted.

"I- I don't know," he responded nervously.

"If I were you, I would start thinking. Human flesh is easy to burn," I threatened.

"I swear I don't know! All he said is that he'd make sure to put an end to Rebellium tonight! He didn't give details," he blurted as he pulled his face away from my fire.

I took in the information, deciding what to do with it. I couldn't waste more time here; I would need to warn everyone as soon as possible, since they were probably already on their way. I reached into one of the pouches on my belt and pulled out a sleeping dart. I jabbed it into Bryce's pale neck and he passed out immediately. I didn't have any more time to waste on this loser, and I didn't want more unnecessary blood on my hands. I let him fall to the ground and I made my way into the town.

I knew I was close when a proper path was in place to guide me back to town. Instead of heading straight to the center, I decided to take a nostalgic detour. I walked on that path again- the one I walked the night my world was flipped upside down; the path that led me to The Phoenix that night. I closed my eyes and took a deep breath as I walked through that empty part of the forest. I didn't even need to have my eyes open to know where I was going.

As the cold air filled my lungs, a distant memory intruded my head. I closed my eyes again, and behind them was another flashback. I was about five years old, running through the town, except I wasn't just running- I was chasing something. I was chasing a light- something that looked like a butterfly made of glowing flames, and just like now, it led me into the same dark, hazardous forest.

I remembered stopping my chase when the butterfly flew into the forest. I was far too afraid of that forbidden forest where not even The Crow's eyes surveyed the area. Out of fear, I turned around and ran back home. Little did I know, I- The Phoenix- was inside that forest, sleeping, waiting until it was time for me to wake up.

The closer I got to civilization, the more crows began to scatter the area. Their beady eyes scanned our every move and caught every mistake, but I had grown immune to their threat. One look from me was all it took for it to burn up and be carried away by the wind as ashes. Besides, I knew The Crow was expecting me tonight- so they had nothing to report back. I pulled up my hood and walked through them as if their eyes weren't piercing into me.

I walked through the streets that I've walked millions of times, but they didn't feel familiar anymore. Shattered glass littered the streets, still stained with blood- innocent blood. The streets were empty and there was no one in sight, which could only mean one thing- there was a public execution going on right now. I took one last look at the mundane, gray town and I made a run for it. *Next stop: the execution stage.*

I ran as fast as I could through a torn down version of the town that existed in my memories. I turned the corner and there it was in all its glory- the execution stage. The stage that held all my sins, my biggest regrets, and the biggest decision I'd ever made. I could still hear the echoes of all the screams that escaped the lips of those I'd murdered on that stage. The stage where I'd spilled the blood of countless rebels, and even my own father; the very stage that created the spark that set the world on fire.

All the remaining civilians that either weren't dead or held captive, crowded around it as they witnessed the circus before them. Dead bodies garnished the stage floor, luckily not yet enough to where I couldn't count. The process was a lot different than usual; there was only one executioner- he wore a Crow mask and a black robe instead of the standard Hunter uniform. What really caught my attention was the weapon- he was using an ax. I felt sick to my stomach thinking about how much pain those poor people had to endure before they eventually bled out. At least with a rifle, the death was instant.

I clenched my fist in fury, and my blood, which ran cold only an instant ago, was now boiling. I scanned the crowd, and my fury intensified every time I spotted a child in the throng. Their innocence was being exploited like this, all over lies and a vile desperation to control. The expressions in the crowd varied from disgust, to horror, to pride. In the crowd, I even saw bodies of civilians that had tried to escape on the ground with bullet wounds. This world was truly *putrid-I can't wait to burn it to the ground.*

A young woman was dragged by the hair onto the stage by a Hunter. She was already in bad condition; her arm was wounded and poorly bandaged, and she looked like she hadn't had a proper meal or sleep in weeks. The girl was forced onto her knees and her hands were tied behind her back. Something about that woman triggered something in my memory, and it irked me that I couldn't figure it out. *Her red dress, tanned skin, wounded arm.*

She looked up at the executioner's ax and the doe-eyed look on her face was what did it for me. I felt heavy chills rush throughout my body, leaving me frozen. I was the one who had put the bullet through her arm; she was the woman I chased all those weeks ago, and the first rebel to ever escape my grasp. *I guess her luck has eventually run out,* I thought as she squeezed her eyes shut, and tears fell from them. *No, her luck hadn't run out yet, because this wasn't going to be the end of the line,* I thought as I hovered my hand over the handle of my sword.

The brief period of time that separated that woman and the gleaming blade of the ax from meeting went by in slow motion. Just like last time I was on that stage, the world around me blurred and time ceased to exist. I heard the faint sound of guitar strings plucking somewhere in the distance as the cold, nuclear breeze hit my face. These feelings reminded me that this run-down district was once my home, *and I will make sure home feels like home again.*

I charged toward the stage at full speed, catching the attention of several civilians whose faces flooded with fear and confusion upon seeing me. I pulled out my sword before jumping as high as I could. My wings aided me in the jump, and with that small jump, I flew up into the air, and dropped down onto the stage in front of the deviant woman. Before the executioner could drop his ax, I stopped it mid swing with my sword- shielding myself and the woman.

His mask covered his face, but I didn't need visuals to see the shock. I heard hundreds of gasps in the crowd as I struggled to push back the heavy ax.

"I swear . . . I won't let you die," I grunted, and I could feel the woman's eyes on my back.

After merely holding off the giant ax, I managed to push it back as I swung my sword with all my force- sending it flying away from us. The stage shook as it hit the ground and the crowd gasped again. I then put all my strength into one punch and slammed the executioner in the jaw as hard as I could- knocking him to the ground. I stabbed a sleeping dart into his neck and a paralysis one immediately after. I proceeded to then grab my sword and slice the rope that restrained the deviant woman's hands.

I could tell a million thoughts flashed through her head when I looked into her eyes again. I knew she recognized me from the bittersweet look of gratitude mixed with the grudge she held toward me painted on her exhausted face. I tried to channel all the shame and regret I felt into my face for a second as I looked her in the eyes.

"Run as far as you can," I ordered quietly, and her look tensed up. Eventually she nodded and the gratitude in her face overtook the grudge. She stumbled off the stage before running as fast as she could. *She's still just as fast as the first time,* I thought.

I turned my eyes to the crowd and all their wide eyes were glued on me. I saw disdain, relief, hope, and fear all over their faces. Just as Guido had predicted, some of them held their hopes with me, while others wanted me dead.

"I know most of you expected to see me again, but with a bullet through my head," I began, but all the rest of my words had completely slipped my mind, so I took a deep breath before continuing. "I was once like you all- brainwashed and oblivious to the cruelty around me, and I hate to break it to you, but before the truth can set you free, you're going to hate it," I added. I watched everyone trying to desperately drown out my voice, because they knew that they were not allowed to believe what I was saying, even if they wanted to.

"All we hear must be right, right? The Crow's truth is the only truth, right?" I asked the crowd before continuing. "We just bite our tongues, turn our heads, and close our minds- it's what you're all doing right now. We look away from the truth because we're afraid of what will happen if we believe it . . . but I promise you, there's nothing to be afraid of anymore."

I scanned the crowd again one last time before finishing off my monologue. *These gray faces will smile again*, I thought as I looked at their apprehensive expressions.

"I don't care if I have to burn this nation to the ground, because we *will* rise; a new, free nation will rise from the ashes, because I vowed to save this desolate land- and that's what I'll do 'till my very last breath," I vowed before spreading my wings again.

Everyone's eyes were fixated on me, not even blinking. They were in shock that the forbidden legend of The Prophet was actually real, and that a phoenix was standing right in front of them.

"If you all want to get out of this alive, *run for your lives.*" I gave them one last warning. *Whether they see The Prophet, a deviant, or Phoenix Euphema, I will lead them to salvation,* I thought as I took off, flying far away from the crowd. *Just hold on a little longer . . . this nightmare will be over soon.*

I flew over the walls and tried to fly back to the base as fast as I could. I needed to reach everyone and warn them of The Crow's plan before they reached the district's walls where all the Crow soldiers were stationed. My heart began to race as soon as I realized that the survival of hundreds was now riding on how quickly I reached the army. A wave of relief hit me once I saw a large mob of marching rebels in the distance. I lowered down to the ground as fast as I could, because they were in close proximity to the district.

I had a rough landing and I ended up falling right in front of everyone. They stopped abruptly upon seeing me.

"Phoenix? What are you doing? Retreating wasn't part of the plan!" questioned Daxon, who was leading the group, which led me to wonder where Asier was.

286

As I struggled to catch my breath and formulate my words, I managed to blurt out, "They have troops surrounding the walls! They're planning an ambush!"

"What?" barked Khalon, who was standing next to Daxon. Several gasps erupted from the crowd.

"We'll have to change our strategy immediately," Fremont suggested.

"We'll storm District Four regardless of the troops guarding the walls. The only difference now is the caution we'll take and our readiness to fight right off the bat," explained Asier, who emerged from the crowd and made his way to the front.

"But, Asier . . . " Daxon began to express his concern.

"You'll fight off the troops on the outside of the gates like we always have, while I and a few others mount the invasion from the inside. You're all trained well enough to fight off those weak soldiers, even in large quantities," he explained confidently. It shocked me how he was able to come up with such an efficient plan on the spot under so much pressure.

"Phoenix, Valerie, and I will invade the prison and free the rebels, while one of you will distract and fight off the guards as the prisoners make their run for it," Asier continued.

"Who will that be?" I asked.

"One of the leaders, or a member of your squad. We need someone experienced, but we'll cross those waters when the time comes," he once again strategized effortlessly. It was apparent why he was the lead commander.

"Proceed with caution, my soldiers. It's now or never; this is the fight of our lives! This will be the battle that ends this war!" Asier announced as he raised his arm. Everyone responded by kneeling down, placing their fists on their chests, and thrusting the other in the air.

"With your hearts held high, run toward freedom!" he exclaimed as he threw down his arm.

Everyone shot up and scattered as they fearlessly charged toward the district. Everyone ran except me and Asier; we stood still as everyone ran around us. He stared up at the sky, and I could see that behind that fearless demeanor, he had a million thoughts running through his head. I wonder if in those millions of thoughts, there was any doubt somewhere lurking in that busy head of his.

"I don't know if I made the right choice, but no one ever knows the outcome of their decisions until they make them," Asier said without breaking his gaze. It was as if he'd read my mind. "Let's go, Phoenix."

We were toward the rear of the mob, so we ran forward, hoping to run into Valerie on the way since we needed her for the prison invasion. The gate walls were finally visible, and it wasn't too long before I heard sounds of explosions, guns firing, and screams in the distance.

"The battle has commenced," Asier informed. He was very calm and collected about the whole thing; he ran forward with no fear of what awaited him.

"Hey, Phoenix," he said, and I turned to face him.

"What is it?"

"Whatever you do, *do not look back*," he advised sternly. "Like always, run and never look back, no matter how hard you want to."

I nodded in response, and he again turned his gaze forward. I didn't understand if he meant that literally, or figuratively. *Is this to tell me to not back down, or is he just telling me to literally not look behind me?* I desperately tried to configure the meaning, but I knew I would soon figure it out- probably sooner than later.

Sounds of screams, grunts, guns firing, swords crossing, explosions, and bodies hitting the ground, all simultaneously filled the atmosphere. I struggled to keep my gaze strictly locked on Asier in front of me to avoid seeing the carnage around me. No matter how hard I tried, I caught glimpses of Crow soldiers and rebels I'd seen every day for these last few weeks, all getting annihilated left and right.

I just swallowed hard and kept running forward without looking back, just as Asier had advised me.

That's how it was for a while, running through a parade of death and violence with a blind eye. We ignored the bodies of our comrades as they fell around us, until I felt something slam against my shoulder, forcing me to stop. Asier stopped too, but he seemed reluctant to do so.

"Don't turn around," I heard Asier's deep voice warn me. This time it sounded heavy and distraught, like he had already seen what was behind us.

I felt a strong urge to look back despite Asier's warning; it was like a force was pulling my head to turn around, and I gave in, *although I wish I hadn't*. My body turned completely cold upon witnessing the barbaric sight now before me. My mouth hung open and my eyes were glued to the ground. My body began to involuntarily shake before my knees became too weak to hold me up. In front of me lay the hope of a bright, promised future, in a pool of deep, crimson blood.

Lamie lay motionless on the cold, desert ground with blood oozing out of his mouth and nose, as bullet holes punctured his small body. The world around me ceased to exist as I watched his face slowly drain of life. I managed to move enough to where I crawled toward him, picked up his head, and lay it on my lap. A single tear fell from each of his eyes as they met mine.

"Miss, I-I'm . . . not scared anymore," he grunted with his last breath and his beady eyes looked at me one last time before shutting forever.

I covered my mouth with my hand to stop myself from crying. The feeling I was having reminded me of what I'd felt when Nila was killed, but ten times stronger. I felt the grief and sorrow slowly morph into rage, and the world around me gradually tinted red as disdain and rage consumed my judgment. Crow soldiers surrounded us in hopes of capturing me, and I gently laid down Lamie's head on the ground and picked myself up. I felt the temperature around me rapidly increasing.

"I WILL KILL YOU ALL!" I screamed, and without warning, flames ravaged and engulfed the scene.

The flames were so hot they instantly incinerated anything they touched. Agonizing screams of Crow soldiers filled the air as they were reduced to ash. I didn't care if they were human or feathers- neither of them had a speck of humanity. I drew my sword and prepared to kill anyone who I laid my eyes upon, but before I could get the chance, I quickly came back down the second my eyes landed on Lamie.

His face was pale and lifeless, but it was at *peace*, and that simple fact put me at ease. I bent down and picked his light body up. I felt a heavy shadow drape over us as I carried him through the remaining flames and ashes.

"I'll carry you away from the fire," I mumbled to him as if he could hear me. "I'm not the hero the world wanted, but you always believed in me . . . and yet, *I failed you*," I added as my voice heavily quivered. "Forgive me, Lamie." I whispered and felt a thick lump grow in my throat, but no tears would fall.

I scanned the field for Lana, who was already busy aiding injured soldiers. When I finally reached her, she turned to face me, and she covered her mouth in horror.

"Please take him. I can't bring myself to leave him on the battlefield," I begged as I handed his body to her. When she grabbed him, her eyes immediately shed the tears mine couldn't.

"Thank you, Lana, and please . . . please survive," I begged without turning to face her. I immediately took off, and I knew if I turned around again, it would be too much to bear.

I regrouped with Asier, who waited right where we left off on the outskirts of the flames. His wide eyes failed to hide his devastation at Lamie's death, and there was fresh blood as well as a few feathers stuck to his jacket; I could assume what happened while I was gone. We wasted no more time, and ran, and this time, without *ever* looking back. Once again, I was dreadfully reminded of how malevolent this world was, and why I set my sights on saving it. I wasn't going to let any more innocent blood be spilled like that; I will not look back, and I will not regret it, because I will *never* regret dying for the restoration of humanity.

Chapter 21

The battlefield was already significantly emptier. Our forces were outnumbering theirs for now; I just hoped it stayed that way. With the emptier field, it was much easier to spot Valerie amongst the others. It was apparent that she too had been fighting; she had a layer of sweat on her face and a few rips in her clothes, revealing bloody scratches underneath. I sincerely hoped that she hadn't seen Lamie's corpse, but judging by her calm demeanor, she most likely hadn't.

It was hard to conceal the grief on Asier's face, but he knew it would only cause more trouble if he let his anguish cloud his mission. It made me wonder even further, *what kind of hell could he have gone through to remain so composed in moments like this?* But then I recalled the vision I had of him, and it made more sense; I could only wish to be half as strong as him. Before we snuck through the gates, we were stopped by the rest of the leaders, along with Aurora, Guido, and Nyrual. They had also visibly been roughened up a bit.

"So, big man, which one of us is going to distract the guards for the prisoners to escape?" Daxon asked the question Asier seemed to be avoiding.

"You know I don't like choosing for you," he responded with annoyance.

"Well, you're the commander, Asier, so it's your job to answer the question," Khalon insisted passively.

"I'm not choosing in situations where your lives are at such sparse odds. It's a decision you have to make- not that I will enforce. So, whoever is brave enough to follow, start walking," he instructed before turning away.

They all sighed in response and looked at one another. It was obvious no one really wanted to do it, but there was one person in particular who seemed most uneasy- Fremont. He shifted his eyes between the others, then dropped his head down and fiddled with his cape.

"I'll do it!" he exclaimed. He was building up courage to volunteer, which explained the unease just now.

"It's too risky and you know that-" Khalon began, but Fremont cut him off.

"I get it, I'm not particularly the strongest of the bunch, but I still have what it takes!"

"Fremont . . ." Daxon began in a discouraging voice, and along with Khalon's reluctance, it set something off inside Fremont.

"How can I call myself a leader if I've never proved myself as their leader? What kind of leader would I be if I let all those people get slaughtered in those cells like a coward?"

The tension in the air was heavy and the silence only intensified it. No one, not even Asier, said a word. I'd never really noticed it until now, but Fremont was right, he was usually thrown in the background and never really given a chance to prove himself. Maybe because he's the youngest, or because they believed he was the weaker of the four, but I understood exactly what it's like to feel the need to prove your worth- to prove that you're not *weak*.

"I can be a good commander . . . so please . . . for once, let me prove it to you," he pleaded.

"Show me then, Fremont," said Asier, finalizing his decision. "Dedicate your heart until the end." He turned to face everyone, but Fremont in particular. A smile grew in the corners of Fremont's lips, and he nodded in response.

"We'll get going now; this will not be a goodbye, this is a see you all later. Don't any of you dare die on me, got it?" said Asier. Everyone nodded.

"Best of luck you guys. I expect to see you all again," added Guido. Asier, Valerie, and Fremont nodded and proceeded to walk away, but my feet couldn't seem to move.

"Phoenix?" Aurora asked.

"Give it your best you guys, you have homes and open arms to hurry to," I uttered. I wanted to tell them that we had to come home together, but it just wasn't realistic. I had so many other things I wanted to say to them, but I couldn't articulate the right words, nor did I have the time to try.

"We promise," Nyrual answered with a smile before he, Guido, and Aurora came in for a group hug. I had been in District Four all day, yet this hug was what felt most like home. I wanted it to last forever, but we had to let go. When I turned around to join the others, Aurora's grasp on my wrist stopped me.

"Please . . . don't go . . . at least not before I say goodbye," she implored in a shaky voice. Her words and her tone stabbed like a knife into my chest.

"I don't intend to, Aurora, but I can't say with certainty this isn't the last time you'll see me," I answered softly, yet somehow my answer dug the knife even deeper.

I couldn't look back, so I just kept walking and hoped Aurora's hand would let go, and it did. The others had stopped at the gate to wait for me, so when I got there, we entered immediately. Sneaking in was far too easy and the inside was awfully quiet- *too quiet*. I expected an ambush as soon as we entered, but there was none; almost like they *wanted* us to come in through here.

"Me, Valerie, and Phoenix will find the control room for the cells, and when you see the doors open, that will be your cue to do what you have to do to get them out into safety, got it?" Asier explained to Fremont. He replied by nodding.

"Keep a low profile until you get the signal. It might take a while," added Valerie.

"We'll be on our way then; good luck and don't die, okay, brat?" Asier told Fremont before parting ways.

As we headed toward the prison control warehouse, my head began feeling light, and my chest felt heavy. I chose to ignore it and kept running, but then something strange happened. A face flashed momentarily in my head; *those emerald eyes . . . mother.* I felt as though I was transported somewhere that was no longer in the present. I was back in the yellow field behind our small wooden house. I had tiny hands and feet, and my eyes were still filled with gentle innocence. I was smiling- I can't remember the last time I smiled that genuinely. I wasn't alone either- my mother was there with me in between the flowers, picking them so she could make a living for us.

"Why do we have so many of these flowers, Momma?" I asked her. Her long locks of dark hair blew in the cold wind- hiding her beautiful smile.

She knelt down to my level and picked a daffodil from the ground. "They symbolize rebirth and transformation. Just like your name, Phoenix," she answered briefly and far too complexly for my young, feeble mind to understand. Little did I know then that she was selling the idea of rebellion every morning under my nose. I simply stared at her with wide eyes before something caught my attention.

"Look Mommy, this one is white!" I shouted in excitement, and she giggled.

"Isn't it pretty?" she asked.

"What does this one mean?" I asked again as I admired its delicate beauty. She didn't have an immediate answer this time, so instead, she pondered an answer for me.

"It tells us that it's a beautiful thing to be different," she finally answered while looking at me. "In a field of yellow daffodils, it's okay to be a white one," she added while smiling at me, and I smiled back.

I didn't understand any of this back then, but it's clear as glass now. She knew I was different then and would only grow to be more

different later. She understood me best because she was different too-
a deviant stuck in a world of followers. She was the white daffodil in
a field of yellow ones.

I simply blinked and I was brought back to the present. I shook
my head and placed my hand over my now pounding forehead. I had
stopped running, and the others stopped too. I don't know how long
I was gone for, but I assumed it was only an instant. *Why am I
remembering you right now of all times?* I thought as I pulled the loose fabric
of my cape over my mouth and nose.

"Why'd you stop? You alright?" asked Asier.

"I'm fine," I answered with uncertainty, because I certainly
didn't feel fine, I felt as though something was pulling me away- back
to the place where it all started.

"Are you sure?" he asked again.

"I need to go back to the stage," I shouted abruptly, realizing
how out-of-the-blue it must've sounded.

"Huh?"

"I just have a bad feeling. I don't have time to explain, nor do I
know how to, but I just really feel like I have to go," I spewed out,
probably making no sense, but right now that was the least of my
worries.

"So, you're gonna run off just because of some random hunch?"
Asier asked with an unexpected coldness, and it made my stomach
turn.

"Me and Asier can handle the control room," Valerie added
unexpectedly. "Do what you have to do and regroup as soon as
possible." Her boldness caught me by surprise, and I could tell I
wasn't the only one. I didn't like the idea of taking orders from
Valerie, but I had no time to be picky.

"Best of luck, you two," I said hesitantly with a weird feeling in
the pit of my stomach. *Are you trying to get rid of me?* I wondered. Deep
down, I still distrusted her intentions, and I was not comfortable with
the idea of leaving her with Asier alone.

"Don't hesitate, either run now, or stay." Asier must've noticed my reluctance.

The tone of his voice did not match the look in his eyes, which were glossed over with worry. I scanned Valerie's eyes in an attempt to read her, but my mind was too distracted to focus. She was a hard one to read, but there was one thing I saw every time without fault- *guilt*. It was always the first thing I noticed, because we share the same pitiful look in our eyes.

I turned in the direction of the stage, spread my wings, and took off without another second to spare. I just had to trust that if it came down to it, Asier would be strong enough to defend himself against whatever she may scheme. I flew through the forest to avoid drawing attention to myself in the town and landed in close enough proximity to the town center. I pulled my hood back up and dashed through the same worn down streets of the district town I'd run through thousands of times before.

The town was in complete disarray. Buildings were burning, glass was shattered, and everywhere I looked, there was drying blood on the streets. I peeked through windows where frightened children hid in the shadows as their parents cradled them in attempts to fight away their fears. Despite all the visible unrest, *it was dead silent*. Not a breathing person in sight on the streets, and that was the most unsettling part. It was disturbing but expected; these poor people had been silenced against their will.

I crept through buildings to avoid being caught, and gradually made my way to the stage. When I arrived, relief brushed over me after finding it empty. However, that relief was short-lived, as I speculated that the emptiness could be due to arriving *too late*. I hid behind a bush next to the stage and sat there, trying to calm myself before I lost control again. I practiced some breathing techniques Lana had taught me to regulate anxiety, but I was interrupted as soon as I heard footsteps that sounded like they were approaching the stage.

I turned myself around as quietly as I could to avoid being spotted, and saw a tall, lanky man, seemingly in his early forties, climb the stage and idly wait there. The longer I stared at his features, I was able to recognize him as the mayor's brother, Secretary Devrim. It was disturbing to think that I had killed his brother on that same stage just a few weeks ago, and even more disturbing that he was my dad, making this man my uncle. I saw his head turn in the slightest, and a grin grew on his lips. I turned to face what he was grinning at, and I saw someone in a long, black robe approaching the stage.

It was only after I really focused that I recognized the robe as a deviant robe- the same ones they wore during executions. The hood concealed their face with a shadow, but they wore a long, black dress underneath, so I figured it was most likely a woman. Maybe it was the familiar height and posture, but it felt as if the person beneath that robe was not a stranger.

They elegantly climbed the stairs of the stage in an oddly noble manner, which indicated their higher class. My suspicions were about to be answered, for the woman had yanked her robe off. Underneath the robe, a woman with hip-length, deep brown hair, fair skin, and emerald eyes hid; it was no other than Cordelia Euphema- my mother. *What the hell is she doing here?*

Intensity filled both their faces- like they were about to settle something once and for all. A million questions circulated in my head, but rather than freaking out, I decided to eavesdrop and find out for myself. The suspense and confusion triggered my fight-or-flight, and I caught myself instinctually hovering my hand over my sword.

"Cordelia Wolfe, in the flesh. I've heard my fair share of rumors, but I'd never imagine you'd still be so beautiful," he fawned with a dark grin on his lips.

"Spare me the flattery and let's cut to why we're both here," she responded with hostility.

"Not one for small talk, huh? Fair enough, you've been forced to keep quiet for years now-"

"But that's about to change," she cut him off.

298

"Oh yes, the little runt's gonna save our asses. How's the cub doin' anyway? She sure grew up fast enough to kill her own father."

A shadow grew over her face for a second. "Did he know . . . about her?"

"It was rumored that you took refuge in a neighboring district, but besides me, no one knew which one; it didn't help that your disappearance was relatively unknown to those beyond District Five civilians, and also that he had almost no interest in the civilian files, so far as he was concerned, your survival was nothing but a rumor."

"But you knew, so why did you keep it from him? What did you gain out of it?"

"If he knew you were a rebel on the run and then named his daughter Phoenix, he would surely kill you both, and I couldn't bear to watch you and my precious niece get slaughtered," he answered sarcastically.

My mother rolled her eyes. "I didn't come here to play around."

"I'm the only one who knew about your dirty little secret in full detail, Cordelia, and I knew it would be amusing to see how it all panned out. The idea of watching you run like a mouse from a fire as all your secrets came to the light was exciting," he began before scoffing, "but it definitely took a turn for the worse. I guess that's what I get for protecting two deviants."

He approached my mother until he was only inches away from her. "Who knew little Phoenix had it in her, to end up just like her mommy," he said to her and began to approach her more, ". . . I suppose the apple doesn't fall too far from the tree."

He put his hands on her shoulders which she responded to by harshly shoving him away from her. Her eyes followed him with an intense look of pure repulsion.

"I think it's only fair that I ask a question too, Cordelia," he insisted, staring her down without blinking an eye, "so answer me this . . . why did you deviate?"

"I never cared for patriotism, nor did I care for rebellion, but when *he* offered me to your brother like an object, I witnessed firsthand the lengths people were willing to go for power." She paused to collect her words. "I grew to hate it all; the people, the nation, the ideas we blindly abided. Corruption and injustice- it doesn't discriminate even against those who are said to be on top."

I felt sick simply imagining the suffering my mother must've been subjected to. She was forced to be District Five's puppet for years, and her father was the one pulling the strings. They traded her dignity for power; *but this will be the last night, Momma.*

"Well then, I think it's time to settle this once and for all. It's a shame Wolfe had to wait this long for justice, but today his killer will get her retribution," he said as he inched closer to her. "Every rebel will finally be extinguished, and you and your daughter will merely mark the beginning."

"This forsaken nation has to burn to the ground for a phoenix to rise from the ashes," she began, placing a hand on his chest. "For a new nation to rise, this one has to fall," she spat, and without warning, pulled out a knife and swung it, slicing the tie off his shirt, and he drew back- seemingly unfazed by the move.

He glanced down at the damage and looked back up with a lustful look in his eyes. "There was always something about you, Cordelia," he said lecherously, "You've always carried the true strength and intelligence of a Wolfe, *up until the very end.*"

"If I die, you're coming down with me," she asserted as she swung at him again. "I owe it to my daughter to kill you!"

"Oh, nothing would make me happier than being the one who gets the pleasure of taking your last breath!" he exclaimed enthusiastically as he dodged her knife.

"Burn in hell," she growled as she continued swinging.

"If it's real, I'll make sure to drag you down with me."

It shocked me to see how natural combat and defense came to her, as it was a side of her I had never seen before. He pulled out a sword from the sheath hidden on his back and swung it at her. She somehow managed to block it every time, but I could tell she was beginning to struggle. If luck was keeping her alive, it had to run out eventually; she tripped on her dress and had no way of dodging his swing on time. Nothing made me more sick than seeing such vulnerability on my mother's face. *I will never let you die.*

I flew toward the stage as fast as I could and in the blink of an eye, I was in front of my mother, and underneath his sword. I didn't even have time to draw my own, so in a moment of panic, with my bare fist, I punched the blade as hard as I could, and the sword flew out of his hand. The blade managed to graze my forearm a bit- ripping my suit and drawing blood. Oddly enough though, I didn't feel the sting; it must've been the adrenaline.

After blocking the swing and knocking the sword out of his hand, I jump-kicked him, which knocked him back pretty far, so much that he almost tripped on impact. A stunned expression painted itself on his rugged face as soon as his eyes landed on me; it was a combination of astonishment, disbelief, and a hint of unease. I turned around and saw my mother's face flooded with relief- relief to be alive, and relief to see that after all this time, *I was still alive.*

"Is . . . is this an angel who's just flown down from our dark sky?" he asked with a disturbing flush on his face. Eccentric behavior definitely ran in the family.

"Not an angel, but a phoenix," I responded with pride and my head held high.

"So, you're still alive, huh? It's a real shame though, little niece. If the prophecy you rebels preach so avidly is correct, that means you're on borrowed time."

"I'm well aware," I answered indifferently.

"And it doesn't bother you? Gosh, you deviants are so strange-"

"Alright, freak, you will answer *me* this time," I cut him off demandingly. "If you knew everything about us, then why didn't you snitch?"

"Darling, we've been through this before; you were destined to be a fighter since you took your first breath of air," he began, and I immediately regretted asking. "With all the strength and intelligence of a Wolfe, I knew you would be of great use, so ratting you out to my brother would have just been a waste of a precious soldier." He paused, then asked, "Don't tell me you forgot our deal?"

"What deal?" my mother asked, completely lost. It totally slipped my mind when I presented the question that this would all be news to her.

"I didn't know you took refuge here until little Phoenix here qualified to be a Hunter candidate. I did my own research and discovered all your dirty little secrets, such as being the one responsible for killing Mayor Wolfe, and letting the District Five rebels escape unpunished," he explained as he paced the stage, "but to answer your question, Phoenix, my desire to watch justice prevail would be fulfilled once I watched Cordelia's dark past catch up to her, and what better way than to have her own daughter become the top Hunter and Executioner, and eventually be the one to put a bullet through her head?"

"What was the deal?" my mother repeated sternly. Her voice shook and her fists were tightly clenched.

"She was under the impression that naming her after a rebel folktale was the only crime you've committed, but even then, that was worth execution for the two of you. So, I told her, if she became a Deviant Hunter and Executioner for District Four, I'd spare both your life and hers; it was gonna be our little secret," he explained, "but of course, I wasn't planning on keeping you two around for too long- I'd make her kill you before eventually killing her myself."

Memories resurfaced of the wretched day he came to me with that offer. I almost wanted to vomit after listening to him, while all the emotions I felt back then tumbled on me like an avalanche. I'd thrown my entire life and peace away to serve as his puppet, and I realize now that his mercy was nothing more than a front; *beware of false prophets that come to you in sheep's clothing.*

"I'm going to rip you apart-" I threatened before I felt a small hand hold my arm back from below. I looked down to see my mother restraining me.

302

"No . . . It will be me who puts him six feet underground."

"But Mother-"

"Phoenix, please. This is my battle to fight; I have to kill him myself in order for me to be *freed*," she implored with desperation.

With all the torment his bloodline, along with her own, had caused her- this was the only way for her to feel like she was finally freed from their strings. We all had our battles to fight, and I supposed this was my mother's. After taking that into consideration, I lowered my sword; I surrendered this battle, not because I'd lost, but because I knew she'd win it for us.

"Thank you, my beautiful girl," she said softly. I felt a dense ache in my heart when I heard her utter those words. I turned away and faced the town in an attempt to keep my composure.

"Even if you lose- you have to live," I pleaded without looking her in the eyes, because if I did, there's no guarantee of what I'd do next.

"Same goes for you, dear; dedicate that burning heart and seize your victory," she replied as she picked up the sword from the ground, "Remember, our fate is always in our hands." I froze at her words, because it wasn't my first time hearing that. Asier always told me the same thing, but it felt so real now that it was coming from my mother too.

I spread my wings and turned to face her one last time. "Don't let this be the last time, Phoenix," she finished.

Maybe it was the tears building up in her eyes, or the quiet crack in her voice- but I turned around, took off, and I didn't dare to look back. It was the first time I'd seen so much genuine pain in her face, and that only made it sting so much more. I fought back, with every cell in my body, the urge to go back and throw myself into her arms. Perhaps I had fought against the strongest weapons, genetically modified soldiers, and even entire armies- yet *this* was my toughest battle, because my heart had already accepted everything.

That was probably the last time she would see me alive.

Chapter 22

The entire trip back all I could think about was my mother, and her words, which echoed in my head over and over again. Now it was not only Asier, but my mother too. The more I heard it, the harder it was becoming to push the possibility away. I wondered as I flew past dozens of gray, run-down buildings, *do I really have to die today?*

The thing I knew for certain, was that the only way to end The Crow's tyranny was to eliminate him. His impact on this world had become far too prominent to reverse. No soldier, weapon, or bomb could kill him either; he had modified himself far beyond the body of a human being, making him practically immortal. It would take a huge amount of power to kill him, and I supposedly had that power nestling inside of me; the power of The Phoenix- enough to set the world on fire . . . *but why did it always have to end in ashes and bloodshed?*

My mind had completely trailed off as I flew through the district's livestock plains. When I reached the outskirts of the town, another pounding sensation pulsed through my head. When I shut my eyes, I had another flashback, except this one wasn't mine. An image of Astrid and Lanon flashed in my head; she was asleep on his shoulder, while he looked off into the horizon with his arm protectively wrapped around her. I could almost feel this vision- the serene surroundings and his arm draped over me. The gentleness of their embrace radiated that strongly.

"I'll always be there to lead you out of the dark- even when you don't want me to," Astrid's soft voice muffled in my head, ". . . because *I love you.*"

It were as if a spark had fired in my brain, and that's the last thing I felt before getting knocked back to reality- quite literally. I was falling, and there was a restricting grip on my neck. When I hit the cold ground, the wind was knocked right out of me; on top of that, there was something strangling me and pulling me down to the ground by the neck, restricting my airflow. Before I could pass out, I gripped onto whatever was around my neck. It burned and disintegrated the second I touched it, and the ashes blew away with the wind. I coughed and gasped desperately, struggling to regain my breath.

Once I sat up, ominous chuckling and deep laughter came from behind me, and my heart dropped as the sound entered my ears. I turned slowly around, but to my surprise, no one was there. I looked all around me, but not a soul was in sight. I looked up to check the sky, and there I found a delicate, white bird floating through the indigo skies, carrying an olive branch in its small beak- just like the legends once told.

The same bird that symbolizes nothing but peace and love was gracing me with its presence in the epicenter of a bloody war. *Why would you come here?* I wondered as it flew around with no direction, *why here?* I was so focused on the bird, that I didn't notice the sharp sword charging straight at me until it was only inches away. I barely dodged it by rolling to the side, missing it barely by a second; *that was too close.* I looked in the direction from which the sword had flown from, and there I found what I was looking for- The Crow.

"Don't you think it's a bit of a bad time to be skywatching, little girl?" he taunted.

He no longer wore his eyepatch, revealing his spine-chilling crow eye that squinted whenever he grinned. I picked myself up and stared intensely into his daunting eyes. One of his eyes might have still been human, but they were equally sinister and full of malice.

"I didn't come here to have a staring contest, darling."

"Neither did I."

"Then what are you waiting for? For me to attack first? Or has The Phoenix lost her flare?"

"I-I didn't come here to fight . . . not anymore, at least," I stuttered.

"I'm sorry?"

"We don't have to fight to the death, Lanon," I uttered, and the grin on his face fell and grew cold.

"I don't know where you got that name from, but that's the last time you speak it," he threatened with wrath in his voice. From beneath his cape, a strong, dark wing poked out and shot out toward me- striking me and knocking me back several feet.

I grunted at the impact as I landed roughly on my chest. I rolled over and caught a quick glimpse of the dove, still aimlessly drifting through the sky. Maybe I hit my head too hard on impact, but I saw images of every person I cared for, flashing in the dark sky; *I have something to live for now, and I don't want to die today.* What I would do next would hurt my pride beyond repair, but I got on my knees and began pleading.

The Crow broke out in laughter. "What is this? Is the oh so prideful Phoenix actually getting down on her knees and begging *me* for mercy? I never thought I'd see the day!" he exclaimed in amusement as he approached me.

"I've finally found something more important than pride- more important than this damned war. There are people I'd die for that I want to *live* for. I want to live for those people *I love*," I finally admitted, and it was like a fog was cleared in my heart. My heart was capable of loving, and I was no longer afraid to admit it.

The Crow's laughter only got louder, which stung even more. "What happened to all that fire you once had, Prophet? This can't be the same soldier who has over fifty kills and captures- the same one who believed she could pose a threat to the empire I've created."

"A real soldier knows when to put their arms down- especially when they're losing something worth more than the victory," I refuted sternly from the ground. "Please, I know you know what it's like to love someone," I supplicated, and The Crow's eyes widened. "She loved you and she still does, that's why she's holding up her promise after all these years; I know you loved her once and I know you never stopped!" I risked it all by shouting those words, and the look on his face was pure carnage. If looks could kill, I would certainly be dead.

He responded to my spew by punching me in the face so hard it knocked me back down to the ground. I could feel my cheek throbbing, and the pain was so profound I could feel it pulsing throughout my head. He then proceeded to kick me even harder in the back, thrusting me yards away. The pain was exceptional, but I remained strong- convincing myself it wasn't the worst pain I'd felt.

I rolled over on my back and slowly opened my eyes to the groggy world which seemed to be running in slow motion again. I tried to keep focus on the dove in the sky to keep me from slipping away- but it was nowhere to be seen. I turned my heavy head to the side to avoid losing touch with my surroundings, and that's when I *really* realized where I was. What I thought was just an empty field by the gate wall appeared to actually be a battlefield.

Small pools of blood that had begun to dry dyed the brittle, yellow grass and rough, barren earth. My best guess was that that blood belonged to those who'd tried to escape the district and were killed on the spot by Hunters. Right next to a large, crimson puddle, I saw something that made the world around me stand still. At the base of a tree stump, a singular white flower danced in the breeze of the bitter wind.

The green stem had been stained red; *I suppose you've been drinking more blood than water these days.* It was a stunning white daffodil, but this time, it was alone- without a field of yellow daffodils. The truth was, there were no more yellow daffodils, only white ones that pretended to be yellow so they wouldn't get cut. Even without the field of yellow daffodils, it still stood out on its own.

The world had paused completely, all except the flower drifting on the cold, nuclear wind, which blew right through each of its delicate petals. The breeze stopped, and a small white bird landed on the tree trunk behind the flower. *Fly away, dove . . . as far away from here as you can,* I internally pleaded. When it began to peck at the white daffodil, I vaguely remembered my mother once telling me that the white ones symbolized the yearn for transformation; *and I have the power to bring that transformation.* I turned to the dove one last time; *truth is, peace was never an option.*

His hands lifted me off the ground by the collar of my jumpsuit, and I courageously stared into his daunting eyes. That alone was all I needed to relight my fire.

"Have you ever heard the story of the phoenix?" I asked him out of the blue.

"What?"

I turned to the dove again, who had knocked the daffodil into a pool of blood. The flower's purity tarnished as carnage stained and spread throughout each petal; *this new beginning will be carried by the blood of those who died trying.*

"It's simple- a bird was engulfed in flames and reduced to ashes," I began, and I extended my arm to the dove, "and from those ashes, a phoenix was born- the symbol of rebirth," I finished, closing my hand into a fist, and remorselessly setting the dove on fire.

The Crow turned away to witness the dove incinerating, and while he was distracted, I took the opportunity to kick him off me with all my strength. He let go of me and knelt down on one knee while clutching the spot I'd kicked. He stared me down as I now fearlessly hovered over him.

I drew my sword and aimed it at his face. "You'll be the next bird to become a phoenix, Crow."

Before I could get a response, thousands of crow feathers flew out at me, obscuring my view of him. I heard him stand up, but because of the feathers, I couldn't see where he was going. I put my arms up to shield myself, which proved unnecessary as every feather that came near me burned before it could reach me.

I refused to let him escape again, so I had to attack now before he had the chance to flee. I caught a glimpse of his silhouette behind the barrage of feathers which had begun to diminish. I gripped my sword and charged at him without a second to spare.

"The sooner I kill you the better!" I shouted and blindly swung my sword. The barrage ceased, and there he was- standing and waiting for me with his blade out too.

"Why the rush, Phoenix? Let's enjoy this," he said in a growly tone and a smirk on his face as he blocked my swing with his own sword.

"The only thing left to do is kill you. I'll avenge every person who's died under your reign," I grunted while pushing to overpower his sword.

"How can you deem yourself any better than me when all you've ever known is killing too?" he asked in an attempt to gaslight me into surrendering again.

"That won't work on me anymore, Crow, because I no longer regret killing all those deviants," I retaliated, and a puzzled look struck his face. "I don't regret killing them, because they don't regret dying for their cause. So instead of regretting their deaths, I will make sure their deaths are not in vain."

As soon as I finished, he laughed his bone-chilling laugh. "My! How noble of you!" he mocked as he swung at me with full force, and I struggled to hold off his sword. "You can keep convincing yourself all you want, little Phoenix, that where the blood has dried- there is no sin."

"If there's one thing I've learned, it's that to feel guilt is to feel *human*," I refuted courageously as I used all my strength to send his sword flying. My blade managed to graze his bicep, inflicting a relatively deep wound.

He merely flinched from the gash on his skin. Like before, a barrage of feathers charged at me, but this time, there were sharp feathers among them. I tried to dodge them, but some of them managed to slip through. They ripped through my jumpsuit and left cuts on my thigh and arm, and a deep one on my cheek. The stinging feeling lingered for a second or two, but it was far from enough to bring me down.

After all the feathers stopped, I was left with no time to react to The Crow launching at me at full speed. He kicked me in the chest, knocking me to the ground and then pinning me down with his knee on my chest. I struggled to breathe beneath him until my body instinctively switched on its fight-or-flight reflexes and heated up like hot metal, enough to where his skin would burn on contact. He immediately removed his knee, and I rolled over, coughing intensely as I slowly sat up. He came up behind me and lifted me up by grabbing a handful of my hair.

"What are you really fighting for, Phoenix?" he mumbled into my ear, his breath on my skin filling me with goosebumps.

"I want everyone to live freely. . . for every person to see the sun."

"But what if there's no one left to fight for?" he asked ominously.

"What?"

"You want freedom in this world for the people you love to enjoy it- am I right?"

"Where are you going with this?"

"Would you still fight for this world if there was nothing left for you to fight for?"

"What are you talking about?"

"Why don't you take a look at the world for yourself through *my eyes*," he said before placing his hand on my left eye, and it burned until he let go of me. I fell to the ground again and grunted as I placed my hand over my eye, but the burning feeling stopped as quickly as it came. I slowly opened both my eyes again, and that's when I realized what he had done to my vision- he had lent me a crow's eye.

"I'll show you a little of what my lovely eyes have captured around here."

Was I prepared to see what was waiting for me? I asked myself. I had a really bad feeling about it, but I had no other choice than to watch. The first thing I saw was an aerial view of the battlefield outside the gates through the clearest, high-definition lens. The war was being showcased to me through the eyes of a bystander- a bird flying through desolation.

People fought barbarically; so many bodies, feathers, and so much blood covered the hard, desert ground as a thick layer of smoke filled the atmosphere. It was a disturbing sight- but my eyes had seen it all many times before.

"Humans are such selfish creatures- designed to fight and kill over even the feeblest disagreements," he prefaced. "In the world I've fought so hard to create for all these years, no one should ever have to disagree with one another, because there's nothing to disagree upon when were all living the same life, under the same rules."

My whole life, this propaganda created by The Crow of him being a savior who built a nation up out of ashes, had been forcefully pushed onto us, and we'd always been strictly reminded that his way was the *only* way. After living with the rebels, I saw their perspective, and why they fought so desperately against this world he'd created; they showed me the potential we could have as the human race if we overthrew him, and if we carried our own lives in our own hands. Right now, I was witnessing something far from the two; The Crow's real, unfiltered perspective, stripped of propaganda from either side, all showcased through *his* eyes, and hearing his reasoning from *his* mouth.

"Disorder is the embodiment of war, and rebellion is the epitome of disorder. Rebellion threatens the system I intricately created to avoid disagreements among each other that would lead to bloodshed like this, which is why I do not tolerate any sort of deviation, and have set my sights to eradicate it," he explained. "What you are watching right now, is one race- the human race, divided in two and fighting each other to the death; this is an unfortunate product of disruption, and the chaos caused by those devils who threaten the intricate beauty in control and sequence."

As he spoke, it was easy to see why The Crow had this nation wrapped around his finger; he was a great manipulator, and it was hard not to fall for his words, especially in times of great desperation. It was interesting to see the logic behind the madness in The Crow's mind, but I didn't want to keep listening; I was in too deep to back down now.

"If you're trying to make me doubt, you're going to have to try a lot harder than that," I challenged.

He remained silent, and the crow that surveilled the scene only seemed to inch closer to the gruesome battle. I watched the battle for what felt like an eternity, and the silence on The Crow's part was the most eerie. I didn't understand why he continued to show me this- until the view drifted to some familiar faces.

In the middle of the field, Daxon and Nyrual fought off soldiers side by side. Daxon's leg was bleeding and looked to have been shot, while Nyrual also bled from an injury on his arm. Both were visibly worn out, and I could tell they were barely standing at this point. The sight made my heart beat uncontrollably with dread, and I wanted more than anything to fly over there and help them. The bird moved away quickly, but I was secretly grateful, as I didn't know if I could bear to watch that any longer.

It flew over more fighting and corpses before reaching another familiar face. Khalon was on the ground; he too had been shot above his hip and was unable to stand. Rebels around him fought off the soldiers as he attempted to drag himself away from the action. In the background, I caught a glimpse of Guido, although I immediately wished I hadn't. He was leaning against the gate wall; his eyes were shut and his head was dripping with blood.

The sight drained all the blood from my body and my eyes began to water. My knees grew weaker and weaker as this played out, but I couldn't exactly look away. Just like a flashback, shutting my eyes couldn't make it stop. When I thought it couldn't get any worse, Aurora appeared, running to Khalon's aid; she was generally unscathed besides a few scratches here and there, and that brought me some ease.

"Khalon!" she cried out as she ran toward him.

"Aurora, run back!" he shouted and she stopped in her tracks. Her face flooded with fear as her eyes landed on a grenade which fell right at her feet.

"AURORA, RUN!" he shouted so loud it sent chills throughout my body. Aurora turned around and tried to run, but she was unable to react quick enough. She let out a horrific scream before the explosive went off.

Smoke clouded the scene, but a crow's vision was so defined that I could still see clearly, although I wished I couldn't. Aurora's small body slammed against the gate wall, leaving behind a large crack on the wall, and a splatter of blood as she dropped to the ground face first. She rolled onto her back; her legs were oddly contorted, and blood trickled out of her mouth and broken nose. People called out her name, but there was no response; her eyes remained shut.

I found myself unable to move; my body was stiff and trembling, and tears were uncontrollably spilling from my eyes. I covered my mouth to stop myself from screaming as my heart banged against my chest in slow, hard-hitting beats. It was hard to tell if Guido and Aurora were alive, but after witnessing that, the chances seemed minimal. My body grew weaker by the second and my breath was caught in my throat.

My delusional mind began to wonder; *was there any way to save them now?* The surveilling crow shut his eyes, and now we were in a different location looking through the eyes of a different crow. We were at the dreaded stage- the place where it all started. I didn't even have to see anything to know what I was about to witness was going to traumatize me even further.

"This one's from a few minutes ago, I saved it just for you," The Crow prefaced.

My mother and Secretary Devrim were going at it. My mom had the sword, and he had the dagger. For a brief moment, it consisted of them mostly dodging each other's attacks, which only made my anxiety skyrocket. Finally, my mother managed to catch him off guard, and she dug the sword straight into his chest. He let out a blood-curdling scream as my mother dug the sword deeper and twisted the blade. Before I could even begin to feel relieved, I saw him reach for something in his belt with his last bit of strength.

"No!" I screamed as if it would do anything- as if my voice could reach her. He placed the barrel of the gun on her chest, and before she could do anything-

The bastard pulled the trigger.

Blood splattered on him and dripped down from her chest. She slowly let go of the sword, and they both collapsed to the ground. The crow flew over the grotesque scene, and I saw something that made me sick to my stomach. With his last ounce of energy, he reached for my mother's limp hand, and held it as they drifted into eternal darkness.

"What a touching ending," taunted The Crow, but I was too speechless to reply. My tongue was dry, and my heart was caught in my throat. I couldn't speak even if I wanted to.

I was paralyzed from the series of traumatic sights, but contradictory enough, my mind was blank; my head couldn't process everything my eyes had just witnessed. I could go on about how my heart felt like it had stopped beating, or how I couldn't breathe beyond shallow breaths, but it would all be an understatement. I just witnessed the only people I had and cherished in this world be killed in HD through the keen eyes of a crow.

After about a minute of trying to pull myself together, I noticed through my tear-blurred vision that The Crow was gone. I never saw or heard him leave, but I wouldn't have been able to stop him if I tried- every muscle in my body refused to move. I closed my eyes to cool down, but whenever I closed my eyes, I saw *them*. I wondered how or if it could possibly get worse, and then I remembered- there was only one person I hadn't seen yet.

Before I could even finish that thought, the crow eye opened to the last place I wanted to see right now- the *control room*. A crow must've been sitting right at the window frame, because I had a front row seat. *Asier won't go down that easily,* I convinced myself silently, trying to grasp onto the pinch of hope and optimism I had left.

"All we need is a few more, but you've got the pattern down- all the cells will be open in no time," Valerie praised, and she seemed different from any of the versions of her I'd seen so far. She had a soft edge when it came down to Asier.

I didn't have to see Asier smile to know he was content right now; being with her was everything he'd wanted since the day she left. They had seemingly managed to figure out most of the code to open the cells, and they were still going at it when The Crow abruptly appeared at the door. My heart dropped to the pit of my stomach the second I spotted him; *so that's where you ran off to.* They both immediately turned around as soon as they heard his menacing chuckle, and their faces reflected shock and dismay in their purest forms.

Asier pulled out his gun and shot at him with no time wasted, and The Crow dodged it, but only by a few inches. While all that was going on, Valerie blocked them out and continued to swiftly push an array of buttons in what seemed to be a premeditated order. That caught The Crow's attention, and he pulled out his gun and shot straight at her, but instead of instantly dodging it, she used that split second to press one final button, which she pressed with all her might. She somehow still had enough time to dodge it, but by dodging the bullet, it shot through and broke the computer system they were using.

I assumed the button she pressed was to unlock the prison doors for rebels, but nothing seemed to happen after she pressed it- nothing visibly changed, and no noise was made. To make matters worse, the computer system was now destroyed, so there was nothing we could do to finish the code.

"So, this is what you've been up to, you dirty traitor," The Crow scorned.

"I was never on your side to begin with," Valerie responded with resentment.

"You do know how we handle treason in this nation, don't you, honey?"

"My name is Valerie."

"I don't usually ask for the names of my convicts," he retorted before pointing his gun at Asier. "It's too bad though, I didn't come for you, hun," he added, "I came to see my favorite commander for the last time."

Asier immediately ducked and dodged the first few bullets, but eventually his luck had to run out in that tiny room.

"Asier, watch out!" Valerie shouted.

He tripped over a box on the ground, and there was absolutely no way he would dodge the next bullet on time.

"ASIER!" I shouted off the top of my lungs, knowing he couldn't hear me.

Everything went by in slow motion; The Crow pulled the trigger, and the shot roared *so loud.*

"Val . . ." uttered a cracked, deep voice.

Blood . . . blood everywhere . . . all over him . . .

Asier's lip quivered, and his eyes were shot open as blood dripped on the floor beneath him. Valerie fell to her knees . . . falling into the puddle of *her blood.* She had valiantly thrown herself in front of Asier, *and took the bullet for him.* The bullet ripped straight through her chest and even through the wall behind them. The shot was so powerful, smoke came out of the wound in her skin.

"Valerie . . ." Asier muttered so quietly his voice cracked. I expected a blood-curdling scream from Asier, but instead, only a small whimper escaped his lips, which somehow felt more heartbreaking.

Her face pointed up at the ceiling as glossy tears rolled from her violet-hued eyes. Her legs gave out and she began to fall, but Asier caught her, and held her in his arms. The Crow laughed hysterically, and every chuckle that escaped his mouth made my blood boil. All the pain he caused was nothing more than a wicked game to him.

My desire to kill him was formidable, but it contradicted with my heart, which was too heavy for me to even stand, let alone come close to killing him. I wanted to murder him- for Aurora, for Guido, for my mother, and for Valerie; I wanted to make him suffer- but I couldn't, and that frustration only added to the weight on my heavy heart.

Tears streamed down my face like an open tap, and I punched the ground beneath me. *I couldn't save anyone,* I cursed, *how can I call myself a hero if I couldn't even protect my comrades?* I opened my eyes again, and my left eye was still in the control room. Asier held Valerie in his arms as he stared down The Crow, but their staring contest was about to end. Vicious flames suddenly unfolded and ripped through the room, tearing right between them. They didn't stop there though, they seemed to chase the Crow until his only way of escaping was by leaving the room as a whole; *this was definitely her doing.*

What surprised me most about this whole ordeal, was that Asier let him escape. He didn't chase after him or even attack him in that brief moment when he had the chance. He most definitely had the strength and fury to hold his own and maybe even win right now, but instead, he chose to stay with Valerie in her final moments. Something about that gave me a weird feeling. *But what is this foreign feeling? It feels . . . uneasy.*

As Valerie bled out in his arms, his face had a veil of unmeasurable despair. The pain in his face was unmatched to anything I had ever seen, but who could blame him? The love of his life was slipping away in his arms. He was all alone this time- he didn't have to act strong for anyone. Unlike him though, Valerie had a serene smile on her face as she leaned against his chest.

"Do you remember the day we first met?" she asked in a breathy voice, "and all the days and nights we spent together after that?"

"How could I forget?" His voice faintly trembled when he answered.

"All I ask . . . is that you remember me by those memories and feelings . . . not the ones after," she begged as tears slipped out of her eyes, and I could see Asier fighting back his own.

"I'm sorry . . . I couldn't protect you. All you've ever done is put your life on the line . . . and I couldn't even protect you this *one* time," he cried out, his voice heavily cracking now.

"And I'd do it all over again, Asier."

"We won't be able to share our lives under the sun . . . like I promised you," he lamented with a strong quiver in his voice.

"But you're here with me right now . . . and that's more than enough," she insisted with a warm smile, before lifting her head up to meet her lips with his.

As I watched that, I felt that uneasy, bitter feeling again. It was like a form of fear- *but what's there to be afraid of right now?*

"What you are feeling right now, Phoenix, is *envy*," The Crow informed me like he was once again reading my mind. "It's a poisonous emotion."

I was so engulfed in it that I didn't even notice his return. *So, this is what envy feels like?* I reflected; *am I wrong to feel it now?*

Once their lips disconnected, Valerie mumbled, "Hey, Asier, I'm finally feeling kinda sleepy. . . I think I'm gonna rest my eyes now." Asier ran his thumb over her soft face as her eyes slowly fluttered shut. "Hold onto what's precious to you, Asier . . . it slips away far too fast," she uttered softly before her head fell back, signaling that she had taken her last breath.

Asier hugged her tightly with a dark shadow over his face. There were no tears, but I could see how broken and ripped apart he was without them. Alas, he held onto her tightly in her final moments, *his beloved Valerie.*

I decided I'd finally had enough and placed my hand over my eye and burned the crow eye off my real eye. The ashes stuck to my face with the moisture of the tears that were still falling. I felt the world closing in on me, suffocating me as grief, doubt, despair, and now envy- all simultaneously clouded my mind. The atmosphere around me suddenly felt much thicker and hotter, so I removed my hand from my eye and I could clearly see the huge fire I had involuntarily started.

It was terrifying. It covered the land as far as the eye could see, and it raged *violently.* I had lost my grip, and it manifested into the deadliest of fires. Worse yet, there was nothing I could do to stop it.

"You may be strong, but just like any other mortal, your heart is weak. That speck of doubt that lingers in your heart is easily exploited by your crippling fear of being alone," he spat out. . . *and he was right.* "So, I ask you now, is this war still worth fighting? Is this victory you seek worth it when you're all alone?" He'd asked the million-dollar question that I didn't dare ask myself, but always lingered in the back of my head.

I stood up and attempted to attack The Crow with my bare hands, but I was so weak he restrained me by the wrists with minimal strength. As I replayed the visions of my loved ones dying, that was the question that constantly invaded my head. *What am I even fighting for?* I asked myself as the air got drastically hotter. The Phoenix would soon give up on me too, and I'd be burned by my own crumbling heart, which isn't fireproof.

The Crow let go of my wrists, and my legs gave out on me instantly. I fell to my knees and let out a scream so strong my lungs were emptied of air. Once again, I screamed so loud it could shake the sky to the ground. Hot tears streamed down my face and fogged my vision; all I could see was a never-ending blur of light all around me.

319

"Get a hold of yourself, child!" I heard her voice shout in my head, but I was too far gone.

The flames were catching up to me, because they burned without even touching me. *Is this what it feels like to burn in hell?* I wondered, *is this what I get for all my sins? Everyone has their demons, but have they ever been burned by them? How did I go from feeling nothing at all, to everything at the same time?*

Bright fire surrounded me, and yet the world felt darker than ever. It was dead silent, and only the sound of embers cracking and fiery wind blowing filled the air. I always wondered what lay beyond the shallow darkness we saw when we closed our eyes, so I closed them, and let the flames cradle me to that eternal sleep; it was only fitting that that's how my story ended.

I was all alone now . . . *and forever.*

Chapter 23

Silence resonated, until a distant voice disrupted it, followed up by a grunt and the sound of a blade ripping through flesh. I shot my eyes open, and there he was, *running through the flames*. Asier sprung from the floor and threw himself onto me, sending us both tumbling to the ground. He pinned my arms down beside me, and I didn't know why, but I began resisting. I kicked and tried to free my hands, but he was exponentially stronger right now.

"Let go or you'll burn too!" I cried out, but he ignored me.

"The day you refused to kill me was the last day you would spend alone, Phoenix." His voice grew more gentle with every word. "You haven't been alone since I met you. . . and you never will be," he added, making me freeze up.

His dark hair stuck to his sweat-covered face as he spoke above me. "Valerie told me before she died, *'Hold onto what's precious to you, it slips away too fast,'*" he quoted with visible grief, "'. . . so that's what I'm gonna do."

His touch softened, and instead of holding me down, he *held* me. After a moment of needed silence and embers cracking, he slid his arms under me and sat up, holding me tightly against him. He laid his chin on my shoulder and tightened his grip, holding me like he was afraid I would slip away at any second. Even as we sat in between the searing flames, his touch somehow remained the warmest feeling.

"I'll make sure you come out of this alive so I can take you to see the stars again- I'll take you every day if you want," he mumbled into my ear, raising goosebumps across my skin.

Tears began to involuntarily slip from my eyes with every soft promise he made. It amazed me how such simple words and gestures from certain people could hold so much volume. That's the power we as human beings all held; we could inflict the deepest wounds, but also mend the most lethal ones.

"But-" I began in a strained voice, but he cut me off because he knew what I was going to say.

"This world is *ours*, Phoenix. Our destiny is ours for the taking," he refuted.

The light emitting from the fire was blinding and demanding to be seen, yet the only thing I could focus on was Asier. Rather than pushing him away this time, I wrapped my arms around him and squeezed. My hand wandered to search for his, and when I found it, I intertwined our hands. Without words, his calloused hand was telling me that he would fight beside me as long as life permitted us. My heart chose to believe him- and that set it ablaze.

I wasn't alone after all.

He lifted his head and I looked into his eyes as he looked into mine. It felt as if Asier's resolve and strength transmitted every time I wandered through the skies in his eyes. The blue flames in his eyes swirled with a hope so profound that no tragedy could ever put them out- it was a blissful feeling to get lost in them. The fire around us began to slowly diminish, or maybe they just felt less searing.

That's when I noticed that we had occupied all the space between each other. Our faces were mere inches away, and the realization made my face grow hot. The tension between us was escalating, and I began to feel a bit self-conscious and awkward, so I decided it was probably time to stand. I let go of his hand and stood up, which he responded to by also standing. I dusted myself off before taking a deep breath and pulling my sword from its sheath.

"I cannot give up- even when the weight of the world is pinning me down," I declared with determination.

A smile grew on Asier's face. "That's right, brat."

If I didn't have enough of a reason to bring The Crow down before, I definitely did now. I was determined to avenge everyone we'd lost on the way. Freedom *will* be ours, and the sun *will* shine on the new nation; I was determined to see this through to the bitter end.

I took a few steps forward, and as I walked through the fire, it opened up a clear path for us; the flames once again worked for me. I followed the trail of drying blood on the ground until it led me to none other than The Crow, who was eerily healing himself. I assumed Asier was responsible for the wound and the sounds I heard earlier. His forearm was sliced from top to bottom, but the wound was already closed and his skin was growing back in mere seconds; just the sight of him gave me the worst bloodlust.

I gripped my sword and charged at him, and by the time he heard my footsteps, it was too late for him. I extended my wings and I sprung up in the air, then brought my sword up over my shoulder and channeled all my energy into one fierce swing. I looked into his eyes as I did so, and for once, a look of trepidation flashed through them. As I came down, I swung my sword and struck him. Blood stained me as I sliced another wound from his shoulder to his chest.

He grunted loudly and almost fell back from the impact. He held his shaking hand over the wound, coating his hand in thick, warm blood. The sound of his jumpsuit and flesh ripping was music to my ears, and seeing the crimson blood drip down my sword was so satisfying. If anyone could hear my thoughts right now, they would think I was a barbaric psychopath- *and they would be right*. All I wanted was to kill him slowly in the worst ways imaginable for every single life he'd taken.

He tried to extend his wing and swing it at me, but I moved swiftly and sliced it before it could even open all the way. It regenerated much faster than I expected, and it took me by surprise when it slammed against me- throwing me against a tree. I grunted as I hit the ground and tried to stand up before it could strike me again.

It charged at me again, but this time, Asier emerged from the flames and sliced it before it could reach me. He ran up on The Crow and kicked him in the jaw, then in what seemed like the blink of an eye, he took out his sword and swung, spinning his whole body with the swing. He managed to graze his arm, but that was the extent of it; The Crow had released his swarm of feathers to push him away before Asier could do any more damage. The surge of feathers concluded as fast as it appeared, and once the air was cleared- The Crow too had vanished.

"Damn it!" cursed Asier.

"He can't run forever. I swear the next time I see him will be the last," I pronounced as I furiously tightened my grip on my sword.

I let out a heavy sigh full of disappointment and grief and I turned toward Asier, who had his gaze glued to the ground. He put away his sword, leaned against a tree, and sat down- letting out a deep sigh as I did. I joined him, leaning against the other side of the same tree. The ground was cool and covered in a thin layer of soot and ash. The breeze felt colder than usual, and the dark clouds appeared full of water. Small droplets fell on my bare skin and grazed my small wounds. They felt especially cold in contrast to my burning skin.

Soon enough the drizzle turned into a light shower- amplifying the already freezing temperatures. I pulled my hood over my head and used the loose fabric at the front of my cape to cover my nose and mouth. I brought my knees up and cradled them to keep warm. The weather was a perfect reflection of how I was feeling right now.

"Rain in a desert, huh?" Asier broke the silence.

"Trees and vegetation in a desert, huh?" I responded.

"Shitty climate for a shitty world I suppose," he added, and I giggled. It then fell silent again for a while, which was dangerous for me right now, because it left lots of room to think about everything.

Asier had also pulled up his cape, and he too looked lost in his own head. He looked down at his feet blankly with his tired eyes. He was always hurting much more than he let on and was constantly trying to suppress it. There was a fresh wound in his heart now- one that would surely be impossible to heal. When Valerie died, she undoubtedly took a piece of him with her.

"I wanted to fight him, so I wouldn't have to think about them anymore. I thought maybe it would distract my thoughts of them, even just for a second," I admitted.

"What did you see?"

"He showed the world through the eyes of his crows. I watched the battle in action- and . . ." The lump in my throat grew mid-sentence, and I struggled to finish. I knew if I said it out loud, it would confirm that it was all real. "A few didn't make it."

"Is that so?" he asked, but he didn't seem one bit surprised.

"They're gone . . . my friends . . . my mother. . . my *home*," I uttered, completely distraught- but I had no tears left to cry.

"I've been there before too." His deep voice was condoling. "I'm sorry, Phoenix. I really am."

"What happened?" I initiated my inquiry. I always wanted to know why he was always able to sympathize with me so well, and this seemed like the perfect opportunity to pick his brain.

"Nothing worth lamenting this many years later." He immediately shut down the conversation, and it kind of took a jab at my heart. It seemed like every time I thought I gained more of his trust, he pulled away even further. He must've noticed the disappointment drag down my face, because he turned his gaze to the ground and looked to be contemplating an answer.

"Let me just say- The only reason I ever second-guessed putting my trust in Fremont, was because the last time I put my full trust in other's abilities, I lost about half my comrades- the people I considered family," he began, pausing to recollect his thoughts. "You know how hard it was to return alone and have to find a way to tell their loved ones that they were all slaughtered under *my* command?"

I immediately thought back to the flashback I saw of him during the ambush- *that must be what he's referring to.*

"How . . . did you just find the will to keep fighting after that?" I asked from the bottom of my heart. I was more than just a question- it was me asking for advice.

"Like I always say, you just have to carry on their fight so that no matter what, their deaths aren't in vain." He let out a heavy sigh. "I'll stand by the choices I've made 'til the day I die. I'll never allow myself to regret anything, because then *everything* would be for *nothing*."

His response filled me with chills, and I struggled to digest it. I watched the raindrops as they slid off my leather sheath and broke as they hit the ground.

"How many times does the human heart have to break for a hero to be born?" I asked, referring to both him and I.

"Sometimes it takes a massive loss to find a meaningful purpose," he answered.

"I think I've lost just about everything one could lose," I sighed. "I like to believe you first have to go through Hell to find a piece of Heaven," I said, moving my gaze up to the dreary sky, shrouded in fluffy rainclouds.

"You know, Phoenix, you made me remember the core reason I wanted to turn this world around in the first place," he said as he turned to me, but I didn't shy away from his gaze this time. "Back when it was simply about *freedom*- a selfless wish that didn't circulate around death or old feuds from the past, but life and a brighter future; I saw my old self in you from day one," he confessed, then it went quiet for a minute, but it wasn't the uncomfortable kind of silence, it was the kind that comes with reflection.

"Hey," I said, breaking the silence, "why didn't you stay with her? I know you would've wanted to." The raindrops filled the gap between my question and his answer.

"I did, until the bitter end- but she was dead, and there would be no point in staying behind." He answered faster than I imagined he would.

"I'm sorry you had to lose her like that, especially after everything you've gone through with her," was all I could seem to say. She always felt like a taboo subject.

"I believe every person we meet is put in our paths to teach us certain lessons," he prefaced. "She became a shoulder to cry on, a comrade to rely on, and she taught me to find the most hope in the bleakest moments; that's the kind of person Valerie *truly* was," he said as he searched the sky- like he was going to find her somewhere within the clouds.

"She taught me a lot, but she wasn't meant to stay forever. Her moment to leave our lifetime has come, and now it's her turn to teach the angels how to smile on their gloomiest days," he answered with so much tranquility he made both her life and her passing seem equally beautiful.

"Why didn't you go after him?

"What would I have gained out of that? Would my soul be at ease the way it is now if I had chosen to go after him out of vengeance, rather than stay with Valerie in her final moments?" He posed his questions diligently. "We can't let vengeance blindsight us from what's *really* important."

Without fail, my mind was blown by his responses for everything. I suppose you learn a lot after you've been through a lot. Though he was only twenty-four, he had the wisdom and experience of someone who had lived many lives.

"I wish I could think the way you do," I admitted. A sense of guilt weighed on me for making my comrades' deaths about vengeance rather than honor.

"Were you and your mother close?" he asked me out of the blue. It was such a simple yes or no question, but the answer was never that easy.

"Now that I've learned to forgive her, I recall all the good moments we shared that I had blocked out of my memory. I couldn't remember the good part of our relationship, because for so long, I wasn't able to forgive her. Once you learn to forgive, you remember the love you feel for that person."

"Well, if that's not the truth," he agreed.

"I never knew my dad, so all I ever had was my mom and my grandmother. Now that they're gone too, I don't know which is harder- losing a parent, or never knowing them at all."

"Watching them suffer," he answered for me.

"Oh . . . I'm sorry," I apologized awkwardly.

"My bad, my intention was not to make you feel bad for me."

"Do you mind elaborating?" I asked, hoping he wouldn't shut me off again.

"When my dad was killed, he left me and my mom to fend for ourselves. I remember every night I saw her come home from work, exhausted and worn out. She suffered a lot, and I can't help but think that I added to her suffering, both when I was with her, and when I left," he explained, and it was oddly heart-wrenching to hear him talk about his mother. "I was mad at her for silencing me the way the whole world did, but in the end, I realized all she wanted was to keep me safe. The lies killed her on the inside, but they kept us alive."

"Have you seen your mother since then?" I asked.

He was silent for a while before answering. "No. She bit the dust, last I heard."

I mentally cursed myself for asking. "Asier, I'm so sorry."

"Don't worry about it."

It got silent again, but fortunately, Asier broke it before it got too awkward. "I still have to pick up where me and Valerie left off with the coding, so in the meantime, why don't you go see your mother? Say your last farewell?"

"Don't you need help?"

"I can fend for myself, sweetheart," he bantered as he stood up. "As morbid as it sounds, you still have the opportunity, so take it."

The fire had been put out completely by the rain, leaving behind a scorched landscape. The temperature had dropped a lot now that the fire was gone, and the cold breeze was once again at its full potential. I stood up and looked at Asier, his black hair stuck to his wet face which still had some soot stuck to it. We agreed to meet back at the control room before going our separate ways.

I flew above the town directly to the stage to avoid any sort of confrontation on the ground. I subconsciously scanned the town to see if I could find any traces of The Crow, but as I expected, there were none. I knew he was hiding somewhere, and in his condition, he couldn't have gone too far. An ordinary man would've surely died from his wounds, but his body was far from ordinary now.

When I arrived at the stage, I lowered myself slowly, preparing myself for the most heart-wrenching goodbye I would ever have to give. With dread I climbed the stairs on the side of the stage, and after just a few steps, I could see their bodies- soaked in blood and rain with their weapons on the ground beside them. The Senator still had the sword in this chest, which was a bit disturbing to see- even for me.

My eyes disdainfully fell on their hands which were still connected, and it made me sick. I drew the sword out of the man's chest and furiously kicked him away from my mother. His body rolled a few feet away, leaving my mother and I some space. I threw the sword down onto the ground and kneeled down next to her. I stared at her cold, pale face, searching for the right words despite knowing she wouldn't hear a single one.

I observed her face as raindrops fell and dripped down her pale cheeks. "You told me to not let that be the last time," I lamented quietly. "I kept my side of the deal, Momma, why didn't you?" I asked with a shaky voice. Whatever child-like innocence I had left seemed to shine through as I spoke.

Long, dreadful minutes passed, and the rain had soaked me completely. It was funny because I know if she were alive, she'd yell at me to cover up or else I'd get sick. Oddly enough though, I wasn't cold; I felt numb from the inside out. I couldn't take my eyes off her either- even in death she was still so beautiful. Her dark locks were drenched, and some strands stuck to her face. I tried to focus on the features of her face, rather than the bullet hole through her chest.

Like I had explained to Asier, now that I understood and forgave her reasons for becoming distant, and recognized everything she did for me, I was able to reminisce on the good memories my heart had blocked out. I recalled the times she would comb through my messy hair, and the times we ran through our daffodil field; when we'd sell the flowers together, and when she'd carry me home after a long day. Her love for me was so real that she ran through Hell for me, and I foolishly pushed that love away.

"You ran through the flames for me," I began to say, but I choked up on my words. "This time, I was supposed to run through them for you," I added, and by the time I finished my sentence, I was fully sobbing. "Why couldn't you just wait for me?"

I covered her with her cape, and picked up her freezing hand, which was wet with blood and rain. I took it in mine and her frosty hands quickly warmed up in mine. My tears camouflaged with the rain, but I could still feel each one as it ran down my cheek. Each salty tear burned the cut I had across my cheekbone.

"What I wouldn't do to hear you say the name you gave me just one more time," I said between tears.

I laid down next to her and shifted myself to a position where my head rested on her punctured chest. I shut my eyes and let myself get carried away by the sounds of the rain for a little while. Despite the off-putting circumstances, laying my head on her brought me so much tranquility that it could put me to sleep if I allowed myself to.

"This isn't a goodbye, it's a see you later," I murmured. "I'll meet you in the afterlife, Momma."

I was comforted by the idea that if there was an afterlife, I'd see her again soon enough, but truthfully, if there was an afterlife, she would have a reserved spot in the heavens, whereas I'll be going straight to Hell. I pushed that thought away and continued to idly lay with her. I knew I had to get back to Asier soon, so I closed my eyes, and cherished *every last second*. As soon as I made up my mind to sit up, something inexplicable happened, and I froze up completely.

She had been dead for hours, so there was no possible way that her heart could beat . . . *but it did*. This entire time her chest had been hollow, but as I lay there, I heard a gentle rhythm, and I felt her chest rise and fall against my face. I immediately shot my eyes open, and kept my head in place to assure that I wasn't just imagining anything. My doubts were erased as soon as I felt a hand rub my head.

As it gently stroked my hair, the shock kept me immobile. There was no one else around, and I didn't hear anyone approach me. Once the initial shock passed, I sat up fast and prepared to attack, but my guard fell once my eyes fell on something they couldn't believe they were witnessing. Mother's eyes fluttered open, and there was a smile on her lips that were once blue. I sat there with my hand on my chest to make sure it didn't stop from the shock.

My mind was flooding, but simultaneously empty, so even if I could find words to say, my tongue was frozen and unable to speak. I watched the gentle rise and fall of her chest as she breathed air into her previously empty lungs. I didn't even realize I was holding my breath until I felt my own chest aching.

"How . . ." I began, but I couldn't finish. I had far too many questions

At first she struggled to sit up, but eventually managed to hold herself up as if she wasn't fatally wounded. Her dress was still torn and stained crimson red, but there was not so much as a scratch on her skin.

"My girl . . . my Phoenix," she said in a shaky voice as if speaking was normal for her right now. She threw herself into my arms, and I almost fell back, but I managed to keep my balance. My body struggled to react, but eventually my arms willingly wrapped around her. I breathed in her familiar floral scent, the smell of *home*.

"Why did you ever lie to me?" I asked, but I wasn't particularly mad. I wasn't looking for an apology, I just wanted an answer. "You won't walk or turn away from me this time. I deserve to hear the truth from you."

She broke from the hug and looked me in the eyes. When I looked inside hers, I could see every struggle she faced hiding beneath the tears that were welling up. She looked away from me when she realized I knew most of the answer. She struggled to answer for a while, which resulted in a tension-filled silence.

"I didn't want you to live in fear like I did," she eventually admitted.

"Explain," I said sternly.

"I didn't want you to grow up in the cruel, organized world that I did, but I realized too late that my decision to deviate would end up hurting you too, and that guilt made me push you away." She paused to answer the part she dreaded to say out loud and the part I dreaded to hear. "As you grew up, you became colder and more distant, then one day, you qualified to be an Executioner . . . and the thought that my own daughter could become my greatest enemy . . . frightened me."

She couldn't look me in the eyes, and it made me wonder if the shame just wouldn't let her. I wasn't necessarily surprised or disconcerted by her answer, but only because I had already come to that conclusion myself. However, now it was more than a speculation, because hearing it from her solidified it.

"You gave up your life of comfort for a child you didn't even want- just for her to grow up to become the incarnation of the very thing you hated."

"Call it selfish, but I didn't care for the rest of the world- I only wanted the best for you, and the rest didn't matter to me," she answered. "This world is violent, cruel, and unjust, and I knew I could never change that, so if you had to become a Hunter to avoid being the prey, then so be it," she said as she gently stroked my hand.

"It won't be in vain . . . I will make your sacrifice worth it, Momma."

"But . . . why did it have to be you?" She bit her lip to fight back tears.

I caught myself trying to disguise my own overflow of emotions just out of habit, but if there was ever a time to expose my vulnerability- it would be now, with her.

"Maybe it's by chance, or maybe it's the only way my soul can ever have some redemption, but one thing is certain though, and it's that I will go through with it to the bitter end," I disclosed as I proceeded to stand.

My legs felt unusually heavy, like they didn't want me to walk away. The truth was, I didn't, but I knew I had to. I had a world to save, and even if all I wanted was to lay in her arms for an eternity, I couldn't let her hold me back when I was so close. Her cold hands wrapped around my wrist and pulled me back, begging me to stay.

"Being faced with death made me realize all the regrets I carried; all my mistakes flashed before my eyes, and now I've been given another chance to be the mother you deserve. So please, Phoenix, I want to show you the love I should've given you all these years," she pleaded in desperation. I had never heard or seen her like this before.

My lips quivered and refused to move. "I'm sorry, mother . . . but this is goodbye," I uttered as I pulled away, freeing my arm using every ounce of strength in me. I turned away from her and began to slowly walk away.

"Please, don't go," she pleaded on her knees with her arm extended toward me.

I turned back around. "What's the point of being strong if I can't protect the ones I love?" I asked as my eyes pierced into hers.

That question spoke a million words to her, and her arm lowered as she stared at me with her glossy eyes. Tears streamed down her face, but she didn't try to stop me anymore; she knew it was a futile effort. I turned around again, and as I began to walk away, I heard her call my name.

"Phoenix," she called out again, and against my will, my legs stopped. I looked back one last time, and she had a smile growing in the corners of her lips. "If you're choosing to fly . . . *show me how high you can go.*"

Her pain was replaced with pride, and a radiant smile grew on her cheeks that were still wet with tears. I turned back around, got down on one knee, placed my fist on my chest, and kneeled to her with utmost respect. She caressed my face one last time, staring into my eyes as she ran her finger over the tender slit on my cheek. I grabbed her hand in mine and kissed it before standing up.

"I love you, Momma." The words slipped off my tongue, and I felt as though a weight I had carried my whole life had been lifted off my chest.

"I love you too, my Phoenix. I always have, and always will." With that, I looked up and took off into the sky.

My trip to the sky didn't last long, because it quickly became too dark to see. Although the sky was obviously dark, it felt unusually dark, at least until I realized . . . that's because I wasn't *really* in the sky right now. I fluttered my eyes and concentrated as hard as I could, but in turn, my wings suddenly faded into embers. Gravity dragged me down the twilight sky faster than I had ever fallen, and before I could hit the ground-

I woke up . . .

I gasped for air like I was drowning and panted like I had a limited air supply. My eyes shot open, and I was back to where I started- on the stage, covered in blood and ashes, accompanied by two corpses. I was soaked by the rain now and still lying next to my mother's deceased body. I quickly sat up and looked around me, dazed and disoriented.

How was that all a dream? I wondered with a knot in my stomach. The disappointment I felt from the realization was immeasurable, but the sense of ease I felt in my heart was still unperturbed. Even if it was only a dream, it still happened, even if it was only in the depths of my subconscious.

That dream held a lot of firsts for me, firsts that I would never let go. It was the first time I demanded an answer from my mother, and it was the first time she opened up to me; It was also the first and last disagreement I ever had with my mom, and the first and last time I told her I loved her. I knew it wasn't what she wanted, but she knew it's what *I* wanted, and that's the moment I *truly* understood what love was.

The Phoenix fought against The Crow because Astrid promised she'd always be there to lead Lanon out of the dark, and that's what she's doing- even if that meant they had to be enemies. Valerie was another fine example; she loved Asier and everyone in Rebellium so much that she ran off on her own to find a way to save them herself- even if it meant they had to hate her first. Lastly, my mother- she knew I would die if I ran off to complete my mission, but she let me go anyway, because she loves me, which meant supporting the decisions I make. All these examples I've encountered have led me to one solid conclusion; *love wasn't always about walking the same path as someone.*

Without making it a big deal again, I stood up, spread my wings, and took off into the sky- for real this time. Despite everything that had happened, I had a sense of peace of mind; I felt as if everything was finally falling into place, and I was finally understanding the mysteries that kept me up at night. I felt as light as a feather as I flew over the gray buildings- I thought I might even touch the sky. As I flew toward the control building Asier was waiting in, I glanced at the indigo sky where the dark sun was beginning to set for the last time.

Next time the sun sets, it won't hide behind the darkness.

Chapter 24

Immediately upon entering the tall tower, I sprinted all the way up the stairs, and the number of doors was overwhelming. I had no idea which room Asier was in, so I took a peek in all of them. As I walked into the first room, the heart wrenching sight caught me way off guard. Pale, dark-haired Valerie lay limp and lifeless in a pool of crimson blood, which sullied the gray, fire-damaged, cemented floors. The sight reminded me so much of my mother's death scene, because even in death, they still looked undeniably beautiful. The contrast between the large, bloody hole in her chest and the serine look on her face was terribly unsettling. The harder I looked at her face, the more my eyes were convinced they saw a smile on her lips.

Only after her passing was when I really put into perspective how young she actually was. She too was in her early twenties, but right now, she appeared even younger. The deceased had such an indescribable innocence to their faces, because in death, there is no sin that can be committed; at that point, we're all just the shells of the person we used to be. It was hard to believe she ever carried out all the heinous acts she'd committed; it was hard to believe she was ever a villain, but the truth was, she was never a hero nor a villain, she's always just been a soldier- fighting for a better life.

I glanced at Valerie one last time before running off to search for Asier. I felt a massive lump in my throat after seeing her lay in a pool of her own blood; an immense guilt came over me as I remembered how I foolishly felt envious of her, even if it was just briefly. Envy was truly a poisonous and vile emotion.

I checked about ten empty rooms before finally finding Asier. As I walked in, he and I immediately exchanged looks, and something came over me when I laid my eyes on him, like some sort of internal gratitude. I saw the confusion on his face upon seeing the small smile lurking in the corners of my mouth. Despite losing all of the people I held close, I was grateful to at least still have Asier around.

"Should I even ask why you're smiling or why you took so long?" he asked in his usual apathetic tone.

"Honestly, probably not," I replied, because honestly, I wouldn't even know where to start, nor did we have time to right now. He looked dissatisfied with my answer but did not attempt to interrogate any further.

"Well, in the time you were gone, I was able to completely deactivate the security system. Now all we need is to push this button to open the cells and the exits."

"Didn't you and Valerie already do that downstairs?"

"I'm honestly not sure what she was having us do downstairs, because all of the cell controls were up here," he explained and put his hand on his head. "Whatever she was coding downstairs must've been important for her to prioritize it."

"Yeah, I remember her pressing a button before she-" Before finishing, I stopped myself after realizing how insensitive it would have sounded, but it honestly made it more awkward.

"Guess we'll find out," he said, throwing his rifle over his shoulder and adjusting his cape. "Ready?"

"Now or never, commander."

"Let's hope Fremont doesn't shit his pants," he teased and then pressed the button. "If we get there fast enough, we can probably help him distract the guards too," he suggested, and I nodded in response.

We ran down the stairs and through the narrow halls as quickly as we could. The lights blinking from the terrible maintenance of this torn-down building gave it an eerie feel as we ran through every gray corridor. The atmosphere felt increasingly heavier as we passed the room Valerie was in.

"Later, Val," Asier subtly murmured with a dark gloom over his face.

Besides his typical indifferent expression, the shine in his eyes was absent, and they appeared to be in a distant daze. For most people that gesture would seem like nothing, especially considering the type of relationship they shared, but if you knew Asier, you knew that's just him. I'd like to think that under different circumstances, he would've given her the farewell she deserved, but for now, it was better left unsaid.

The run from the control building to the prison tower was short; all we had to do was cross over a small hill. Asier abruptly stopped when we reached the peak of the hill, which caught me off guard. Immediately after stopping he pulled his hood over his head and threw himself onto the ground, pulling my arm and dragging me down with him. The ground was cold and muddy from the rain, and from this angle, the tall gates obscured any view I once had of the sky.

"What was that for?" I asked, irritated.

"Unless you're trying to have an unpleasant encounter with those gentlemen, stay low," he ordered in a whisper.

I looked up as much as I could without being spotted and saw a long line of heavily armed and well-trained soldiers encompassing the entire tower, eliminating all chances of getting in or out. They weren't there before, so I'm guessing The Crow must've caught onto our plan and sent them recently. They alternated between facing the tower and facing our direction, so there was no room for slip ups on any end. They looked highly alert, so I'm guessing they heard the cells opening from the inside and were just waiting for that first unlucky deviant to run out blindly. I scanned the area for any traces of Fremont, hoping he had managed to hide before the guards got there.

For a while it was silent- almost too silent. I could hear the wind blowing against my cold, red ears, and the crows cawing in the distance. It wasn't until now that I noticed there were no sounds coming from the outside of the gates anymore. There was once a time when I was afraid of too much noise, but now I was afraid of *silence*. Silence signaled when a battle had ceased; *but who claimed the victory?*

It wasn't even a minute before the silence was shattered by the deafening sound of a shotgun. First one shot, then two, then three- all back-to-back and faster than I could turn my head. Three soldiers fell to the ground and the rest of them turned around and frantically searched for the source of the bullets. Their search was interrupted almost immediately when an array of smoke bombs went off, completely shrouding the perimeter. I could hear the chaos and panic in the soldiers- but even that was interrupted by the sound of an actual explosion.

The explosion opened a large hole in the gate wall within closest proximity to the exit of the prison. The exit was open, but there were still no prisoners in sight. Debris and rubble crumbled all around the area, obscuring the soldiers' sight even more. Beyond the thick cloud of dust and blue-colored smoke, I spotted someone in the distance as they climbed over a small hill near the prison. They were carrying a large flag with a sun painted over top of the black Crow symbol. I squinted my eyes, and it was none other than our dear Fremont.

It was like the smoke had dissipated around him only; the view of him standing tall and proud while holding the flag was so clear. You could see in his eyes he was terrified, but nonetheless, his courage concealed any fear of his. He looked toward the prison and now you could see a crowd of people at the exit. He lifted the flag up and pierced it into the ground. The dirty-blond-haired boy held his heart and courage out for the world- like a true commander.

339

"REBELS, CHARGE!" he screamed at the top of his lungs and mobs of captives began to pour out of the prison and dashed toward the hole in the gate.

The smoke had begun to blow away with the wind, and soldiers shot at and charged toward the prisoners. A few unlucky rebels were in the range of the fired bullets, and I watched them fall to the ground one by one. I tried to stand to run and help, but Asier held me back sternly.

"We need to stay back, Phoenix!" he warned. I tried to figure out why he wouldn't intervene, but it was quickly answered when a series of explosions went off. The ground under us vibrated vigorously and I sheltered my head with my arms as dirt and debris flew around us.

"Fremont!" I cried as soon as it hit me that he would get caught in the chaos.

"Stop, Phoenix!" Asier yelled, "have some faith in him!"

"But he's going to die!" I shouted back.

"We have to have trust in our comrades," he explained more calmly, but with intensity in his voice.

I didn't respond, and instead turned back to the destruction; Fremont was still on the hill, and I could vaguely see people still running out of the prison. My muscles tensed, but I was relieved to see that everything was going according to plan; Fremont was safe, and the prisoners were escaping with minimal casualties. I tried to detense completely, but I just couldn't, and it made me abundantly anxious- like I knew something bad was going to happen. *It was all just too good to be true.*

Once the explosions ceased, there were no more soldiers-standing soldiers at least. It was silent once again, and that only worsened my anxiety. I felt like my heart was going to rip out of my chest- that's how fast it was beating. Me and Asier finally sat up once we thought the coast might be clear. We got up and began to run toward Fremont, but we both froze when we saw *exactly* what I dreaded happening.

The tranquility of silence was always broken by the sound of gunshots.

Three, four, five shots were heard, and three, four, five bullets punctured Fremont's skin. My mouth hung open and I couldn't react beyond just staring. A Crow soldier had remained hidden, and now he was approaching the hill whilst holding a ticking bomb- planning to take Fremont, himself, and the remaining rebels down with him. Even with a punctured shoulder, torso, chest, and leg, Fremont bravely dashed toward the soldier and tackled him to the ground, away from the range of the rebels.

I promptly ducked and Asier followed my lead split-seconds before the explosion went off. We weren't in close enough proximity to where it would harm us, but debris was still a factor. I squeezed my eyes tightly shut as the ground rumbled; whatever bomb that soldier had was made to cause considerable damage. I laid there in the dark for a while, only opening my eyes when the smoke and dust was remotely cleared. Asier immediately stood up and searched the area for traces of Fremont, but all we found were a bunch of dead soldiers and small craters as we made our way to the hill.

It wasn't until we got to the bottom of the hill that we found something. I looked up and saw that the flag was still standing, somehow, and beneath it was none other than Fremont. We dashed up the hill as fast as our legs allowed us until we finally reached him. He must've pushed the man with the bomb down the other side of the hill, and away from the rebels; unfortunately, he got caught in the middle- quite literally. His body was scattered with scratches and bullet wounds, and his face coated in gunpowder and dirt.

"I . . . d-did it . . . Asier . . . I t-told you guys I could do it," he stuttered before choking on blood. "Tell me, Asier . . . did I do good?" he asked in a shaky voice.

As harrowing as it was to watch, my eyes were glued to him. Me and Asier both kneeled down beside him as he uttered his final words. Fremont lifted his blood-covered hand slightly, and Asier grabbed it, clutching it firmly as Fremont took his last breaths.

341

"You guys c-came," he said in an ailing voice.

I was confused as to what he meant until I turned around and saw Daxon and Khalon come up behind us. A flood of relief washed over me to see that they were still alive and in one piece. They both kneeled on one knee, putting their fists over their hearts and one to the ground. They were bowing their heads, and I could tell they were holding back tears.

"I saw everything- and you did amazing. You were a phenomenal leader," praised Asier, and I watched a feeble smile form on Fremont's pale lips. "You can rest now, *Commander Fremont.*"

Tears slipped out of his weary, brown eyes that were struggling to remain open. His breathing reduced little by little until his eyes eventually couldn't stay awake anymore. His breathing stopped, his smile fell, and his eyes shut slowly- never to open again. Asier grabbed the hand he held and laid it over his bleeding chest. Daxon reached under his cape, unclipped his commander badge, and placed it gently in Fremont's hand.

"I'm sorry for ever doubting you, brother. You were more of a commander than I could ever hope to be," Daxon repented with sorrow.

"Until we meet again, my brother," Asier said somberly before standing up.

Amid the grief, my mind began to trail off into places it shouldn't. I began to think back at all the lives that had been lost because of how long I was taking to win this war. This became less of a death issue, and more of a prevention issue, because no one could resurrect the dead, but as Fremont demonstrated- anyone could save someone from dying. *For a person that's standing over a mountain of corpses, why did I think I could save anyone in the first place?* I asked myself.

"I- I couldn't save him," my voice involuntarily murmured. I lifted my eyes from Fremont and saw Asier, who was glaring at me, then switched his glance away from me.

"A part of being strong is accepting the fact that you can't save everybody," he said as he looked off at the destruction in the distance. *I knew he knew that better than anyone; he knew what loss was.*

He walked away after that, leaving me with Daxon and Khalon. I didn't know if I was just too distracted to notice before, but only now did I see the eyepatch over Khalon's right eye. His left eye, however, was glued to Fremont, and welling up with tears. He'd watched Aurora and Fremont die in one day, and had to be feeling defeated.

"Where's everyone else?" I asked naively as if I didn't already know the answer. Guido and Aurora dying while Nyrual fought on his last leg had replayed in my head nonstop since the second I saw it.

"Lana is treating them inside the basement of the prison," Daxon answered, and my body froze up completely. My eyes widened from his answer, because it was definitely not the answer I was expecting.

"W-what?" I asked blankly, confusing Daxon.

"They're all in there. Lana, The White Raven, and the rest of the nurses managed to get everyone in there right before the swarm of guards decided to encompass the area," he explained, which didn't help the shock in the slightest.

"S-so, they're . . . alive?".

"A bit knackered and maimed, but definitely still breathing," Khalon answered this time.

Once again, I hadn't noticed I had stopped breathing until my lungs started burning. I felt as if the heaviest weight had been lifted from my chest, and I could finally breathe again.

"Do you think . . . I could go see them?" I asked hesitantly. I didn't know why, but it felt more like I was asking myself for permission, rather than Daxon and Khalon.

"I don't know if they're awake, but you can go check," answered Khalon.

"I think I'm gonna go too, I need to lay down for the next ten years," added Daxon while trying to crack his back. "You need to come too, Khalon. That bullet wound and eye aren't gonna heal themselves."

Khalon was leaning against the pole of the flag, clutching his bandaged wound. The vision of him bleeding out on the battleground reoccurred to me, and I immediately felt chills cover my body. Even in his severely wounded state, that didn't stop him from coming out and praising Fremont's heroic act. Unfortunately, instead of coming out to praise him, he ended up coming out to say goodbye to his dear friend for the last time.

Daxon and Khalon were both heading back inside, and I followed along. We passed countless empty, rusted cells as we made our way down to the steps that led to the basement. This tower was occupied as a prison, but within the building, we passed several rooms with hundreds of small screens that broadcast the eyes of the crows scattered around the district. It was one of the few places within the district where you could see the eyes- but of course, it was completely off limits to regular civilians.

Once we reached the bottom steps, I saw bunches of people scattered around on the ground. Most were already bandaged up and resting, but some were still being tended to by the nurses of Rebellium. My mind subconsciously panicked when I scanned the room and saw no signs of my friends, even though I knew good and well that they were alive. Daxon and Khalon headed toward a door, so I figured everyone was behind it. Upon entering, my eyes went to the rifle, bow, stash of arrows, and violin leaning against the wall, and my heart began to race. I turned my head slightly and there I saw Aurora, Guido, Nyrual, and Lana. Thick tears immediately began to well up in my eyes.

Guido was bandaged up and sound asleep on the ground, his head resting on a soft pillow. Nyrual was laying on his back as he was being tended to by Lana, and looked the least wounded out of the three. Aurora was awake and leaned against a wall, and she was also the first to notice us as we walked in. There was a loosely wrapped bandage around her head, but you could still see her groggy eyes shift their focus to us. A big smile formed on her weary face, and I immediately dashed toward her and threw my arms around her as delicately as I could to avoid hurting her.

"Thank goodness, you're alive," she mumbled, "I knew you would make it."

"You're all alive," I uttered desperately, and I couldn't stop the tears from falling this time. I began to think I'd cried more tears today than I probably had in my entire life.

"Phoenix!" Nyrual exclaimed excitedly as he tried to stand, but Lana pulled him back down.

"You can rejoice after I'm done with you," scolded Lana, making everyone giggle.

I struggled to release myself from the hug; after watching everyone almost slip away, I didn't want to let go ever again. Against my will, I released Aurora and she leaned back, visibly in pain. Daxon also leaned against a wall next to Khalon, who laid down as soon as he got the chance.

"How bad is the damage, Lana?" I asked timidly as I dried off my tears.

"Nyrual here had a couple bloody wounds, but no serious injuries. Aurora has a spine injury, broken nose, and her head was split a little. Guido probably had it the worst; he has a bullet puncture, fractured arm and back, and his head was gashed. Depending on how his back heals will determine his ability to walk again," she explained, trying to hide any visible dismay. As selfish as it might've sounded, I wasn't too worried about the damage- I was just relieved to know they were alive.

I moved over to sit next to Guido and began to stroke his soft curls. We all sat in silence for a while until a loud ruckus down the hall caught our attention. Only a second after, a rugged, tan, dark-haired man with bright green eyes barged in with a nurse following close behind him.

"This is her room sir, but she needs to rest-" the nurse began to explain but was cut off by the man.

"AURORA!" the man shouted and fell to his knees in front of Aurora, who was now covering her mouth from the surprise. Her eyes were forming tears along with his.

"Daddy . . ." she mumbled before throwing herself into his open arms.

"My dear, you're okay. You're really okay," he reassured himself as tears slid down his wrinkled cheeks.

"How did you get here?"

"I came as soon as I found out you were here. I just ran and hoped I didn't get caught."

They embraced for a long time before finally breaking the hug. He cupped her small face in his rugged hands as he ran his thumb over the cuts on her cheeks. In the commotion, the bandage from her face unwrapped, revealing a freshly stitched gash on the top of her forehead extending to some point on the top of her head. It also unveiled the gnarly scratch across her nose bridge.

"My dear, look what they've done to you," her father lamented. Aurora just smiled in response. After a second her smile began to fade, and her face filled with shame. She moved her gaze down to avoid eye contact, which puzzled her father.

"What's on your mind, darling? Are you in pain?"

"You're probably ashamed of me, aren't you?" Her voice quivered.

He let out a deep sigh followed by a brief moment of silence. "I've never been prouder of you than I am right now, Aurora," he confessed with the warmest, most genuine smile I've seen. A smile that didn't need words to show the pride and love he felt for his daughter.

I decided to give them some space and let everyone else rest and recover. I made my way toward the screen room I passed on my way here, but it proved to be more difficult than expected. This place was dimly lit, and the sun had almost completely set, once again enveloping the world in inescapable darkness. To top it off, the stairs were steep, and the corridors were worn out and eerie, making it spine-chilling to put it lightly.

When I reached the door, I felt something grab my shoulder, and I involuntarily gasped before turning around instinctively drawing my handgun. A small flame formed in my hand out of fright, and it lit up the surroundings, revealing the person behind me- Asier, as per usual.

"Don't wet your pants now, brat. It's just me," he mocked.

"Don't you get tired of coming up behind me like that?" I scoffed.

"Did I really scare you? My bad, princess," he mocked again, and I punched his arm.

"You're lucky I didn't swing with the flaming hand," I said, and Asier chuckled.

I tried to open the door, and I wasn't surprised to see that it was locked, but I had to brainstorm a way to get in without a key. Asier sensed my struggle, and he walked up to the door.

"I know a way to get in," he informed me.

I raised a brow at him and turned to the door. He stepped back a bit, gathered up as much force as he could, and then kicked the door down in one forceful kick. The heavy, metal door fell, making a blaring noise as it hit the ground. *Well, I guess that's one way to get in.* The print from his combat boot remained etched on the door, which was now fully on the ground.

I peered inside before walking in. The room was brightly lit from the hundreds of eyes in that room, and then I saw a man with a Hunter badge on his uniform, who had a petrified look on his face as soon as his eyes landed on me. I was shocked more than anything to know there was a Hunter in the building this whole time, and that he was just hiding in here; *I supposed they were making any useless coward a Hunter nowadays.* I slowly and calmly approached him, but even then, he drew back in response.

"C-Crimson Hunter!" he exclaimed, stuttering my name. It was oddly satisfying to know they still cowered at the sound of my name.

"Sorry, man, but I have business here and you're in my way," I warned menacingly. The man tensed up but maintained his composure. He proceeded to pull out his gun and aim it at me, but too bad for him, he was far too nervous and slow.

I pulled my handgun out faster than he could pull the trigger and put a bullet between his eyes. Blood splattered on the screens behind him, and he flopped onto the ground. It was unsettling even for me to see how sometimes I could still kill with such little reluctance.

"Nice shot," Asier praised, "now, what's all this?" he asked, visibly disturbed.

"His eyes," I responded vaguely.

I skimmed through the screens, feeling intrusive knowing I was peering into the lives of every single citizen in District 4 against their will. Children sheltered in their parents' arms, families hiding in the shadows, the same look of torment on every screen. My eyes were pulled toward the screen broadcasting the stage- where you could watch convicts get their brains blown out in H.D. I scanned and scanned but had no luck finding a single trace of The Crow.

I was incredibly frustrated with myself for playing along to his game of hide and seek and still having no leads on his whereabouts. He was probably fully healed by now, which meant we were at a big disadvantage, especially since over half our team was out of commission. I didn't want to lose more people, so this needed to come to an end now. Time was still running, and it would not wait around for me to catch up.

As relieved as I was to know my comrades were alive, seeing their injured states replaced the grief I was feeling with guilt. Ultimately, I was the one who dragged them into this, and the reason they were fighting for their lives right now. For whatever deranged reason, they'd chosen to fly with a phoenix, even though they were not fireproof.

I hope this world burns with me, but I hope I don't burn you.

Chapter 25

"Where are we going?" called out Asier between breaths as he ran behind me.

"To end this once and for all," I answered, purposely sounding overly confident.

"And how exactly are you going to find him without a lead?" he asked, but I let his question hang in the air unanswered.

I didn't know where I was going but searching was better than idly standing. For my entire life, whenever emotions were involved, my fight or flight reflex has always been *flight. Run away, turn away, and it will go away,* I would tell myself, but not this time; this time I had to turn around and *fight.* I wouldn't let personal conflicts keep distracting me from what was really at stake here- the entire world. I was here to kill The Crow, and if I had to lose my sanity chasing him through every corner of the world, then to hell with my sanity.

I hadn't noticed that I'd subconsciously led us back to the plains I scorched just a few hours ago until I noticed the layer of black soot covering the brittle vegetation. The wind here blew so gently and quietly- it was the calm before the storm. I saw a black feather floating through the gentle wind, and my eyes followed it to the ground. I knew he was near, and he had the same intention as me; he wanted to end this *now.*

Suddenly, the atmosphere was suffocating, and the aura grew malicious. Asier and I looked around simultaneously, and we saw nothing at first glance. I adjusted my eyes to the darkness, and on top of the tall gate wall, I saw something that never failed to chill me down to the bone. The devil standing on the gate wall with his black wings spread so broadly across the twilight sky- The Crow's silhouette. I had seen The Crow with his wings spread before, but this time was completely different. There was an even more sinister aura to him- like he was losing grip of the last bit of his remaining humanity.

At that moment all I could do was gawk at him. Part of me wanted to run as fast and far away as I could- *Phoenix Euphema*- but the other side of me spoke louder and was drawn to the danger- *The Prophet*. My surroundings lit up as I spread my own fiery wings. Delicate, bright, crimson flares emitted from both sides of my back, and this time, they were larger than ever, and twice as bright as usual.

"Take me with you," Asier requested, and I shot him the dirtiest of looks.

"Are you out of your mind?" I asked coldly in an effort to deter him.

"I have a plan, and I brought a *special weapon*," he explained, but I still wasn't convinced.

"Bringing him down requires more than a bomb Asier-" I began before he cut me off.

"It's not an ordinary bomb, brat. A chemist in Rebellium constructed it with energy emitted from *your* flames," he explained, and I looked at him as confused as ever. I'm sure he noticed, because he proceeded to explain it further. "A shot from a regular pistol will set it off and at the very least would debilitate him significantly."

"It's dangerous-" I began and once again he cut me off.

"Simply *existing* in this world is dangerous, so what's your point?" he refuted. "This is the fight of our lives, and I'm not backing down."

"Endangering you is unnecessary. I have the power to end it myself," I insisted.

"This isn't just your battle, Phoenix. Remember that." I was already conflicted, and he continued to try. "Please, Phoenix, let me do this for my comrades."

"But-"

"Besides, I promised I wouldn't let you die today. I'm not losing another comrade to this war."

Though Asier had managed to convince me, I was still reluctant to say yes. I had a terrible hunch about bringing him, but I knew this was something he had to do to be at peace with himself. He was certainly skilled enough to, so- *so why do I still doubt him?*

"I know you're doubting me, and that's why you won't agree," he speculated.

"What- no!"

"I've seen trust lead us to victories, and I've seen that same trust kill over half my comrades,"- he paused to take a deep breath- "But whatever the outcome turns out to be, *never* regret making the decision to trust."

I let his words sit in the air. I had heard a similar lecture from him before, but this time, I actually had to apply it. I'd learned throughout this journey that to doubt is to be human, but learning to trust and confide in others was too. I looked him in his eyes; years of pain, hope, and grief, all engraved into every millimeter of his eyes, but what I didn't find there were any traces of regret.

He always explained to me how he carried on with no regret in his heart, because he was busy making sure his comrades' deaths were not in vain. I closed my eyes briefly and concentrated with that thought in mind, then I began to feel the faint presence of hundreds of people around us. Rebels wearing black capes surrounded us; all the soldiers he had lost, and a lot of them *I had probably killed.* Among the crowd were people I recognized too- Nila, Markus, Fremont, Valerie, even my mother.

I opened my eyes when I had made up my mind. He was right, this wasn't just my battle, it was also a battle to every comrade we'd lost along the way. It wasn't even my battle to begin with, but wherever they all are, they're putting their trust in us to end it for them. If both the living and dead trusted me, I would trust them too- by trusting Asier.

"Well then, let's go. We don't have much time," I concluded, and I saw something light up in Asier's eyes. "Let's set this world on fire."

I clutched onto him firmly and took off into the sky, painting it red as we dashed through it. I looked down and was alarmed to see so many people through the dim town lighting. Citizens and the previously captive rebels had come out of their shelters and began to rage through the town. Those loyal to The Crow fought back the raging citizens who had now chosen to deviate. Whether they were fighting or spectating, everyone was outside to witness the revolution, and the sight truly adrenalized me.

I landed me and Asier on top of the gate wall a safe distance away from The Crow, who looked as though he had not moved an inch the entire time. The wall was narrow, but wide enough to walk on it comfortably. It was about ten feet wide and around a hundred feet tall, which was a long way down. It was quiet and still for what felt like an eternity; no one spoke a word, and no one moved a muscle.

"Get down!" exclaimed Asier, and he pushed me to the ground with him.

Sharp, black feathers bombarded us, but each one burned before it could even touch us. In between the barrage, I caught glimpses of what The Crow was doing behind the feathers. He had a large syringe in his hand, and he jammed it right into a vein in his arm, shooting whatever substance was in there straight into his bloodstream. He grunted loudly, and a sheer layer of sweat formed on his face from the injection; whatever he was doing to himself seemed to cause a strong reaction. When the feathers began to dissipate, behind the flames and the feathers, was the most frightening sight I would ever witness in my eighteen years on Earth.

His human body was slowly morphing into that of a crow. Every second that my eyes remained glued to him, the less he looked like a man, and more like an infernal bird. All I could do was stare open-mouthed out at the horror in front of me. All traces of his humanity were gone; and he resembled a real crow from top to bottom. Horrified screams came from below, and it only went to verify that everyone else was seeing what I was seeing, meaning that it was all *actually* happening. I willed my legs to stand, but my eyes never left the beast in front of me. The approximately thirty-feet-tall Crow turned his head toward me and Asier, and before I could react, he let out the loudest screech in history.

I thought my eardrums would burst as he released the most blood-curdling cry straight at us. I felt as if all the air had been extracted from my lungs while simultaneously feeling each and every harsh beat of my rapidly pounding heart. I tried to keep up my fearless demeanor, even in the face of a man-made demon. As his wide beak closed, his large beady eyes burned right through me.

Something indescribable fired up inside me the second his eyes settled on me. The world grew hot, and tinted crimson; all the flames in the world could not compete with me right now. My wings grew to be more than just wings; a phoenix was forming out of the meek torch that resided within my heart, and before I knew it, it made its presence known, and let out its own high-pitched battle cry. With its beak aimed at the sky, it screeched louder than The Crow, and the sound was like nothing I'd ever heard before- like an eagle's screech mixed with a lion's roar.

I extended my arms out as flames, and embers formed the body of a resplendent bird. I was the same as him now- the vessel for a large phoenix constructed out of my internal flame. I wasn't sure what everyone else was seeing, or if they could still see me amongst the blazing feathers of this bird, but I turned to look at Asier, who was still next to me, watching me with wide, dazzled eyes. I saw my glowing reflection in them.

"Grab on," I ordered, and my voice seemed to echo. He swiftly snapped out of his trance and gripped onto the feathers on my back- well, the phoenix's back.

The Crow flapped his wings and soared into the sky, flying at a relatively slow speed due to his large size. I prepared to take off, and I unexpectedly shot through the sky at an exceptional speed; *who would've guessed phoenixes were so fast?* I flew straight at him with my vast speed, but he moved just in time to dodge. I missed colliding with him only by inches, but that didn't mean he was in the clear.

Asier released his grip off me and drew his sword as he fell. I felt my heart drop all the way to the pit of my stomach when I saw Asier falling. I immediately dashed to catch him, but before I could get in his way, he swung his sword and sliced into The Crow's flesh. The Crow screeched and I immediately caught Asier midair. It was insane how much trust he could have in a person to trust me to catch him midair.

"Inform me of your plan next time, idiot!" I rebuked, but Asier didn't react.

The Crow's blood was on Asier's face and sword, but thankfully he was unharmed. The Crow dashed at us but missed as Asier motioned me to fly above him. He once again let go and struck him from above, wounding his wing. He let out another screech that roared through the sky as the sword tore through his flesh.

Once I caught him, he let go again almost immediately. This time, he simply landed on The Crow's back instead of attacking. He gripped his sword so tightly the veins in his arms and hands were pronounced, and his knuckles were white.

"This one's for my comrades," Asier grunted with vengeance as he stabbed the sword right into his back, "and this one is for the life you ripped from me and many others," he added as he stabbed his bloody blade back in. His face was shadowed with disdain and pure hatred, looking almost possessed. The Crow screeched with every stab and began to fly unstably and disoriented.

"What's wrong? Why aren't you laughing now, bastard?" Asier asked, sounding almost unrecognizable, though I recognized this tone of speaking- it was *bloodlust*.

I saw him hold the bomb he was referring to and that was my cue to get ready to catch him. I flew toward The Crow, but this time we wouldn't be so lucky. I felt the wind get knocked out of me as his large, heavy wing swung at me with such incredible strength. The phoenix I had manifested dissipated into small embers, and I was flung onto the gate wall with so much impact that blood came out of my mouth.

I was in so much pain I thought my body would surely go into shock right then and there. It felt as though every bone in my body had just shattered, and no matter how hard I tried, I could not catch my breath. The taste of salty, metallic blood lingered in my mouth and my eyes failed to focus. Through my blurred vision, I was only able to see muted colors and opaque, undetailed figures, but I was able to decipher a large black bird charging at me. When my eyes finally cooperated and focused, I saw The Crow holding out his sharp claw, and was getting ready to rip me apart.

I attempted to sit up, but the pain was so excruciating that I let out an involuntary scream. All I could do then was close my eyes, and guard myself with my weak arms. Before I shut my eyes, I saw Asier jumping over The Crow's shoulder. I closed my eyes for what I thought would be the last time; *I was surely about to die. . . right here . . . right now.*

They say when you're about to die, you see your life flash before your eyes, and it was true, because I had seen it once before . . . *so why is it that I didn't see anything just now?* Before I could even ponder an answer, I felt a warm liquid splatter all over my face as the air filled with the smell of *blood*. I felt no pain, and I was still alive- *how is that?* With great dread, I opened my eyes, and everything beyond that point was in slow motion.

I lied earlier when I said The Crow transforming was the most horrifying sight I'd seen, because this definitely topped anything this morbid world had to offer. My mouth hung open, and my eyes bore the doe-eyed look; that's when I realized that look wasn't only for people seconds before *physical* death, it's also for people who had just died *internally*. I witnessed it all in slow motion- Asier in front of me, acting as a shield in midair against The Crow's claws. His blood danced in the air as a gash ripped through his chest all the way up to his left shoulder. Even as The Crow's claws ripped through his flesh, he managed to throw the bomb directly at The Crow's chest in midair, and it clung onto him like a magnet. He reached for his pistol with his injured arm and shot directly at the bomb. His aim was always incredibly precise, and this was no exception; he hit the target right on the first try. The world began to run at its regular speed again as soon as I heard ticking coming from the bomb.

"Phoenix!" Asier grunted as he threw himself onto me, launching us over the edge of the wall.

He hugged me tightly as we free-fell, and I could feel his warm blood seep into my clothes as he clutched me. My eyes moved up as the bomb went off, still attached to The Crow's body. A bright explosion erupted in the sky, tearing through the hollow darkness. The impact caused the top of the wall to crumble, meaning if we had stayed there, we would've been caught up in the explosion too.

I panicked upon realizing we would soon hit the ground, so I squeezed my eyes shut, and used up the last bit of energy I had to create wings. Luckily, they summoned, but I didn't have much control as we spiraled rapidly toward the ground. I tried to lift us, but it was futile- I could only lessen the impact of the fall. Once I recognized that, I immediately flipped us around so that I was on the bottom, and I would take the majority of the impact. I shut my eyes tightly as we were about to hit the ground. I didn't even feel the pain from the impact; just like that, the world simply went blank.

Once again, I found myself in never ending darkness, unable to move a muscle. I felt as though I had broken multiple bones, and now there was the added feeling of suffocation. *Where am I? Why can I feel everything, but not see or move a thing?* I wondered all these things yet did not find myself closer to any answers. I still had my sense of smell, and I could smell something like an earthy cologne mixed with smoke and blood. Excruciating pain aside, I felt rather warm- like I was in somebody's embrace.

The more I seemed to tune back into reality and my surroundings, the more I began to realize, they weren't pleasant ones. I focused harder, and heard muffled voices, which sounded distant from me. I felt a subtle vibration going through whatever I was leaning on, like the feeling of being up against a laughing body.

Digesting all the stimuli around me was how I gradually gained back my consciousness. As I had presumed, it sure was a laugh I was feeling, and now I could hear it too; the laugh that made my blood boil, yet run cold at the same time. It was The Crow laughing victoriously.

There was an arm wrapped around me, and a hand squeezing my arm painfully tight. I couldn't feel the ground underneath me, so without opening my eyes, I concluded that I was somewhere in the sky being held up by The Crow's arms. He held me with so much built-up rage in his tight grasp, but behind this extreme itch he had to kill me, I felt something beyond that. There was a part of him that was holding onto me as if he was afraid that if he loosened his grip, *I'd slip away.*

"Both your leader and precious little Prophet are about to bite the dust," The Crow goaded and laughed sinisterly. "I've won this war, filthy devils. The rest of you, surrender now and re-establish your loyalty before you join them."

Your leader? I repeated to make it make sense, and then everything came back to me at once. Last time my eyes were open, they watched Asier be severely wounded- maybe even fatally. The sight of the gash across his chest from The Crow's claws was etched in my brain. I remembered the sound as they tore through his flesh, and how his warm blood felt on my skin. Fury rushed through my veins at the thought of The Crow possibly taking someone else away from me, and it was enough to open my eyes.

I opened them up to hundreds of people scattered throughout the plain field that was once covered in dying trees and was now scattered with thousands of black feathers. I didn't look up at him yet, because I felt his eyes crawling on my skin. Call me crazy, but I could've sworn I felt his grip on me soften.

"You're mine now, Phoenix. You've lost this battle," he proclaimed quietly, and something told me he wasn't necessarily referring to *me.*

When I felt his gaze move away, my eyes looked up at him- utterly repulsed. The wounds Asier had inflicted on him were almost completely healed and he looked roughened up at best. It must've been one of the side effects from the syringe; whatever wounds were inflicted during the large crow stage would heal almost immediately once he was back to his original form. I took a closer look at his face and his expression was softer than expected; I even saw a glimpse of anguish in his eyes, but it was quite short lived. It quickly turned back into that ruthless, malevolent grin he always wore.

Almost nobody in the mob kneeled in submission like he'd ordered, and this was their way of revoking their loyalty to both The Crow, and the nation in its entirety. He lifted his hand to the audience to show them a trigger button in his hand, but I was unsure of its purpose or what it could've been connected to.

"See this lovely button I have in my hand? I have one for every district. It's connected to a series of big *fireworks,* as I like to call them," he prefaced, "and I don't have a problem blowing this feeble town with all of you in it to the ground, so I would suggest being docile, and surrendering before it's too late," he threatened, mostly targeting the rebels.

The way The Crow spoke to his subjects was so different from the way Asier spoke to the rebels. Asier didn't have to beg or use threats to gain their obedience or loyalty, he just received it unconditionally. The Crow's finger hovered over the red button, which presumably would blow the town to smithereens once pressed. After another long moment of utter silence, still, no one kneeled. His eyebrows furrowed, and his finger sat directly on top of the button.

"Fine then. Hell knows I tried," he concluded. "*Farewell, District Four,*" he uttered, and finally pressed the button.

My heart dropped when I realized what that actually meant; my home was about to be obliterated along with all the people in it . . . *and there was nothing I could do to stop it.* A loud panic surged from below, and I expected a deafening explosion to follow it up. After the longest second of my life, all remained *still.* The Crow furiously pressed the button repeatedly until he accepted that it was defective. He squeezed it so hard in his hand that it broke into pieces, which he let crumble from his hand onto the ground.

"*Valerie . . .*" he mumbled under his breath, "rot in hell."

I was confused as to what she had to do with any of this, or why he would mention her now of all times, but then I recalled *what* she was doing before she was shot. She must've anticipated him leveling the city with everyone in it to threaten everyone into submission. It made more sense now that The Crow suddenly went over to the control tower to eliminate her and didn't just casually stumble in there to kill Asier like he'd claimed; he knew what she was doing all along, but he was too late to stop her.

"*I wouldn't celebrate so early- because dead or alive, I'm still your leader, and now, you're gonna wish those bombs had gone off instead,*" he asserted *iniquitously.*

"Don't be so sure, Lanon," I interrupted in a deep, vengeful voice. The words just slipped out without me even thinking about them.

He looked down to face me, and his eyes widened a considerable amount as soon as they met with my face. Vulnerability looked strange on him, but man, did I enjoy it. His malicious expression fell, and was quickly replaced by confusion, rage, and prominent melancholy. Once again, something told me it wasn't me he was staring at, it was-

"*Astrid?*" he uttered in disbelief. For a second there, he looked and sounded just like any other regular, heartbroken man.

"Don't play with fire, Crow," I warned, and this time, it was actually *me*.

I took advantage of his distraction and brought my hands up to his arm that was wrapped around me, and a bright light and scorching heat emitted from them; his arm resembled hot metal when put under fire. He immediately grunted and pushed me away from him. For some reason, I hadn't registered that we were on top of the gate wall, and I was hanging off the edge the entire time with his arm being the only thing stopping me from plummeting down. I free-fell for only a second before halting my fall with my wings. I flew back to the top and tumbled as soon as my feet hit the wall.

"DAMN YOU, PHOENIX!" he screamed with formidable wrath as he clutched his burning arm. I hadn't witnessed that much fury on him before, and it sent an array of chills down my spine.

I tried standing up straight, but I was far too weak to stand on my own. I pulled out my sword to lean on for support and lifted my head toward him. I saw hundreds of black feathers orbiting around him and a few shot out like comets in the sky. I fell to my knees again- I was just far too weak. I could barely catch my breath or even stand on my own, so *how am I ever going to keep up with him?*

My vision began to blur, and I was certain I was going to pass out again. Before my senses could fully give out, something caught my attention from below.

"PHOENIX, PHOENIX, PHOENIX!" I looked down to the ground and saw my friends, my town, all cheering my name.

My whole life I grew up hiding and hating my name, but right now, it sounded like the most beautiful song. It didn't stop there; the rebels got down on one knee, held one fist to their chest, and lifted the other to the sky. The others watched, confused, because this was probably the first time regular civilians were exposed to this salute, but they quickly followed behind them.

Just like that, I found the drive to fight again. I leaned against my sword as I pulled myself back to my feet. I looked down again, and saw all the Rebellium leaders kneeling as well, even in their weak states. I saw Nyrual struggling to kneel too, but Guido and Aurora could not kneel due to their injuries, but they still threw their fist in the air and held the other to their heart.

Someone was missing from the group, and I scanned the dark area in panic until my eyes finally landed on him; Asier, leaning against a tree with a pool of blood under him, but even then, he too was saluting. I chose to ignore the blood and his gruesome injury and just focus on the relief I felt to see him still alive and conscious.

"Victory will be ours," I mumbled before choking on my own blood.

"You're already one foot in the grave, darling. Why don't you just give it up before causing another scene?" The Crow sneered.

"Because I *never* leave business unfinished."

"Phoenix, we both know we'll burn in Hell after all the lives we've taken and all the suffering we've caused," he provoked. "Regardless of what you do now, there is no redemption. Your hands will *always* have blood on them."

"Just because you and I are going to Hell doesn't mean the rest of them have to live in it. This nation deserves to be free under an un-eclipsed sun, and the only way for that to happen, is for us to *die*."

"Don't waste your last breaths on some sappy speech," he snarled.

"Are you that eager to be killed by The Phoenix?"

"I'm glad you brought her up. I can't wait to finally put an end to her petty, century-long grudge too."

"Who are you trying to fool, me, or yourself?" I chose to refute in a much calmer tone. "She loves you, and I bet you anything that love is still there."

He paused for a moment, never once breaking his intimidating eye contact. "Phoenix, you know just as well as I do that emotional ties *always* turn the hunter into prey, and in this world, *only the strongest can survive.*"

He stood and stared at me like I wasn't there. It had felt like this for a while now, but right now, I knew especially that he was talking to *her* through me. It was hard to tell what he was feeling through his eyes since only one was actually his, but that one eye was all I needed this time. The eyes are definitely a portal to the soul, and his eyes too admittedly began to remind me a bit of the sky, because like the very sky, there was still a faint light in the midst of all the darkness.

He pulled out another syringe from beneath his cape, and paused to stare into my eyes before stabbing the syringe into his arm again. This time, his look had a sort of unhappiness to it. Feathers flew all over the place as he once again morphed into a full-fledged crow. This time, it was more unsettling, because he would die as this horrible, artificial monster he had turned himself into, and not the human underneath. It was pitiful to know the darkness and greed for power would ultimately kill him before I could.

Through the barrage of feathers, I could see The Crow's body being enveloped by black feathers until there was no more trace of man. It was a great visual of how Lanon's heart and soul had been consumed by the darkness that accompanied his great power. Once the enormous bird stood before me again, he flew up into the air, waiting for me to join him. He placed himself in the sky directly in front of the silver moon, perfectly exhibiting the outline of the beast, which contrasted so eerily with the moon's delicate beauty.

I shifted my eyes to the stars, taking them in for the last time, and praying they would guide me to victory tonight. I closed my eyes and felt the hands of everyone we'd lost in this battle pick me off my feet and hold me up. My legs felt light again, and strength surged through me as our comrades surrounded me. The scores of lives I'd taken no longer pulled me down; instead, they held me up.

An explosion went off inside me, once again manifesting into a phoenix, and honing its power to its fullest potential. My body burned in the best way possible, and the surroundings glowed brighter than every light in the world; a preview of how bright the days would look after this. My wings spread out and without much time to react, shot me into the daunting sky.

Chapter 26

I shot through the sky like a comet entering the stratosphere. The sound of everyone calling out my name echoed in my head as I chased The Crow across the sky. The delicate flaming feathers of the phoenix ripped through the darkness of the night with each movement. The Crow flew much faster than he had previously, so it appeared he too had saved his full potential for last.

I once again found myself- a wolf- chasing its desperate prey without letting up. In less than a month, I had gone from being the hunter, to being the prey, and back to the hunter again. Never in my eighteen years did it ever cross my mind that my prey would ever be The Crow himself, the mighty leader that managed to wrap a nation around his finger, and could bring even the devil to his knees. Never did I imagine that I would be the one to end the war that burned out the sun.

Our chase quickly became exhausting as we both hunted each other aimlessly. I could feel all the energy slowly draining from my body, and maybe even my life force. At this point, I wasn't just a vessel for The Phoenix, I *was* a phoenix- a bird made up of flames- and every fire had to eventually burn out. I saw The Crow's movements hinder as well, and I knew he was growing tired like I was; his movements weren't as well calculated as before. He was beginning to slip up- and one slip up was all I needed.

I stopped in midair for a second to gather up all the energy I had and put it into one final, powerful dash. The Crow stopped, thinking he was winning, and that mistake would ultimately be fatal. I took that opportunity and charged straight at him at what felt like a thousand miles per hour. My wings became flaming blades and as I charged at him, in a zig-zag motion, I burned right through The Crow's body from top to bottom.

A roaring, blood-curdling caw echoed throughout the land and skies as I burned through his feathers and flesh. After that grand move, I ended up right above him- though I was utterly drained. I felt like a withering flower, but I had to gather myself and finish him, because this battle was still far from over. *I had no choice but to win,* I reminded myself.

Since I was now fully under the supernatural power of a phoenix, that meant every movement, and every instinct, was programmed to kill him- and that was all. I didn't have to strategize an attack, everything I did was out of instinct; my brain knew exactly what to do to kill him. He was weak and burned out at his point, but so was I. I didn't think I could physically do much more, but I fought against the strain no matter how difficult it was.

Underneath the faux, flaming phoenix I was engulfed in, I pulled out my sword from its sheath- the very sword that Astrid once used on him. I brought it above my head, and with every last bit of energy and power that remained in my body, I would use it in this *one final strike.* All the fire and energy that had engulfed me until now, I transferred onto my sword. A giant, flaming phoenix emerged from the blade while flames and embers surrounded and emitted from me. I felt every last bit of my strength draining as the fires grew brighter and stronger.

Just before I swung, I felt two weightless hands place themselves on top of mine, gripping the sword with me. When that happened, the flames grew almost threefold- which was quite a sight to behold.

I looked over my shoulder and saw a beautiful, olive-skinned woman with dark, curly hair who wore a look of intensity- *Astrid, The Phoenix.*

"It's over, Crow," we said simultaneously, and clutched the handle so tightly my knuckles turned white.

With The Prophet and The Phoenix's power combined, we swung the sword down with all our force, right down and across The Crow's chest. The phoenix on the blade snaked its way throughout The Crow's entire body, leaving a large opening at the heart, which shone brighter than anything my imagination could even fathom. The Crow let out a final cry, so loud it shook the heavens and the Earth. It rang so loud it roared throughout the land- a sound the world would never forget.

He tried to fly higher and conceal himself in the dark clouds with the last bits of strength he had, but it was futile. I threw the sword straight into the bright gash in his heart, increasing the blinding light, and emitting waves of crimson flames which scorched the night sky, painting it a *bright, crimson red.* I flew straight into the light in his chest-

And I knew that was the last thing I would ever do.

I looked down one last time, and before the light blinded me, I saw *them;* they were all watching me, kneeling, chanting, sobbing. I saw Aurora meekly playing the violin with tears in her eyes, and it made me happy that this was my last memory of her. Nyrual wore a proud smile on his face, despite the tears running down his eyes. Guido was reunited with his mom and sister, and they all cheered me on from below. Daxon and Khalon kneeled with their fists to their hearts, and I even caught one last glimpse of Asier- the man with the skies in his eyes that started it all. There was a proud smile on his weak face, and with everything I had just seen, a smile painted on my lips.

I looked back up, and beyond the light in The Crow's open chest, I saw The Crow's human silhouette trapped in there. The light had become too bright to keep my eyes open, so I closed them and let myself drift. I felt like a cloth that was being unraveled- like the light was splitting me apart completely. Oddly enough, I felt, heard, and saw *nothing*. It was like passing out, but instead of never-ending darkness, it was never-ending *light*.

It was finally time to let go of the skies I loved the most. As I fell into the sky, I finally surrendered to the wonder of it all. I surrendered to the beauty behind the sky, the stars that guided me to this point, and the mysteries behind the sun.

I did it, I painted the sky red, *I thought as a final tear slipped from my eye.*

With every end comes a new beginning. May my flames burn bright and light the path for the new tomorrow.

May the skies bury me now.

Dying was not what I had envisioned, but I was certain I had died. I could see everything from a third-person perspective now, so I supposed this is what people meant when they said our souls left our bodies after death. Following the diffusion of the light, an explosion of thousands of feathers from The Crow's faux body erupted and scattered all over the landscape. The sky had also died down, and was no longer that ravishing crimson color.

In the midst of the feather rain, I saw my body along with The Crow's. We both hurtled straight toward the plains within the district, which were now coated by a thick layer of black feathers. It was disturbing to watch my limp body falling, and that's when the question arose; *why is my soul still stuck here?*

Mine and The Crow's bodies hit the ground quickly, but a thick accumulation of feathers stopped the fall from being too morbid. My body bounced off and rolled over, landing face down. The Crow had landed on his back and was tattered from head to toe. His jumpsuit had been ripped all over, and bloody wounds, burns, and bruises covered his whole body. As for me, my jumpsuit had been torn, revealing wounds and bruises here and there, though most of my damage had been internal.

I heard people shouting my name, but all sounds were muffled. The part that caught me- well, my soul- by surprise, was that The Crow had not died in the attack. Before I could even begin to wonder how, an abstract sensation overcame whatever was left of me; it's like I was fading, and something was dominating my existence.

"It's me, I'm not done with you yet," said the voice that always chimed in my head- Astrid's voice.

Once again, before even wondering what she meant by that, she answered me. Particles and ashes began dancing in the air and swirling like a tornado, but they were not just any ashes, they were Astrid's ashes, ashes that had been scattered on her grave. They eventually began to form something, like a human sculpture. I felt my presence growing weaker and weaker, and before I knew it, Astrid's soul had dominated my own and it flew right into the body of ashes.

The girl's soul was strong, but not strong enough to overpower me. Her soul was still in here, intertwined with mine, but right now, she is merely spectating. I didn't intend to keep it for long, so I hope she understands. I opened my eyes and looked down at my arms made of my own ashes. I used my flames, ashes, and Lanon's feathers to create a temporary body, because I still had business to take care of *myself*, not through another person.

Everyone around us was staring in utter confusion. None of them knew who I was by my appearance alone- and I could bet most of them didn't know me by my name either, since I was practically eradicated from history. I didn't care about them seeing me though, there was only a specific group that needed to see me; in fact, it was *crucial*.

I looked down at the mess in front of me. At my feet were hundreds of thousands of feathers scattered on the ground, and atop a bed of those feathers lay the young girl and Lanon- *my love*. His eyes were shut, and he was one foot in hell, but I knew his heart was still beating. I could see the slow rising and falling of his exposed and bleeding chest.

I turned to face the crowd again, and I spotted a group of elders congregating within the mob. Their eyes remained glued to me, and they didn't move an inch. They stood there, hypnotized as memories flooded back to their heads. Their wrinkly eyes glossed over as a veil was lifted from them. They are the ones who have been around since the day of The Old-World Revolution, and they were repossessing their memories prior to The Crow's reign.

He had brainwashed the people who lived before the nuclear attack, and in turn also his reign, in order to forget every detail of their lives without him as their leader. The only way to get those memories back was to see something from the past- but nothing of that sort existed anymore, Lanon made sure of it. Up until now, they had no recollection of life before the day The Crow won his tainted crown.

"*Please, let me go!*" I heard a childish voice yell inside my head. It was the girl; she was fighting for her soul back. *I had to make this quick.* I didn't intend on staying long, but I had to put an end to this war the *proper way.*

I looked down at Lanon, and his eyes were wide as a doe's now. He looked me up and down, and with just a quick glance at me, he became the weakest man alive. His eyes were glossed with tears, but they spoke all the words he couldn't get out. All the memories he tried to block out came crashing back to him like an avalanche.

"Lanon." I threw the first stone.

"Astrid," he replied with a broken, raspy voice.

I kneeled down and crawled up next to him, then hovered over him. His face had aged a bit from when I last saw him, but considering he was almost a century old, he aged well. He had a blacked-out crow eye in one socket, and the other remained the gorgeous ocean blue I remember losing myself in every day.

"The battle is over, Lanon. The worst is over now."

"Why . . . Astrid?" he said and coughed. "Why didn't you just kill me?"

"I have a lot left to say, and there's nothing left to fight."

"Why couldn't you just let me die in peace?" he asked with audible anguish. "Without ever seeing you again?"

"Do you really . . . hate me that much?" I asked, disheartened by the question.

"You betrayed me, fought against me, and then made it your mission to kill me for almost a century . . . *I hate you, Astrid . . . I hate everything about you,*" he scoffed with torment in every word, pausing to meet my eyes, "yet, I don't understand . . . *why do I still care about you?*"

"Because you know I still love you. I always have and I never once stopped."

"So . . . why?" He could barely speak at this point, but I knew what he was asking.

"Do you remember those days at the park? When we would sit under the sun?"

"I try not to."

"Do you remember what I said?" I asked, but he remained unresponsive. "I promised I'd always be there to lead you out of the dark, even when you didn't want me to."

"By killing me and destroying everything I worked for?"

"Power and greed have consumed you completely, Lanon. After you killed me, I realized nothing in this world would be enough to stop you, so as much as I love you, after all the devastation and death you caused, you don't deserve to live."

"Does that make you any better?"

"No. My efforts to bring you down have caused a fair share of devastation too. My part in this war is as big as yours, which brings me to why I'm here- to take you to Hell with me," I concluded.

"Astrid-" he began, but I cut him off by crushing my lips against his.

This kiss was more than just a kiss- it was a peace treaty. I felt his warm tears on my face. I could feel his pain, and he could feel mine. I could feel his heart break when he realized this wasn't just any regular kiss, *it was a goodbye kiss.*

I pulled away, and full tears were streaming down his face. "Astrid . . . your lips- they're cold." A few more tears slipped down his cheeks. "How could I have done this to you?"

"It doesn't matter anymore, because you'll be joining me now," I reassured.

"This isn't a goodbye?"

"No. We'll be together again, even if it's in Hell." I paused for a second, then asked, "Will you follow me, Lanon?"

His response was a soft nod. I lifted him up and held him in my arms, which had begun to crumble back to their original state. I felt the girl's soul fighting for dominance, and she was winning. I saw the main leader of Rebellium staring right at me as I disintegrated. He leaned against a tree, painting the ground under him deep red.

"You've done well, commander," I praised, though it didn't seem like he cared about what I had to say. He was intently focused on the girl on the ground. "Her survival will depend on her willpower. I purposely didn't use all her life energy," I said in answer to the question I knew everyone was wondering.

"You're leaving?" a familiar voice in the crowd asked me. I turned and I smiled when my eyes met hers.

"I fulfilled my promise, and my time here is long overdue," I answered briefly. "Thank you, for advising them, *my white raven*," I added and a smile spread across her face.

I finally closed my eyes and engulfed myself and Lanon in the hottest flames I could manage. Immediately, my artificial body disintegrated, and Lanon's body incinerated almost immediately as well; now, we were both reduced to nothing but ash. I split my soul away from the girl's, and it returned back to her body. I let my soul be carried away by the wind, along with mine and Lanon's ashes. As our ashes blew across the desolate land-

That was the last of us in this world.

I found myself yet again in solitary darkness upon gaining complete control over my soul again. I spent so much energy coming to terms with death for so long, and now that I was faced with it, I was debating if I should open my heavy eyes, or just let them finally sleep. I had prepared myself for the moment it was time to finally let go . . . *so why couldn't I? Why did I feel this urge to wake up?* I had fulfilled my mission here, *so what was holding me back?*

"*Wake up, Phoenix.*"

"*Phoenix!*"

"*Please wake up!*"

Voices around me were calling, and with every word I heard, it was like I was being reeled back to life. My senses returned slowly, and that's when I knew it wasn't even a question; I had no choice but to wake up. No matter how hard it was, no matter how much it hurt, *I would wake up.*

I was in such indescribable, excruciating pain I thought that even if I woke up, I'd die immediately. Every bone in my body felt broken, and my insides were turned to hot mush. My head was pounding vigorously, and I couldn't catch my breath, nor could I even move a single muscle. I approached it by attempting to take small, baby steps, like moving one finger at a time.

After what felt like an eternity, I managed to make my middle finger twitch. Slowly that one finger became two, then three, then my whole hand. My lungs began to cooperate a bit and were finally able to take shallow breaths enough to keep me alive. I could hear more clearly now too, and I heard something dragging on the floor near me, followed by grunting. I recognized that deep grunt anywhere, so I pushed myself to open my eyes.

I fluttered them open slowly, but they felt heavier than they ever had. My head was laying on a considerably thick layer of black feathers, and I saw people surrounding the area, though no one approached me- all but him. A trail of blood followed him as he dragged himself with one arm.

"A-Asier," I managed to mutter, which was a bad idea, because I barely had enough air in my lungs to breathe.

373

I forced my limbs to cooperate and move, but only my arms responded- and my movement was eminently limited. I willed my arms to grip the ground and pull me since my lower body would not respond. One arm at a time, I dragged myself along the ground towards Asier, who had collapsed on his back. I was certainly pushing my body; I could tell by the blood coming out of my nose. After dragging myself for an eternity, I finally reached Asier, and collapsed onto his right shoulder- opposite of the wound extending from his chest to his left shoulder.

"I told you, you'd make it," he gloated in a raspy, strained voice.

"I don't know for how long. I'm in so much pain I think I'd rather just die," I replied, also relatively strained.

"I don't feel any more pain, so I suppose that means I'm dying," he said with a breathy chuckle. "I think I can hear the angels sing."

Large tears began to well up in my eyes. "Why did you jump in front of me, you idiot?" I cried onto his shoulder. My tears were threatening to escape; I didn't know how they hadn't already. "I can't lose you too, Asier. It's not fucking fair."

"Phoenix. You need to see this through. You have to be strong-"

"I'm tired of being strong; I'm tired of being brave- because I'm not!" I cut him off. "*I'm scared, Asier* . . . I always have been." I paused when tears started to stream down my eyes like waterfalls. "My whole life, I've lived without wanting anything, and now that I finally find something I want, it's taken away from me, and I can never have it; they're taking you away from me too, Asier."

I know my words got to him, I could tell by the time it took him to respond.

"Then hold closely the short moment in time we shared together, Phoenix, even if it wasn't the best time."

"You weren't the best part of my life . . . you were the reason I wanted to start living it," I confessed, and tightened my grip on his arm. "Asier Jovano, you made me feel hope for the first time, the second I looked into your eyes."

"Phoenix . . ." He barely managed to get the word out. I could tell he was struggling with every breath.

"You reminded me of what it means to be human," I added, then laid on his chest for a short while without either of us saying a word. It was such a comfortable silence.

He lifted his arm slightly and wrapped it around my back. Even though we were both dying, I had never felt as safe as I did right now. My eyes looked up at the sky, and it only accentuated the beauty of this moment. The dawning sky today was so . . . *bright*. It was painted in a way I had never seen before; a giant, blinding sphere came up slowly, as myriad hues of mellow pinks and blues swirled in the sky around it. I never imagined it would be so red; it was like the sky was bleeding.

"At least I'll get to see the sunrise once before I die," he said, shifting his eyes from the sky back to me. "Sunlight looks good on you, brat."

We observed our first dawn, as we both fought to keep our eyes open. Between adjusting to the new brightness of the sky, and the overflow of emotions, I could not stop the tears from falling, so I witnessed my first dawn through blurry eyes.

"I hope when our souls are reborn, we end up together in another life, because if there's one thing I know for sure, it's that we belong together," I confessed between sobs. He moved his arm from my back and clutched my hand, interwinding his cold fingers with mine.

He lifted his arm with the wounded shoulder and moved my tangled hair behind my ear. I felt my face warm up, which contrasted with the rest of my cold body. I lifted my head slightly, and he moved his hand to the back of my head and began to pull it toward him; that's when I realized- he was pulling my face toward his. I closed my eyes, and he closed his as our lips met.

I immediately noticed that his lips were still remotely warm, but I knew it wouldn't last for long. I felt my heartbeat sync with his as it slowly faded, little by little. I opened my eyes slightly and saw he had opened his, and the bright light of the rising sun reflected in his gorgeous blue eyes. I saw his gaze slowly shift back to me, and a tear slipped out as he shut his eyes again. *He had chosen my face to be the last thing his eyes saw when the very sun was right in front of him.*

I closed my eyes again, and my tears joined his. I felt the very moment my heart shattered; when his lips stopped moving, and the hand he had kept on my head slowly fell to the ground. His fingers that held my hand fell limp, and his lips went cold. I dropped my head to his chest again and squeezed my eyes as tight as I could as I sobbed quietly, gripping a handful of his bloody shirt as I cried. I could no longer feel a pulse in his chest, nor did I feel the gentle rise and fall of his breathing. Just like that, the man that taught me to forgive myself and learn how to love life- *was gone.*

I looked around me- the once gray town was now scattered with thousands of black feathers. That's when I also noticed every single person around me was kneeling. All on one knee with their fists to their hearts; they were saluting him and the death of the strongest commander this world ever had the pleasure of knowing.

"I promise the world will remember you the way I remember you, Asier Jovano," I whispered into his shoulder. *How can I forgive this world for taking you away from us?*

As I cried, I was hit with the disturbing reality- *no one was there.* No one was hearing these promises or questions. My hands couldn't touch him anymore, and my voice couldn't reach him anymore. I closed my eyes and all I saw were his; the eyes that set the world on fire, and that up until the very last second, never lost that hope.

I couldn't move my head, but I could shift my eyes enough to witness the first and last sunrise of my life. Though I had finally stopped crying, this brought more tears to my eyes. *I won-* I had officially completed my mission to resurrect the sun, and free every person under it from The Crow's tyranny. The sky I loved was alive again, and the sun no longer had to hide from humanity. This war was finally over. *It was all over now.*

I had the weight of the world lifted off my shoulders, yet I felt heavier than ever. It was like gravity was crushing down on me. Every single plea telling me to stay alive echoed in my head, but my body wouldn't listen. I saw the sunlight glisten against the frosted leaves as my eyes drifted more and more out of focus. The world around me faded gradually as each second passed, and all I could focus on was my life slowly slipping away from me.

We always imagine death to be a sudden, horrifying experience, but it was quite the opposite. I wasn't afraid at all, I had no regrets, and I was comfortable with this being the conclusion to the story of my life. I was content with the stories that would be told of my life- my legacies and accomplishments as Phoenix Euphema. My lips curved into a smile as I closed my eyes for the last time-

And took my final breath of faintly radioactive air.

Chapter 27

I was lying down on a hard surface, and I no longer felt any pain. I fluttered my eyes open and was immediately dazzled by a warm light shining down on me like a spotlight. I felt so comfortable and had a weird sense of safety and stability. I lowered my gaze and saw something wrapped around the pinky of my left hand- a delicate red string. I followed the string with my eyes, and a few tangles and loops later, it led me to the other end. Once my eyes adjusted to the brightness, I saw that it was Asier on the other end; the string was wrapped around his pinky too.

There was a peacefulness washed over his sleeping face, reminding me of the look Valerie had on her face when she passed. It didn't seem like he was dead- more like he was just sleeping and lost in a lovely dream. I had never seen him look so serene and relaxed. His short, raven locks fell over his face- falling on his sleeping eyes that would never open again. There was no gory wound on his shoulder, and no blood nor sin staining his grace.

I felt myself growing drowsier by the second and my eyes began to involuntarily close again. I stared intently at the sight of the red string on mine and Asier's fingers as my sight went out of focus. The string was eminently tangled, but never torn.

I found myself stranded in a deep abyss of darkness when I 'opened' my eyes again. Wherever I was, it was dimly lit. I looked up and this time Asier stood in front of me, looking down at me with a weird sort of blueish halo around him. I noticed he and I still had the string attached to our fingers. Without a second thought, I jumped up and threw myself into his arms.

"I have to go now."

"No," I refused.

"Until we meet again, Phoenix," he said, ignoring me as he spoke one last time before letting go.

I held onto his arm tightly, but my arm involuntarily let go too. He turned away and walked into a bright light in the distance. As I ran and reached my arm out for him, I tripped over myself. I fell to my knees, and I tried to stand up, but my legs wouldn't move. With the last bit of strength I had, I reached out for him again, but he never turned around.

"Please don't go, I can't do this on my own!" I pleaded in tears. "DON'T GO, ASIER!" I screamed so loudly my voice cracked.

"You're not alone, Phoenix, never forget that," he said right before disappearing into the bright light.

After he vanished, he took the light with him, leaving me alone in the blinding darkness. Before the darkness engulfed me again, I looked down at my hand and somehow the string was still there, still intact. It was being stretched beyond the capacity of a regular string, but it wasn't pulling me toward him. That red string- it can be stretched and tangled, but never broken- just like our bond.

"Wake up, Phoenix!" a high-pitched, child-like voice called out.

"Phoenix, wake up! You're having a bad dream!" It was the same childish voice again.

I fluttered my weary eyes open to the brightest lights shining in my face yet again. I was beginning to wonder when all these stupid dreams would end. I squinted and raised my hand above my face to filter the brightness a bit; I still wasn't used to this new sun. I saw a bright, green leaf fall from the tree hovering above me, and land next to me on a bed of equally green grass. I had never seen vegetation look so lush and green, nor had the sky ever appeared so bright.

"C'mon Phoenix, your life is falling away from you," the voice said again, and I instinctively turned to the side- only to find that no one was there.

Come to think of it, everything around me felt empty and hollow. My heart rate didn't spike, nor did my body react to anything around me, and there sure was a lot to react to. Something was definitely off, and that's when I realized. . . *I was supposed to be dead.*

"Is this the afterlife?" I intended to ask, but my voice made no noise. My mouth moved but no sound came out.

"Phoenix, you must find yourself," is all she replied. Not that I expected a logical answer, seeing as she didn't even hear my question in the first place.

I stood up from where I was previously laying, and then I recognized where I was immediately. I was laying on the hill I always crossed on the way to my house- the one I would stargaze at. I heard a gentle guitar strum in the background- the Bardman that would always play. To top it all off, a glowing butterfly landed on my shoulder, and it felt so nostalgic. *Where would it lead me this time?* I wondered.

It flew into the forest, and I chased it, nonchalantly jumping over my dead body on the ground. It led me along a short trail that led to a large tree. As I approached it, I noticed that someone was leaning on it. I looked closer, and much to my dismay it was another clone of me. *Just how many Phoenixes are there?*

The butterfly landed on the clone's shoulder, which was sleeping soundly, with its head slightly tilted to the side. I reached out to touch my sleeping clone when I realized my hand looked very different; it was a lot smaller and child-like. I turned to the side and a big mirror was conveniently leaning on a tree. I saw myself- but it wasn't quite me- it was me as a child.

"Find yourself, Phoenix," the words echoed again, and I couldn't tell if it was inside my head or out loud, since all of this was inside my mind.

I turned to the sleeping adult version of me. I reached to grab her shoulder, and I shook it. "Wake up, Phoenix, you're dreaming," I actually said this time.

A hand grabbed my shoulder and I flinched. I turned around and saw a figure that's been burned into my brain from the moment I first set eyes on it. A white-robed rebel with a bird mask and mouth cover.

"Astrid," I uttered, and sound actually came out again.

"You need to wake up, Phoenix."

"I'm dead, I can't just wake up."

"You're not dead until you decide so."

"What?"

"Why do you think you're still here? You're still tied down to the Earth because deep down you still want to live. You need to re-find yourself to wake up, Phoenix."

"Why is that?"

"You don't want to let go of this world because you're not ready to let go yet- the world still needs you."

"They don't need me; I already did what I had to do."

"Your mission might've ended there, but your life doesn't," she explained. "You've freed the world and brought back the sun, Phoenix, there's nothing you can't do. The world needs guidance from a natural-born leader like you."

I didn't really have an answer for her. I wanted to wonder why she was choosing to confide in me yet again for such a major role, but I guess it didn't really matter, and it wouldn't really change much. Once again, I remained quiet. I tried to collect my thoughts and figure out what I was feeling, but I was still as numb as I was when I was fully alive.

"What is this anyways? Another dream you're directing?" I asked

"You're in a coma," she answered blatantly.

"Huh?"

"You were on the verge of death, but like I said, you couldn't let go just yet."

"How long have I been out for?"

"About three months."

"What?" I asked, genuinely astounded by the answer. "How?"

"Your body took quite the blow; you should be dead, but obviously there's a reason you're not," she explained. "You created all these strange scenarios to get you to find that sense of purpose and finally wake up."

"I . . . don't want to," I answered hesitantly.

"Your conscience says otherwise."

I listened to her and tried to process her reprimands. My existence was limited in this state- like I was stuck in a lucid dream. I couldn't feel a thing, and I didn't seem to have much control over my own mind. There was deafening silence around us, and the only sound that could be heard were her words replying in our heads.

The truth of the matter was, somewhere deep in my heart, I did want to wake up. Maybe Astrid wasn't really here talking to me; maybe *'Astrid's'* voice had been my own all along. Afterall, The Phoenix wasn't just Astrid, it was a hybrid of her and I. I might've burned myself out, but my heart still beat, which meant I still had a chance to live the life I fought so hard for.

"Do . . . do I deserve another chance?" I didn't know who I was asking anymore, but I needed an answer.

"Everyone deserves a chance at happiness," someone responded, but I wasn't sure who anymore. "Live out the victory you fought, cried, and bled for."

"Thank you," I replied, and someone else replied simultaneously.

The robed figure took off her mask and mouth cover, and underneath was a bright-eyed, curly-haired woman smiling at me- Astrid, of course. I'd seen her in memories, visions, but she lived purely in my mind. This encounter was still within my head, but this felt like the most intimate meeting we'd had because it felt like she was actually next to me. She was smiling and had a genuine look of gratitude.

"Good luck to you, Phoenix. Until we meet again," she said before fading. The great Phoenix, Astrid Eleodoro, had finally found peace, and now it was my turn.

I wanted to see the blue sky- to live with the sunlight on my back. I wanted to experience living in a world without shackles; free from the birdcage we had all been confined to, because I was a phoenix-born to spread my wings and soar through the sky. Amongst all the reasons I could name, the most prominent reason was still seeing *their faces* smile again- the world I left behind.

Once that final thought crossed my mind, the darkness no longer felt as dark. It felt more like a veil- like something was merely blocking the light from entering. My senses progressively returned to me, until I could fully feel my limp body lying on top of a soft mattress. My body felt much heavier than I remembered, my back was sore and corroded, and my limbs were debilitated and heavy.

A faint pain lingered throughout my body, and it felt as though little critters were crawling all over me. My mouth and throat were considerably dry too, and my eyes felt glued shut. All that aside- there was one feeling I couldn't ignore; there was an incredible warmth on my chest, and for once I didn't feel cold. It was as though I was lying beside a fire, but I didn't hear the wood crack, nor was I suffocating from any smoke. My body was idle for far too long, until my muscles began to twitch in response. The warmth I felt concentrated on my chest, slowly migrated to my face, and the brightest light lay over my heavy eyelids.

This exact process happened and repeated for God knows how long. I didn't recall much more- only that distinct warmth and bright light. As time passed, that light wasn't the only stimulus anymore. I heard muffled sounds around me, and I could feel more of my body. This continued until I finally got to the point where I believed I could try and move, and my body would actually respond.

I focused on moving my eyelids, because I wanted to rip this dark curtain off once and for all. I lifted my heavy lids and was almost blinded when I first opened my eyes. I quickly shut them, and slowly fluttered them open this time, looking down as I did so. The dark, wooden ground looked almost golden against the light, which was a little too bright for me right now. I gradually moved my gaze up and that's when I realized what I was seeing. A tear escaped each eye, and I was unsure if it was from the light, or my emotional response to the light.

Tears slipped down my cheeks, but *the sun* dried my teary face. I squinted my eyes as I faced the window where my gaze met with the brightest star- the one that had illuminated my darkness all these days that passed me by. The sun I had fought so hard to resurrect was now fighting to resurrect me. I swallowed a hard lump in my throat, and my pain went down with it. I wiggled my fingers and toes, and the movement slowly crawled up my limbs.

I raised my arm up and brought my shaky hand up to my face; blood still ran through the prominent blue veins in my hands. The sun glowed against my pale skin, and my hands didn't feel drenched in blood as they once had. The sun has dried them for me too, and where the blood has dried *there is no sin.* I put my hand down and pushed the rest of my body to move enough to where I could sit up. I lifted myself with my frail arms and prayed my back could support me as I sat up.

My legs were far too weak to stand, and my back wasn't strong enough to hold me up, causing me to fall forward onto the ground right in front of the large window. I held myself up with my arms and crawled right up against the window that extended from the ceiling to the ground. I mentally prepared myself to peek outside and admire the world that had resumed while my life was on pause.

The concrete ground was dark and wet from rain that must've fallen not too long ago. The rain had washed away the blood that once stained the gray streets, along with all the carnage that once took place here. The light reflected so gorgeously on all the wet surfaces it gracefully touched. For once, people walked the streets without fear, and kids played with the sun glowing against their red cheeks. The town had already begun to rebuild and the workers' skin glowed golden as the sun reflected off their humble sweat.

As different as it looked now, this was still my home- this was still District Four. The town that once existed under an eclipsed sun, now thrived under a blue sky where the sun seemed to shine brightest. All our pain wasn't in vain, and that would've never sunk in had I not opened my eyes. This was truly the sweetest victory after the toughest battle.

After a long time of restabilizing myself, I finally managed to get my legs to stand. I still felt incredibly frail- but I was grateful for even being able to move. I was in a pampered room and judging by the surroundings outside and the luxury inside, I knew I was in the mayor's old mansion.

I browsed through the closet parallel to the bed and noticed that all my things had been moved here; *I guess this was my home now*. I found my Rebellium cape on a hanger deep within the closet, and although it was probably strange to wear this now, I wanted to wear it for everything it stood for *now*. I wore it over top of the loose white T-shirt and pants I was currently in and made my way toward the door after lightly fixing my hair.

I took a cane from the mansion to help me stand and walked through the town and the streets that were all vacant now- though I knew exactly where everyone was. I had caught a glimpse of a sign stuck to a tree outside the window I peered through, which informed of an event that would take place today at the town center stage. *Funny how some traditions never die.*

The sunlight followed me as I walked toward the stage, and the whole world was so unusually bright my eyes still had trouble adjusting. The sky was much bluer than usual, and the clouds adorned it perfectly, no longer just serving as eerie decorations in the sky. There was just so much to take in, but I had my mind set on one thing right now, and that was making it to that stage. Once I arrived, I hid underneath the hood of my cape, and went through the back to hide myself from the crowd.

I took a deep breath, and the frost didn't burn my lungs this time. I slowly moved one foot at a time, making my way toward the stairs that led up to the stage where Aurora, Nyrual, and Daxon gathered. I closed my eyes, and lifted my head to the sky, walking proud with my head held high as I made my way up each step.

The crowd immediately hushed as soon they saw me climbing, but I remained hidden behind my cape. I looked in front of me and everyone's jaws had fallen to the ground. I put my hood down, closed my eyes, and took a breather before facing the crowd. Loud, frantic cheers erupted in the audience, and I opened my eyes back up; there they were- the faces in the crowd *smiling*. Corruption had finally lost to the strong flames of humanity, and now home finally felt like home again.

My name was being shouted in the crowd so loudly even heaven could hear them call it out, just like a certain little boy once told me. Just when I thought the moment couldn't get any better, they all knelt down on one knee, and put their fists to their chest. Instead of looking down, they looked up at me. Their fists were no longer in the air, now, their other fist hid behind them, signaling that battle had already been won, and it was all behind us now.

I turned behind me, and tears of joy slipped from Aurora's eyes, while Nyrual and Daxon wore the proudest looks on their faces. They all brought me into a tight group hug, and even the sun's warmth could not compare to the warmth of this hug. The sight of my town kneeling with respect against the backdrop of the blue sky with the sun shining down was enough to bring anyone to tears. It was so beautiful, I thought even *the devil could cry.*

Chapter 28

Today was August 22nd, 2099. About nine months had passed since I walked to the stage and took on my title as leader of this new nation. It wasn't just me though; the two remaining leaders of Rebellium, and my old squadmates, walked by my side as we guided this young nation toward the future. Today marked a year since that fateful day we won the most important battle that has gone down in history. It's been 365 days of freedom and sunlight since then, and we're still counting.

While I was in a coma for a total of three months, the nation was regulated by Daxon and Khalon, while me, Aurora, Guido, and Nyrual recovered. Despite our titles, the power rested heavily on the people, and not solely on the leaders. We were informed by the elders that this system roughly resembled democracy- the system this nation followed prior to the nuclear attack and The Old-World Revolution. The nation was finally standing back up now, and it all started here in District Four- the new capital city, which I had now pronounced, *The City of The Sun.*

The once gray town now flourished with color and life that blossomed at every corner. Laughter and noise filled the air, along with warmth and light. This had been most of our first summers with the sun unveiled, and it was unlike any summer I had ever experienced. Wearing heavy layers in August was unheard of, and our skin was no longer so pale it was transparent. Now, we wore light, breathable clothing, and our skin was golden and nourished.

The first thing I had ordered, aside from the reconstruction of District Four, was the construction of a school built in the name of the late Rebellium leader, Fremont. I remembered when he had told me before the big battle that he wanted to be a teacher and teach the kids history- so I tried my best to make his wish as much of a reality as I could. His grandfather ran the school, and I made sure they taught kids the real history of this nation, with nothing hidden from them, nor buried in any propaganda. We buried Fremont in the school garden, and a small monument stands there for him where everyone constantly leaves flowers.

I made sure to have every Crow statue burned to the ground in true Phoenix fashion, and I ordered the construction of Astrid's new grave along with a monument with a statue of her and Lanon. I know it seems foolish to include him in there, but unlike him, I didn't think it was right to eradicate him from history. He was a significant role to say the least, and it only seemed fitting to give him his recognition beside hers.

While on the topic of graves and memorials, I buried both my mother and grandmother in the garden of our old home. I found out later that grandmother did not make it through the initial battle, and she deserved to be buried next to her daughter. I brought flowers there constantly, and I decided today was the perfect day to bring them new ones. Although I no longer lived in that house, nor did anyone else inhabit it, I asked that they leave it untouched to make it my mother and grandmother's resting place.

I found a dress my mother had made me years ago, in the depths of the grand closet built into the room I now resided in. I had saved it for a special occasion, but never wore it because I never found a reason to; now, I didn't need a reason. I slipped it on, and the crimson fabric hugged my upper body and flared like a flower at the bottom.

I fixed my wavy hair quickly before walking out the door, and as I walked through the streets, everyone waved and smiled- something I had never experienced until now. It was a wonderful feeling being recognized and smiled at, and not feared and looked down upon.

Every time I saw children playing outside, I was reminded of a certain boy- one that brought light to my life, even before the sunlight. I pictured Lamie playing with the other kids under the same sun, just like he had always dreamed of. Monuments for him and Valerie were also made, and they were positioned right next to each other as well; I like to think wherever they are, they're somewhere playing together again. I'm sure the sun shines even brighter wherever they are.

I climbed up the same hill the way I always did, and like always, I knew home would be right there behind it. The entire area was painted yellow with hundreds of daffodils growing all over the perimeter of our small home. I went to the back where their golden graves were, and I kneeled and set the flowers down. Piles of flowers surrounded them, and most of them were from me. All the flowers in the world still wouldn't be enough for them.

"Take care of everyone up there for me," I said as I set the flowers down.

Before heading out, I picked a single daffodil from the ground, and walked back toward the town. I walked the same path I've walked at least a thousand times, but this time, it wasn't forced or dreaded as it once was. The past felt like nothing but an old nightmare, and there was just too much to smile at now, and so much to look forward to, that there was simply no time to look behind us. While on the way to my final destination before taking on another busy day, I ran into everyone in the town.

First, I saw Guido and his sister, who he was dropping off at school. His mother was slowly but surely recovering from her illness, and you could see both his sister and mother were proud of the man he had become. He turned and saw me, flashing his same bubbly smile as always. As a result of the injuries he endured during the battle a year ago, he became paralyzed from the waist down, and though some might call it unfortunate, he was still the same, cheerful Guido, and that's all that mattered.

I saw someone running up behind him- it was Lana. They had been going out for a while now, and she was even the nurse that tended to both him and his mother. She also waved once she saw me, and I waved back before continuing my stroll.

It wasn't long after until I ran into Nyrual, who was with Daxon conversing with a crowd of people. They were easily the most interactive with citizens- truly born to be leaders. Nyrual's mom had been cured of her sickness, which had always been his main concern. Daxon found a few of his family members from his old district and brought them back here to live with him.

"Going again?" asked Daxon, referring to the place I was headed to like I did every morning without fail.

"You know the drill," I answered, and they both giggled before returning their attention back to the crowd again.

The last people I ran into were Khalon and Aurora, who married each other about two months ago. I always thought it was weird that it took them so long, seeing as they bickered like a married couple even before sharing vows. Aurora was the only family Khalon had now, besides Aurora's dad, who was in good health and working to rebuild the town. I knew she was nearby before even seeing her by the sound of her sweet violin. It wasn't just her violin though, a guitar harmonized with her notes from the one and only Bardman.

Khalon waved, and Aurora shot me a smile since she was occupied playing her instrument. Khalon still wore an eyepatch, since he lost his right eye in the battle, and Aurora luckily got off with only a scar running down the bridge of her nose. After seeing them, I walked alone for a while, which was honestly what I needed. I loved my friends, but sometimes I needed to be like the old Phoenix, and just be alone to reflect for a bit.

I walked the last bit of the path that led to my destination, and I knew I was there when I saw steps. It was not the stage, but a place that I once scorched and burned to the ground. I had the place redone with marble steps leading to a golden statue that replaced the old statue that once stood.

I walked up the steps and looked up at the golden statue as the sun's light reflected on it perfectly- Asier Jovano's resting place and monument. I replaced the old Crow prayer site with a large, golden statue of Asier. The statue held his sword with a fist to the sky, and I had draped his old, torn Rebellium cape with his commander pin over the statue's shoulders. I thought back to all the people who've become monuments and placed a hand over my heart. If there's one thing this war taught me, it's that legends never die- they simply become a part of all of us.

"It's been a long year, Asier. The sun's so warm, you should see how much it makes everyone smile," I said to the statue as I placed the daffodil at the foot of the monument with the rest of the flowers left for him *every single day*. "I'll tell you all about it whenever I see you again."

This wasn't a story with a sad ending, this is a 'happily ever after,' because I know he and everyone we've lost along the way was out there waiting for me in some distant world. I held onto the hope that whenever our souls were reborn, we'd all be together again. The idea of that couldn't help but make me smile like an idiot while I looked at his statue. As I stood there, a small, blue butterfly landed on the last daffodil I placed down, and I smiled even harder. *Hey, Asier*, I thought, and smiled.

They told him the idea of freedom was crazier than reaching the stars, so he became the sun. I looked up to the sky, and it felt like looking into his eyes again; the only difference this time was that bright blue consumed the *entire* sky. *You did it Asier.*

You painted the sky blue.

Made in the USA
Monee, IL
18 January 2023

25542245R00229